Valley of the Shadow

The Desolate Empire
Book Two

Christina Ochs

christinaochs.com

This is a work of fiction. Names, characters, places, and incidents are the products of the author's imagination or are used fictitiously. Any resemblance to actual events, locales, or persons, living or dead, is entirely coincidental.

First Edition

Cover design by Amygdaladesign.net

Lujin Press
Nashville, Tennessee

© 2016 Christina Ochs
All rights reserved.
ISBN: 0692573593
ISBN-13: 978-0692573594

DEDICATION

To my parents, for lighting the way.

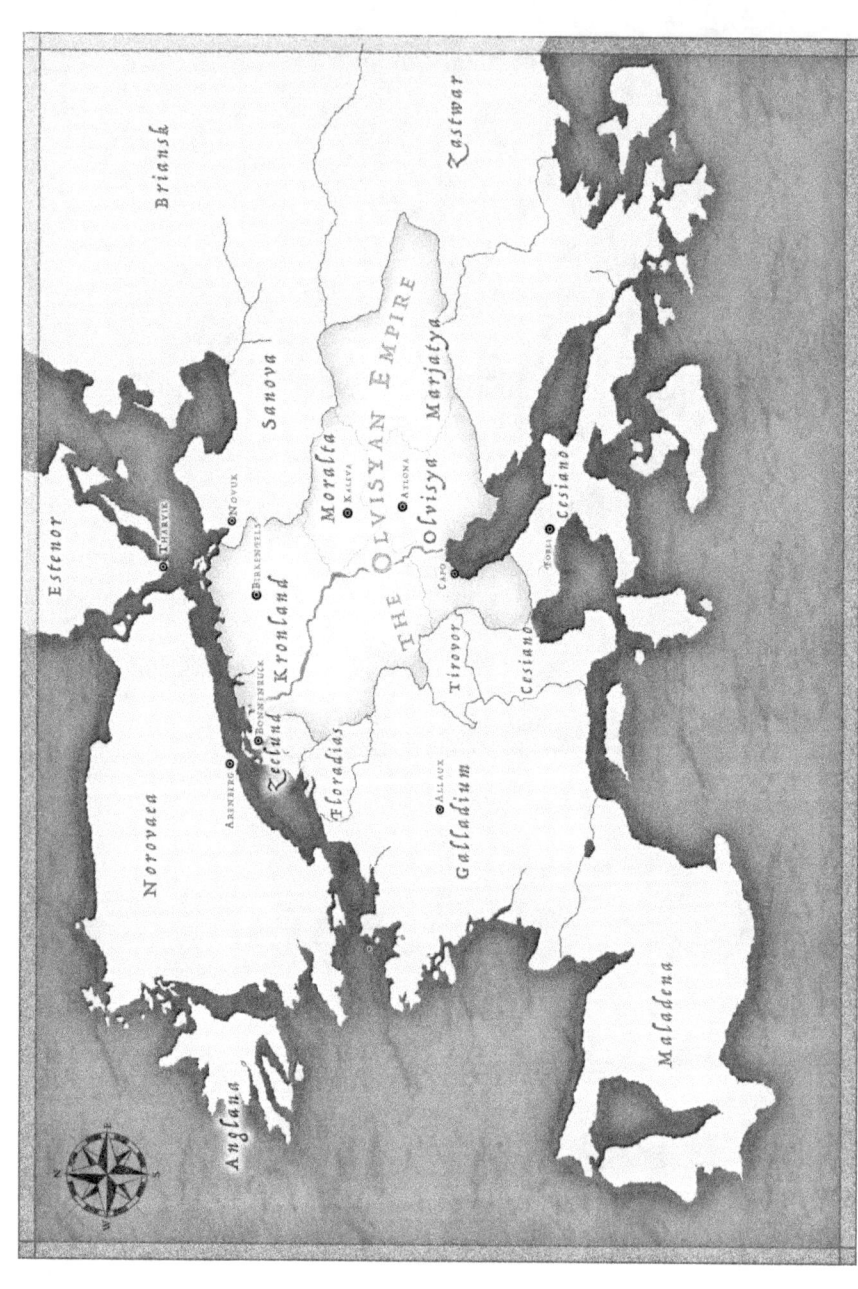

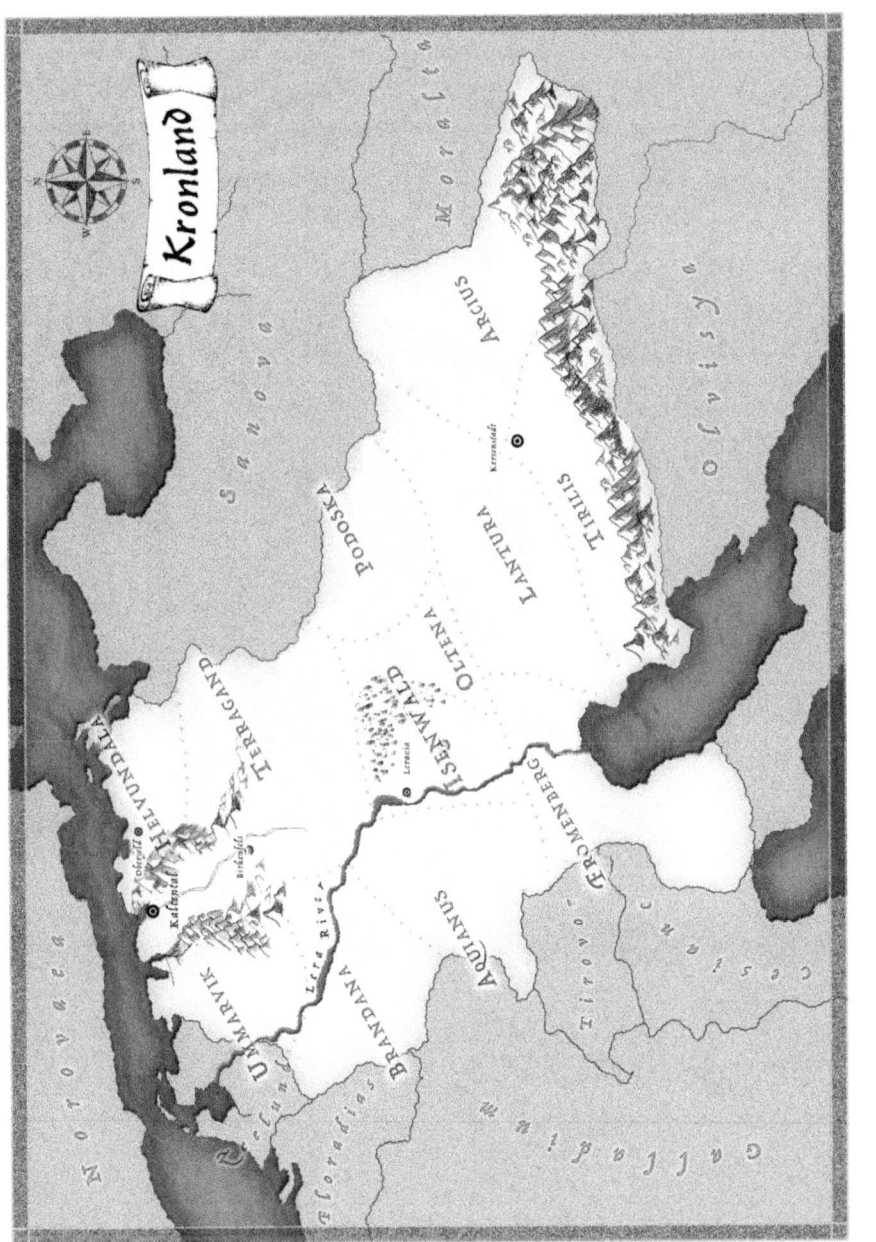

ACKNOWLEDGMENTS

First and foremost, a huge thanks to my husband Ben for making all of this possible.

My beta readers once again took on this huge project. Thank you Clarissa N. Goenawan, Patricia Heinrich Bailey, Cheryl Carter, Natalie Keating and Cindy Borror for your attention to detail and many helpful suggestions.

And thanks to all of those who read Rise of the Storm. You're the reason I keep doing this.

KENDRYK

Somewhere, someone was moaning. First the sound seemed distant, but it came ever closer, finally waking him. He opened his eyes with difficulty, feeling as though weights hung from his lids. Then the pain hit him in a wave, and he bit his lip to keep from crying out. The wave crested and receded just enough for him to tell it was coming from his right leg. Something about that leg niggled at his consciousness, but he couldn't call it forth.

Another wave hit and he cried out before he could stop himself. It was only when the jostling stopped that he realized he'd been moving all along. Light flooded over him, burning his eyes, and through a squint, he saw a face swim into view. It was a woman's, small, pointed and mouse-like, with something like a hat on top of it. Kendryk tried to open his eyes further, but the light was still too bright.

A cool hand touched his forehead and a sharp voice said, "The fever is strong. Send a message that we must stop or he will die."

Kendryk wondered who was dying. He heard a sound of protest, and the sharp voice replied, "Do it. I'll deal with her myself if need be." When the next wave hit, he realized he'd been holding his breath, and a whimper broke out against his will. He felt the cool hand again. "Can you speak?"

After a moment he realized she was talking to him. "I think so," he croaked through gritted teeth, his throat dry.

"Good," she said. "I will give you something for the pain. It won't make it go away altogether, but will help for a time." A spoon materialized above his face and a liquid slid between his parched lips, cooling his throat as it went down.

"Thirsty," he croaked again.

"I know," she said. "But first you need more of this."

He didn't ask what it was, just parted his lips again. The pain returned, but was muted already. He knew what she had given him, but wasn't able to remember its name. He found he didn't care.

With the pain receding to the edge of his consciousness, he tried to get his bearings. He looked up at dirty white canvas, stretched over ribs of light wood. He wondered if he was in a tent, then remembered the motion. No, a wagon. Why would he be in a wagon? He must be hurt and someone was taking him to safety. But safety from what?

He thought hard but didn't find an answer. He decided he might as well ask. "Who are you?" he croaked. The woman was doing something to his leg.

"Sybila," she said. "I'm a physician."

That was good. "Do you work for me?"

"No," she shook her head. "I do not. I'm so sorry."

He didn't understand why she would be and attempted a smile. "It's all right. Who do you work for?"

"Oh dear. You don't remember what happened, do you?"

Kendryk carefully shook his head. He wondered if rocks were rolling around where his brain should be.

"Hmm." She frowned. "I don't wish to upset you because it might kill you."

"You'd better tell me anyway." He tried to smile again though foreboding niggled at him.

"I suppose I should. I'm personal physician to Empress Teodora, and you are her prisoner."

Kendryk felt a vague shock. He tried to remember what had happened, but couldn't. "How?"

"You fought in a terrible battle," she said. "Your horse fell on you and your right leg is broken in two places."

"That's what hurts, then."

"Yes. I'm afraid I had to set it rather violently, at which point you passed out. You didn't wake up again until just now. I worried I'd killed you."

Kendryk's brain tried and failed to make a connection. "What does this have to do with the empress?"

Sybila sighed. "After you were wounded, the empress made you her prisoner. She is taking you to Atlona, where I imagine you will stay for some time." She paused. "If you live."

"So, I might not live?" When he said it, it didn't sound so terrible.

"I don't know," Sybila said. "The broken leg is healing well enough. But the wound around it got dirty and now you have a terrible fever."

"That might kill me." The idea didn't bother him overmuch.

"Yes, it might. It doesn't help that you've been bouncing in this cart for the last six days. I can't take care of you properly."

"Six days? Where are we?"

"Somewhere in Lantura. I've asked that we stop for a day at least, though her highness won't like it. But I'm sure she's eager to keep you alive, so maybe she'll agree."

Kendryk remembered something. "No, she wants to kill me."

Sybila laughed. "Oh, she does. But she has other reasons for keeping you alive and those will win out, I hope."

Kendryk couldn't remember what those reasons were, although he was certain he knew at one time. He was exhausted and had figured out little except who and where he was. He had no recollection of battles or horses or anything else of the sort. His teeth chattered.

Sybila pulled a blanket up to his chin. "I realize you're hot, but it's freezing outside and I don't want you taking a a chill. Try to sleep, and I'll be back soon. Her highness may wish to see you, so try not to be upset if she appears. If you like, I'll tell her you aren't able to speak yet."

Kendryk agreed, though he wasn't sure why. He was suddenly very drowsy, and the light faded as his eyes fell shut.

ARRYK

Arryk read the letter on horseback, then stuffed it into his pocket after dismounting. "The king must see this," he muttered to himself. He entered the palace from the stable-yard, then took the main staircase two at a time, heedless of the mud he left on the Zastwar carpet.

Arryk passed the guards standing at the doors to the king's personal wing as if they weren't there. He knew they had orders to stop him, but they'd never dare. The long corridor was quiet, but more guards stood before the bedchamber. Two doctors conversed in hushed tones at a small table in the corner just outside.

"Is the king alone?" Arryk asked without slowing down.

"The duke is with him," one doctor said. "He asked not to be disturbed."

"Of course." Arryk gave the guards a friendly nod as he pushed the door open. He practiced swordplay with them several times a week. They wouldn't stop him either.

There was sudden darkness inside the bedchamber. Arryk wrinkled his nose at the stuffy air, redolent of illness and ointments, letting his eyes adjust to the gloom. A single small lamp burned in the corner, far from the bed on which the king lay.

Norvel Classen rose from a chair. Immensely fat, he blocked the already meager light. "The king needs to rest," he said sharply, adding, "Your Grace," just a second too late.

"I know," Arryk said. "You should leave him alone so he can."

Classen opened his mouth to reply, but stopped.

4

"This won't take long." Arryk waved the letter and looked for a seat. He found a plain wooden chair and pulled it up to the bed while Classen stood, a disapproving frown creasing his broad forehead.

"Father," Arryk said, "I have more news about Gwynneth."

The king was awake, but seemed barely aware of Arryk. He turned his head slightly and his eyelids fluttered. Arryk took that as permission to go ahead. "Terragand is a disaster." He placed the letter on top of the brocade coverlet. "Empress Teodora has defeated Kendryk and taken him prisoner."

"That's the end of it then," Classen said, sounding rather too satisfied.

"Hardly," Arryk said. "Ruso Faris escaped with a remnant of his infantry and is headed for Zeelund. Arian Orland is also at large with his cavalry intact. But best of all, our Gwynneth still holds Birkenfels."

"That's excellent news," Classen said, although Arryk was looking at the king. "She can trade the castle for her husband's life."

"She will not. My sister is made of better stuff than that. She will hold Birkenfels until I can relieve her. Surely you'll give me permission to sail to Kronland now?" He looked at his father intently, but the king's face was slack and unresponsive. The doctors had said that the attack had taken his speech, but Arryk wondered if Classen had put the story about to keep others away. "Father?" Arryk asked again.

"You should not trouble his highness with this sort of news. It's upsetting." Classen glowered at Arryk.

"It's important." Arryk felt heat rising up his neck, but did his best to stay calm. "Gwynneth is his daughter, and the honor of our family and our country is at stake. What will everyone think if we abandon her? It's a sign of weakness."

"The princess created her own problems and is capable of solving them herself. We will of course welcome her here should the empress exile her along with the prince."

"That is unacceptable." Arryk curbed his temper with some effort. "I refuse to see my sister humiliated in that way. It's time we intervened."

"We cannot intervene now," Classen said. "The empress is far stronger than she was a few months ago. I'm sure she'll meet any attempt to relieve the princess with considerable force."

"Perhaps. But we are more than a match for the empress."

Classen made a huffing noise that might have been contemptuous. "I doubt it very much. I understand Prince Kendryk could match her numbers and yet she defeated him in a matter of hours."

"This latest dispatch says he lost half his army after being struck by plague."

"All the same, Teodora's force is impressive and experienced. Our troops are green and poorly trained."

Since Arryk was responsible for training, he took this as an obvious slur. "Mind your words Classen. You understand little of these matters."

Classen seemed unintimidated. Arryk was not eager for his father to die, but he looked forward to the day he could send the duke to a well-deserved, premature retirement.

"My soldiers may be inexperienced, but they are full of fire. They would give everything to save Princess Gwynneth." He made a note to himself to drill them more diligently. The hunting season had been excellent, and he had neglected his military duties as he often did this time of year.

"It doesn't matter," Classen said. "I too am fond of Princess Gwynneth, but she no longer belongs to Norovaea. This is an imperial affair and we cannot interfere."

"Of course she belongs to Norovaea. If something should happen to me, she will become queen. It's impossible that she lose this fight. I won't allow it."

"It appears you must." Classen looked down at the king's still form. "The king cannot authorize any kind of action."

"You can act for him." Arryk didn't try hiding his impatience. "You do it every day."

"Oh, I can carry on with administrative tasks, but I cannot approve of military action against a foreign power on his behalf. I'm afraid you and the princess must wait until the king recovers."

"He won't." Arryk looked down at his father once more, then stood. "We both know that. We also both know that I will be king when he dies. And when I'm king, we shall sail for Kronland at once. We should do it now, before it's too late. It would have been better if we had helped Kendryk sooner, but we can still do something."

"I don't agree," Classen said. "And as long as your father draws breath, you must do what he orders. He trusted me to let me rule on his behalf, and I will continue to do so. I'm sorry you are not satisfied."

Arryk walked to the door and paused before opening it. "I'm also sorry, but I'm afraid I can't accept your answer. You'll hear from me again." He let the door fall shut behind him with a bang. Classen was far too arrogant. No matter how sick the king was, a royal family member, and not some jumped-up clerk should make the big decisions. Arryk would talk to his brother.

BRAEDEN

"Sir, we're making camp just beyond the crossroads," Trisa said.

"Isn't it early?" Braeden asked. With the days so short they rarely stopped before dark.

Trisa shrugged. "I suppose so. Don't know much except the order came down from the empress herself and Papa wanted me to tell you." Trisa was eager to become a page, though Reno and Braeden both agreed she could start by delivering messages. Braeden thought a twelve-year-old girl was still too young to take into combat.

"All right, we'll come in as soon as I round everyone up."

Braeden had headed up a scouting party since there had been rumors of other cavalry in the area. So far, they had seen nothing, but the land was hilly and wooded, and it was easy for a smaller force to stay hidden. But now, with night falling and snow swirling on the wind, he was happy to stop. By the time he returned, servants would have put his tent up and Janna would have made it warm and comfortable. It was nice to have someone waiting for him.

"Might I stay with you, sir?" Trisa asked.

"Sure." Braeden knew he should send her straight back, but they'd all be on their way in a few minutes.

Braeden told Miro to round everyone up, and an instant later, heard pistol fire. He couldn't see where it came from but it was close. "Form up," he shouted, wheeling Kazmir around to get in front of the others and pulling a pistol from its holster. Then he paused, holding his breath.

More shots followed a few seconds later, whizzing past his head, but not hitting anyone. They were lucky it was already so dark and that they weren't on the road where they might have made easier targets. The dark also meant they should be able to spot muzzle fire if the enemy was close by.

"That way," Trisa said in his ear.

"What did you see?" Braeden asked.

"Flames, little ones, over there near that house."

"Get behind me," Braeden told Trisa, then had Miro bring everyone else up. "Head toward the house and fire at anything that moves."

They moved slowly toward the tall farmhouse, nothing but a shadow against the increasing snow. Braeden didn't want to give the others time to reload, but he didn't want to charge into an ambush either. When the next crack came, he was ready. He saw the flash and fired straight at it, and so did several others. There was a scream in front of him, abruptly cut off, and the thump of a body onto the ground behind him. He hoped it wasn't Trisa, but couldn't look back right now. He kept moving forward and pulled out his other pistol. In the dark there'd be no reloading. But that was also true for the enemy.

He advanced on the house, pistol raised. There was a rustling, the jangling of a harness and he resisted the urge to fire in that direction. Instead, he spurred Kazmir on and came upon them as they were getting away. A few of their number were hurt and trying to scramble onto their horses. It seemed their pistols were spent, since Braeden heard, rather than saw, swords being drawn. He fired at a shadowy shape in front of him and it fell. He drew his saber and Kazmir rushed forward.

Now they had them on the run, but Braeden's blade caught one unfortunate fellow across the shoulder. His armor might have stopped the worst of it, but he was already hurt and slid to the ground under the force of the blow. The rest were getting away. "Hold!" Braeden shouted. It was too dark and he didn't want to risk the horses slipping into a hole in the snow.

He paused until he was sure they were gone and asked for someone to light a torch. He dismounted to look at the fallen man. His horse had run off with the others and his breath came in harsh wheezes. Braeden knelt next to him and held up the light. "Who are you with?" he asked.

The young fellow gasped for air, though Braeden reckoned he might be putting on a show. "Tell me," he said, shaking him by an injured shoulder. The man moaned, turned his head away, and died.

Braeden looked him over. Cavalry, as expected, with the fine armor of a cuirassier. It had been his bad luck he'd been shot in the side, in a small area the armor didn't cover.

Braeden stood. "This is one of Arian Orland's cuirassiers. No other enemy force is this well-equipped. I don't know what he's doing here, but we'd best get back and warn the camp."

They helped one slightly injured hussar onto his horse and hurried back to camp.

Braeden went straight to Prince Novitny, who stamped around in front of a small fire, while he shouted at servants to hurry setting up his tent. The fire snapped and hissed as the wind blew snow across the flames. It was a terrible night to be out.

"I'll tell the empress," the prince said, "but we can't afford the distraction. Orland's force is large enough it won't be easy to beat. And this snow will make it hard to find fodder for the horses. We have to keep moving."

"I reckon Orland thinks he'll rescue Prince Kendryk," Braeden said, pulling off his wet gloves so he could warm his hands over the fire.

"Maybe. Or he'll try to take on Ensden up at the castle."

"Either way, we need to stop him."

"Don't get me wrong, I'd like to. But our mission is to get the empress and the prince to Atlona with no mishaps. We have to defend, not attack. Double the guard tonight," Novitny said. "Set another perimeter so we have plenty of warning if he tries anything. I'll go talk to her highness right now. Be ready to move out in the morning just in case."

GWYNNETH

There was a puff of smoke from the guns and a second later, a tremendous crash. A few chips of rock flew, but the tower held.

Gwynneth forced herself to stand up straight. "Everyone into the cellars," she said. She had hurried into the courtyard from the library after the first barrage. Most of the castle's population had joined her, but she had to get them inside. Another crash followed, a few people screamed, but everyone made for the stairs. She stood outside and counted as everyone went below. Just a few missing.

She looked around for Merton, pounding down the stairs from the wall, following the rest of the guard. "Where is Edric Maximus?" she asked.

"Still in his study, I'm sure," he said.

"Get everyone else below and keep them there. I'll find the Maximus."

"Your Grace, it's not safe."

"I'm sure it sounds worse than it is. These walls will hold well enough."

"But the flying rock. You could be hurt."

"Maybe. But I can't risk the Maximus. Please, go below so I don't have to worry. I'll bring him."

Gwynneth turned away, ignoring Merton's protests, and ran across the courtyard, praying she could get indoors before the guns fired again. She was running up the spiral stairs when the next blast hit. She kept going. If Edric was foolish enough to stay in his study something might fly through his window and hit him. He wasn't that foolish.

He stood outside the study door, at the head of the stairs.

"You must come below," she said.

"Won't it be over soon?"

"Probably not. They needed three days to haul the guns across the river. I imagine they'll blast away until they run out of ammunition."

"That's very inconvenient."

"I'm sorry if it interferes with your work, but you must come down. Bring what you can." She didn't give a fig about his work, but he was useless to her dead.

He pointed to a folio tucked under his arm.

"Good," she said. "Then come." A blast hitting the walls just outside drowned out her words. It was gratifying to see Edric flinch. That took some doing.

"They won't break through, will they?" he asked as he followed her down the stairs.

"I doubt it. The weakest spot is at the gate, but they haven't found an angle that can reach it. So now they're trying the other side."

They paused at the foot of the stairs, and waited for the next round. "So he's trying to batter the wall down," Edric said.

"Yes, he's trying. But he won't succeed. He's got to do something, of course. I'm sure Teodora is furious that I'm not cooperating, and she needs me to surrender before I can get help. At best, he might hope to intimidate me into surrendering."

"I find that hard to believe," Edric said.

"You know me that well at least." And it was true. Much as Edric had hurt and angered her in the past, he was one of the only people who knew what she'd done. So he understood better than anyone why she had to atone for it now.

There was a quiet space. "Now." Gwynneth gathered up her skirts and ran across the courtyard. Merton waited at the heavy door and opened it just wide enough for them to slip inside. Everyone had crowded into storerooms at the foot of the stairs. They weren't comfortable, but better than the dungeons.

Gwynneth had planned for this and stocked the cellars with food that could be eaten cold, barrels of water, and plenty of heavy blankets. Hopefully they wouldn't stay here long. At the rate he was firing, Ensden would run out of shot before morning.

"I don't suppose he can keep this up for long." Merton looked pale.

"No, he can't," Gwynneth said. "It's a good show, but completely useless for him. Best of all, he'll be out of shot and powder when my brother comes."

"You seem very certain of your brother," Edric said. "I wonder he's not here yet."

"There've been complications." Gwynneth was still unwilling to believe that her own father hadn't come to her rescue at once. "But I'm certain Arryk is on his way by now."

"I hope so," Merton said. "Even if they can't break down the walls, they might break down our nerve."

"I should think not," Gwynneth said. "And please keep your misgivings to yourself. It's up to us to set a good example to those who aren't as strong. There will be no talk of surrender. Anyone who does so will find themselves keeping Count Balduin company in the dungeon very shortly." Gwynneth wished she could find a use for Kendryk's unpleasant, unfortunate cousin, but for the time being, he was just another mouth to feed.

"Of course." Merton was still a bit pale around the gills. "I apologize, Your Grace."

"See it doesn't happen again." Gwynneth kept her tone stern. She hated being hard on him, but Merton was a stout as they came and she wanted him to help keep up everyone else's spirits. She didn't want to do it alone, though she would if she had to.

With the great door shut, it was much quieter in the cellar. After a while, people talked softly, and Maryna led a group of children into a corner to play a game. Gwynneth sat on a pile of blankets and tried hard to keep her thoughts from Kendryk. Whenever she thought of him, she felt her resolve weakening. Even if he hadn't been hurt, she didn't want to imagine what Teodora might do to him.

She glanced across the room at Edric Maximus, talking with some of the soldiers. It would be so easy to send a messenger to Count Ensden, surrendering Edric and the castle in return for Kendryk's life and safe passage to Norovaea for all of them. It would be over and Teodora wouldn't be able to hurt any of them again.

Gwynneth hardly dared admit it, but she wondered if Arryk would ever come. Winter was setting in now and crossing the sea would be difficult. And by spring it would be too late. She thought she'd stored enough food to last a year, but the cook had quietly shown her meat already rotting and weevils in the flour. They would starve by spring.

But she had promised Kendryk. And worse than thinking about him suffering was picturing the disappointment in his eyes when she told him she hadn't been able to keep her promise. She had seen it once and couldn't bear remembering it even now. It wouldn't happen again.

TEODORA

Teodora paced the length of her tent while Sybila stood calmly at the brazier, warming her hands. The sharp wind of a winter storm made the canvas walls snap and and icy air crept into every gap. But Teodora was warm.

Maybe because she was angry. It was bad enough that her doctor had more or less ordered her to stop her entire army in the middle of nowhere, but she also had the nerve to give Teodora instructions on how she ought to handle her captive.

"He's slipping in and out of consciousness," Sybila said, "but you can visit him for a short time."

"Good," Teodora said. "I'll try not to be too horrible."

"Your Highness, with respect—" Sybila began.

Teodora knew her well enough to expect that she wouldn't want to hear Sybila's next words. "What?" she asked, impatient.

"I realize you are feeling triumphant, and rightfully so. But the prince is still near death. If you upset him too much he might succumb to the fever within hours."

"Yes, I understand," Teodora grumbled. "A dead prince does me no good at the moment. I hope I can kill him later, if his wife refuses to cooperate."

Teodora wondered if there was a way to force Gwynneth to surrender the castle and the priest, but still kill Kendryk after that. Her victory would then be complete.

In the meantime though, it was time to pay Kendryk a visit. Outside, Teodora wrapped her heavy fur cloak close against the biting cold. Once she entered the hospital tent, it was warm again.

A light flickered near Kendryk's head, and she sat on a stool someone hurriedly pulled up for her. He looked quite white and she would have thought he was dead if she hadn't seen the slightest movement of the blanket over his chest. She stared at him until his eyes fluttered, then stayed open. The first thing she spotted in them was fear, but then he smiled.

She smiled back. "It's lovely to see you, darling."

Kendryk nodded pleasantly, though she was sure she was the last person he wanted to see. But it was true he'd always had good manners and too much composure for her liking.

"You look dreadful." She pretended concern, putting a hand on his forehead. Sybila hadn't been wrong about the fever. He was burning up.

"Oh dear, you're in terrible shape." She pulled back the blanket, picked up one of his limp hands and put it in hers. "I don't want you to die. Do you understand?"

Kendryk nodded again, though his eyes were so glazed over she doubted he comprehended anything.

"I can't stay here, and I can't leave you here either. Arian Orland's been sniffing about and I can't give him a chance to rescue you." She had hoped to finish off Orland, but he'd disappeared and Prince Novitny was adamant about getting her and her prisoner to Atlona first. It was maddening, but she knew he was right. After nearly losing her capital earlier in the year, putting her base at risk was unacceptable. Bad enough she'd had to leave it this long to take care of Kendryk.

It hadn't escaped her that Kendryk winced when she said Orland's name.

"You'd like that wouldn't you? He didn't help you when you needed him, but he could redeem himself now. Well, I won't allow it." Her words were angry, but she felt happy. She kept holding his hand. "I have good news I wanted to share with you. Not only are you completely defeated, but the Marjatyans won't trouble me anymore. They will need years to recover from what I've done to them."

Kendryk smiled pleasantly, his stare still blank. He'd probably forgotten who the Marjatyans were, even though their rebellion against her must have been his greatest hope. According to Sybila, he'd awakened without knowing who he, or

Teodora, was. It rankled that he had no recollection of her marvelous victory, but with any luck those unhappy memories would return as he recovered.

"And now that I have you, sweetheart, I'll get the rest of Kronland to behave too. Terragand is practically mine." She paused and frowned, thinking of Princess Gwynneth still in her way. "I suppose you're wondering what's to become of you."

Kendryk nodded politely, though he seemed uninterested. No matter. That would change soon enough.

"You will be my guest," she said. "You won't be comfortable, but I won't give you the worst cell in the Arnfels either. If your wife behaves, you might not spend the rest of your miserable life there. I'd like to make an example of you, but my advisers tell me I might cause more rebellion if I had you beheaded. It would give me immense satisfaction, but I must be practical."

Kendryk appeared far too unconcerned at the prospect of beheading.

She smiled at him bracingly. "Now I'm ordering you, as your sovereign, to stay alive. You are no good to me dead. Is that understood?" She gave his hand a squeeze for emphasis, then dropped it and left him.

JANNA

The wind changed direction, blowing sleet into Janna's face. She pulled the hood of her cloak farther forward, but then she couldn't see. Not that she needed to. Zoltan, the old warhorse, obeyed instructions perfectly and failing those, just followed the horse in front of him. Janna fell asleep in the saddle more than once, to awaken with a start and see she was still moving at the same pace in her same position in the column.

But when the wave of nausea came on, Janna barely had time to leap from Zoltan, and vomit into the frozen grass at the roadside.

"I hope it's not plague," she moaned.

"How long have you felt this way?" Nisa was already next to her. She'd been riding in a wagon alongside.

"It came on just now." Janna stood up, a little shaky.

Nisa laid a cold hand on her forehead. "You're not feverish. I doubt it's plague, though I have an idea of what it might be." She smiled.

Janna remembered and shuddered.

"When did you last have your courses?" Nisa asked, practical as always.

"I don't know." Now she considered it, well over a month. "I thought it was the stress of being on campaign."

"That rarely includes being sick the way you are," Nisa said, with a meaningful look.

"Oh." Janna looked for Zoltan, who stood waiting for her nearby. "Are you sure?"

Nisa shrugged." It seems natural."

"I suppose it is. Should I tell him?"

"Right away. He'll be thrilled."

Janna mounted Zoltan, wincing as she did so, and looked down at Nisa."Will he? Some men aren't happy about it."

"Pfft. Those men don't want a future with their women. Yours does." Nisa smiled over her shoulder as she climbed back into her wagon.

"I think so," Janna said. "I hope so."

"Are you sure?" Braeden asked when she told him after making camp that evening.

"I seem to have the symptoms," Janna said. "Nisa believes it, and she would know."

Braeden pulled her into his arms once they'd entered the tent. "It's never happened to me before. I never wanted it, to be honest."

"But it's all right now?" Janna looked into his face anxiously even though he was grinning.

"More than all right. It's a surprise, but I love the idea of being a father, having a child with you. Do you suppose it'll grow up to be a hussar?"

She smiled up at him. "I don't see why not. Although I'd wish for more peaceful times, and work."

"You're right," Braeden said. "Peaceful would be better."

"He could still be a splendid horseman," Janna teased.

"Oh, I'm hoping for a girl. It's hard to keep 'em interested once they turn fourteen, but every now and then you get one like Franca. Wouldn't that be something?"

"A girl." Janna was laughing now. "She'll have to be very different from me."

"You're turning into a splendid horsewoman yourself." Braeden started undoing her dress.

"Adequate perhaps. And that only because Zoltan is splendid."

"Was," Braeden said, sliding her dress down and lifting the hem of her shift. "He's rather old at this point. Like me."

"You're not old. What are you doing?"

"Seeing if anything's there yet." They both looked at her middle. It didn't look like she'd gained any weight.

"I suppose it's still early for me to get fat."

"I can't wait." Braeden picked her up and laid her on the cot. "You'll be very pretty when you're fat."

"Not too fat I hope. Zoltan will complain."

"He won't." Braeden lay down next to her, and put his hand on her stomach. "He's used to carrying someone my size, with armor."

"True." She turned toward him. "I'm glad you're happy about it."

"I am. Mostly."

"Mostly?" She wondered what the catch was.

"Completely. But I'm worried, too. Being pregnant and having a baby while we're at war could be dangerous for you."

"Isn't the war over?"

"Who knows? The empress is in a strong position, but things change quickly. Just think of how promising Prince Kendryk's affairs looked a few months ago."

Janna shivered and pulled the covers over both of them. "You're right of course. But there are a lot of other pregnant women about and many who've already had children. If they can do it, so can I." Though she'd never say so, she didn't look forward to being sick every day while it was so cold and unpleasant on the road. Even inside the tent, she never felt warm until she'd been snuggled up to Braeden under the fur robes for hours.

"You're much finer than they are," Braeden said, stroking her hair. "More delicate. You belong in a nice house, with a doctor close at hand, where it's warm and dry with plenty to eat. A winter campaign is always miserable."

"We'll be in Atlona for the winter, won't we?"

"Depends." He smiled again. "We can get married there. Maybe you can wear that dress again. If you don't get too fat in the meantime."

"The empress dress?" Janna poked his chest playfully. Both of them remembered the night of Janna's debut at the palace with some fondness. "But we don't have to get married if you don't want to. I never thought I'd say this, but I don't care about that."

"I do," Braeden said, looking earnest. "You're a respectable woman and you're having my child. I want everyone to know you belong to me."

"I like belonging to you," Janna whispered, and blew out the lamp.

ANTON

"They're coming," Anton said. "But I get Orland's horse."

"You're welcome to it," Gerd said. "You'd be smart to stay out of the way and let someone more experienced handle him."

Anton shrugged. He wasn't afraid of Count Orland. Not too much, at least. He'd seen him beat a boy with the butt of his pistol for putting on the wrong harness, and the boy still couldn't eat anything but porridge. Couldn't talk, either. But Anton was smarter than that, so he didn't worry.

Snow had fallen in light flurries all day, and now it was almost dark. Servants were building fires and setting up tents, but Orland and his officers remained mounted, discussing something. After sneaking out of the forest where they'd been hiding from the empress, they were approaching the besieged castle and the count seemed preoccupied.

For all he liked to talk about women, he clammed up the moment someone mentioned Princess Gwynneth, and made the others shut up too. The other boys said she was very beautiful, so Anton thought the count would want to talk about her more. Maybe he wouldn't, because he was such great friends with her husband. Anton was disappointed that they hadn't been able to rescue Prince Kendryk. He didn't see why they couldn't fight those Sanova Hussars. When he was a grown man, and a cavalry trooper himself, he'd find a way to beat them.

Anton edged closer. Part of being smart meant paying attention so you knew what was about to happen before it happened. When the count was ready to dismount, Anton would be there the second he was needed; not a moment too soon or too late.

"It makes no sense," Commander Schurtz was saying. "The King of Norovaea's own daughter. If he lets the empress capture her, he will look like a fool who can't take care of his family. Bad enough he let the empress have the prince."

Orland shrugged. "Word is that King Andres is ill, but Prince Arryk surprises me. I thought he'd be here by now, king or no."

"We'll have to act without him," someone else said.

Anton darted forward as Orland dismounted, tossing the reins in Anton's direction without looking at him.

"If we can," Orland said. "I want to count Ensden's troops, and see how well entrenched they are. I'm not sure what Faris is doing in Zeelund. He's a resourceful fellow, but I doubt he'll find the money to rebuild his army."

"Maybe he'll borrow it, like the rest of us." Schurtz laughed.

Anton moved as slowly as he dared while holding Cid who had his nose in Anton's pocket, looking for treats. The officers hadn't noticed him yet and he wanted to hear more.

"Can't imagine those Zeelund bankers extending him much credit," Orland said. "They used to turn their noses up at me."

"But not anymore, eh?"

"Oh, I have collateral now," Orland said, and they laughed.

Anton didn't know what collateral was, and why it was funny. Then the talk turned to some woman Count Orland knew in Zeelund, and then to the count's wife. Anton didn't quite understand what they said, but turned red all the same. He didn't see why these men were so interested in something boring like women when they had such splendid horses and armor and could fight just about anyone they wanted to.

Anton liked taking care of Cid, Orland's enormous, bad-tempered black stallion. There wasn't much competition for tending him. Anton knew how to handle him, though. So far, he hadn't met a horse he couldn't handle.

Anton got Cid ready early the next morning, but then Orland and his scouts went ahead and there would be no news until they returned. Everyone else camped at a safe distance from the castle, on the other side of the hills that surrounded it. They were very near Ensden's army, but the freezing weather meant everyone kept to themselves. It was much too cold to pick a fight.

Snow covered the ground, but underneath it, everything had been burned. They'd had to range far to find fodder for the horses. Anton nearly killed himself running around getting hay and oats from the wagons parked throughout the camp, but at least that kept him warm.

Orland returned by early afternoon. Anton could see on his face that he was angry, so he stood back. The count leapt off of Cid, and threw his helmet on the ground, letting fly a string of curse words that Anton hadn't heard before. Which was saying something. The clang of metal on the frozen ground made Cid shy, but Anton was right there to grab him.

Schurtz dismounted as well. "It's not impossible," he said.

"Not impossible," Orland replied, "But almost. Ensden knows what he's about and is dug in as well as any I've ever seen. We could ride right over them and they wouldn't budge. And those guns will make mincemeat of us before we get that close."

"What will it take?" another officer asked.

"Another ten thousand at least," Orland replied.

"That many?"

"Well, perhaps a few less. But we need overwhelming numbers against that position. Foot and horse. And artillery. As many guns as we can get."

"Where do we get 'em?" Schurtz asked.

"I'd hoped for Norovaea, but I won't wait for them any longer. Tomorrow, we march west. Our best hope now is to recruit whatever friendlies we can from the rest of Kronland. With any luck, Faris will come through sooner rather than later. I'm sick of dealing with this scorched earth. There should be plenty of food to the west, and if they don't give it up cheap, plenty of plunder as well."

Anton liked the sound of that, and smiled as he led Cid away.

ARRYK

Arryk left the king's chambers, striding with great purpose until he was out of the wing. Once the double doors closed behind him, he sat on the nearest bench and stared out the window at the snowy garden. Lights glimmered from tall windows across the courtyard, but the pale blue palace walls looked chilly and blank. Arryk sometimes wondered if he was the only person living here who had real, hot blood running in his veins.

He hoped he'd made it appear that he had a plan, but the truth was, he didn't. The people around his father were old, cautious, and frightened of shaking the stability and prosperity of Norovaea. It never occurred to them that Norovaea could become far greater. They acted like the affairs of the empire to their south wouldn't affect them, but Arryk couldn't believe that Teodora Inferrara's overreaching didn't bother anyone here.

Once the empress vanquished Kronland as she had Moralta and Marjatya, she would turn her gaze north. She needed to be stopped sooner rather than later. Arryk had been so hopeful when Kendryk had taken his surprising stand in the Landrus matter. Arryk considered his brother-in-law a good-hearted fellow, but a light-weight in military matters. So it had been beyond frustrating to watch Kendryk and Gwynneth stand up to the tyrannical empress without being able to help. He was certain Kendryk would have been able to defeat her with his help.

He needed the support of someone who cared about Gwynneth as much as he did. Arryk stood and made his way down the corridor more slowly. He and his brother shared a wing on the other side of the palace, though they seldom saw each other. Arryk was outdoors all day, every day, while Aksel rarely ventured from his rooms.

When he approached Aksel's suite, the outer door stood ajar, so he walked in. His brother was hard at work in his laboratory, standing at a plain wooden table with lamps flickering at each corner. He peered over the rim of his spectacles and said. "Stay there and don't move until I say so."

"Good day to you too." Arryk grinned.

"I'm not joking. This compound is highly volatile." The boy poured a yellowish substance from one beaker into another, looked at it closely, then scrawled something into a book that lay open next to it. "Interesting." He pushed up the spectacles that had slid down his nose.

"Boring," Arryk said.

Aksel shook his head and clapped lids on a few bottles. "What emergency brings you here?" he asked. "Come, let's sit." He took a stack of books from a bench, placed them on the table, and they both sat.

Arryk handed over the letter.

Aksel read it quickly, frowning as he went. "Poor Gwynn," he said. "I hope she's holding up well."

"She'll be all right. She was always the toughest one of us."

"True." Aksel handed the letter back. "But it's still hard, and even worse for Kendryk. Clever of Gwynn to keep the castle; perhaps she can make an exchange."

"Why does everyone keep saying that?" Arryk snapped. "It's the last thing she should do, and she won't. We must relieve her."

Aksel raised his eyebrows. "Does Father agree? Or maybe I should ask—can Father agree?"

"Of course not," Arryk said impatiently. "He can't speak, and that idiot Classen is lily-livered as always."

"Classen is no idiot. He just doesn't agree with you."

"I don't need him to agree with me. I need him do his job and let me help our sister."

"He won't."

Arryk hated Aksel's matter-of-fact tone. "He won't right now. But the two of us can convince him to change his mind."

"Classen will listen to me even less."

"He can't ignore the two of us together," Arryk said.

"He probably will."

"I won't tolerate it." He'd never been so frustrated in his life. "Everything he has, he has because of Father. He's a nobody without him. But we are princes of the blood. Our opinions matter."

"No, they don't. Unless you're king, no one cares."

"I could act on my own." Arryk wanted to shout at someone, but it shouldn't be his little brother, even if he was being thick. "If I go, Classen won't be able to stop me, especially if you support me."

"Of course I will support you," Aksel said. "You should do whatever is necessary to help Gwynn and Kendryk. But that means nothing. I'm not involved in politics, and everyone sees me as a crank, possibly mad. If I speak, no one would pay attention."

"I can't bear this."

Aksel sighed. "This is hard, and I'm sure it's even more awful for you, since you're the man of action. Do you know what I think?"

"What do you think?" Arryk slumped against the wall.

Aksel leaned forward, his light blue eyes intelligent and alert. "Father won't live much longer; I'm sure of it. And once he's dead, you can do whatever you think is best. In the meantime, you can prepare. Even if Father gave the order, you couldn't leave today. You must prepare ships and muster all of the troops. It might take weeks or months to get ready."

"So father dies at some point, and then I'll need ages to prepare."

"No. Prepare now. The moment you become king, you'll be ready to sail for Kronland. Classen can't stop you from outfitting ships and gathering troops."

"I need him to authorize funds," Arryk said glumly.

"You have some personal means, don't you?"

"Not enough to pay an army."

"You don't have to pay them yet. Do you have enough to hire ships and feed soldiers until they sail?"

"Maybe. I'm not sure."

"Find out then. And I'll give you everything I have if you need it. My income isn't as large as yours, but I hardly use it. I have a fair amount piled up. You're welcome to all of it."

"You're a genius, and a very good sort." Arryk clapped Aksel on the shoulder, and then stood. "I'll do just that. I'll have my factor liquidate everything he can, and hire ships. If I need more, I'll let you know."

"Go get our sister," Aksel said. "I know you can."

KENDRYK

A cold wind blew straight into the wagon, slicing through the heat of the fever, and Kendryk wondered if death had come for him. Didn't the fairytales say that the King of Death and his black horse rode an icy wind? Kendryk shivered, then reminded himself he didn't believe in fairytales.

The wagon stopped and someone pulled up the blankets he had thrown off and put something on his head. The wagon moved again and wheels clattered on cobblestones. They were in a city. He tried to think of which one, but had to ask the young man who walked next to the wagon and was charged with guarding him.

"We're in the capital, finally," the man said, his relief obvious.

"Which capital?" Kendryk still couldn't get his brain to work right most of the time.

"Her Highness's." The fellow seemed offended. "Atlona."

"I've always wanted to visit."

His guard laughed. "You won't see much of it I'm afraid. You're headed straight to the Arnfels. Dungeon, most like."

Kendryk felt oddly satisfied at the idea of a dungeon. Surely that would be better than bouncing in a cart all day. With any luck, he'd catch a cold and die before things could get any worse.

The wagon bumped through the city for an eternity. At some point, it went uphill at a sharp angle, the wind stopped and they came to a halt. Sybila's voice shouted orders, there was a banging on the wagon and suddenly Kendryk was being carried away from it.

He wondered where he was, but saw nothing but snow swirling above him and stone walls all around. Next, he was inside. It was dark at first, but then torchlight flared. They carried him up some stairs and put him down.

Sybila's face swam into view. "You've made it," she said cheerfully.

"It seems I have." It would be rude to die when she had gone to so much trouble to keep him alive. She'd even tried to make sure he wouldn't be too crippled. He knew there was no point in that, but it was kind of her anyway. "Is this the dungeon?"

"Oh no." Sybila laughed. "I doubt you'd survive two nights down there. Dreadful place. No, the empress has given me complete discretion in your care and I intend to take advantage of that. You are inside the Arnfels castle, and heavily guarded, but you won't go to the dungeon until you are well."

"So I can die there?"

"I hope not." Sybila's face disappeared, Kendryk heard footsteps and a door closing. She came back. "I don't want it put about, but if I can manage it, you'll never see the inside of that dungeon. There's a plan afoot to exchange you for someone or other—I can't give you details of course—but if all goes as it's supposed to, you'll be released as soon as you're well enough to travel."

Hope surged in Kendryk's chest. In the past weeks, he'd begun to recall almost everything. He remembered Gwynneth's promise to hold the castle and he'd asked if she still did. No one would tell him, but if hope of an exchange remained, perhaps she had succeeded. He prayed that she would not give in.

Someone had built a fire and the room seemed pleasant. He didn't mind staying here. He would spend the rest of his life in this place if it meant his family and Edric Maximus were safe. A tear leaked from one eye and he blinked back the rest, mortified.

Sybila misunderstood. "I don't want to give you false hope, but I think a little bit will help you. I hope it will be easier for you to heal if you have something to look forward to."

Kendryk nodded, then closed his eyes. There was nothing to look forward to.

GWYNNETH

The bombardment continued until morning. Only the children slept. It was uncomfortable in the cellar, but the racket outside was more unnerving. When it ended, Gwynneth waited another hour before leaving the cellar to see what was happening. Across the river the gun emplacements were quiet and the smoke had blown away. Merton came up next to her and handed her a glass. She looked at each piece in turn. There were no crews to be seen. It was bitterly cold and had been colder during the night.

"No doubt they're huddled around campfires, trying to thaw out," Gwynneth said.

"Perhaps they've used up all their shot," Merton said.

"I hope so. They will send for more, but that might take weeks. I think it's all right to come out, but give the order that everyone is to stay vigilant and indoors as much as possible."

Once everyone was out of the cellar, Gwynneth took to her chamber. She was so tired and cold. It hadn't been too difficult to put on a brave and cheerful face, since she was confident they would not be hurt, but the long sleepless night had worn on her.

Someone had built a fire in her room so she kicked off her slippers and slid into the cold bed with her clothes on. She was dozing off when her maid Catrin bustled in and put another blanket over her. Gwynneth kept her eyes shut and soon fell asleep. She woke up a few hours later with a mouth like cotton and a pounding head.

When Catrin reappeared, Gwynneth asked for food. A tray of bread and stewed meat came in due course and Gwynneth forced herself to eat half of it, then laid down again and drifted off, wondering vaguely what the children were doing.

She woke up nauseous and vomited into her chamber pot. Catrin came running, but Gwynneth was sick until she was sure there couldn't be anything left in her stomach. "Don't let the children near me." She panted, wondering what sort of plague she could have picked up while living in such isolation.

After more rest, she felt better. She doubted she was terribly ill, and she ought to show herself. Gwynneth worried that if she disappeared for any length of time the others might lose heart.

She slept well that night, but was ill again the next morning. By noon she knew what was wrong. She dragged herself out and went in search of the children. Andres was playing with the nurse, while Devyn chased the carpenter's daughter all over the castle in some kind of game. "Where is Maryna?" she asked the nurse.

"Gone up to see the Maximus."

Gwynneth had to smile. Maryna was so like her father and fascinated by what Edric Maximus was doing. For a five-year-old, she was very devout and understood more about the gods than most adults.

She made her way up the winding stairs to the study. It was dark, the window closed against the chill wind, but a fire burned in the grate and a few lamps stood on the tables. Gwynneth paused in the doorway looking at Maryna's curly blond head bent over a large book, with Edric next to her.

"You know that word," he said. "It was in the last sentence."

"It's beauty, isn't it?" Maryna asked, excited.

"Exactly. But it has a different ending because of the case. Do you see?"

"Yes." Her curls bobbed. "It's very hard, though." She made a face, then saw Gwynneth. "There you are, Mama. Are you better now?"

"I am." Gwynneth smiled and crossed the room to plant a kiss on her daughter's head.

"I hope it's all right she's here," Edric said. "She's so interested, and very intelligent."

"Just like her father." Gwynneth felt suddenly wistful. She missed Kendryk so much it was almost unbearable. "It's fine, though her nurse will be coming for her. It's time for a bath."

"Will you come back tomorrow?" Edric smiled down at her.

Maryna nodded happily. Her nurse appeared in the doorway.

"Might I speak with you for a moment, Your Grace?" Edric asked.

Gwynneth handed Maryna off, then closed the door behind her. "What is it?"

"I heard you were ill, and was concerned."

"Oh, it turned out to be nothing."

"If I may be so bold Princess, I have an idea what it might be."

Gwynneth raised an eyebrow. "Why am I not surprised."

"So, I'm correct in assuming you are pregnant?"

Gwynneth stared. It seemed impossible to keep any secrets from him. Finally, she said, "I'd prefer not to tell everyone right away. Just in case something happens."

"Of course. I would offer congratulations, but I'm not sure ..."

"You may," Gwynneth said. "And I'm sure it's Kendryk's."

"You are?"

"You are unbelievably insolent." She paused and took a deep breath. She already knew it did no good to lose her temper with him. "And yes, I'm sure. I needn't explain myself to you, so I won't be sharing any details."

"No, no of course not. I meant no offense."

"Somehow I doubt that."

Edric sighed. "You always assume the worst of me, I'm afraid. I only have your best interests at heart."

"Forgive me if I don't believe that."

"I hope you will come to realize it in time. But you must believe I care a great deal about your husband."

"That's the only reason I haven't turned you over to the empress, though I confess that the more I miss him, the more tempted I am."

"I don't blame you. I'm tempted myself."

Gwynneth sat down as a wave of fatigue washed over her.

"Are you all right, Your Grace?"

"Yes. But I don't know how much longer I can bear it. I can't sleep for wondering what's happening to him, what awful things that woman might do to him."

Edric came around the desk and sat across from her. "I know you don't believe, Princess, but we must trust in the gods. That faith will sustain Kendryk through everything and will help you as well."

"I wish I could, Maximus, since I'm sure it would be comforting."

"I pray that you do. And I will never stop praying for a miracle that will return your husband to you and the children."

"Thank you for that at least." Gwynneth stood. "While you're at it, please pray for another miracle that sends my brother here."

ANTON

Even though hundreds of wagons had gone before him, Anton was scared. He did his best not to show it, set his jaw and hoped no one noticed his white knuckles. He was leading two spare mounts across an ice-covered river into Brandana, and the horses didn't like it any more than he did.

Count Orland ordered everyone spread out in all directions so the ice didn't carry too much weight in any one place. The danger of being attacked during such a crossing was high, but there'd been no reports of enemy forces in the area.

"Brandana should be friendly," Gerd said. He'd crossed the kingdom several times already, traveling from Lantura to Zeelund and back with Ossian Schurtz's troops. "Princess Floreta is a great friend of Prince Kendryk's." He made it sound like he knew all of these people personally, although Anton doubted he'd ever so much as seen them at a distance.

But Anton kept his mouth shut. Gerd was a good source of information, as long as you sorted out the lies, which was easy enough.

"Do you think she'll give Count Orland the troops he needs?"

"She'd better," Gerd said, as they stepped onto solid ground. Anton almost sighed with relief, but stopped himself and kept walking along as casually as if they'd been on a road all along.

"What do you mean?" Anton asked. "What if she says no?"

"Then I imagine the count will have to burn things. He'll start with a few villages, somewhere the princess can see them. If she doesn't give in, he'll plunder a larger town, hopefully a rich one."

"She won't like that," Anton said.

"Of course not. But it's the fastest way to get her to help. She'll do anything to make it stop."

They were both quiet for a while. The path up the riverbank was steep, and the ground uneven until they reached the road. Even though he'd become much tougher, Anton was out of breath, and his feet hurt. His old shoes had fallen apart, so he had taken the boots off a dead soldier not far from the Birkenfels battlefield. Poking around amongst the corpses, he thought of the woman they'd met the first day out of Kaleva, and how shocked his mother had been that she would steal from the dead. Much as he missed his mother, Anton was glad she'd never find out he'd become one of those people.

At first, Anton was happy to see snow-covered fields and cozy farmsteads with smoke rising from stone chimneys. There was ample hay here, and Count Orland was offering good coin for it. Anton supposed he would try to stay on the princess's friendly side. It was a relief to have fodder so handy, after so much scrounging in Terragand.

On the second day, they reached a crossroads, and then everything changed. The land was as devastated as it was in Terragand. Worse, there were dead bodies everywhere. Here, the people hadn't had a chance to find safety in the castles and towns. Most had been slaughtered where they stood. Anton wondered who'd do such a thing, remembering the Kronek farm.

"We'll find the princess tomorrow," Gerd said. "She might know."

The next day, they traveled through a huge, dark forest. Great, bushy fir trees grew close in on the road and the count ordered everyone on high alert in case of ambush. Anton peered into the trees until his eyes crossed; it seemed impossible that anyone could get through those branches without making a huge racket. But he was nervous all the same, since he hated being exposed on the road like this.

It was late afternoon when the woods opened up and a great castle appeared in the distance. It had four black towers that rose high above the treetops and tall black walls disappeared into the trees on either side.

Gerd came running from the front of the column. "Come with me," he gasped, grabbing Anton by the arm. "Princess Floreta is in that castle and you need to help with Cid while the count gets ready to pay her a visit."

Anton was glad once again that no one else wanted to take care of Cid and took him to get water while Count Orland and his officers changed into their parade armor. It was said the old princess had a weakness for good-looking men, and no one could deny the count cut a fine figure in his black armor inlaid with gold. Anton also noticed that Commander Schurtz wasn't going. He wasn't good-looking at all, and his manners were terrible. The old princess wouldn't like him.

Anton and Gerd helped the count into his saddle because his armor was so heavy. Cid stamped and snorted, not liking the extra weight, but the count gave him the spurs and they trotted into the distance.

Anton hoped it wouldn't take too long. Gerd assured him it would. "She'll probably have him stay to dine," he said.

"In that armor?"

"He can take it off." Gerd smirked. "The old bird would like that. No doubt he'll have to use some sweet words with her."

"Ugh." Anton hated the idea of flirting with anyone, especially a wrinkled old noblewoman.

"He's good at it," Gerd said. "Lots of practice."

"Ugh," Anton said again.

The count returned long before sundown. He was in a fine mood, even tossing Anton a copper along with Cid's reins. That was good. He hoped to find woolen socks to buy, since his boots were too big. Then Anton loitered behind the men in case he heard something interesting.

"We're in luck," the count said. "The old lady is desperate for help. We'll have all the fodder and supplies we need."

"Any idea who did this?" Schurtz asked. "They say Barela went west after the battle, but this isn't his style."

"It's not Barela," the count said. "It's Tomescu."

Anton drew his breath in sharply.

"Who?" someone else asked.

"That woman, friend of the empress. Everyone says she's part wolf, though I doubt it." The count laughed. "Though according to rumor, she has the most unnerving eyes. Hope I get to see them for myself someday."

Gerd looked at Anton. "Know her?"

Anton swallowed hard. "I think I've seen her. In Moralta." It seemed so long ago, but the fear came rushing back like it had happened yesterday.

Gerd looked put out. He hated it when someone knew something he didn't. "Did she look like a wolf?"

"Not exactly. Though she had these strange animal eyes and I could swear she was sniffing the air the way a dog does when it's on the trail of something."

Gerd stared. "Whose trail was she on?"

"Mine, I think," Anton said. He'd tried very hard to forget all about that awful day.

"Did she find you?"

"I think she knew I was there, but she didn't do anything. Obviously, or I would be dead."

"I wonder why she left you alone?"

"Don't know. Don't want to talk about it," Anton said, turning his head away so Gerd wouldn't see the tears that welled up suddenly. He pretended to adjust something on Cid's harness.

"Have it your way." Gerd shrugged, then talked about what they might have for supper all the way back to the horse lines. He'd probably like it if no one else found out about Anton's brush with that woman.

Anton hoped they found her and killed her. He wished he could do it himself after what she'd done to his little sister. Even though he wasn't yet a good enough fighter to take her on himself, he liked being part of such a large, strong force. No matter what happened, Anton swore to himself that he'd never again be weak and helpless and scared like he'd been back then. He didn't care what it took.

ARRYK

"Will those be enough?" Larisa asked, the wind yanking her hair out of its braid and whipping it around her face.

"They'll have to be," Arryk said. They stood at the Arenberg docks where Arryk was overseeing the preparations of his invasion fleet. An icy wind drove sleet into his face, but those working on the ships had to carry on in spite of the weather. Arryk needed to set a good example.

As usual, Larisa didn't seem to notice the terrible weather. "It doesn't seem like those are enough ships to hold so many troops."

"I'll find more somehow, though it'll take time and a lot more money."

"Your poor sister." Larisa stared at the water. "It would make me crazy, not being able to fight."

Arryk looked at her sideways. He loved looking at her though he tried to be circumspect in public. "But Gwynn isn't a soldier like you. I'm sure she's bored, being cooped up in a castle, but she'll pass the time reading and discussing philosophy most like."

"Ugh," Larisa said.

"She got that from grandmother. Aksel did too. I'm the only one who's not a scholar."

"Thank Ercos for that," Larisa said, punching his arm. "I would never let a scholar into my bed."

"It's *my* bed I've been letting you into lately," Arryk said, feeling warmer at the thought.

"Only because a palace is better than a barracks. What will we do on campaign?"

"You'll lodge near me wherever we are. You're one of my senior officers, so it makes sense."

"It does. I'll be able to advise you at all hours of the night." She threw him a smile and he nearly went weak in the knees.

He had promised himself he wouldn't fall in love, but it was too late. It had been too late the moment he met Larisa Karsten, the top pupil at the Arenberg military academy. All of the male cadets had been in love with her, and a fair number of the girls as well. She looked a veritable goddess of battle; nearly as tall as Arryk, slim and strong, with blond hair in a braid to her waist, bright blue eyes and a rosy complexion that turned golden brown in the sun.

She'd bested him the first time they sparred with swords, and from the moment she had him on the ground, a blunted steel tip at his throat, he couldn't think of anyone else. He even stopped visiting a certain Arenberg actress and ignored his father when he tried to bring up princesses suitable for marriage.

It had taken months, but one night when they were on training maneuvers on the northern islands, she had crawled into his bedroll. That had been nearly two years ago and they had spent all but a handful of nights together since. For all that, she never let on how she really felt and it frustrated him.

"Why so grim?" Larisa asked. "You'll figure something out, I'm sure."

"I hope so. The problem is, I can't get all the ships I need to carry enough troops down the river to Birkenfels. I need to bring at least fifteen thousand soldiers and the ships must be able to navigate the river so I can't take anything very big. I don't know how I'll do it in less than a year."

"That's much too long. Won't your sister run out of food by then?"

"Probably," Arryk said miserably. "I also don't see how I can launch a surprise attack from the river."

"You can't." Larisa was as blunt as ever. "Count Ensden is experienced enough that he'll be watching the river." She turned and looked at a large merchantman being unloaded. "That one alone could carry hundreds of troops."

"I wish," Arryk said. "But even if she could run the river, I can't afford more than a few ships that size."

They were silent for a moment. Larisa chewed her lip while Arryk became increasingly wet and miserable.

"Why must you take the river?" she finally asked.

"It's the most direct way." He'd never considered another.

"True. But is it the best? Why not come over land?"

"From where?"

"Someplace with a nice beach and where you're likely to find allies."

"Allies?" Arryk hadn't considered that either, but liked the idea of getting help. "Would anyone be willing with the empress so powerful?"

"Maybe. What about Helvundala? Isn't the princess there Kendryk's aunt?"

"She is. And Helvundala has nice flat beaches."

"It's perfect." Larisa took his arm. "You can land on the beach, gather up allies and march on the castle in force. Even better," she dragged him along the dock until they stood in front of the merchantman, "you can use ships of this size to carry troops and horses over."

"I still can't afford to buy them."

"Don't then. You can borrow them, rent them, confiscate them, whatever you need to. And you won't need that many because you can make several trips. Load them up, take the troops over, unload them and bring them back a few more times. You'll need a few days with good weather, but you can manage that by spring."

"I like it," Arryk said. He would have to redraw all of his plans but since he had nothing but several pages of mad scribbles it was no great loss. "Come back to the palace with me. I'll need your help to work it all out."

JANNA

"I never thought I'd be happy to be back," Janna said after she, Braeden and Reno Torresia had passed through Atlona's outer gates.

"It's nice to have friends already here," Braeden said.

Reno knew they planned to marry as soon as possible and said they should come straight to his daughter Adela's house in the old town. Senta had been staying there, helping with Adela's baby.

"If you're not too tired, you can stay for a few hours. I'm sure Senta will want to feed you and fuss over you," Reno said with a friendly wink for Janna.

"I can't wait to see her." Janna brought Zoltan to a sudden halt, unable to hold back a noise of dismay. The heads of the Moraltan rebels were still on top of the city's inner wall. By now they were mostly bone and hair, but grisly all the same.

"At least Prince Kendryk's head isn't up there yet," Reno joked. "Though it's true it would be fresh and pretty."

"Oh Holy Mother!" Janna said. "Surely the empress won't ..." She was angry with Prince Kendryk for starting so much trouble, but she didn't wish for his death.

"It's unlikely," Braeden said quickly. "Her Highness has gone to a lot of trouble to keep Prince Kendryk alive. As long as his wife holds Birkenfels, she won't kill him. Probably."

"The poor man." Janna was happy to look away from the heads and up at the Arnfels instead. An enormous mass of stone, it lacked the imposing grace of a castle like Birkenfels, though it must have been three times as big. "Do you suppose he's in the dungeon?"

"I would think so," Braeden said.

Janna fell in next to him. "Is it very terrible in there?" Braeden had never

39

talked much about his brief stay there after he'd defied the empress by arresting Daciana Tomescu.

"I imagine it's worse in the winter, being so cold, but either way, it's dark and there's nothing to do. He's more likely to die of boredom than beheading."

That didn't make her feel much better and it was a relief to lose sight of the castle in the narrow streets. Then she forgot all about it once she saw the many shops and pretty houses. It had been so long since she'd been in a real city. She'd spent most of her last stay in Atlona in the Sanovan camp near the imperial palace.

"You must do some shopping while we're here," Braeden said. "I want you to have plenty of warm things, and pretty ones too."

"That would be nice." She smiled at him. "Though I'll soon be too fat for most of them."

"Adela might have a few things you can use," Reno said. "You're of a size with her."

"I'll ask Senta," Janna said.

It didn't take long to find the tall, narrow, crowded house. Adela lived inside with her husband and baby, but so did her husband's parents, his brother and wife, and two younger sisters. Senta had been packed in with the baby, but she'd rejoin Reno in the camp soon.

Senta had seen them coming and ran out into the street to greet them. Reno jumped down from his horse, picked her up, swung her around, then kissed her long and deeply. Braeden and Janna couldn't help but grin at each other. With any luck they'd be the same in twenty years.

Braeden lifted Janna down, then handed the horses over to a young trooper responsible for getting them back to camp.

Janna was scarcely on the ground before Senta enveloped her in a hug and soon they were crying and talking over each other.

Still holding onto Janna, Senta led them inside. They all barely fit into a small front parlor. "Adela will be here as soon as the baby is awake," Senta said. "In the meantime, you must tell me your plans."

"We plan to get married," Braeden said.

"I should hope so," Senta said. "It's much nicer to do it before she shows. I'm still angry that I couldn't wear my best dress because I was too fat."

"Can you get that dress again?" Braeden asked. "You know the one ..."

"Of course I know. The empress dress. When do you want to do it?"

"Tomorrow," Braeden said, and Janna laughed.

Senta shook her head. "I doubt it can be done. We must find a temple and a priest, and plan for a little party. A week?"

"A week will be perfect." Janna wondered how they could arrange anything in such a short time. "Please let me help."

"Absolutely not," Senta said. "I am happy to do this. I have wanted nothing more than a wife for Signor all these many years and I could never find a girl good enough for him. This is a dream come true for me." She put her hand over her heart and Janna worried she might cry again. "I was not even so happy when our own Cara married."

"That's because she married that silly fop," Reno growled.

"Edwyn is a very nice young man," Senta said. "Though he isn't a soldier and takes a bit too much care with his clothing, but he adores our girl."

"He adores her because she's as silly as he is." Reno shook his head.

"It is true, they are very silly together," Senta agreed. "They will do well at court I think. But I am happier about these two. Just look at them. Not silly at all."

"That's a relief," Braeden said.

Senta insisted they stay to supper, which was a crowded, lively and delicious affair. Senta and Adela shouted at each other over the din, arguing about which temple to use and where to hold the feast.

"Oh, I don't want a feast," Janna said. "It's too much."

"Just a little one," Senta said.

"You must let her," Adela said. "Mama loves feasts and Cara's mother-in-law planned hers. I'm surprised there wasn't bloodshed."

Janna looked at Braeden, who shrugged and grinned. They both knew Senta and it was best to let her have her way.

They walked back to the parade ground after supper. The sky had cleared and it was a cold, starry night. Janna looked down as they passed the inner wall with its heads, but after that they both enjoyed the view. She linked her arm with Braeden's and laid her head on his shoulder as they walked.

"It seems so long ago that we went to the palace," Janna said. "I feel like a different person."

"Much has changed," Braeden agreed. "For the better, I hope."

"Oh yes." She smiled up at him. It was true, she was mostly happy now. She still remembered Anyezka and Anton with a pang, and thinking of having a baby of her own sometimes caused her a bit of wistful pain. But she was so much stronger now, and she had Braeden. Together, they would keep this baby—and any future babies—safe.

KENDRYK

Though Kendryk was miserable and in pain, he couldn't complain about his treatment. He understood little of medicine, but clearly Sybila was good at what she did. Unsurprising, if she served the empress herself. Still, he wasn't sure if he would survive, or if he wanted to.

For all he knew, his family were refugees and Teodora had killed Edric already. She might just be keeping Kendryk alive to hold leverage over any other rebels. Or she wanted him able to mount the scaffold without help. Much as he didn't care if he lived or died, the very idea of that gave him chills. The pain itself wouldn't be any worse than what he'd already endured, but trying to be brave in front of so many who wished him dead seemed almost impossible.

"Why so gloomy?"

He started, since he hadn't heard Sybila enter the room.

He smiled back at her friendly face. "I can't imagine. Maybe I'm offended because no one invited me to the victory feast."

"Better that no one did," Sybila said lightly. "You'd be the main dish."

"True," Kendryk said, unable to keep smiling for long.

Sybila fussed with his bandages and made tsking noises over them.

Kendryk wrinkled his nose. "Is that smell coming from me?"

"I'm afraid so. That wound is still festering, though your fever isn't so bad. I worry I'll have to take the leg, or at least part of it."

"I don't suppose it makes much difference, does it?"

"You might die if the infection spreads."

"I think that would be best."

Sybila stopped what she was doing and sat down next to him. She took one of his hands in her tiny, warm one. "I wish you didn't feel that way."

"Can you blame me? I've lost everything, and I doubt I'll get it back. I'll never see my wife and children again and I'm responsible for my country's destruction."

Sybila sighed. "It's not as bad as all that."

"It is."

"No, it's not." She got up and closed the door after looking down the corridor both ways. She sat back down and took both his hands in hers. "Now, you must promise me you will tell no one about this. The empress is certain of your ignorance, so you mustn't let on, no matter how much she goads you."

"I promise." Kendryk's heart suddenly beat much faster. What the empress's friends considered good news might be rather different from what was good for him.

"There is a great deal of hope," Sybila said. "Your wife still holds the castle of Birkenfels and refuses to treat with the empress."

The relief washing over him was so profound he trembled and had to gasp for air before he could speak. "Thank the gods. I hoped she would, but I worried the castle might not hold."

Sybila seemed to understand and stroked his hands until he could master himself. "It has, according to the last news I received. And as time goes by, she might be persuaded to surrender in exchange for you."

"I don't want her to," Kendryk said. "I made her promise not to."

Sybila pulled back a bit and frowned. "Goodness, that's rather strange."

"I have my reasons."

"I'm sure you do." Sybila looked at him searchingly. "Now, it's possible the empress will mention it. She would very much like to have that castle and the priest your wife still shelters. You won't consider an exchange with him?"

"That's exactly what I won't consider, and I made my wife swear not to as well. If he falls into the empress's hands, then all of this was for nothing."

Sybila squeezed his hands while shaking her head. "I admire your principles, even after what you've been through, though I don't claim to understand. You could be reunited with your family and live in comfort in Norovaea. Who knows what might happen after that? You are still very young. You might even see Terragand again someday."

"I can't do that. I won't do it." Saying the words helped prop up his resolve, because Kendryk had to admit that he would do just about anything to see Gwynneth and the children. And the idea of living in peace somewhere nice became more tempting as every day passed with nothing but chilly stone walls around him.

"Please give it some thought. You are still unwell and I'd hoped to give you something to look forward to."

Kendryk smiled. "You've made me feel much better. If the empress had given me the same news, I might have suspected her of lying. At least now I'm no longer worried about my family."

"Count Ensden still besieges the castle."

"Gwynneth won't give in. And before long, she'll receive help from somewhere. I'm sure of it."

"I'm glad you're a bit more hopeful. Now I want you to concentrate all of your will on healing. A great deal might still happen and you will be better able to face it if you are well and strong and in possession of both legs."

"I'd prefer that too." Kendryk managed one more smile before she left. As soon as the heavy door closed behind her and he heard the key turning in the lock, he screwed his eyes shut. He had done his best to put his family from his mind because the thought they might already be dead was too painful. But now he could allow himself a little hope, he tried to picture them in the castle, safe behind its thick walls. It would be hard to wait for help but Gwynneth was strong and she'd keep the children in good spirits. He just hoped they knew he was still alive and that the knowledge would comfort them.

TEODORA

"He must be better by now!" It wasn't a question. Teodora had waited more than long enough.

"Better yes, but still not strong, and I worry his leg isn't healing as it should." Sybila was unflappable as ever.

"Can he carry on a conversation?"

"Well enough."

"That's all I need." Teodora rose from behind the table and Sybila stood as well. "You'll accompany me to the Arnfels. I don't wish him to die of shock when he sees me." She'd welcome an hour away from her never-ending work.

"I've already told him you might call on him," Sybila said. "He'll be as prepared as he can be."

It was a crisp, sunny winter's day, so Teodora went on horseback while Sybila followed in a coach. She'd had little time for outdoor exercise since returning. Though the nobles of Olvisya were falling into line well enough, they still complained and stalled at every opportunity. One would think a penny of tax had never been collected from any of them, and considering her lily-livered forebears, that might well be the case. They'd become accustomed to her way soon enough, even though it cost her every waking hour.

She rode straight into the courtyard of the castle, dismounted and went in. Sybila would be there soon but Teodora wouldn't mind a moment alone with her prize. It was reassuring to see guards lining the corridor outside his room deep inside the fortress. She didn't like that he wasn't in the dungeon, but didn't see how anyone could attempt a rescue as things stood. She couldn't think of who would try.

A guard opened the door and Teodora swept in, wrinkling her nose at a faint smell of putrefaction; Sybila was right about his wound.

"Bring light," she ordered the guard, who materialized with a lamp.

Teodora advanced on the bed. The little prince was asleep. She took the lamp and nodded dismissal at the guard. She stood at the foot of the bed for a moment and studied him. He looked far better than he had on the road. It probably helped that Sybila had cleaned him up. He'd even had a recent shave, assuming such a baby needed one. She took a step closer, and he opened his eyes, blinking against the light. She allowed herself a moment to enjoy their beauty before moving closer.

"Your Highness," he said, his tone as courtly as always.

"Prince Kendryk," she said, just as politely, wondering how much longer she'd address him that way. That was up to him. She sat down on the edge of the bed. "I must discuss a few things with you."

"I thought you might." He still wasn't as cowed as she would have liked. That would change soon.

"First, I'd like to let you know that your wife and children are safe and well, for the time being."

"That's good," he said calmly.

"That can change quickly, I assure you."

"Really?"

"It can. They are in my custody and are being treated as befits their station. Should you fail to agree to my proposal, that will no longer be the case."

"I'd like to see them."

"What?"

"If you have them in custody then I'd like to see them. My wife or daughter please, so they can verify that they're being treated well."

This was unacceptable. Sybila had done her job too well and he was feeling a little too good. Teodora put one hand on his thigh and pressed down.

He yelped, but quickly clenched his teeth and was quiet. She kept the pressure on. He turned pale and started shaking.

"Your Highness, please!" Sybila had come in, and snatched up Teodora's hand. "You're hurting him. Even the smallest bit of pressure ..."

"Oh, I'm sorry," Teodora said, her eyes never leaving Kendryk's. "We were just talking. My hand must have slipped."

"Please be more careful, Your Highness." Sybila was too comfortable around her. They had been in school together and Sybila had delivered all of her children, but it didn't excuse her lack of proper deference. Teodora would have to have a word.

When she turned back to Kendryk, he'd recovered a little.

"I'm afraid I can't allow your family to visit," she said sweetly. "Too risky."

"Then I can't agree to your proposal, whatever it is."

"Your agreement isn't required in any case. You will abdicate as ruler of Terragand." She paused here and watched him. He hadn't been expecting that, judging by how he turned paler than she thought possible.

There was a long silence and it was gratifying to hear how hard his breath was coming. "As it turns out, my agreement is required. My charter clearly states that—"

"Oh, not that damned charter again!" she exploded, standing up. "Your charter is irrelevant. I am nullifying it and creating another one."

"You can't—"

"Yes I can. Who will stop me? One of your many allies?"

That hit its mark. She stood over him, smirking at his trembling lip. "Furthermore," she said, "Terragand's new charter allows me to choose its ruler. And you're in luck; your family name will live on. Your uncle Evard Bernotas will be the new prince of Terragand."

If she had liked him in the least, the wounded look in his eyes would have been unbearable. Fortunately, she hated him more than anyone. She stared at him a moment longer, then turned on her heel and left the room.

ARRYK

The end when it came, came quickly. Arryk received a message from Classen in the middle of the night. He threw on a dressing gown and ran, meeting Aksel in the corridor. They hurried to the king's chambers. Several doctors clustered around the bed, but made way for the princes.

"What's happening?" Aksel asked.

"His breath is leaving his body at last," a doctor said.

"Why now?" Aksel wondered.

Another one shrugged. "Hard to say. Since the attack several months ago, he has lost one vital function after another. It was only a matter of time before either his heart or his breath stopped."

The king was very quiet, but clearly struggled to breathe.

"Father, can you hear me?" Arryk asked, moving closer. The air in the room was still and oppressive. Taking just two steps required huge effort.

There was no response besides an increased wheezing which went on for a few moments, then stopped. The room was completely quiet.

Finally, one of the doctors felt for a pulse. "It's over," he said. "Andres Roussay the Fifth, King of Norovaea is dead. Long live King Arryk the Eighth."

He'd expected this for so long, but it still seemed unreal. To his surprise, Arryk wanted to cry. He'd never been close to his father, but as parents went, he'd been all right. He'd always been there, and now he was gone. Arryk glanced at his brother, who stood as if frozen, looking down at his father's body. He was unsure of what to do next, and so was everyone else, it seemed. Then he realized they were waiting for him to act, which paralyzed him completely.

He ventured a glance at Norvel Classen, then wished he hadn't. The enormous man had fat tears running down his cheeks and couldn't contain his sobs. He had probably been closer to King Andres than anyone else in the world.

That helped. Arryk walked over to Classen and clapped him on the shoulder.

"Thank you for your loyalty to my father," he said. Classen looked up at him in surprise. "No, I mean it. We've had our differences, but you were a great help to my father and he trusted you with good reason."

Classen nodded, unable to speak. Arryk squeezed his shoulder and moved on. He thanked the doctors, then put an arm around Aksel, still standing at the bedside.

"Shouldn't I be more sad?" Aksel whispered. "It just doesn't seem real."

"It probably won't for a while."

"Now what?"

"Now we let the doctors do what they must and we go back to bed. Tomorrow I'll figure out what to do."

In his chamber, Larisa was up and waiting for him. "One of the servants told me," she said. "Are you all right?"

"A bit stunned, though I'm not sure why. He was ill for so long." Arryk sat down heavily. "I was so anxious for this, but now I feel bad."

"He was your father." Larisa came over and sat on his lap, wrapping her arms around him. "Of course you feel bad. Oh, and congratulations, King Arryk." She kissed his cheek.

"Thank you. A doctor already said something about that and at first I didn't realize he was talking about me."

"You'll get used to it. Not so used to it that you'll do without me, though," she said gravely, looking into his eyes.

"Of course I won't do without you. I need you more now. I have no idea what I'm doing." And it was true. He'd never given much thought to the actions required of a king and assumed he would understand his role because he'd been born to it. Now he realized he didn't know the first thing about ruling. He needed to rescue his sister, but aside from that, a whole country now waited for his next act. It was overwhelming.

"I can't advise you on how to be king, but I can help you with military matters." Larisa laid her head on his shoulder. "And other things." She patted his knee.

"Good." He pulled her closer. "That's all I need from you."

He'd need to find someone to give him political advice soon. It was annoying, but that someone would likely be Classen. So much for sending him into immediate retirement.

TEODORA

"Your Highness, I'm afraid these terms are ..." Evard Bernotas looked at the document, the quill poised above it.

"Different," Teodora offered. "Different from what your forebears were given and from what your nephew ruled by. But the times are also different. What seemed sensible a thousand years ago no longer does. We don't live in times of robber barons and kings who ruled by courtesy, if they ruled at all. Our enemies have created powerful kingdoms with powerful rulers and the Olvisyan Empire must keep up."

"But ... but according to this, Terragand is no longer a sovereign kingdom." The duke put down the quill. "I do wish to rule, but not under these terms."

"Then I will find someone who does." Teodora smiled and reached for the quill. "I imagine someone like Aidan Orland won't turn up his nose, and he also has a suitable heir. Perhaps even more suitable than yours."

There was a long silence while the duke's jaw worked and his face turned varying shades of red and purple. Teodora hoped he survived the stress. Others could take his place, but she'd have to argue all of this again. It was uncomfortably warm in her private study, perhaps because a wintry late-afternoon sun warmed the room through the tall windows, or perhaps because Teodora's frustration was rising.

"So, if I sign this document," the duke said slowly, "Terragand becomes a kingdom with the status of Moralta or Marjatya."

Teodora nodded.

"I will be just a governor, ruling at your pleasure."

"You will be more than a governor. You will be a prince, and a hereditary one at that. Barring outright rebellion, I cannot remove you or your heirs from your position. What's different is that you will no longer print your own currency or be able to treat with foreign powers. Your treaties with countries like Sanova and

Norovaea will need to be rewritten, though I imagine terms can remain the same."

"I doubt Norovaea will agree to that," the duke grumbled.

"We'll worry about that later," Teodora said, handing the quill back. "Any more questions?"

The duke took the quill, but laid it down again. "I'd like money," he said flatly.

Teodora laughed. "I'm giving you a kingdom, and you want money? You can't be serious."

"I'm very serious. You're giving me a kingdom which has been half destroyed."

"Because of your nephew's foolishness, which you supported."

"I did not." A vein throbbed in his temple. "I was completely opposed and told him so."

"And yet, you fought off the hussars at the gap, and stood beside Kendryk on the field at Birkenfels." She didn't need to bring up the fact that his wing had crumbled first and he had surrendered to Demario Barela in less than an hour of fighting.

"He had my son." The duke gritted out between clenched teeth.

"I understand," Teodora said. "I would have done the same had it been one of my darlings." In truth, she wished Elektra were in someone's dungeon, preferably dying there, so someone else could be her heir. She was still amazed she'd somehow produced such a plain, stupid girl and was certain it hadn't come from her side. The Inferraras might be a touch eccentric, but they always possessed striking looks and some measure of intelligence. Common blood must be hidden somewhere in her husband's impeccable lineage.

"The fact remains that Terragand is devastated, and I don't have the funds to restore it." The duke drummed his fingers on the table.

Teodora felt her blood rise. If anyone in this room was entitled to a tantrum, she was, not this supplicant. And yet, she was tired of delays. She wanted this wrapped up now. She had to remind herself that part of being a wise ruler included moderation of one's temper, in spite of annoying subjects.

Teodora drew a deep breath and pondered while she calmed herself. She didn't want to start handing out money. If she did, there would be no end to the petitioners. But it was true that Terragand could not meet its new and increased tax obligations in its current state.

She thought of the look in Kendryk's eyes when she presented him with this document and that decided it. "All right then; sign this at once, and I'll see you get a loan from the treasury."

"I'll want better than the usual terms," the duke said, quill poised once more.

"Of course," Teodora said. It was no wonder Prince Kendryk hadn't loved this uncle. He was quite horrible. "How does a five percent discount from the usual rate sound?"

"Ten," the duke said.

"Seven," Teodora replied, anger leaking out around the edges of her voice.

"Done." And Evard Bernotas signed the new charter of the Imperial Kingdom of Terragand. Kendryk was no longer a prince and no longer had a kingdom.

JANNA

Janna's first wedding had been terrifying. She'd been so young and Dimir was a stern, distinguished stranger. This time she was excited and happy, but she had to wait. Senta hadn't been able to line up both a temple and a feast as quickly as she'd hoped, so it was nearly a month before the ceremony could take place. Senta wouldn't let Janna help, so she occupied herself by shopping for new clothes and altering the ones Adela gave her to wear later in the pregnancy.

After a string of dark, rainy days, the day of the wedding dawned cold and sunny. Braeden had hired a fine carriage and Senta brought the dress over the night before. To her relief, Janna hadn't been sick in the morning in over a week.

Braeden wore the same suit he had worn to the empress's feast the previous summer. He helped Janna into the dress, then stood back to admire her. "You look perfect," he said. "Senta will be so pleased."

Janna laughed and took his arm. "What about you?"

"I'm very happy." He handed her into the carriage and climbed in after her. It was warm inside, so they were a bit disheveled by the time they arrived at the little temple in the old city.

"You are supposed to wait until after." Senta shook her head as she repaired Janna's hair.

"That horse left the stable some time ago," Braeden said, patting Janna's bottom, though she couldn't feel his hand through the voluminous skirts. It seemed neither one of them could stop smiling.

They both gasped with pleasure as they entered the temple. It was small and over one hundred years old, a beautiful example of the ornate style of that time. A famous Cesiano artist had painted the icons at the high altar and gold leaf adorned every cornice and crevice.

An elderly, dignified priest presided. The ceremony was short and simple, with only the Torresias, Novitny, Franca, Miro and Adela's family present.

Franca even wore a dress, though she looked very uncomfortable.

"You didn't have to," Braeden said, when she came to offer her congratulations.

"I felt the occasion demanded it, sir," she said. "Though if you don't mind, I'll change into something more comfortable for the feast."

"I don't mind too much," Braeden said, laughing at her obvious relief.

The feast took place at a small inn not far from the temple. They gathered in a room toward the back and a jolly innkeeper brought trays of food. The guests may have been few, but the food was plentiful.

Janna thought the whole roast pig provided more than enough meat, but it was accompanied by four kinds of sausage, from very mild to a spicy Marjatyan variety. There were dumplings made of herbed bread, thick noodles blanketed in cheese and onions, several different stewed vegetables and fruit, and the wine flowed freely. Through the open door, Janna spotted a table laden with cakes and pastries. She wondered who would eat all of it.

Everyone had just settled down to loaded plates when there was a small commotion.

"I didn't know you were in town, General," Braeden said, jumping up upon seeing a dark, wiry man wearing black velvet adorned with puffs of gold lace stride into the room.

Janna recognized Demario Barela under the enormous black hat with its plumes of red and gold. The rest of the wedding party, bride and groom included, looked dull by comparison.

"I've just arrived from Kronland." Barela swept off his hat and executed a courtly bow in front of Janna. "I was looking for your superior officer," he added, nodding at Prince Novitny, who raised a goblet in his direction before downing its contents, "and was told there was a party going on. I hate to miss a party, you know." He winked at Janna, who promptly blushed. "I understand congratulations are in order."

Janna, blushed some more when Barela then greeted her in the Maladene fashion. This exotic custom started with a nibble on her fingers, followed by a kiss on each cheek and one that lingered on her lips. Fortunately, Braeden didn't seem the least bit offended by the attention paid his wife, and gave the general over to Senta, who became uncharacteristically flustered at similar treatment.

Once he'd kissed all women present, was seated and provisioned, General Barela said. "I have interesting news from Norovaea."

KENDRYK

Kendryk opened his eyes and blinked when the door burst open and lamplight flooded the room. Only one person made this sort of entrance. He tried to prepare himself for whatever it was she might put him through.

He was strong enough now, so he pulled himself into a sitting position. "Your Highness," he croaked, his throat parched, and not just from lack of water.

"Please, don't get up on my account," Teodora said, an unpleasant smile fixed on her face.

"I won't then," Kendryk said, before reminding himself to mind his tongue. He didn't need to make things worse than they already were.

She pulled up a chair and sat so they faced each other. He studied her face for any new signs of strain or weariness. It was hard to tell.

"So," she said. "It seems Sybila has worked a miracle and won't need to saw off your leg."

"She's an excellent doctor."

"She is. I must confess that I'm sorry about your leg. I would enjoy watching her cut it off."

"Why are you so horrid? Isn't it enough that I'm here, in this condition? Besides, I'm sure you could have someone hack off my leg anyway, if it would make you happy." There didn't seem to be much point in being polite.

"Somehow, it's never enough," she said, with a smirk. "Though I bring news that might make you feel even worse."

She must have captured his family after all. He thought he'd been prepared for this, but still felt it like a punch to his chest. He resorted to his old training to keep his face neutral no matter what. Her victory might be complete now, but he wouldn't give her the satisfaction of seeing him break down.

"But first," she said, in that same smug tone, "I'd like to ask you one more time to abdicate as ruler of Terragand."

"What are you offering in exchange?"

She laughed and struck his wounded leg. It no longer hurt as it once had. He didn't even flinch.

"You're not in a good position to negotiate," she said.

"It's not a negotiation. I doubt very much that you can offer me anything that would force me to abdicate."

"Your family—" she began.

"If you have them, show me." He was determined to call her bluff, even if it killed him. "It shouldn't be that hard to arrange. That I haven't seen them means that they aren't in your power, or you've murdered them already. In either case, you can't sway me."

"You think you're so clever, don't you?" she asked, her mouth tightening.

"Not really." He let his head fall back against the pillow. Arguing with her wore him out quickly.

"In any case, I was only asking for your permission as a courtesy, since I don't need it. I might as well give you the news."

He nodded, wondering if he was prepared for whatever she was about to tell him.

"You are no longer Prince of Terragand," she said. "I have removed you from your position and given it to your uncle Evard. He kindly agreed to a new charter as well."

"He's a traitor," Kendryk said. "It's still illegal and no one else in Kronland will accept it."

"Princess Zelenka already has."

"Everyone knows she's your toady."

"It doesn't matter." Teodora tossed her head. "As far as everyone is concerned, you are no longer a prince and you no longer have a country."

Kendryk was certain she would not get away with this. This new charter was nothing more than a piece of paper, and unless every last one of the other Kronland rulers ratified it, it had no meaning. "I refuse to agree to this arrangement."

"Your agreement isn't required, though it would bring Kronland into line faster and I wouldn't need to kill half the population."

"You'd do it anyway, just for fun." Kendryk wished she would go away. The meaning of what she had done was finally trickling into his brain and he now had to fight for composure. Illegal as it was, he realized she could do this because no one could stand against her. His kingdom was gone.

"Maybe I will," she said, and stood. "I hope you aren't offended if I no longer address you as prince. You are now just Kendryk Bernotas and not entitled to any special treatment." She walked to the door and called into the corridor. A guard came. "Take Master Bernotas to the dungeon."

She turned to Kendryk once more. "I hope you enjoyed the sunshine today. You will never see it again."

ARRYK

If Arryk hadn't felt like a king until now, that changed with the weight of the long fur cloak with its twelve-foot train on his shoulders, the heavy jewel-studded crown pushing down onto his head, and the ancient forked scepter of the Roussays in his right hand. By the time the old Maximus pronounced him sovereign over the lands of Old Norovaea and all of the Northern Sea, and he saw the faces of everyone in the temple gazing at him reverently, he thought he might be up to the task.

That feeling didn't survive the day. As he had feared, Arryk found he couldn't do without Norvel Classen. In fact, there was no one suitable in the entire country to replace him.

It had never occurred to Arryk that he should cultivate political in addition to military advisers. Everyone at court worked for Classen, or at least sympathized with him. Arryk's friends and supporters were young military officers with no political clout or experience.

"I'll be honest," Arryk said. He sat at his father's desk in his father's study the day after the coronation, going over papers with Classen. "I wanted to replace you, but I don't know how I can."

"You must do so before long," Classen said. He'd been uncommonly kind and patient, showing Arryk what went into ruling. It was clear that the king had left his heir woefully unprepared to step into his shoes, though it was true Arryk had shown little interest in being guided. It occurred to him that Gwynneth would have relished this and excelled at it. Not only did Arryk not understand much of administrative matters, they also bored him to tears. And now that he'd spent a few days at a desk, he was even more eager to set out for Kronland.

"Can you help me find someone?" Arryk asked. "Although you are welcome to stay on a while, if you don't mind."

"That depends," Classen said. He looked like he'd lost several stone in the past few days and it didn't suit him. "Do you still insist on this ill-advised action in Kronland?"

"I do."

"Then I cannot in good conscience stay on."

"Why not? You need do nothing on that score. I just need someone to manage things here. I'd hoped Aksel might want to, but he has no interest."

"And very little knowledge. No, it's better he stay in his laboratory for now, though it would benefit us all if he started to take an interest in politics."

"I don't even know what he does in his laboratory."

"Develops high explosives, last I heard."

"In his rooms? Right here in the palace?" Arryk thought of how close they were to his own.

"Where else? Don't worry; he's working with small amounts so will only blow himself up if something goes wrong."

"That's not very comforting."

"He's careful. He's safer in there than on campaign in Kronland."

"I don't think we'll be there long. I'll help my sister and come back right away."

"It never works out as easily as you think. You can expect to be there many months and lose many soldiers. But I can't convince you. Until you have been at war you can't know."

"Have you been at war?"

"Yes, long ago." Classen nodded. "For a short time. It was enough."

"I must go, no matter what."

"I see." Classen sighed heavily. "Then you leave me no choice. For the good of the country, I'll take care of things while you're gone and look for my replacement. I'm afraid I won't find anyone before you insist on leaving."

"Thank you," Arryk said. "I'm very grateful and I won't forget this." When he returned from Kronland, he'd see that Classen was richly rewarded for his service and then he could retire. One of the best things about being king was the ability to dole out favors. Arryk was already making sure that his closest friends and their families were well-provided-for. He needed to work especially hard now to develop his own loyal following.

With domestic matters settled for the time being, Arryk prepared his ships and soldiers. He planned to land his entire force on the beaches of Helvundala in just a few weeks' time.

GWYNNETH

So many weeks had gone by unchanged that it was almost a pleasant surprise to spot a messenger bearing a white flag. Almost. Gwynneth was certain no message would bring good news for her.

"Shall we receive it, Your Grace?" Merton asked. They stood on the castle walls, looking down over the still-raised drawbridge.

"Why not? I doubt it's anything we want to know, but that doesn't matter." Neither one said it, but one of the few events meriting a message was Kendryk's death. Gwynneth tried to prepare herself. Whatever the news, she couldn't fall apart in front of everyone.

"Do you suppose it's a trap?" Merton looked concerned.

Gwynneth leaned over the parapet, pulling her cloak close as the wind whipped around her. She saw one horseman. "We have a clear view in all directions. No one else is coming. Take the message and ask if a reply is needed. If so, he can come back later. Post everyone we have at the gate in case he tries something."

Merton soon returned with a small pouch in his hand. "No reply needed," he said, looking pale. He was probably as worried as she was about its contents.

No point in keeping them both in suspense. She opened the pouch, her heart in her mouth, her stiff cold fingers fumbling with the Imperial seal. The letter inside was in Teodora's own handwriting. Gwynneth read it quickly, relief washing over her in such a powerful wave she had to lean against the wall. Anger soon followed.

"Prince Kendryk is alive. But the empress has done something outrageous." Gwynneth handed the letter to Merton.

"Can she do that?" he asked after reading it.

"Not legally. But who's to stop her? No one is coming to help us, let alone prevent her from anything." Gwynneth was unable to keep the bitterness from her voice. "I must speak with Edric Maximus," she said, turning toward the tower.

She hadn't seen him in some time. This pregnancy, her fourth, left her feeling melancholy and she feared seeing Edric too often would weaken her resolve. He remained concrete evidence of Kendryk's plight and the easiest way to end it. She didn't want to be tempted. But she was tempted no longer.

The study door was ajar and she knocked softly before pushing it open.

"Your Grace." The Maximus stood. "Is all well?"

To her surprise, she found herself weak in the knees and sank into a chair. "There's been a message from Teodora," she said, handing it to him.

His face drew into a frown as he read. "This might do it."

"Do what? This is a disaster, and no one can stop her."

"No one is stopping her right now." Edric handed the letter back and came around the desk to sit down across from her. "But that will soon change."

"I don't see how. It's been months and there's no sign of my brother. If he doesn't come, who will? I try not to lose hope, but it's becoming more and more difficult."

"The waiting is difficult, I agree. I've had all-consuming work to keep me distracted but you've not been so fortunate."

"I can't help but worry about running out of food."

"That won't be for awhile, will it?"

"No, not for several months. Some things have spoiled, but we can make it through the spring. After that ..."

"Something will happen by then. You must believe it, Princess."

"I have to, or I couldn't bear it. But if Arryk hasn't come by now, he won't. I don't know what's kept him or what has happened. The empress doesn't mention defeating him in battle and I'm sure she wouldn't hesitate to rub my face in that if she could."

"Princess, please. Please don't despair. This letter means the tide is about to turn."

"I don't understand."

"Teodora has overreached herself here. The rest of Kronland won't stand for it."

"They've stood for it so far."

"They weren't directly threatened before. This is different. It's a clear message from Teodora as to her intentions. This forces the Kronland rulers to choose sides, because if they allow this to stand, all of their rights are in jeopardy."

"Will they all see it that way?" Gwynneth couldn't trust the flicker of hope.

For once, she wanted Edric to be right.

"I'm sure they will," he said, his voice firm. "And I have faith that rescue is at hand. If not from your brother than from someone else."

"Falk or Dahlby, maybe," she said, even though she didn't believe it. "They were always the most sympathetic to you and to Kendryk and most jealous of their rights."

"Can you picture Prince Falk taking this news calmly?"

She almost smiled. "No, I cannot."

"Neither can I. This forces him to act, and I'm sure the other northerners will feel the same way. The Princesses Kasbirk and Martinek may well join them."

"Oh, if only," Gwynneth said. "I suppose this also means that Kendryk is still alive, if she had to formally take Terragand from him. Oh gods." She put her hands to her mouth as the terrible thought struck her. "I hope he can bear it."

"He can. The gods will give him the strength he needs. I am convinced he still has an important part to play. I may as well tell you now because I'm so close. By sunset tomorrow, I will have completed my translation of the Srolls."

Gwynneth stared at him. She had known he was working on a translation, since Maryna talked of nothing else, but for the first time, she realized what it meant. "All of them? In Olvisyan?"

Edric nodded and looked down at his ink-stained fingers.

"Well," Gwynneth said. "You've managed to impress me."

"That in itself is an accomplishment." Edric cracked a smile. "I didn't know if you would care."

"I do," Gwynneth said, surprised that she did. "In fact, I should very much like to read them."

"You would? Now I'm truly surprised."

"It's time I saw what all the fuss is about."

ARRYK

"Why did you do that?" Larisa asked. She was almost in tears. Arryk had never seen her so distraught.

"I thought you'd like it." This was a bad time for a spat. He was overseeing the embarkation of his troops and trying to keep track of what was happening in the chaos on the docks.

"Like it? Why in the world would I want to be a duchess?"

"Would you rather be a princess? I'm not sure if I can manage that. Queen I can, probably," He grinned at her, hoping to get a smile. He wasn't supposed to marry a commoner, but he'd do it if that was what she wanted.

"Stop it." She scowled. "You know that's not what I mean. I don't want a title from you."

"Why not? It's no problem for me, now that I'm king."

"You really don't understand, do you?"

"Understand what?" A rearing horse not keen on going up the gangplank distracted him.

"Are you listening to me?"

"Yes, yes," he said, turning his back on the horse. "Now, please tell me why you're unhappy."

"I don't want anything to change between us, just because you're king now. I've told you before, I don't want titles or money or anything else like that from you."

"You've said that, but surely you don't mean it. You're rich now, and have one of the highest positions in the land." Arryk's father had had mistresses; often more than one at a time. The king had given them gifts—splendid ones like mansions, estates and jewels. He'd thought to do better by giving Larisa a title.

63

"Highest paid whore, more like," she said, her lips in a white line.

"You can't be serious. No one would ..." Even as he said it, he realized that was exactly what everyone would think. In one night, Larisa had gone from being an anonymous girl who sneaked into his bed to being the king's mistress. He had hoped to improve her life, but maybe he'd been wrong. For the hundredth time, he wished he had a quicker mind, or someone in possession of one to advise him on these matters.

"See? Slow as you are, Your Highness," she said in a mocking tone, "you must realize how it looks. But it's more than that. It's that I don't want anything from you. I just want you. Nothing else." She stood in front of him, her eyes wide and angry.

He stared back, uncomprehending.

She tossed her head, made an indignant noise and started to walk away.

"Wait!" he shouted, grabbing her arm. He suddenly realized what she had said. "Are you saying you like me, and not just because I'm king?" He had always been in love with her, but assumed she was only with him because of his position.

She dashed the back of her hand across her eyes. "I seem to have fallen in love with you. I'm sure I'll regret it."

As her words sunk in, warmth spread through him. Suddenly, there was no icy wind, no spray blowing in from the sea, no ten thousand soldiers and horses and ships surrounding them. "What?" was all he managed after a long moment of silence.

"You heard what I said." Her eyes were flashing now, no longer tearful.

He swallowed hard. "You won't regret it. I swear it. And if you like, I'll undo the duchess thing, if I can." He doubted it was possible, but for her, he'd find a way.

"All right," she said, a smile reaching her lips, though she quickly looked stern again. "Please do it as soon as you can, before someone finds out. But first, let's board this ship and rescue your sister."

TEODORA

"General Barela requests an audience with you, Your Highness," Brytta said. "If it's too late, I'll tell him to come back in the morning."

"No, I'll see him. He might have important news." Teodora hoped her tone was neutral, though she thought she detected a fleeting sly look on Brytta's pretty face. "I won't need you any more tonight," she added.

Teodora had been at her desk for at least twelve hours. She stood up and stretched, wishing she had a moment to let her hair down and change into something less formal. She stopped herself. They hadn't seen each other in several months and she must not appear overeager.

Teodora pasted a noncommittal smile on her face, though her heart beat so hard she was sure the whole palace could hear. The door opened and he stood before her.

"Your Highness," he said, with that smile she loved. He bowed, but she crossed the floor to him in a few steps, and he straightened up, taking her hands in his. He raised each of them to his lips before pulling her in close. "I've missed you terribly, Your Highness."

"I wonder." She pulled back. "You've been having all of the fun, while I've been stuck here by myself." She suddenly realized she was starving. "Have you dined?"

"I have," he said. "I stopped by a friend's wedding just now."

It was annoying that he hadn't come straight to her, but she concealed it. "An important wedding?"

He shrugged. "Not particularly. They are unusual in that they seem to be happier than most."

"How lovely," she said, her tone making it clear she didn't care. "You don't mind if I have a bite?"

"Not at all. I can tell you the news in the meantime."

"So there is news." She pulled the bell rope. "Please tell me you caught Count Faris, or killed him."

"I did not. I apologize." He waited for her to sit, then took a seat across from her. "Count Faris made it over the Zeelund border before I caught up with him. He had less than three hundred soldiers. I would have pursued, but my queen is in particularly delicate negotiations with Zeelund right now."

Teodora snorted, realizing too late it was not an inviting or ladylike sound.

"Oh, I know," he said, flashing a grin. "I work for you, and I am of course in love with you, but she is still my queen. It is a shame. You would be a much better one. You would make Maladena great again."

To her chagrin, Teodora flushed with pleasure. Perhaps he wouldn't see in the dim light. She hated how she was unable to take the upper hand with him, as she did with most men. "So, you didn't catch Faris. Did you find out what he's up to?"

"Yes, I did. He's going to all of the bankers, trying to raise money."

"Will he succeed?"

"I don't know. The Zeelunders would like to keep me occupied in Kronland as long as possible. That way I cannot torment them in Floradias."

"You can hardly blame them. I suppose the question is, will they give Faris enough to matter?"

"I hope not," Barela said. "He is a poor risk, and those bankers are people of business. They will think twice before throwing their money away on a general who has just been so soundly defeated."

"That is mostly good news."

"Yes. But there is bad also. While I was on my way back to you, I received word that King Andres of Norovaea finally died."

"Oh dear."

"Yes. I was already in Arcius, or I might have marched back into Terragand. I hope I did the right thing coming here."

"You did. Is there any word of what Prince Arryk might do? Though I suppose I should call him king now."

"Everyone knows Arryk wants to help his sister. But he has no party of his own at court and no understanding of what he must do to rule. It is likely he is being advised by those who worked for his father. They will counsel caution."

"Will he listen?"

"From what I have heard, probably not."

"So he might already be in Kronland."

"Very possibly. But even if he has succeeded in landing a force during the winter storms, they are untested and untrained troops. Norovaea has not been at war for twenty years and Arryk is an inexperienced commander. Until now, he's spent all of his time hunting and wenching. Not a serious person."

"Indeed." Teodora looked up as a maid brought in a tray and some wine. "He doesn't need to be serious to cause me a great deal of trouble."

"No he does not." Barela's face was grave. "I think Count Ensden will stop him for now, as long as he is alone."

"But will he be alone?" Teodora stabbed at a piece of meat with her fork. "I worry he will gather allies in Kronland."

"Perhaps. The Kronlanders are angry with you about the way you've treated Prince Kendryk."

"I was within my rights!"

"Of course. But they all now worry it could happen to them. Their charters torn up, they themselves replaced by more cooperative family members."

"I want them to worry, but not enough to rebel. Enough to cooperate."

"It's hard to find that balance, is it not? I do not envy you, my love."

"I must strengthen my forces." She had lost her appetite but none of her determination. "What if Arryk invades and all of Kronland rallies behind him? Ensden must stay at Birkenfels and you are not enough to meet the rest, brilliant as you are."

"I know that. I am also temporary. Queen Beatryz might call me back to Floradias at any time."

"I don't think I could bear it." Teodora burst out before she could stop herself.

"You can. You are the strongest person I know." He sat down next to her, then took her hand. "But you needn't be strong tonight." He kissed her palm.

Teodora felt herself going soft inside, but yanked her hand away before it got worse. "I always have to be strong, especially with you," she snapped, standing and pacing to the far side of the room.

He stood as well, but didn't follow her. "You don't, my love." His voice was soft. "But I understand if you don't believe me. Perhaps it will be better if I showed you."

She stayed in the shadows, willing herself not to move from the spot. But when he came to her and pulled her into his arms, she didn't fight him.

ARRYK

"There's a storm coming," Larisa said, standing next to Arryk on the Helvundala beach. The clouds were black, and rolling in fast. "You should bring the rest tomorrow."

They had sailed from Arenberg right after dawn with slightly over half of Arryk's forces. Even though it was still winter, it had been calm and sunny, and the Maximus said all omens showed that Ercos smiled upon this day and Arryk's mission.

The wind that had been merely brisk onshore was much stronger at sea and the sun soon disappeared behind high clouds. A crossing that should have taken five hours took nearly eight instead. It was early afternoon before they first set foot in Kronland.

Arryk watched boats ferrying soldiers ashore. Horses were led through chest-high waves that seemed to grow in strength and height. "A storm won't blow over by tomorrow, or the next day. It could last a week. I can't delay that long."

"Stupid," Larisa said.

"It's Your Highness." Arryk smiled at her. He didn't stop until he got a half-smile back. "I need your help, please."

She sighed. "Let me return with you. I'll be anxious."

"You'll worry about me?" As concerned as he was about the weather, he still felt light enough he thought he might float away whenever he remembered she was in love with him.

"Yes. I'm a worse idiot than you are."

"It's a good thing, too." He couldn't stop smiling. "But no, I need you here. Hansen will oversee getting everyone organized and making camp. They'll stay here until I've brought over the rest."

"Will one trip do it?"

"I think so. I counted a little over nine thousand here, so less than half remain in Arenberg. In the meantime I have a mission only you can carry out."

"You're just saying that."

"No, it's true. No one else can handle a cranky prince as well as you."

That brought a smile. "You're right. I have some experience with cranky princes. What must I do?"

"Take twenty soldiers and ride for Prince Bronson's seat at Oberfeld. It shouldn't be over fifteen leagues."

"Is he friendly?" Larisa frowned, pulling on riding gloves and shouting for her horse. Arryk had already seen the beautiful gray—a gift from him on her last birthday—come off the ship.

"He ought to be. His wife is Kendryk's aunt, and he's been a vocal supporter of the religious reform. With any luck, he'll join us on the march south."

"What do I say to him?"

"Send my greetings and give him this." Arryk handed her a letter. He'd had Classen help him compose it. It was a formal appeal for Prince Bronson's aid in removing imperial interference from northern Kronland once and for all. "Come back as quickly as you can with his reply. If he doesn't agree, ask if we might at least receive peaceful passage through Helvundala. We should have enough supplies to make Terragand without his help."

"He'll help," Larisa said, putting the letter in a pocket inside her coat. "I'll use my feminine wiles," she joked.

"Ercos save us all." Arryk nearly kissed her, but caught himself, and performed an awkward salute instead, which made her laugh, then turned back to the ships.

GWYNNETH

Gwynneth read all day, every day, for two weeks. She hadn't realized how long the Holy Scrolls were. She'd never cared before. Maryna sat next to her, reading each page as her mother finished. When Gwynneth put the last page down, her head ached and her eyes watered. But she sensed something else. A tightness inside her had relaxed. Maybe she no longer felt so alone, and that the gods were looking down on her, even caring about her.

Then a wave of sorrow washed over her as she carried a sleeping Maryna to the nursery. She would give anything to talk to Kendryk right now. He would have been thrilled at her interest and help her understand what she had just read. She went to her room and sent her maid to bed. Gwynneth wondered if she'd be able to sleep tonight. She pulled her chair close to the hearth and stared into the dwindling flames.

From childhood she had learned that the Holy Scrolls were dictated by the gods themselves to Teodora the Holy and her followers many centuries ago. But the words of the Ancient Tongue intoned by clerics were different from those she'd just read on the page. She knew they were the same words, since she didn't doubt the accuracy of Edric's work, but reading them herself was both comforting and unsettling. She wondered if praying would help her understand.

The fire burned down to coals, but Gwynneth stayed motionless in her chair. She closed her eyes. Praying was harder than she expected. This was so different from the formal prayers of the temple and memorized words recited at bedtime. This was a conversation with the gods and she wondered if she was good enough to talk to them directly.

Her eyes flew open. She shivered and reached for the heavy woolen shawl draped over the back of her chair, pulling it around her shoulders. Gwynneth had never been humble, but for the first time in her life she felt inadequate. She didn't like it.

And yet, something tugged at her mind and wouldn't let her rest. She had the strong impression she wouldn't until she at least tried to communicate with the gods. It was tempting to shake off the sensation, to dismiss it as superstition brought on by fatigue or the overwrought emotions of a difficult pregnancy. But she couldn't fool herself. She would have to try.

Even though the room was dark, Gwynneth closed her eyes. "Holy Vica, please help me," she whispered.

To her surprise, help did come, as she realized who she could talk to now. It was long after midnight, but she went upstairs anyway.

She found Edric still in his study, scribbling away on some new project.

"I can come back if it's too late," Gwynneth said, peeking around the door.

"No, please, come in."

She took her usual seat, relieved that a fire still burned in here. She had nearly frozen in her cold bedroom. "What you've done is incredible. I wish to apologize."

"Whatever for?" Edric put down his quill.

"For assuming this was nonsense that didn't matter. For not having faith."

A broad smile transformed his stern face. "You have faith now?"

"More than I did. Perhaps not as completely as you'd like, but you've changed my mind." Gwynneth twisted her hands in her lap. "Also, I prayed just now. I've prayed before of course, but this was different. I did as the Scrolls said and talked to the gods."

"And it worked." He was still smiling.

"Something did. I don't understand what happened, but I'm different now. I learned so many new things as I read the Scrolls, I'm sure I don't even comprehend them all. It changed me somehow, I'm certain of it." Gwynneth ended with a whisper.

"I'm so pleased, Your Grace. I've long prayed for this moment."

"Thank you." Gwynneth had to pause and stop the quiver in her voice. It was bad enough she had to admit she'd been wrong about this. To weep in front of Edric, kind as he was, would have been the worst. "I hope it's all right that I still have a lot of questions. And many doubts, I'm afraid."

"There's nothing wrong with that. We all of us start with a mere kernel of faith. With study, prayer, and the help of the gods that kernel will grow into a mighty tree with roots so deep it cannot be shaken. But that can take years."

Gwynneth smiled. "A kernel describes rather well the amount of my faith. But even that seems like a miracle."

"The gods did that. That's why everyone needs to read the Scrolls for themselves."

"Yes, you are right. At last I understand why Kendryk was so excited about your work. How will we get the Scrolls to anyone outside these walls?"

"I must make more copies. Even if we remain trapped here, there might be a way to get some out. I am sure many in Ensden's camp hunger for the truth."

"We have no printing press and no way to get one, but I'll send you everyone in the castle who can write. We'll make copies until we run out of ink." She jumped up and paced the room, more excited than she'd been since before the war. "You know," she said, turning to look at Edric, "I believe we will receive help soon. The gods will make it possible."

"I agree. Help might be taking so long because I needed time to finish this work."

"You may be right." She took both Edric's hands in hers. "Thank you for being patient with me. I will do everything I can to see that your teachings are spread everywhere when we get out of here. I swear it."

ARRYK

By the time Arryk reached Arenberg to retrieve the rest of his army, he felt lucky to be alive. The wind and seas had risen, making the return journey terrifying. Arryk had been at sea often, but never on one this high and rough. He didn't know what to do. He needed to return to Helvundala today or it might be weeks before they could try again.

"Your Highness," the captain said, as he readied to disembark and gather the rest of his army. "A storm is moving in fast. I doubt we'll make it back ahead of it."

"We have to," Arryk said. "We can't delay any longer; half my army is over there."

"As you say," the man said unhappily. "Just wanted to say for certain I'm not in favor."

"Don't worry," Arryk said glumly. "There's no question who's responsible if this goes wrong." He hated this part of being king. At first, he enjoyed doing whatever he wanted but he'd soon learned that the problems were his as well. And there were so many problems.

In spite of the terrible weather, his officers loaded the ships quickly. Most of the soldiers had stood shivering on the docks for hours, so didn't mind being packed onto crowded decks for a change.

Though wet, tired and hungry, Arryk didn't rest until he'd accounted for every person, horse and barrel. Then he boarded the last ship sailing out of the harbor. It was growing dark, and the wind howled through the sails. The captain shouted orders and sailors took in most of the canvas. Arryk decided he'd give every man who climbed the rigging in that gale a silver coin upon their safe arrival.

Arryk saw that the ships ahead of them had done the same. Now the wind might blow them anywhere. At the moment it pushed them in a southerly direction, but that meant they wouldn't make landfall with the rest of his army. He would worry about that later. First, he wanted to get everyone onto dry land safely.

As the dark gray sky grew black, the waves rose higher. The ship pitched into deep troughs and back out again. Every now and again, on the crest, Arryk spotted other ships. He tried to close his ears to the panicked shrieks of the horses below decks and the moans and vomiting of the troops above. This was bad, he told himself, but nothing like a battlefield. He'd never been in battle, but knew it must be worse than this. If he had any hope of saving his sister, he would have to bear this without fear or complaint.

The ship's pitching increased as the night blackened. A few lamps were lit, and some cold food served, although most were too nauseous to eat. Arryk had a sailor's stomach, but anxiety gnawed at him, making his heart pound and his head sweat under the woolen cap someone gave him. He offered some vague prayers to Ercos, but couldn't remember the right words. He doubted the gods cared anyway. These ships that looked so magnificent in harbor were only toys to them.

The ship creaked alarmingly but held. Surely it had survived much worse. After an eternity, a cry came from the mast. The lookout had spotted land, or rather, lights on shore. Arryk hoped the lights were those of his soldiers' camp. He also hoped they weren't warnings of rocks. Earlier, they had landed on a five-league-long stretch of smooth beach, but he knew of a few rocky areas to the east. He hoped they hadn't been blown that far off-course.

The lights came closer; perhaps they would drop anchor soon and launch the small boats in the morning.

Suddenly, there was a sharp lurch and a terrible cracking noise. A wave washed over the deck before the ship righted itself and Arryk felt his feet slide out from under him, the water dragging him back toward the sea. He flung his arms out, grasping for anything he could get hold of, and caught the rail. He held on tight as the water smashed him against it, but it didn't carry him off. Someone shrieked nearby and he hoped they hadn't gone overboard.

When he found his footing again, he looked for the captain, who shouted, "Rocks!" with a wild look in his eyes.

Arryk cursed under his breath as the captain shouted urgent orders. He doubted anyone heard them above the howling wind and the horrific tearing noises of the ship coming apart.

Arryk gripped the rail, frozen. He knew he needed to do something, but didn't know what that should be. Others looked to him to give orders or set some sort of example, but even a king wasn't able to keep a ship from sinking.

Someone plucked at his sleeve. "Your Highness." It was a young trooper he recognized, but whose name he didn't remember. "We must jump before the ship is destroyed."

"Jump?" Arryk stared at the boy. "I can't leave the ship," he said lamely.

"You must," the boy said. He looked like Aksel, though taller and without spectacles. Arryk remembered now his name was Magnus something-or-other. "If you are lost, all of us are. It's no good to sacrifice yourself."

He saw the sense in that, though it seemed so unheroic. The deck was pandemonium, barrels and people sliding everywhere while many jumped overboard.

"We must swim away from the lights," Magnus said. "Away from the rocks."

Arryk nodded and walked to the other rail. He spotted the captain again, still gripping the wheel. "Come," he shouted at him. "The ship is lost. You must come."

The captain stared at him blankly.

"I'm ordering you," Arryk shouted, shaking off Magnus tugging at him again. "Abandon ship!"

And then someone shoved him over the side. He hit the water feet first. The ship was halfway submerged already. Horses swam out from a great hole in the hull, crowding the area around the ship and making it even harder to swim. The freezing water teemed with soldiers and went up Arryk's nose when a wave came from nowhere. He started swimming. He kept bumping into horses and hadn't gone far when he heard a huge cracking shriek as the ship came apart completely.

Arryk swam harder and tried to ignore the nightmare around him. Most of those in the water couldn't swim, but he didn't know what to do for them. He forced himself to tread water until he oriented himself, finding the lights on shore and striking out to the right of them.

Next to him, someone shouted and flailed. He took them around the neck, as he'd been taught and swam toward what he hoped was the shore. The waves were so strong and the water so cold he feared he wouldn't survive long enough to reach land. He could only use the one arm because he refused to let go of the person he was holding. That slowed him down, but as his panic subsided, he realized the thought of being unable to save even one of his soldiers was unbearable.

He breathed slowly, settled into a rhythm, letting the waves pull him along, praying they would carry him to land before he died.

KENDRYK

Someone had noticed that Kendryk hadn't touched the small amount of food or water they put into his cell twice a day. He'd hoped they'd let him fade away, but wasn't that lucky. The torchlight burned his eyes as the two guards dragged him out. He could barely walk and the fact he hadn't eaten made him even weaker.

"Easier just to carry him," one of the men said, picking him up like a child. "Lost a bit of weight, have you?"

Kendryk let himself go limp, but it didn't seem to make a difference. He'd never been big to begin with and starving himself didn't help.

The guard carried him up the stairs and into a room that wasn't a cell. He saw a patch of blue through the bars of a high window. So it was daytime. He wondered what time of year it was. Maybe it was already spring.

The guard dumped him onto a table. "You should eat something," another one said. "It'll be a lot worse for you if you don't."

Kendryk shook his head. He had decided the best way to thwart Teodora while putting an end to his misery was starvation. At least it didn't hurt.

"Have it your way then," the guard said. "Hold him down, boys."

Someone pinned his arms to his sides and someone else held his legs. The man who'd been speaking grabbed his nose and pinched hard. When Kendryk finally gasped for air, he poured water into his throat. Most of it went into his lungs and he coughed so hard he thought that might kill him.

"That won't do," someone said. "Should we call the doctor?"

"I'd rather not. She always gets so high and mighty telling us what all we did wrong. One more time, shall we?"

A bit of water went down, but surely not enough to matter. Then they tried forcing down some kind of runny gruel, but that didn't work either. Kendryk was beginning to hope he might thwart them by choking to death. Finally, they left him alone on the table unrestrained, but too weak to move. All the coughing had tired him out even more. He fell asleep looking at the patch of sky.

When he opened his eyes again, Sybila looked down at him disapprovingly. "Why must you be so difficult, Prince?"

"Not a prince anymore," he croaked.

"Whatever you are, I can't let you die. What I'm about to do is extremely unpleasant and I'd rather not. Please eat and drink a bit so I don't need to."

Kendryk shook his head.

She sat on the edge of the table and took one of his hands. "I know this is terrible for you, but the empress will not let you die and there's no point in trying. Your wounds healed well, so your will to live is irrelevant. You might be here for some time, and it would be better for all of us if you cooperate."

Kendryk shook his head again.

Sybila dropped his hand. "For someone who's lost the will to live, you're terribly stubborn." She stood. "I hate to do this, but you leave me no choice."

Kendryk couldn't imagine what would be so bad. More choking perhaps.

Sybila rummaged around some things on another table for a few minutes, then ordered the guards to hold Kendryk down again.

"This has to go down his throat, but not into his lungs," she said, holding up a funnel with something that looked like a reed attached to it. It wasn't too big, but Kendryk didn't see how she could force it in.

As it turned out, she could. He felt like his throat was being torn out and thrashed so hard Sybila had to stop and call for another guard. He held Kendryk's nose until he gasped for air, and another held his tongue down while Sybila shoved the reed into his throat. It scraped and burned all the way down and made it difficult to breathe, since it took up all the space in his throat.

He must have turned some awful color because he heard Sybila say, "Let his nose go, by the mother. He needs to breathe."

He didn't stop fighting, but he wasn't strong and the guards were. Sybila, tiny as she was, could have held him down if she weren't otherwise occupied. Once she had the funnel positioned, she poured liquid into it from a small flask. Kendryk didn't notice that. He noticed when the reed came out, because it hurt far more, and then he coughed for a long time after.

When he lay back on the table, completely spent, Sybila stood over him. "It will be worse next time," she said. "I must do it every two days and your throat won't have time to heal. Please think about that before you refuse food and drink. I'll send you only thin porridge. I assure you that's all you'll want to swallow."

Kendryk closed his eyes, and she gave his hand a pat and disappeared. He would have to find another way to end this.

ARRYK

Arryk lay on the beach, waves washing over his legs. He was so stiff he could hardly move, but knew he had to before he froze to death. That would be more embarrassing than drowning.

It was getting light. Horses and soldiers wandered about the rocky beach, but corpses of both lay everywhere. He dragged himself to his feet. A sharp wind hit him and he realized his clothes were still soaked. Now he had to hope that Larisa or Bronson Falk would find him, and quickly. But before that, they needed shelter.

He heard a moan nearby and looked down. The young trooper who'd pushed him overboard lay near his feet. He'd remembered his name now—Magnus Torsen.

Arryk bent down to him. "Are you all right?" he asked.

Magnus rolled onto his back. "You saved my life, Your Highness."

He must have been the one Arryk grabbed. Arryk grinned down at him. "You saved mine first, giving me that shove."

Magnus sat up slowly, his teeth chattering. "It had to be done. I apologize."

"No need." Arryk grabbed him by the hand, pulling him to his feet. "But now I need your help again. We must find shelter soon if we are to survive this day." The storm hadn't abated and the wind drove sleet against them from the lowering clouds. "Let's round up those who can move and get them out of the wind. We must gather the horses before any more wander off."

"My horse." Magnus's voice wobbled. "I can't lose him. My family could hardly afford one."

"You will have another," Arryk said. "No, you'll have two. The finest Norovaean stallions. It's the least I can do."

Magnus opened and closed his mouth, and before he could say anything, Arryk clapped him on the shoulder and said, "Come, before we all freeze to death."

79

Once the others realized that Arryk was alive, things happened quickly. He ordered the wounded gathered into the shelter of some tall rocks and someone built a driftwood fire. They caught dozens of horses and herded them into a makeshift pen, girded by rocks on one side and clusters of soldiers on another. The wind remained strong, but the day grew a bit warmer.

Magnus, as energetic as Arryk had suspected he might be, found a village less than a league away and sent someone to take a message to Prince Falk. Arryk hoped Larisa and the rest of his force were nearby as well.

He had just warmed up enough to realize he was hungry when two laden carts lumbered out of the distant woods and down to the beach. A stout fellow with a leathery face drove the first. "We was told the King of Norovaea is here."

Arryk stepped forward, conscious of his bedraggled appearance. His wet hair had dried into salty ropes and his face was burned from the wind. "King Arryk, at your service," he said, hoping he looked the part well enough.

The fellow seemed delighted. "Never thought I'd live to see this. A king in the flesh. Your messenger came through the village and told us about the wreck. I'm sure our prince will come to collect you. In the meantime we've brought bread and ale. It's simple fare but it'll keep you alive a bit longer."

"We're very grateful. You'll be rewarded as soon as I meet the rest of my force."

"No need," the fellow said. "All of us here are eager to fight the empress."

"That's exactly what I mean to do."

Larisa arrived before evening, at the head of a long string of wagons bearing tents and supplies. She brought enough troops to set everything up, but left the bulk of the force behind with Prince Bronson.

"We'll take you to him tomorrow, Your Highness," she said, her tone strangely formal.

Arryk tried to catch her eye and smile, but she refused to look at him. He was sure she was angry with him, but hoped she'd visit him later anyway. If she hadn't appeared by the time he was ready to sleep, he'd send Magnus, who now followed him everywhere, puppy-like, with an order for her to attend him.

He had just shed his damp, salty clothing and slipped on someone else's dry shirt and breeches when the tent flap opened.

Arryk grinned. "It's good to see you."

Larisa was on him in two quick steps. "How dare you," she whispered, then shoved him in the chest so he fell back onto the cot. She slapped his face. "How dare you frighten me like that." She slapped him again. "I told you not to go without me. I told you to wait."

When she tried to slap him again, Arryk caught her arm and pulled her down next to him. "You were right. I'm sorry." He tried to look her in the eye, but she turned away. "I'm so happy you're here. I feel like such an idiot."

"That's because you are," she muttered, and then he realized she was crying. He'd never seen her cry.

He let go her arm and pulled her close to him. "I'm sorry," he whispered again. "Please don't be angry with me. I can't bear it. I need you to help me right now. Once we've sorted out this disaster, you can be as angry as you like, but until then, I need you."

She looked up at him, dashing the tears away. "All right," she said. "How bad is it? Can we still go to Terragand?"

"I don't know. There are no more than a few hundred survivors here, but perhaps some of the other ships made it to safety. I'm sure we'll find out in the next few days. How did you find Prince Bronson?"

"Grumpy, but willing to help. He doesn't have a large force—perhaps three thousand untrained militia."

"That's not enough. But surely there are others. We must contact Ummarvik and Podoska. Counts Faris and Orland are still at large and I'll send messengers to find them. It'll take time, but it'll be enough."

"Your sister doesn't have time."

"Not much. But she'll have to wait." Arryk knew he should be more worried about Gwynneth, but his relief that Larisa was talking to him and not hitting him was so great he didn't much care.

"We'll go to Bronson tomorrow and you can talk to him. Maybe he'll be nicer to you."

"If he wasn't nice to you, he'll be sorry." Arryk grinned, putting both arms around Larisa and pulling her onto the cot. She made some grumbling noises, but let him.

BRAEDEN

"It's time we found a house," Braeden said. He and Janna sat at the brazier inside the tent one chilly evening. She was trying to mend one of his shirts in spite of the poor light and fingers stiffened by the cold.

"Now? We won't go on campaign as soon as the weather improves?"

"I doubt it. Seems the empress wants to keep us close by to see what King Arryk does. It could be months before we go anywhere, and I want you safe and comfortable until well after the baby is born, whether or not I go out."

"You'd go without me?" Janna looked a little alarmed.

"Come here," he said, pulling her over to sit on the cot next to him. "Only if I must. I know you're bound and determined to come, baby or no, but don't you see the sense in staying here until it's born?"

To his relief, she nodded. "It's true I'll feel better with Senta and the girls close by. But if you go, I'll join you as soon as the baby is big enough to travel."

"We'll worry about that when the time comes." Braeden kissed the top of her head, and put his hand on her now more prominent belly. "How's she doing in there?"

"Active for a girl."

"You're sure it's a girl?"

She smiled. "Just a feeling I have. And you're right. A house would be nice. I get so tired of the dirt and stench of the tents. I don't think I'm acquainted with anyone who doesn't smell like horse."

"Nothing wrong with that." Braeden elbowed her to show he was teasing.

"Of course not. But I don't mind a change."

"I'll search for a house tomorrow. We're not drilling the next few days so I can take leave."

"I'm coming with you."

"Are you sure? We'll have to walk all over the city."

"I'd like that. There's so much I haven't seen yet."

He liked the idea. It would be fun to run about, just the two of them. He already had a few houses in mind. Even though Janna seemed to handle the pregnancy well, sometimes he worried about her. He'd caught her crying once or twice when she thought she was alone, and knew she still mourned the children she'd lost. But when he tried comforting her, she'd dry her tears and say she didn't want to talk about it, that she was happy and it was most likely the pregnancy making her emotional. He hoped a change of scene might lift her spirits.

To his surprise, she didn't like the first house.

"It's much too tall."

"How's that? It looks rather grand." Braeden had pictured something very nice for her. He didn't want it said that an officer's lady of his rank didn't live in style, and he wanted her to get back at least a little of what she'd lost in Kaleva. He'd spent a few days in a merchant's house there and had been impressed by its simple luxury.

"It does. But it's too big for the two of us."

"Three." He reminded her with a laugh.

"A third tiny person. She'll take up no space at all. And think of all the stairs. I get tired at the very idea."

She had a point. She would only get bigger, and going up and down stairs wouldn't be much fun.

"I'll hire servants. All you have to do is sit in a little parlor while they fetch you everything."

"Don't be ridiculous." She took his arm, and they walked away, while he looked over his shoulder at the handsome gray house, apparently not to be theirs. "I don't want a lot of servants. I've become more useful in the past months. All I need is someone to cook and do heavier cleaning. Unless you want me to do the cooking." She grinned up at him.

"You'll get a cook," he said a little too quickly. The few times she had attempted something as simple as soup or porridge had been notable failures. "You'll need a nurse for the baby too."

"Someone to help for the first few weeks. After that, I want to do everything myself. I realize it's a lot of work. Anyezka was only a few months old when I married Dimir and she cried all the time. When a baby cries, its mother should be there if she can."

"I should have known you'd have your own ideas about child-rearing." He'd never considered it at all. Until now, babies hadn't been real to him. If anything, they were reason to pity his comrades when he heard plaintive wails at all hours of the night. And the poor little buggers died all too often, sometimes before they could so much as say a word. Braeden didn't even want to think about that.

"I'm looking forward to it all. Where's the next house you wanted to see?"

"You won't like it either." Braeden was feeling a little downcast. He'd been so certain she'd want something big.

Janna stopped in the street and turned to him. "I know what you're thinking but I don't want anything grand. Just something comfortable. One or two servants to cook and clean. What about near Adela's house? She and Senta will be more help than anyone else when the baby comes."

"The houses in those streets are so small."

"Yes, but they're very pretty. Shall we see if any are available?"

"If you like. It's a long walk. Sure you don't want to go tomorrow?"

"I'm sure." She took his arm. "It's a lovely day. Why don't we go to your factor and see what he recommends?"

"Good idea."

Silbershmid was a small, dark man who lived in an enormous house near the main temple. He took one look at Janna and said, "I have exactly the thing. My nephew just bought it as an investment, and it's quite lovely. Not too big, but fine enough for someone of your rank."

They followed him down a narrow alley, and out onto a sunny street; a pretty residential one so common in Atlona. They passed larger stone houses, made another turn and came upon a row of smaller stone and half-timber houses. Silbershmid fumbled with a large ring of keys and finally found the one he wanted. They had stopped in front of a house at the end of the row. With only two floors above the ground, it was shorter and wider than other houses on the street. A cross street sloped off to one side.

"It has a garden," Silbershmid said, as he opened the door.

"I would love a garden," Janna said.

"I know," Silbershmid said.

That was news to Braeden. He didn't take Janna for the gardening sort, though he reckoned she'd had experience with farming.

With large windows on the three unattached sides, the house was sunny and light. Janna exclaimed with delight as they entered. It was open, with the dark beams of the ceilings just over Braeden's head, so he didn't have to duck.

They looked at the garden first. It was rather bare, but it was still early enough to plant a few things. Maybe Braeden could get Trisa to help for a few days.

Janna pronounced the small kitchen satisfactory, then lumbered up the stairs with surprising energy. Braeden needed only a glance at her happy, glowing face to decide he'd pay whatever was asked.

Silbershmid seemed surprised that he didn't try to bargain him down when he named the price, then shrugged. "I told you it was perfect. I can always tell by the look of the lady what is needed."

"That's a rare gift my friend."

"That's why I'm very rich." The little man smirked.

ARRYK

"I thought you weren't coming," Prince Bronson said, his craggy face unsmiling. Arryk found him unnerving. The Princess Rheda, Bronson's wife and Kendryk's aunt soon joined them. A trim, dark-haired woman with bright blue eyes, she reminded Arryk of Kendryk and he liked her at once. A young priest wearing all black followed her into the room. She introduced him as Father Anselm, a devoted follower of Father Edric, now known throughout Kronland as Edric Maximus.

"This is a military discussion," Bronson growled at the two of them. "You're not needed here."

"You're wrong," Rheda said calmly. "This is more than a military matter. Everything depends on religious reform. Without it there is no point."

Bronson grumbled but said no more. They sat in Prince Bronson's audience chamber, inside his magnificent, though damp and drafty palace. Arryk didn't mind. It was nice to be out of the wind, Larisa at his side.

He'd promoted Magnus Torsen to lieutenant and left him in charge of rounding up the wreck's survivors. Most of the ships had reached a small harbor before the worst of the storm hit. Only the last few out of Arenberg had run aground. Arryk was optimistic.

He knew the war had started because of religious problems, but wasn't sure what they were.

"Erm," he said. "I quite agree." He didn't know what else to say, but Larisa jumped in.

"I'm afraid his highness has been preoccupied with preparations for the invasion and we're not up to date on the latest developments. Perhaps Father Anselm can fill us in later?" She turned her most dazzling smile on the priest, who blushed, then nodded.

"If you must," Prince Bronson said.

Arryk then proposed which allies might be approached next and his plans to contact Faris and Orland.

"Orland's in Brandana last I heard," Bronson said. "The empress has sent marauders there and he's chasing them down. Faris is in Zeelund, trying to raise an army. Don't know when he'll be ready. As to Ummarvik, Prince Ossian is a fool and won't do much to help. He talks a good story, but that's all."

"I'll ask anyway," Arryk said. "What about Princess Martinek, in Podoska?"

"She might help. It's hard to say. Those Martineks are a strange lot, though they don't shy away from trouble."

"I'll send a messenger," Arryk said.

Prince Bronson then excused himself, leaving him with the princess and the priest.

"Tell him, Anselm," Rheda said.

Anselm looked nervous. He'd been regarding Arryk closely, to the point of making him uncomfortable. "Your Highness," he began, then paused, clearing his throat. "Are you familiar with the Quadrene Prophecy?"

"The what?" Arryk asked.

"You've heard of the work of Edric Maximus?"

"We've heard a little in Norovaea, but I never had time to study his writings." In truth, pamphlets of Edric's most famous sermons had arrived in Norovaea months ago, but Arryk had never bothered to read them. He was sure Larisa hadn't either.

"Then I'll start at the beginning," Anselm said. "The Holy Scrolls tell of a great battle between the forces of light and darkness. The forces of light will prevail by the efforts of a young prince, who comes from the north to defend the truth. Originally, Edric believed that Prince Kendryk was the foretold ruler."

Beside him, Arryk felt Larisa sit up straight. "Go on," he said, wondering where this was leading.

"At first it seemed obvious to everyone that Prince Kendryk was the ruler of the prophecy. He did so much to defend Edric Maximus and defied the empress herself. All of us were sure he would prevail."

"But he didn't." Arryk's confusion mounted.

"No, he did not." Anselm looked sad, and Princess Rheda's eyes glinted with unshed tears.

"So Kendryk is not the ruler in the prophecy?"

"It seems not. The great battle still lies ahead, but Kendryk is in captivity. According to the last message we received he was near death. He might not even be alive."

The princess wiped her eyes.

"Gods, I hope you're wrong." Belatedly, Arryk remembered he shouldn't swear in front of a priest.

But no one seemed to mind. "I hope so too," Anselm said. "Even if he is not the prophesied one, he has done the Faith a great service and we owe him a debt that can never be repaid. But the fact remains we need that ruler to lead us to victory." Anselm paused again and gave Arryk a meaningful look.

Larisa elbowed him in the ribs. Arryk jumped. "Oh surely, you don't mean me." This was appalling. He didn't even care about religion, though he didn't think it was the right time to say so.

"Of course I mean you," Anselm said. "You fit the prophecy perfectly."

"I thought Kendryk did," Arryk said, feeling put out.

"To be honest, the prophecy is not all that specific. It says that the ruler is young and will come from the north, that he's a prince, not a princess and will defend the truth."

"I'm not a prince," Arryk said, relieved to find this loophole. "Not since last week."

"I'm sure it's not meant so literally," Larisa spoke up, placing her foot firmly on Arryk's.

He knew she wanted him to be quiet, and he was happy to oblige.

"Exactly," Anselm looked pleased. "And it makes sense it could be you. You're here at our hour of greatest need."

"That's very interesting. I will pray about it." Arryk supposed there wasn't too much harm in playing along for now. He was sure the prophecy was nonsense and once he'd liberated Terragand he could return to Norovaea. He didn't plan to take the empress on directly if he didn't have to.

ANTON

At first, chasing Daciana Tomescu all over Brandana was fun. But they never caught her and she never stopped killing and burning. Anton was starting to feel frustrated, but then the count received word that King Arryk of Norovaea had landed in Helvundala and was gathering allies. He asked the count to meet him in Terragand where they would be joined by Count Faris, coming from Zeelund with a new army.

It had taken several weeks for the count's forces to get back to Terragand to meet the king and Prince Bronson, and then they had to wait for Count Faris. The king didn't want to wait any longer, but the count convinced him they needed experienced infantry and the several dozen big artillery pieces Count Faris was bringing.

The count said something to his own officers about the king's troops being inexperienced, but Anton expected a king could afford the best soldiers. Besides, anyone looking at King Arryk was bound to be impressed. He looked like a golden god from paintings Anton had seen in temples. He was tall and on the slender side, though he seemed strong and quick, and wore his long blond hair braided down both sides and loose in the back. Anton used to think hair like that was for girls, but it didn't look like that on the king. His face was strong, with sharp cheekbones, and his blue eyes seemed to pierce right through you.

He looked exactly like a barbarian king should, and Anton was sure no one could withstand him. He rode at the head of a troop of young officers who all looked a lot like him, and at his side rode a beautiful, very fierce-looking duchess. Anton liked looking at her but was a little afraid of her too.

They joined up with Count Faris's army as they marched into Terragand, and he'd brought a great deal of artillery. The terrain became hillier and it took a long time to drag the big guns up the steep slopes and carefully bring them down the other side. Everyone able was drafted to help. Anton helped with the horses most of the time, but sometimes he jumped in when a big piece rolled too fast, or refused to budge uphill. The rainy spring weather didn't help, and the roads turned into thick mud churned up by thousands of feet and hooves.

He was relieved when they reached Birkenfels. They had been this close before at the beginning of winter, when Count Orland decided it would be too hard to take Ensden on by himself. But this time, there were far more of them. King Arryk alone led over twelve thousand troops, of both infantry and cavalry besides the count's eight thousand horse. Prince Bronson led a force of about two thousand, but they were militia, not seasoned professionals.

Even though the enemy had sentries posted in the steep hills around Birkenfels, it only took the count and the king a half day to kill all of them. Then they posted their own guards so no one would bother them while they put the big artillery pieces into place.

It took almost three whole days to get them up the steep hillside. The horses weren't able to pull them all the way because the ground was too rough, so every man and boy and a few strong girls dragged them with ropes. Sometimes it took an hour to move just a few feet. Anton had never worked so hard in his life.

The sun finally came out and it got warm. Anton peeled off one piece of clothing after another until he wore nothing but his breeches. At last they had the guns at the crest of the hill overlooking the castle and he saw his chest and arms had turned quite tan. He also had what looked like muscles.

Even Gerd seemed surprised. "You don't look like the wind will blow you away now. But Ensden's guns still might."

Enemy guns didn't scare Anton. He'd been spending so much time with theirs, they seemed like furniture. The crews were jolly sorts though rather deaf. They'd each named their pieces and were in friendly competition with each other as to who would blast the greatest holes in the enemy lines. For the first time, Anton thought that when he grew up, perhaps he wouldn't become a cavalry trooper after all. It might be fun to fire off these great things instead. Maybe one of the crews would let him help during the battle.

By the fourth morning, the guns were in position, overlooking the huge enemy camp below. Above that stood Birkenfels Castle. It looked tiny compared to the vast army spread below it and it seemed stupid that no one had conquered it. If Ensden had put his guns up here months ago, he might have been able to drop balls right into the castle courtyard.

Anton said as much to one gunner, who roared with laughter, showing a mouthful of blackened teeth. "She's got good range, our girl does, but not that good. We'd have to be half a league closer. And Ensden's guns don't have the range ours do."

"It looks closer than that."

"It's a trick of the eye. That valley below us is nearly a league across. We'll only be able to hit the edges of them."

"What good will that do?"

"Oh, plenty. We'll soften 'em up just enough that the cavalry can slice right through. Then when they're all in disorder, the infantry will go in. And that should just about do it."

It sounded simple enough. Anton couldn't wait for his first real battle. If he wasn't needed with the spare horses, he hoped they'd let him stay up here and help with the softening up.

That night, Anton slept on the hillside with the gun crews. They expected the fighting to begin at first light. But right before dawn, Gerd came huffing and wheezing up the steep slope, carrying a small lantern. "You're needed to help with Count Orland's horse. He has a new page and she's afraid of him."

Anton snorted. "What good is a page who can't help with the horse?"

"She's the daughter of one of his father's friends. Had to take her on after Cid kicked the last one in the ribs."

There was no chance of becoming a page if you weren't high-born or had good connections. Anton wasn't keen on baby-sitting a fancy girl who didn't know how to handle a warhorse, but he was excited about being so close to the action.

He went in search of the page and found her holding Cid's saddle while a horse-boy Anton didn't know tried to hold him still.

"Here, let me." He took the saddle and walked right up beside Cid, who calmed down and stuck his nose in Anton's pocket, looking for the treats he always carried. Today it was half-rotted carrots, but Cid didn't care and crunched happily while Anton saddled him.

"Thank you," the girl said. She had hair the color of the carrots in his pocket and front teeth that stuck out. "I'm Lotta, and I'm no good with horses."

"I'm Anton, and I am. Just do what I tell you. What else do you have to do?" Anton figured she wasn't half ready and wouldn't like what the count did when he came and found out. Those front teeth could still look a lot worse.

"Um, load pistols? And get some swords? There's a great pile outside his tent but I can't make out—"

"Come on. I know what he needs. I'll show you. Loading pistols is hard and slow, but he might already have some loaded. We'll do more after he's gone."

She gulped. "Do I have to bring them to him during the battle?"

Anton stared at her. "That's what pages are for."

"But I'll be scared."

"I expect so. Most everyone will be, except for me."

"You've been in a lot of battles?" she asked as Anton picked out a sword, a battle axe, two sabers, an arquebus and two pistols.

"A few," he said. "Though this is the biggest so far."

"Oh good. Can you stay with me? I'm really scared, but it'll be better if someone experienced is close by."

"Sure." Anton handed her the pistols. "Put those in the loops in his saddle. Make sure the butts are facing back."

They had finished loading up the weapons when Orland appeared. "What are you doing here?" he asked when Anton handed him a saber.

"Showing Lotta around."

"Good. Can't believe my father saddled me with such a worthless brat. Stay with her. Can you ride?"

"Yes." Anton didn't mention it was because he "borrowed" Cid late at night when no one was about.

"I want you at the back of the first rank. It'll be hot, and I'll need reloaded pistols in a hurry. One can reload and hand them to the other who'll bring them to me."

Anton was disappointed. He was the faster reloader, so Lotta would have to carry them in.

She looked like she was fighting tears.

"What's wrong now?" he asked after the count had disappeared into his tent.

"He called me a brat. He can't do that."

"He just did. He's that way with anyone who's displeased him. Once you learn everything you won't make him angry anymore and it'll get better. Now, where's your horse?"

Her pony was saddled and ready to go. "Is it battle-trained?" he asked.

"I don't know. Does it matter?"

"It matters a lot. If he isn't, the first bit of gunfire will spook him. I'll find you another."

Anton found a horse for himself. He chose a young charger named Timur and another smaller one for Lotta. She was bigger than Anton—he reckoned she was at least fifteen—but she seemed scared of big horses.

It was already bright and sunny a half hour after dawn. There was to be no surprise with a force this size and the racket they'd made getting the guns up on the hill, not to mention the sentries they'd killed.

Anton found Orland's standard in a sea of banners and horses, and said, "Come on," spurring Timur while Lotta followed. Once he spotted the purple plume waving from Orland's black helmet, he stopped and looked around. They were surrounded by horses and armored men. This was sliver of the whole force since King Arryk was off to the left somewhere and Count Faris behind.

The cavalry spread out among the trees at the base of the hill, out of range of Ensden's guns. Pike and musket ranged behind, but the cavalry would have to get in pretty far before the infantry could advance.

Anton's heart pounded. He'd loaded up Timur with all of the pistols, shot and powder he could carry, and Lotta already held two loaded sets. She was pale and her teeth chattered, but he hoped she'd be able to do her job.

It seemed they stood there forever, though it probably wasn't more than a few minutes. Suddenly, the guns let loose. The whole hillside shook and the noise, echoing through the valley, felt like it came from right above his head. A few horses jerked nervously, but everyone stayed put. Count Faris had been very strict in his orders. With the enemy so well entrenched, the guns would fire a long time before the cavalry moved in.

The guns roared again, more ragged this time. After the first barrage, they fired as fast as they could and some crews were faster than others. Anton saw nothing but armored backs and horses in front of him. Smoke drifted down from the hillsides, but the air was still mostly clear. Judging by the shouting and screaming from the enemy camp, some of the rounds had found their mark. Then there was the pop of musket fire and some whistling noises through the branches. The enemy was returning fire.

A restless murmur spread through the troops.

"Hold," the count said. "It's not time yet."

The pop of the muskets continued, but none seemed to hit their mark. They wouldn't be able to find good targets in the trees, and most were still out of range. If anyone got hit wearing armor, they would barely feel it. Anton had none, so if he got hit, he'd notice.

After a while, he got used to the sound of the guns. Even Lotta, who'd been looking green, seemed to relax. That was good. Then, there were explosions in the distance. Those would be the enemy's guns, across the river. They were still out of range, though.

Suddenly, there was a commotion to the left and Anton watched King Arryk's cavalry move out.

"Vica's tits!" the count swore. "It's too soon. Send him a message—oh, never mind. We'd better go now." He slammed down his visor with its grinning death's head, raised his saber and shouted, "Forward!"

The horses ahead of Anton moved, so he followed. He glanced to his right and shouted, "Go!" at Lotta, who had frozen. He grabbed her horse's harness and pulled. It started walking, too. They went slowly while they were in the trees. It was a long way to the enemy lines and they mustn't tire the horses with a long gallop before the charge.

Out of the corner of his eye, Anton watched the Norovaean cavalry pull ahead, the king at the front. They didn't seem worried about sparing their horses.

"What's the fool doing?" a trooper near Anton asked. "All by himself out there. Someone'll pick him off."

Anton thought that would be a shame, though King Arryk presented a tempting target. His armor was all gold and over his helmet he wore the fur of a great white bear, it's jaws gaping wide.

Count Orland wasn't going to let him stay out there by himself and Anton watched Cid pull ahead. He urged Timur to a trot, and picked up speed as the ground grew more even. He still couldn't see what was ahead, though now musket balls whistled closer and a horse crashed to the ground behind him. Anton pretended he hadn't noticed and urged Timur forward. King Arryk was still out ahead, but not by much.

Now the shrieks were louder than any Anton had heard before, followed by crashing thuds and the awful screams of people and horses. They had come into range of Ensden's guns.

The Norovaeans were taking the worst of it, although Anton felt rather than saw cannonballs landing around him. He gritted his teeth and spurred Timur on. If they went far enough, the balls would pass overhead and into the ranks behind them.

Ahead of him, he spotted Count Orland's plume, but nearly fell off as Timur came to sudden halt. It seemed they had reached the front lines. Ensden's infantry stood massed before them while his guns landed shot behind them. They were trapped.

The count turned toward them. "Don't stop now," he shouted. "Their lines are thin and won't hold if we go straight in. It'll be ugly, but it's the only way." With that, he faced forward again and pulled out two pistols.

Anton looked for Lotta and didn't see her, so he got two more pistols ready and looked for a path forward.

For the next moments, he was confused. He lost track of the count, and several horses rushed past him. One went down right next to him and he yanked Timur out of the way. The horse's rider was thrown off, but got back to his feet, fumbling for a weapon. A spear-point came from nowhere, pushing through a gap in his armor near the throat. There was a spray of blood and he fell again.

Anton looked around wildly. He wondered if he should fire the pistols, until he remembered the count needed them.

He took a deep breath and urged Timur on, keeping an eye out for that spear. The enemy soldier holding it had disappeared, so he kept going forward. He spotted the count off to his left, in the thick of things. Anton went straight for him and shouted as soon as he got behind Cid. "Sir, your pistols."

The count turned in his saddle and grabbed the two Anton held. In one fluid motion he fired one, then the other at a right angle, away from Cid's head. Two enemy pikemen fell and Anton had two more pistols ready when the count turned back. He took back the two empty ones. Somehow, he'd have to reload in the middle of this.

He had two more already loaded, and when the count turned back to him again, he shouted, "reloading," so the count pulled out his saber and slashed about until Anton handed him the pistols. The noise filled Anton's ears and he wondered he could hear at all. Smoke and dust and awful smells swirled around his head.

"We have to get to the king," the count shouted. The pressure in front of them had let up because much of the enemy had gone left. Anton handed over two more pistols, then drew a sword sheathed in Timur's saddle. He couldn't remember putting it there. Though he didn't know how to use it, it was better than nothing.

The count, Anton, and a few others, pushed to where they saw King Arryk and a few of his officers in a sea of enemy. More of Orland's cavalry came up behind them and they bore down on the enemy to their left.

When Anton saw he wasn't in immediate danger with the enemy focused on the king, he sheathed the sword and reloaded a few more pistols. By now, the count was cutting his way through with his saber and Anton couldn't keep up, so he just handed pistols to all who needed one. He kept an eye on Orland's purple plume and another on King Arryk's white bear's head.

Ossian Schurtz galloped past, then wheeled back when he saw Anton. "Get whatever pistols you have to the king," he said. "He's in trouble."

ARRYK

Until now, Arryk had imagined a battle would be more fun and less terrifying. It started out well enough. The great guns overhead made a tremendous noise and Arryk knew the enemy would falter at the sound. He also knew he should wait, but every second that went by meant less enemy left for him to kill. He didn't want it said that he'd never even joined the fight before it ended.

Larisa anticipated his order, and before he spoke, she said, "Wait," rather sharply.

Arryk pretended he didn't hear and shouted the order to move forward anyway. He knew the others would be eager to fight too. The way ahead was clear and he urged his horse to a trot, then a gallop. He didn't see the enemy but they had to be near.

Arryk caught sight of spear tips and shiny helmets ahead when a whistling overhead and horrid sounds behind him nearly caught him by surprise. His horse kept moving, even though Arryk's first impulse was to run away.

But he couldn't run. He was the king and everyone was following him. He would have to keep moving and hope a cannonball didn't take him. That would be a terrible end. He wondered if he should pray but didn't remember the words to any prayers. So he made a silent promise to the gods to read everything Edric Maximus ever wrote, no matter how boring, if they would just spare his life, and Larisa's.

She was still at his side, and pulling ahead. He spurred his horse to catch up to her. After the shriek of another cannonball the officer on his left disappeared. Arryk forced himself not to look. He needed to keep his eyes trained on what was ahead. And that was infantry and they were ready for him.

Since Count Ensden knew they were coming, he'd had plenty of time to get everyone into position. They had dug trenches and put spikes into the ground, and in between, pike stood waiting for him.

The plan had been to have the artillery soften up the infantry positions before sending in the cavalry, but Arryk had moved too soon and they still stood firm. There were a few gaps where the guns had hit their mark, but those filled in quickly.

Arryk drew his saber, but the enemy was still out of reach and his horse wouldn't ride into the lowered pike. He'd have to wheel around and try again. There was a terrific noise on both sides of him and he realized that both Larisa and someone on his left had fired pistols.

Arryk fumbled for his own. He could shoot well enough, but wasn't prepared to do it at a full gallop. He pulled his horse up well before they reached the pike, pulled out both his pistols and fired them into the front ranks. There was already so much smoke it was impossible to tell if he'd hit anyone. But then Larisa peeled off to the right and his horse followed.

Now he remembered their training. His own second rank would come up and fire next and they would keep going until the pike square crumbled.

When he headed back, he saw the damage the enemy artillery had done. It looked like half his cavalry was gone, pounded into the mud in a bleeding mass. He worried he might be sick, but Larisa shouted at him again. "Hurry up and reload."

By some miracle, she had already reloaded while Arryk fumbled with his pistols, hands shaking. Larisa grabbed one impatiently and finished it before he reloaded the other. He remembered Count Orland suggesting he have a page accompany him with loaded pistols, but he'd forgotten to do anything about that.

When they reached the front again, most of the enemy pike had disappeared. Arryk wondered if they'd retreated, but there was the glint of muskets an instant before an explosion of noise and smoke. This was worse. The muskets had greater range than his pistols and he had no idea where his own musketeers were, if any survived at all. He'd placed them behind the cavalry which meant they were being pummeled by the guns as well.

He took a deep breath and spurred his horse on. If he died right now, at least it would be facing the enemy. His horse veered around the body of a fallen horse and officer. Arryk, caught by surprise, fell off. In spite of his heavy armor, he rolled onto his shoulder and got back up again. He looked for his horse but it was gone, along with the pistols still holstered in the saddle. Cursing under his breath, he drew his saber, just in time to meet a halberdier who'd come from nowhere. The man wore little armor and went down in a spray of red when Arryk sliced his blade across his neck. He grabbed the halberd, though he didn't need it and looked around wildly for Larisa.

She was on the ground, on her hands and knees, next to her thrashing horse. "Oh gods," Arryk said, certain she'd been hurt.

Larisa got to her feet unsteadily, grabbed a pistol from the saddle and shot the horse, then pulled a flail from somewhere else. Arryk remembered laughing at her when she practiced with it; now as it hissed around her head, he was glad she never listened to him.

The muskets ahead still fired, but more raggedly now. Faris's guns were doing their work and the enemy was slowly diminishing. But there were still too many, especially because most of Arryk's cavalry was now on foot. At least some were still alive, though Arryk didn't know how long that would last.

There was more shouting in his ear. It wasn't Larisa—she was several paces ahead, cutting a path with her flail. He turned and saw a boy with a horse standing at his elbow.

"Your Majesty, here's a horse," the boy shouted.

Arryk laughed. He couldn't believe his luck. Maybe he'd be reading sermons after all.

"His name is Timur and the pistols are loaded," the boy said.

Arryk vaulted into the saddle and spurred into what remained of the enemy line. A rising breeze blew the smoke away and he noticed they had made progress. To his right, Orland's cavalry chased infantry down the riverbank and behind him marched rank upon rank of Faris's pike.

The castle seemed so close now he could see the hinges on its massive gate across the moat. Around him, his own troops ran forward and he urged the horse on. He came to the top of a small rise that led down to the river and saw waves of humanity crowded at its banks.

There was no bridge but everyone who could was getting into boats or heading upstream to a ford. Troops fanned out all around the castle walls and soon there was no sign of the enemy.

Arryk stopped for breath and wiped the sweat from his face. His hand came away red. He didn't feel hurt and wondered if it was someone else's blood. He looked to the sky, surprised that the sun had moved so far west. Had they really been fighting all day?

Everyone milled around the castle walls expectantly. The orange Roussay banner fluttered from the highest tower above the Bernotas blue and Arryk realized with a sudden surge of excitement that he had won a great victory. The drawbridge lowered and the gate opened. Arryk rode forward, crossing the moat. He couldn't wait to see his sister.

GWYNNETH

Exhausted, hungry and ragged, Gwynneth didn't feel the least bit like a princess. It didn't help she was hugely pregnant. The baby wouldn't come for several months, but she was certain she was about to burst. And over six months of siege had done nothing for her looks, she was sure. She'd ordered them to open the gate when it was clear her brother had won the battle, then made her way down from the top of the tower.

Arryk rode into the courtyard on a horse that was too small for him, throwing off a bloodstained fur as he dismounted. Gwynneth would have run to him, but she could barely walk. Arryk ran to her instead, and swept her off the ground as if she were still a girl of seventeen. By the time he put her down, she was sobbing. Mortified, she buried her face in his shoulder. He held her close, stroking her hair and murmuring something in Norovaean into her ear.

She pulled herself together with an effort, wiping her eyes with her apron.

He looked down at her, his eyes crinkling the way she always remembered. "What are you wearing?" he asked. "You look like the maid."

"Whatever fits." It had been so long since she'd smiled, she thought her face would split. "This dress belonged to the baker's wife. She used to be on the larger side, before we went to half-rations."

"We'll find you something suitable soon enough." He put his arm around her shoulder and steered her back toward the castle. "Are you all right? And the children?"

"We're all well, though rather hungry," she said. "Almost everyone's survived, but I worried about having enough food to last another month." Only one old woman had died on one of the coldest nights; that everyone else had remained healthy was yet another reason to convince Gwynneth the gods were watching over her and her mission. "I'm so glad you're here; I have to admit I'd nearly lost hope." While she led him into a tiny parlor in the castle living quarters she barely registered everyone else rushing down stairs and out doors to greet their liberators.

She grabbed a girl running by and told her to have the children brought down to see their uncle. Arryk had met Maryna a few years before on a visit to Terragand while Devyn was a baby, but he'd never seen little Andres, who was just now learning to walk.

The two of them sat at a small table grinning at each other. Then his face sobered. "You must know that father is dead, Gwynn. That's why I didn't come months sooner. He'd had some kind of attack last summer and wasn't able to speak after that. Classen wouldn't authorize any military action, so I had to wait."

She had suspected her father was dead, but hearing it was still a blow. She couldn't speak for a moment. "Poor Papa. Did he suffer very much?"

"No one knows. It didn't seem like it. The times I saw him, he was hardly conscious."

"That's a mercy then. I was sure something awful had happened, because I knew you would have helped if you could."

"I was ready to come as soon as I heard what Kendryk did with the priest. I'm sorry I took so long but I'm glad I wasn't too late."

"Not too late for us, thank the gods. But too late for Kendryk, maybe."

"What do you mean? Surely he still lives."

"I hope he does. The last word I received was from the empress telling me she'd had him deposed and ordering me to vacate the castle as it no longer belonged to him. Even if she didn't kill him, I don't know if he would have survived that. It must have broken his heart."

"I have heard no word of his death. Come now Gwynn, don't despair. He's tougher than he looks."

"But he was hurt." The tears she'd been holding back so long welled up again. "And it wasn't just from battle. I'd done something terrible before and he was already so sad, and then he had to burn everything, and I don't see how he could bear it all."

"I can't imagine you doing anything that awful and he did what he had to. It is very much in Teodora's interest to keep him alive."

"Or to let us believe he was alive. She still kept hoping I'd turn over Edric Maximus or the castle to her."

"Well, now you're free and she has no hope of that, there will be no point in pretending Kendryk's alive if he isn't. I doubt you'll be in suspense very long."

"If he's dead, I'm sure I won't survive it." She felt like she was hanging on by a thread. The joy of liberation was being replaced by a creeping fear that Teodora might punish Kendryk for her defeat here.

"I'm sure he's fine and you will be too," Arryk said stoutly. "Now, I want to send you and the children back to Norovaea as soon as possible. You can take care of things for me there, since I've had to leave Classen in charge, which I don't much like."

"Why not Aksel?"

"Oh, he's more peculiar than ever and has no interest in anything but his experiments. You'd be better at it anyway. I'll make sure that Terragand's borders are secure and find a way to free Kendryk. With any luck, we'll have made Count Ensden a prisoner and can trade him."

"Teodora won't do it," Gwynneth said. "She won't free him for any reason now she can't get the castle and Edric. And I'm sorry, but I'm not going to Norovaea. I'm staying with you and we're not stopping until we've beaten down the gates of Atlona and freed my husband."

Exhausted as Gwynneth was, she couldn't rest yet. She'd ordered hers and the children's things packed since she planned to join Arryk on campaign. Balduin Bernotas still languished in the dungeon and must remain a hostage, so she'd leave a garrison at the castle to keep it from falling into Evard's hands.

Arryk was no good at making those kinds of plans, so she sent him off to play with the children and gave all the orders herself. After arranging everything, she went back to the little parlor to see what letters needed to be sent, now she could send them. She'd no sooner sat down, than there was a soft knock. "Come," she said, hoping whoever it was wouldn't take long. It was well after midnight and she struggled to keep her eyes open.

She jumped out of her chair as Arian Orland entered, alone. He closed the door behind him, but stayed on the opposite side of the room.

"Might I have a word with Your Grace?" His tone was very different from what she'd ever heard before. "I won't take long; I can see you are exhausted." That was a kind way to comment on her faded appearance.

She stared at him hard for a moment. He looked as good as ever, but she felt nothing, not even anger. Best to finish this now. "All right." She sat back down without offering him a seat.

He took a few steps toward her, then stopped. "I need to know," he said. "Is it mine?"

Such an unexpected question nearly sent her into hysterical laughter. She pushed it down. Whatever had passed between them, he had helped free her now and didn't deserve to be insulted. "It's not," she said softly, shaking her head. "I'm sure of it."

"Oh." He seemed disappointed.

"It's for the best, I think."

"I suppose it is. I wouldn't have minded, you know. Does this mean you were reconciled with Kendryk then, before the end?"

She nodded, unable to speak, thinking of that last night.

"I'm glad," he said. "At least in some ways. I wanted to apologize in any case. I've never had many true friends, and Kendryk was the best. My behavior was disgraceful."

Mine was no better, she thought. She didn't want to discuss this, but it had to be done. "Might we please forget this and not speak of it again? I still have so much to do."

"Of course," he said. "I don't wish to cause you any trouble. But I want you to know something before I go." To her shock, he went down on one knee. "I will only speak of this once and never again unless you wish it, but I must tell you I still love you."

She stared at him for a moment, then shook her head. "I'm sorry, but I don't believe you. You behaved terribly toward me. You wouldn't do that to someone you loved."

"Forgive me," he whispered. "The thought of losing you drove me mad. But now I want nothing from you except that you let me serve you in any way you see fit. I will do anything for you."

"Anything?"

"If you ask me to throw myself off the top battlement of this castle, I'll do it right now without a second thought."

"Don't be ridiculous; I would never ask such a thing."

"I know. But you could, and I would do it. I've done you a terrible wrong and the gods are punishing me."

"Punishing you?"

"By making me love you when there is no hope you will ever feel the same way."

"There's no need to be so dramatic. And please ..." She stood and walked over to him. "Please stand."

He rose slowly. She didn't like him towering over her, but looked up at him anyway. "I thank you for helping my brother win this battle. He told me you

102

saved his life by sending your page to him with a horse. You don't owe me anything further."

"Please don't say that." His voice trembled. It was hard to believe he was the same man who'd destroyed her life last summer. "Please, let me do something, anything."

She wanted to send him away, but then considered she shouldn't squander this opportunity. It wasn't as though she had all the allies she needed. The combined force had taken terrible losses that day in spite of the victory. She still needed help.

"All right," she said. "I'll tell you what you can do. I want you to find a way to rescue Kendryk."

She relished the shocked look on his face. It would have been much easier to jump off the tower.

He composed himself quickly. "Very well, then. I'll find a way, if I have to break into the Arnfels myself."

"I wish you to succeed, not sacrifice yourself needlessly," she said. "I've nearly prevailed upon my brother to take on Teodora. Without Ensden, she is severely weakened. If we march straight into Olvisya, we may be able to demand Kendryk in exchange for sparing her lands. Or we may defeat her."

"She'll build another army," Arian said. "It won't be easy."

"I don't expect it to be. But I won't rest until my husband is safe with me again, and in charge of Terragand, where he belongs. If you love me as you say, you will swear right now to help me do this."

To his credit, he didn't hesitate now. He dropped to one knee again, and took both her hands in his. "I swear it," he said, placing a chaste kiss on each hand.

ANTON

"More of that Sanovan brandy," Count Orland said, his speech already slurred. He slouched at a table in the library of his own castle at Anglestein.

Anton hesitated, but not for long. He knew better. "That's the last of it, sir." He poured what remained into the goblet.

"It might be enough." The count drained it in one long swallow. "How old are you anyway?"

"Twelve," Anton lied.

"Old enough to need this advice, then." He slammed the goblet onto the table and turned toward Anton. "No matter what happens, never, ever fall in love with a woman."

"I won't," Anton said. "I don't see any reason to."

"You will soon enough, and it will be hard to keep your head. The first time some pretty thing smiles at you, maybe even lifts her skirts for you." The count looked sadly into his empty goblet. "You can have as much fun as you like, let her fall in love with you, even. But never, ever, ever fall in love with her."

"Seems sensible," Anton said. "I don't think I will."

The count laughed bitterly. "That's what I thought, too. But it happened anyway and now I'm as good as dead."

"I thought you liked being in love." Anton wrinkled his nose.

"I used to, but now I'd give anything to stop caring. It's torture when she doesn't feel the same way. And you'd still do anything for her and agree to all kinds of foolishness just to see her smile."

"That sounds pretty stupid." Anton stepped back in case the count tried to hit him, though he was too drunk to have good aim.

"You've got some cheek on you," the count laughed. "But I like how bold you are. Reminds me of myself at your age. Though I was a lot bigger at twelve. Be sure you eat more. Oh, and don't fall in love."

When they had approached the castle earlier that day, a young woman had run out to the stable yard and cried all over the count.

"Stop your caterwauling, wife." The count pushed her away with a sneer, but she still seemed happy to see him.

With all the talk of love and the princess, Anton hadn't realized the count was married to someone else. Anton liked the young countess because she looked a little like his mother, smelled nice, hugged him a lot and gave him sweets. He wished they'd stay a little longer.

But they rode out again the next morning. The countess cried over the count again while he rolled his eyes and pushed her away. She still gave him all the money she had, with papers to get more from a bank when they reached a bigger town. Anton didn't understand why the count was in love with a princess who didn't even like him when he was already married to someone so nice.

They were on the move every day. After liberating Birkenfels, King Arryk and Ruso Faris went south, making sure all of Terragand stood behind them and gathering allies in the rest of Kronland. Count Orland went west to defeat Duke Evard. He was not at his seat, Emberg Castle, though his duchess was. The count gave her two hours to pack her things, then set the place on fire.

Next, they spent a few days at the home of Duke Aidan Orland, the count's father. He had a castle somewhere, but right now he was in a big house in Kaltental, a large northern port city. The count and his father weren't on good terms. There was a good deal of drinking and shouting, but in the end, the count rode out with five hundred soldiers from the duke's militia.

Through all of it, Anton rode right behind the count on his own horse. Skandar was a shaggy gray Norovaean stallion, a gift from King Arryk himself. He was a reward for Anton bringing the king a horse and pistols at the right moment. The count reckoned he'd saved the king's life.

"There's nothing for it," Count Orland had said. "That stupid girl got herself killed, and the king himself rewarded you. Common as you are, you'll be my page now." Lotta had been too scared to follow Anton during the battle and a cannonball hit her right where she stood. Anton was glad he hadn't seen it. The count refused the offers of half a dozen nobles who wanted him to take on their own children, preferring Anton over all of those little lords and ladies.

The count also gave him his own helmet and a breastplate, black just like the count's, with a falcon on the front worked in purple inlay. It was nearly as handsome a gift as Skandar had been, but the count was grateful for making him look good in front of the king. Anton had been sure to tell King Arryk that he'd brought the horse and weapons due to the count's instructions and the king had been very pleased.

Even more importantly—to the count at least—Princess Gwynneth had thanked him personally for saving her brother. When she took the count's hands in hers, Anton saw him turn pale and shaky, which was very funny. Then the princess gave Anton a kiss on the forehead. She really was beautiful, though hugely pregnant. At her side was a little girl, the Duchess Maryna, who reminded him of Anyezka. She smiled shyly at Anton and he couldn't help but smile back, though he felt sad right after. He missed his little sister.

Anton's heart might have exploded with pride except he remembered his mother telling him they owed everything to the gods, and that it was wrong to be too proud. So he made an offering to Ercos in gratitude, and pledged his life to fight the empress until she was defeated. If the gods heard his prayers, Anton would kill her himself someday and be a great hero.

KENDRYK

Kendryk couldn't face Sybila's feeding tube again, so he ate enough to keep her away. He'd first thought he'd pour whatever they gave him into the privy trench, but now a guard stood in his cell and watched him until he choked the horrible food down.

So he wouldn't die that way after all. He still held out hope that he might catch the plague, but because no one ever came near him, he doubted he'd catch so much as a cold. And he couldn't face endless years of this darkness.

He turned on his side to face the wall, and out of long-established habit, sent up a prayer to Ercos before stopping himself. If the gods existed, they didn't hear him. Or he had disappointed them and they had abandoned him. Prayer was a complete waste of time. He drifted into an uneasy sleep, full of nightmares; Teodora's mouth stretched into a grotesque laugh as she shoved a hot iron poker into his mouth. Kendryk woke up with a shout and a terrible pain in his throat.

He lay in the dark, staring straight up, trying to calm his breathing. He started to relax a little when the scent of flowers wafted over him along with a warm breeze. He had probably drifted off again. Propping himself up on his elbows, he looked around.

It was pitch black as always except for the two times a day someone brought food. The fragrant breeze blew over him again. And then he recognized Gwynneth's scent. Perhaps he was dying and the gods were giving him one last good memory before he went.

He closed his eyes and breathed in the scent, then his eyes flew open as someone shook his shoulder. She sat on the edge of the stone bench he lay upon. There was no light but he could see her clearly. Her hair hung loose and she wore a peculiar gown he'd never seen before, but he knew beyond any doubt it was Gwynneth.

"How did ... I ... How?" he croaked, his throat nearly swollen shut.

"Shh," she said, placing one finger against his lips. It was soft and warm, just like she always was. "The gods have given us only a few moments. You must not give up hope. The children and I are safe and well." She looked down. "See? We're going to have another. She'll probably be here before you're rescued, but not too long, I hope."

Kendryk shook his head, disbelieving.

"It's all right," she said, stroking the side of his face. "The gods are with you still, and they're with me too. You must stay strong and be ready. We will be together again soon." She leaned forward, placing a kiss on his forehead. Then she was gone.

Kendryk opened his eyes and felt around in the dark, but there was nothing. The faint scent of flowers lasted a while longer and he lay motionless, breathing it in, allowing hope to creep back into his heart.

ANTON

Anton and the count were escorting Edric Maximus who was spreading the word of the Holy Scrolls all over Kronland. While they were in a big city up north, the count sent Anton to a printer's shop with a large stack of paper, instructions and a hefty bag of coins for the printer.

The big man had grumbled about being too busy until he saw how much was in the bag. "Tell Count Orland I'll have these done in three days," he said. "The boys and I will work all night if we have to."

Anton drove one of twelve wagons sent to pick up the results: several hundred bales of small books, cheaply bound and stamped with The Words of the Holy Family on them. Messengers then carried those bundles to every town, village and farm.

Anton had started reading one himself, but it was boring. There were stories he already knew, like how the Father and the Mother made the world and everything in it. Then there were long lists of rules and names of people who were important long ago, but who'd been dead thousands of years. Their names were hard to pronounce, though he was pleased to discover an Anton among them. He'd been a simple cobbler's apprentice who became a great general and did something holy somewhere near Zastwar. But most of the stories were boring or confusing even though everyone else seemed excited about them.

They liked it even better if Edric Maximus read to them from the book himself. During the days, the Maximus spoke in town squares or in temples, but in the evenings, he sat by the cook-fires and spoke with the soldiers. Anton came close once, but was a little scared by the stern way Edric looked at him. It wasn't unkind at all, but it was as though he could see what Anton was thinking, which was how he'd sneak a ride on Cid after everyone else had gone to sleep.

Still, he liked the sound of Edric's deep, smooth voice, so he hung back in the shadows and listened. The Maximus often recited from memory, even though he held a book in front of him. "For it has been given to you to touch the face of the Father, and he shall hold your hand. The Mother will hold you like a child and her own children will tend and guide you. You shall call upon Vica for wisdom and upon Ercos for strength and they shall hear you."

Edric put the book down. "See, it's quite clear. There's no mention of a priest or priestess here. They are not needed for you to speak with the gods directly. If you pray, they will listen."

"So what's the point then, of priest or temple or Maximus?" A young man asked. Anton recognized him as one of Duke Orland's musketeers.

"Just to help you," Edric said. "It's important for the children of the gods to gather as one and to pray together and learn from the Scrolls. Most of you do not have time to study every word of the Scrolls and sometimes they are hard to understand. It's the job of the priest and Maximus to help you understand. But they are there to help only; they are not higher or better than you."

Edric Maximus said much the same wherever he went. Everyone listened and most of the time the priests and priestesses agreed with him too. But sometimes they didn't, and that was why the count had come along. Princess Gwynneth had asked him to protect Edric and remove anyone who stood in his way. Usually that was someone at a temple who still wanted to follow the old way. That had happened just the other day in Urwessen, a large town in the Brandana marches. The priestess shouted at Edric and told him he was bad and wrong and a rebel. That scared Anton. His father had been a rebel and they'd killed him for it. He didn't want that to happen to Edric.

But the count rode into town with a hundred armed men, dragged the priestess out of the temple and told her to leave. She wouldn't go, so he threw her into the city jail until she changed her mind. He'd done that a few times to a few others, but mostly everyone agreed with the new way. It was fun to be part of it all, though Anton wished they'd get back to fighting real battles.

ARRYK

"They worship you like a goddess," Arryk said. He meant to make a joke of it, but found it unpleasantly close to the truth and couldn't say why it annoyed him.

"Hardly." Gwynneth handed baby Stella back to the nurse before mounting her horse. "The troops like seeing the baby and the other little ones. It gives them something real to fight for. Innocent children they can defend."

"Whatever you're doing, it's working," Arryk said. "They can't wait to fight for you." They were riding back to the town where they were staying for a few days—he couldn't remember the name. They had visited so many towns in southern Terragand and northern Lantura he lost track.

Gwynneth insisted on getting in-person commitments for troops and money from every lord and every town council, no matter how small. She also wanted to make sure that every temple they saw followed the teachings of Edric Maximus. "Religious reform is essential to political reform," she had said when they first set out from Birkenfels. "Those who follow Edric's teachings will not tolerate Teodora's rule. They are your natural supporters."

He wished Gwynneth and the children were safe in Norovaea, but he couldn't persuade her to go. He worried that she was distracting him from his mission. Instead of marching directly to Teodora, who sat virtually undefended in Atlona, they were spending far too much time traveling through Kronland, gathering reluctant allies. The only reason he hadn't already returned to Norovaea was because he wanted to finish Teodora off while she was still weak.

"You don't have to work so hard," he said. "The most important thing is meeting Teodora in the field and defeating her."

"I'm not repeating last year's mistake," Gwynneth replied. "Before we make another move, I want the certain backing of every person of importance in Kronland. We can't sway Princess Zelenka, but we don't need her if we get all the others."

"You've thought about it a lot more than I have," Arryk said.

"I had time, all those months in the castle." Gwynneth smiled at him. "I suppose I learned patience then, and you must learn it now. We'll gather our forces and face Teodora once we have overwhelming numbers."

Arryk worried that losing the last fight against Teodora had made his sister too cautious now, when Teodora was nearly as weak as she had been last year. But he'd long ago learned there wasn't much point in arguing with Gwynneth because she would always win.

They arrived in the courtyard of their temporary home and he swung off his horse, then lifted Maryna from her pony before helping Gwynneth dismount.

Beside him, Maryna piped up. "Might I come to your study later, Uncle Arryk? I should very much like to read that last sermon with you."

Arryk caught Gwynneth's eye and hid a smile. "All right, but you can't stay up past your bedtime."

He'd made the mistake of telling Gwynneth about his vow to the gods during battle while Maryna was present. It had never occurred to him that a child of six might be interested in theology, but she considered herself a good friend to Edric Maximus and was anxious that everyone in her family understand his work.

It had become a ritual most evenings that Maryna sat in a little chair at his feet and read Edric's sermons to him out loud. The first time, Arryk dozed off and was unable to answer her questions about what she had just read. He couldn't bear to see her disappointed in him, so after that he always did his best to pay attention, though he still didn't understand much of it.

That night's sermon was one about the prophesied ruler. "People say you're the prince from the north," Maryna said, frowning. "But Edric Maximus was certain it was Papa. Was he wrong?"

Arryk shifted in his chair. He hated talking about the prophecy. It put even more responsibility on him. "Have you asked Edric?"

"Yes. He says he might have been wrong about Papa, but he's quite sure it isn't you."

Arryk had to laugh. He was more relieved than offended. "Why does he think it isn't me?"

Maryna closed the book in her lap. "I'm sure he's wrong, Uncle Arryk, but he says you aren't pious enough to lead the forces of light." She looked up at him, clearly worried she might have hurt his feelings. "But I've written to him and told him how we're reading his books and how you say prayers with me at bedtime. Maybe he'll change his mind. I think you would be very good at fighting the evil ones. After all, you rescued us when we had lost all hope."

"Come here," Arryk said, picking her up and putting her on his lap. "I might not be pious enough for Edric Maximus, but I don't mind. I suspect only the gods know the real truth."

"You're right, Uncle Arryk. I will try not to worry about it." Her clear blue eyes were still anxious.

Arryk wanted to tell her she was only six and had no business worrying about prophecies of any kind, but he knew that would make no difference. Instead he said, "Why don't we say our prayers now, and ask the gods to worry about it for us. They can give us answers when they feel like it."

Maryna's face lit up. "That's exactly what Edric says we should do. I think you've learned a great deal from his sermons. Tomorrow I'll read from the Holy Scrolls. I'm sure you'll love them."

With all of this religious education, Arryk reckoned he was building up so much credit with the gods, he'd be bullet-proof for the next twenty battles.

ANTON

"They've found him," Count Orland said. "Get ready to move out. We'll go within the hour and the baggage can come later."

Anton sprang into action. Now they would finally meet Duke Evard, he hoped to get a chance to fight. Before getting his own horse ready, he ordered Cid saddled and equipped. He called to Gerd to saddle Skandar next. "We're headed east," he said. Gerd scowled. He'd never taken Anton's promotion with good grace.

"Do it," Anton said, looking forward to the long ride. He worked Skandar every day, but he'd never taken him into a real battle.

Anton had spent hours training him not to flinch at the sounds of battle. He'd started by igniting small amounts of gunpowder near Skandar's head while he ate. Once he got used to that, he led him to the target range where troopers practiced with their pistols, rewarding him with treats when he calmed down. He asked a drummer boy to practice next to Skandar's head and fed him oats on the head of the drum. When the count was away, Anton piled up some of his old, dented armor and make Skandar ride over it, rearing up and trampling it under his enormous hooves. But a real battle would be different.

They rode east at speed. Count Faris had received word that Duke Evard was marching on Birkenfels Castle from the south. Though the empress had given him Terragand, it didn't really count. Count Orland had burned the duke's own castle, his son was a prisoner inside Birkenfels and the palace of Birkenhof was still a charred ruin. It was hard to rule a country without a place to live.

Anton didn't understand why an uncle would fight his nephew, though he thought of Bora and Seko, who'd been uncles of sorts. He would have fought them if they'd given him or his mother any trouble. And it sounded like Evard had given Prince Kendryk plenty of it.

Faris was hurrying to meet Evard, but hoped the count might cut him off first. The castle had a small garrison with few supplies and if Evard attacked it in force, it wouldn't hold out very long.

At the end of the second day, scouts reported Evard a few leagues ahead. They had entered the hilly country around Birkenfels and as far as they could tell, the duke didn't know they were there.

"How many?" the count asked.

"Three or four thousand at most," the scout replied.

"Horse?"

"Only a few hundred."

The count stopped and called his officers. Anton stood at his elbow, ready to help with anything he needed, whether it was a flagon of wine or a message to another part of camp. "Do you think we can surprise them?" Schurtz asked.

"I wouldn't count on it," the count replied. "He must expect someone to stand in his way. But we outnumber him, so we ought to defeat him ourselves. I'd rather not share credit if I don't have to."

"Princess Gwynneth will probably throw you a flower either way," Schurtz said, smirking.

Anton held his breath, but the count ignored Schurtz's insult, which was unusual. He'd once fought a duel with another officer who said the princess looked fat. The fellow still couldn't sit a horse.

After more discussion they decided that Faris was at least two days' march away to the east. "Let's strike right away and see what damage we can do. Maybe I'll get a shot at the old bastard himself. If we have trouble we can wait for Faris," the count said.

Anton was bursting with excitement when they finally made contact. They rode through the trees at a breakneck pace. He couldn't see what was ahead until they splashed through a stream and spotted the silver glint of helmets. Evard's troops were marching down a wide road with trees on both sides.

Anton stayed close behind the count, who rode out in front as always. Once the column was in sight they all yelled at the top of their lungs. The infantry turned in surprise and only a few lowered their pikes. It wasn't enough to stop the horses and the muskets were slow and too few. The count's troops cut through the column with no casualties and then circled back around for the duke.

They had seen him in the middle of the column, and he didn't have time to gather more guards around him. The count ordered the guards killed and captured the duke personally. The duke was mad about that and shouted curses at the count, who just laughed before knocking him in the head with a pistol butt. Then he told someone to carry him to a wagon and chain him to the bed until he could be taken to Birkenfels where he could join his son in the dungeon.

Anton hadn't had so much fun in his whole life and he could tell Skandar had enjoyed himself too. He hoped they'd fight again soon.

TEODORA

"He's here, Your Highness, in your small study," Elyse said. She was Teodora's most level-headed lady-in-waiting and as such was often the bearer of bad news.

Teodora sprang from her chair. "How many? How many have returned with him?"

Elyse sucked in her breath and paused before saying, "I'm sure he can give you an exact accounting better than I can."

Teodora chewed her lip. That was not a good sign. She rushed into the study, Elyse just far enough ahead to open the door and announce her. The first thing she saw was the bald spot on top of the general's head, as he bowed. "Stand," she snapped, waving at Elyse to close the door behind her.

When he lifted his head she had to keep herself from gasping. She'd never seen Niklas van Ensden look so terrible. He'd always had a rather gaunt face, but now it was skeletal. When she last saw him, his dark hair had been graying and thinning; now the little bit remaining was white.

"Your Highness." His voice at least was as firm as ever.

"What. In the name. Of the gods. Have you done?" She tapped the pointed toe of her slipper between the words for emphasis.

"I have suffered a serious defeat," he said, with no change in his tone.

She suppressed the urge to scream, which made her very unhappy. "That's what I've heard." She forced the words out between clenched teeth. "I was hoping I'd been misinformed, or that you'd be able to explain."

"It's true," he said. "I have no excuse or explanation, though I will be happy to answer your questions."

She hated his composure at that moment, though she wondered if she might use it to require him to fall on his sword or some such nonsense. She'd love to do it herself, though her position prevented it. Barbaric as some of her subjects were, they didn't seem to like the idea of a ruler who murdered the unworthy in cold blood. Besides, she might need him later. Best to keep him alive for now.

"Yes, as a matter of fact, I'd like to know how an excellent army like yours was so easily overrun."

"We were outnumbered and outgunned. We might have withstood King Arryk's undisciplined hordes, or even Orland's fine cavalry, but not after Ruso Faris's guns did their work."

"Unbelievable," she said. "How is it he could place them where they could harm you? Did you not have guards placed on the high ground?"

"I did Your Highness, but they were overrun."

She shook her head and turned her back on him. "How many have returned to Atlona?"

"Two or three hundred."

She whipped back around. "What did you say?"

"Two or three hundred." To his credit, he still didn't flinch.

"Out of fifteen thousand? How is that possible?"

"We lost several thousand during the siege. It was a wet winter and there was flux in the camp. We lost some to desertion as well. I am not certain, but I believe there were another two thousand killed during the battle."

"I'm no mathematician, but that should still leave you some ten thousand."

"Indeed." He shifted from one foot to another. "Unfortunately, our retreat was cut off and many thousands were captured."

"What happened to them?"

"I'm not certain, but we heard rumors that most went to fight for King Arryk."

"What?" These were her own troops, veterans of the border wars, of Cesiano and Moralta.

"It was said he offered a piece of Norovaean silver to every soldier who joined his employ and many did."

"Traitors," Teodora hissed, and clenched her fists at her sides. She took a long, deep breath. "How many did you come away with?"

"About three thousand, mostly horse. We did what we could to harass King Arryk's baggage train and pick off his scouts. We met a detachment of Orland's cuirassiers in the field, but they overran us quickly. Those who remained—well, we had no food and very little ammunition. We took what we could from the local population, but they had little enough after the winter. Many of the rest starved or died of exposure."

He looked like he'd come close to being one of those casualties. Better for him if he had.

Teodora badly wanted to throw something, but suppressed the urge for now. Out of the corner of her eye, she saw Elyse scribbling away, no doubt taking detailed notes of everything that was said. She would later transcribe it to the official document. She breathed deeply so she could keep her tone even, then said, "Very well. You can repeat all of that at your court martial."

His face lit up. "Your Highness, I thank you."

It seemed the fool thought he would get a chance at justice.

"Don't thank me until you hear who the judges are. I've half a mind to hand you over to the temple on charges of providing aid to heretics."

That made him turn even paler than he already was.

"In the meantime, there's plenty of room for you in the Arnfels. Give my love to Kendryk Bernotas; you will be neighbors."

His hue became even pastier, but his face remained impassive. If he lived, she might be able to take lessons in composure from him.

JANNA

It started in the middle of the night. Janna sat up suddenly with a moan. It was all right an instant later and she wondered if she'd imagined the sharp pain. She sat up for a few minutes, listening to Braeden breathe. By some miracle, she hadn't awakened him. He was the lightest sleeper she'd ever known.

It came again, sharper this time. Her moan was louder and Braeden awoke in an instant. "Are you all right?"

"It might be time." She held her belly, trying to tell if the baby had changed position or not. It had kicked and moved a great deal in the past month.

Braeden was up like a shot. "I'll send for Senta," he said, "and I'll go for a doctor." He was dressed by the time he finished speaking.

"Don't leave me alone, please," Janna whispered.

"Franca will be here in a moment." Franca was staying with them until the baby came so Janna would never be alone. Braeden ran into the corridor, shouting, "Dura, it's time!" He came back into the room, lit a lamp and set it on the table next to Janna. Another pain came.

"They're so close together, " she gasped. "What if the baby comes while you're gone?"

"Franca's helped deliver a foal or two," he said. "How different can it be? And I'll get Doctor Toure from camp. I'll be back with her before you know it. Now let me get a message off to Senta." He kissed her quickly and disappeared the moment Franca came into the room.

"Not sure what I'm supposed to do," she said crossly. Janna still felt like an annoyance to her.

"Nothing." Janna tried not to cry out at the next pain. "Senta and the doctor will be here soon."

"Thank the gods." Franca paced in front of the bed.

120

"I don't want to be difficult," Janna gasped, "But could you sit down please? You're making me anxious."

"Hmph." Franca plopped into a chair and fidgeted.

Fortunately, Senta bustled in moments later, a cloak over her nightdress. "How close together are the pains?" she asked, throwing the cloak aside.

"A few minutes, I think," Janna gasped.

"It might still be awhile." She took Janna's hand. "It will be all right. Franca my dear, run and get rags and hot water. Make it yourself if you have to."

Franca disappeared.

"Better to give them something to do. I imagine your husband's gone for the doctor, though I hope we don't need her."

Braeden was back before long. "The doctor's finishing up somewhere else," he said, looking worried. "She'll get here as soon as she can."

By now the pains were close together and terrible, worse than anything she'd ever felt. She couldn't hold back the screams, even though she saw Braeden turn pale.

"Shoo, shoo," Senta said. "Better you go keep an eye out for that doctor." After he had gone she turned to Janna. "Those fellows are so tough on the battlefield, but I don't know one who can endure the blood and screaming."

Janna wasn't sure she was able to, either. It went on and on while she lost all track of time. At some point, she noticed light streaming between the drawn curtains. Hours must have passed if it was getting light outside. The light came and went. She hardly believed it could be evening again.

She saw Braeden's face briefly before someone pushed him away. Janna was afraid that if she died she wouldn't get a chance to say goodbye. Another face, a dark brown one, swam into view and disappeared again.

Senta wiped her brow with a damp cloth and a few seconds later there was an unendurable pain. Something was tearing her in half, and all went black.

When she opened her eyes, it was full daylight and someone was crying. Braeden sat on the bed next to her, his arms around her.

"There she is," Senta said. "And a good thing. This little one is hungry."

Braeden carefully propped her up, and Senta put a tiny, shriveled red-faced thing to her breast. Janna saw toothless gums in the wide-open screaming mouth, but it closed quickly enough.

"See, she knows what to do," Senta said.

"A girl." The pride was evident in Braeden's voice. "A perfect little girl."

Janna looked down. "She is, isn't she?" It was true the baby was a bit red and shriveled, but everything else was perfect.

"Just right," Senta said. "She'll pretty up in a few days. I'll go now, but Adela will be here in a few minutes and I'll return tonight."

"Thank you," Janna said gratefully to Senta, who looked as frazzled as Janna had ever seen her. After she had gone, Janna asked Braeden, "Was it very bad?"

"About the worst thing I've ever seen or heard. And I've been in over fifty battles. I don't know how you women keep doing that time after time. But you had trouble that wasn't normal. Good thing the doctor came when she did. She'll be back to check on you."

"It seemed she wasn't coming out like she should."

"That was just it," Braeden said. "She was turned the wrong way and couldn't come out. Seems the doctor had to reach in and turn her around."

""That's what made me pass out," Janna said.

Braeden pulled her close and kissed the top of her head. "I prayed to gods I don't even believe in to give me a cannonball to the gut if it would stop your suffering."

Janna found herself unable to speak, but then the baby wanted more, so she moved her to the other breast. When she was settled, Janna turned her face to Braeden and kissed him long and hard. "I'm glad they didn't answer your prayers. And now, it feels worth it. Look at her. She really is perfect. Except for her head, which has an odd shape."

Braeden took a closer look and traced a finger around the baby's skull. "I think that's from the doctor yanking on it. She said it would come right soon."

"I hope so," Janna said. "Otherwise we must hope she gets your hair so no one notices the shape of her head."

"What'll we name her?" That was something they hadn't discussed. Janna had worried about cursing herself by hoping for too much.

Braeden took a deep breath. "What was the name of the little girl you lost? If that's not too hard."

She realized for the first time she didn't want to cry when thinking about her. "Anyezka. Though I don't want to use that name again. What was your mother's name?"

"I don't remember," Braeden said. "If I ever knew it. I always just called her Ma."

Janna smiled, trying to picture a small Braeden.

There was a long silence. After that first time they'd never talked about his family. Finally he asked, "What about your mother?"

"Iryna." Janna's voice caught in her throat. She did her best not to think about her family, hopefully alive and well in Kaleva, since she doubted she'd ever see them again.

"Iryna. I've known Sanovan girls with that name too."

"That's perfect. Her father is a Sanova Hussar after all."

"And maybe she will be too, someday," Braeden said, putting his finger in little Iryna's hand and smiling when her tiny fingers closed around his.

TEODORA

"This just arrived by messenger from Kronland." Elyse handed Teodora an unopened pouch.

Teodora pulled the message out and read it twice, then crumpled it into a ball and threw it as hard as she could.

"What is it, Your Highness?" Elyse asked.

"More bad news. It seems Duke Evard was unwise enough to run into Arian Orland and allowed himself to be taken prisoner. Is it really too much to ask for competent allies?"

"Oh dear," Elyse said faintly, then crossed the room, picked up the balled-up sheet, opened it and started reading. She could match General Ensden for composure. It hadn't escaped Teodora's notice that delicate little flowers like Brytta Prosnytz made themselves scarce whenever it looked like there might be fireworks. She wondered if the other ladies-in-waiting paid Elyse in sweets or trinkets to induce her to take on the hard duties.

Teodora paced while Elyse read the letter. She was running out of options. Only one person could help her now. "Send for General Barela," she said, and Elyse ran to do her bidding.

He took far too long to come. She must have paced the long corridor in the palace main wing at least four times before he came through a distant door. He was in half armor, sweating and breathless. He still managed a courtly bow. "I apologize, Your Highness. We were practicing maneuvers on the parade ground."

"I see," she said sourly, looking him over. He looked good in spite of his disheveled state, perhaps even more so than usual. He caught her eye and winked, which she found very annoying. It did no good to let a man know you found him attractive. He would exploit it relentlessly.

124

"Come," she said, leading him back to her study. "Out," she waved at Elyse, who scrambled to gather up a pile of papers before scurrying out. Once the door fell shut behind her, she sat at her desk and pointed at a chair across from it. Barela sat down, never taking his eyes off her.

"You might have heard that General Ensden has returned," she said. He nodded and she went on. "In addition to his humiliating defeat he also lost all of his troops, down to a few hundred."

That seemed to surprise Barela, who shook his head and made a sympathetic noise.

"That leaves me with no army at all, aside from the Sanova Hussars and you."

"And I am merely borrowed," he said.

"Beatryz hasn't called you back has she?" The thought struck her like a thunderbolt and she failed to hide the panic it invoked.

"She has not. And she will not before next spring. The truce in Floradias is holding and she is bringing more troops over the mountains in the meantime. But I cannot take on Arryk and his allies alone. Where is Evard?"

"That's the other bad news." She told him about Evard's defeat and imprisonment.

"Your Highness, this is an impossible situation. You must get help."

"From you."

"Yes, I will do what I can. I probably can defeat Faris or Falk by myself, and perhaps Orland also, but not Arryk. I am sure you know he is gathering allies in western Kronland."

"I'd heard rumors, but I keep receiving letters from various Kronland rulers assuring me of their loyalty."

"Oh, they will be loyal to you, until they are not." He shrugged, though his gaze was sympathetic. "The king is making a good case to join him. He throws money around like you throw rose petals at the Feast of Vica. And Princess Gwynneth goes everywhere with him, looking like a pretty vision of the Holy Mother with a newborn babe in her arms, reminding everyone that Kendryk has never seen this sweet little daughter of his. They must both be stopped before they turn every kingdom against you."

"You must do this."

"I cannot. Believe me, I would if it were at all possible. But I know what I can do. And I cannot defeat Arryk Roussay alone."

"Then what am I to do?"

"Send the Sanova Hussars to attack Arryk's allies. Maybe even Arryk himself. Cavalry is excellent for hit and run. Many small attacks will wear him down, though they will have to return before winter."

"I'll send them right now, and if nothing else materializes, I'll send you in the winter. For now, I'd rather keep you close by." She cursed herself for letting this last slip out.

He smiled his dazzling smile. "I'd rather stay close by."

ANTON

The gates of Bernhausen were closed when Count Orland and Edric Maximus rode up to them, Anton right behind them. In the past few months, every town and temple had welcomed them. It had been some time since any had required the persuasion of Orland's Cuirassiers.

Edric Maximus himself went to speak to one of the guardsmen, flanked by the count and another officer. Anton trailed behind. No one ever seemed to question his presence, which suited him well enough.

"We need no changes to our temple here," the guard said stoutly. "We are happy with our priestess and we hold to the old teachings. Please be on your way."

"Might I speak with the head priestess alone?" Edric Maximus asked, polite as ever.

The guard looked uncertain. Count Orland loosened a pistol in its holster and said, "We can kill you lot easily enough and ride through this gate. Better do as the Maximus asks."

"Wait here," the guard said, then returned a scant ten minutes later. "Mother Barra asks that the heretic come alone and she will speak with him."

"Impossible," the count said. "We're not about to let him out of our sight so you can cut his throat. She can come here."

The guard sighed and ran off again. Before he returned, a woman riding a mule approached the gate. She had a plain, kind face and looked older than the Maximus. It seemed they knew each other.

"Edric," she said, smiling though her eyes remained serious. "It has been a long time." She dismounted and walked right up to the Maximus, took his hand and kissed him on both cheeks.

"It is good to see you Barra," Edric said. "Might I have a word?" He took her by the elbow and led her away from the gate.

It didn't take long. They never raised their voices, but it seemed she would not be swayed. Edric Maximus tried to give her a copy of the Scrolls he always carried in his pocket, but she shook her head.

For the first time, he looked upset. "Please Barra," he said, catching her sleeve as she turned to go. "It means your life and the lives of your congregation."

"I know." She kept walking, but slowed down a little. "Just as you risked all to defend what you believe in, I will risk the same. I am sorry." She smiled at Edric, patted his hand and made her way back to the gate.

It happened so fast that Anton almost missed it. The count's saber came from nowhere, slicing across her throat with a hiss and a spray of blood. Mother Barra crumpled to the ground. There was complete silence for several seconds. Then the guards shouted and drew their weapons.

"Take the town," the count said, brandishing the bloody saber. "Do as you wish until nightfall. Then I'll meet with the survivors and they can tell me how they want to continue."

By the time he'd finished speaking, the men at the gate were already dead. The rest of the troops had come forward upon a signal from an officer and streamed through the open gates. Anton drew his short sword and followed the count, but first glanced back at Edric Maximus, who still stood by the gate, next to Barra's body. His face was set and grim, but fire burned in his pale eyes. Anton shivered and looked away.

Within the walls, all was chaos. Horses galloped in every direction, shots were fired, people screamed. The count spurred Cid forward and Anton tried to keep up. They made for the center of town and rode straight to the doors of the temple. A young man in novitiate robes stood in front of them, shaking. He held a jeweled dagger in one hand.

"Halt, in the name of Vica," he quavered.

"Step aside." The count lifted his saber. "I won't ask again."

The man scrambled out of the way and Cid reared up and kicked the enormous doors open. The temple was empty, though tapers burned at the high altar in front of the icon of Vica and incense hung heavy in the air.

"Pull it down," the count said, turning to Anton.

Anton hesitated. He wasn't on the best terms with the gods, considering what they'd let happen to his family, but he knew better than to desecrate holy places. It was bad enough he had ridden his horse straight into a temple, as if it were a stable.

"Now," the count said, raising his saber again.

Anton spurred Skandar forward, up the three stairs to the altar, then puzzled over how to bring down the enormous icon. It hung from the rafters on heavy silk bands. While he looked up, another young officer joined him.

"On my shoulders," he said.

Anton jumped onto the back of his horse first, then climbed onto his shoulders. By wedging his feet between pauldrons and neck-guard he had a steady foothold. He took his sword with both hands and swung at the bands, just overhead now. Two separated completely and a third tore loudly. That left two on the other side.

The officer didn't need to be asked. He walked his horse to the other side of the altar, now wide open, its glittering contents already being scooped into bags by soldiers swarming all around. There was screaming in the distance, but Anton felt heady from the incense and his height and his extreme daring and it didn't seem real to him.

He swung at the other two bands, and the great icon of Vica crashed into the altar below. Anton jumped to the floor and sprang back onto Skandar. The count laughed and slashed at the icon with his bloody saber. Even though nothing had happened yet, Anton was a little worried that Holy Vica might punish them right this moment. But nothing had happened when the count killed her priestess and nothing happened now.

The count grinned at Anton. "Well done. Let's burn it now, and go see what other treasures await us. I've heard this is a rich town."

As they trotted out of the temple, smoke and flames already rising from the wall hangings, the count said, "There's a wagon full of sacks in the square. Grab a few and fill them up with all you can carry. Take any girls you want too, for now or later."

Anton shook his head. He doubted he could find a girl who could help him reload or was good with horses. Gold or jewelry would be better.

By the time he reached the main square, the chaos had increased. A few houses were on fire and people and soldiers ran everywhere. There were occasional screams, but most soldiers were busy getting what they could out of the houses.

"Picked over," the young officer said. He still rode beside Anton. "Let's find another neighborhood." His horse trotted to the left and Anton followed him.

A few streets away from the main square, it was much quieter. There was no one on the street and the doors of the tall houses were shut and Anton supposed, firmly barred as well.

"They won't open if we knock, will they?" he asked, hoping he didn't sound too much a novice.

The officer laughed. "The way I knock, they will." He rode up to a door decorated with elaborate carvings, drew his pistol, shot at the latch and kicked the door open. It took Anton a moment to recover from the noise, but he tied Skandar to a post and went in.

"You start at the top," the officer said. "I'll start at the bottom. If you see a pretty girl, drag her down here."

Anton made for the stairs. This was a merchant's house, much like the one he had grown up in, so he knew the layout. The stairs were of dark, polished wood, with a thick carpet over them. Anton ran up them soundlessly, his sword drawn. He wondered if the people who lived here were hiding or if they'd run off.

Servant's quarters were on the top floor. There wouldn't be anything good there, so he started on the next floor. One room was a nursery, with a terrified old woman holding a baby, sitting in a rocking chair. He darted into the next room without saying a word. This was probably the master's bedchamber and more likely to hold something worthwhile.

Anton opened the drawers of a tall bureau and started rummaging. Sure enough, they had tried to quickly hide the jewelry amongst the clothes. Nothing too fancy, but nice, heavy gold chains and a few pretty pendants of semi-precious stones. Anton pocketed them and looked for a strongbox. If he found one box full of gold and silver coins he'd consider the day a success.

He ransacked the rest of the bureau and wardrobe and found nothing. Dropping to his knees to look under the bed, he stared straight into the frightened face of a girl a little older than he was. She held the box in her arms.

"Give it here," Anton whispered, forgetting to pull out his sword.

She swallowed hard and shook her head.

He heard heavy footsteps on the floor below. "Give it here," he said, "and I won't tell anyone you're here, or the little one upstairs." By now, she'd heard the footsteps, too, and whimpered.

"Hurry," Anton said, putting out his hand. She put the box in it. It was gratifyingly heavy. "Now be quiet," he whispered, before standing and heading to the door.

He was just in time. The officer met him on the stairs. "Anything good?"

"A few trinkets." Anton shrugged, noting the bag bulging with a silver service the man dragged behind him. "Seems no one is home. I didn't bother about the servants."

"Just as well. Let's go."

Anton was relieved to find Skandar where he'd left him. When they rode off, he noticed a few other broken-down doors and wondered if anyone else would go into the house.

What he saw next made him forget all about it. Two men were pulling a young woman out of the house next door by her hair. She shrieked and struggled, but was obviously overpowered. Anton looked down at her, saw a small pale face, enormous eyes, dark hair.

"Mama?" he asked, stunned. Then he blinked. It couldn't have been, she was much too young.

It took only seconds for his confusion to turn to anger and by then they had her pinned up against the wall of the house. One man held her by the arms while another tried to push up her skirts. She'd stopped screaming and struggling and was crying quietly.

"You leave her alone," Anton said, drawing his sword.

"What?" the man pulling at her skirts looked around. "Get in line, sprout. You can have her shortly."

"Leave her alone." Anton pointed his sword at the man.

"Put that little thing away." The man laughed. "And get out of here. There's plenty more in this town."

Anton slashed wildly at his face and the other man reached for Skandar's reins. Skandar reared up and kicked out, just as Anton had trained him, and the man flew against the wall with groan. The other man kept coming at him.

"Go," Anton said. "Run." And with one look back at him, the girl ran. No, definitely not his mother. He swallowed down the grief that threatened to choke him and slashed at the man one more time, bloodying his arm. Then he wheeled Skandar around and spurred him down the street as fast as he could go.

BRAEDEN

"This ought to be fun." Prince Novitny looked pleased. Braeden suspected he'd gotten bored all these months in Atlona. "Our orders are to venture into Kronland as far as we can with the goal of harassing Arryk Roussay's allies. There aren't enough of us to take him on in a pitched engagement, but we can find other ways to make his life miserable." He opened a rolled-up map and spread it across the table. All the officers of the Sanova Hussars were gathered in the dining room of an inn the prince had taken over as his headquarters.

Braeden leaned forward so he could see. He wasn't keen on leaving the girls so soon after Iryna's birth, but couldn't deny he'd enjoy some action.

"Last we heard, King Arryk himself was in Lantura, trying to form an alliance with Prince Benda. If he's succeeded, which is likely, we think he'll go west to Fromenberg next. We won't try to stop him.

"I really want to get Ruso Faris. We pummeled him good at Birkenfels, but he's back. And judging by how he's taken out Ensden, he's stronger than ever. He's the one we need to wear down and keep from meeting up with Arryk if we can. Arryk will need his pike and artillery if he wants any hope of taking Teodora on directly."

"What about Arian Orland?" Braeden asked. He'd been more than a little disappointed that he'd been absent when they fought Kendryk at Birkenfels.

"Too far away for now. Last we heard, he was causing trouble in Brandana, taking that heretic priest to all the towns there. If he comes our way though, I'll be happy to give him a friendly welcome. No, our best chance for action right now is Faris. If we don't run into him, we can go north where Bronson Falk is doing gods-knows-what in Terragand."

"Wouldn't he be easier to defeat first?" Reno asked.

"Maybe. But he's weaker. Much less use to Arryk right now. And we only have a few months before winter sets in and we must come back here. Unless much changes, Demario Barela might go out. He's been training his pike to take on cavalry in small engagements. He'll do well if he wants to go after Arryk or Orland once they're pinned down during the winter."

"So we'll be back by winter?" Braeden asked.

"Late autumn, I imagine. Southern Kronland is already eaten clean and we'll want to be away from there by the time the grass stops growing. I won't risk our horses starving."

Braeden left the meeting feeling happy, but he slowed down a little by the time he reached the house. He didn't know how to tell Janna.

He found her in the garden, sitting in the shade with the baby. It was a warm afternoon and fragrance rose from the flowers she and Trisa had planted in the spring. Bees hummed and Janna and the baby both looked half asleep, propped against the trunk of a large cedar tree. Braeden felt a bit sleepy himself as he lowered himself into the grass, sliding an arm around Janna's shoulders.

"It's wonderful out here, isn't it?" Janna turned to him, smiling, then put a sleeping Iryna into his arms.

Braeden took a deep breath. No point in putting it off. "I'm being deployed," he said.

"What? Now?"

He hated the panicked look in her eyes. "Yes, now. But only for a few months. We'll be back here by winter."

"We'll come along, of course," Janna said, a determined set to her mouth.

Braeden sighed. "I'm sorry little mouse, but you can't. We're traveling fast and light this time and won't be camping anywhere for long. It'll be quick actions and we'll cover a large area. I don't think anyone is taking family."

"But I came last time. I enjoyed that so much and you liked having me along, didn't you?"

"You know I did. But the little one isn't a month old. She's too young for even a regular campaign."

Janna's lip trembled as she looked down at the sleeping baby. He prayed she would see things his way.

She swallowed hard. "When will you be back?"

"October at the latest. We'll spend the winter here together, I promise."

"What if something happens to you?"

"Nothing ever happens to me; you know that." He grinned at her, hoping she'd smile back.

She did, though it was a tiny one. "I know, but I still worry." She looked at Iryna again and sighed. "I suppose you're right. She is still so small and I'd never forgive myself if she got sick while we were on campaign."

"There's nothing wrong with her, is there?" Braeden looked into Iryna's tiny face anxiously.

"Oh no, not at all. Things can just happen so quickly when they're small. All the more reason it's best for me to stay here."

Braeden breathed a sigh of relief, then laid Iryna onto a blanket that Janna had spread on the grass. "I'll miss you, you know," he said, then reached for his wife.

TEODORA

Teodora drummed her fingers on the table. "Let's discuss the Kronland situation. I need details before I decide what to do."

A sigh went up from the twenty members of her council. They had been seated at the enormous table in her largest state chamber for the past three hours. A warm breeze wafted in through an open window and Teodora caught an old nobleman casting a longing glance at the fountain just outside in the gardens. It wasn't as though Teodora had time to enjoy them so there was no reason he should.

"Your Highness," Count Solteszy said, "your victory over Prince Kendryk was overwhelming, but incomplete. The remnants of his armies have combined with those of his brother-in-law. Between them, they hold nearly all of the political power throughout Kronland. This is exacerbated by the aggressive activities of the defrocked heretic priest Edric Landrus. Every town whose temple has gone to his Quadrene heresy has also declared for Kronland's independence from the Empire."

"I want the name of every traitor," Teodora said. "If they think I will forget this when the tide turns in my favor ..."

"Your Highness—"

"Read them. I want to hear the names of each person who dares claim I am not the rightful ruler."

Solteszy sighed and looked down at the document in front of him. "Very well. First, and least surprising is Prince Bronson Falk of Helvundala. We've known for some times he's harbored treasonous ideas and likely even engaged in secret negotiations with Norovaea. He led an army against Count Ensden himself at the relief of Birkenfels."

"His head will be first on the block," Teodora snapped. "Next."

"Princess Galena Sebesta of Oltena. Also unsurprising, since she is Prince Kendryk's aunt on his mother's side. We neutralized her last year and she has not recovered, so even though she is near our northern borders, we needn't consider her a threat right now. It's also possible that holding Prince Kendryk helps keep her from acting against us openly."

"Hmm. See that she is reminded. No further harm will come to her nephew as long as she follows our instructions to the letter, and so on."

"Done." Solteszy scribbled something on his paper. Then he started reading again. "The northerners are proving the most problematic, also not surprising. They were already infected by the spirit of rebellion in Zeelund and no doubt feel Norovaea will offer them protection if they misbehave. We've learned that Prince Ossian Dahlby of Ummarvik has entered into formal alliance with Arryk Roussay, and has appointed Emilya Hohenwart to recruit and lead ten thousand troops, if she can find them."

Teodora's fist slammed down on the table and everyone sitting around it jumped. "Hohenwart? Isn't she one of ours?"

Solteszy consulted his notes. "She was, Your Highness. After working for your uncle, she was in the employ of your cousin, Queen Beatryz, but had a falling out with Commandant Montanez some years ago and has worked for Zeelund ever since."

"Unbelievable." Teodora slumped back in her chair. It hadn't happened on her watch, but it seemed her uncle had let one of his best generals slip away, and her incompetent cousin had done the same.

Solteszy made a vague noise of agreement and continued. "Next is Princess Floreta Bensen of Brandana. She was a highly equivocal supporter of Prince Kendryk—in fact, I would say she hardly qualified as such. But, her land has been subject to the depredations of Daciana Tomescu so she has thrown herself in with Arian Orland, who continues to transport the heretical priest across her kingdom, unhindered."

"Then we have Prince Dristan Fabrey of Aquianus. My sources say he too is on the verge of an agreement with King Arryk. No word yet on the number of troops he may supply. Princess Viviane Kasbirk has formalized an alliance with the king but she only has three thousand or so militia at her disposal. Princess Keylinda Marthaler in Fromenberg has not entered into in-person talks with King Arryk, but we've heard Princess Gwynneth is on her way there right now."

"Would someone like to explain how Princess Gwynneth—" Teodora could hardly get the words out without gagging. "How Princess Gwynneth is roaming all over my empire, inciting my enemies, gathering troops against me, when just a few months ago, we had her cooped up in her castle?" Her voice rose to a shriek. "Anyone?"

Everyone stared down at the table.

After a long, unpleasant silence, a Countess Biaram spoke up quietly. "Your Highness, is there no further way Prince Kendryk can be used to keep her in line even now?"

That was the only name that could make her angrier right now. "Kendryk is turning out to be a singularly useless hostage. I could never have guessed that his wife cared so little for him she wouldn't exchange that priest for him, or the castle. Theirs was supposed to be a storybook romance and they would die for each other. Instead, she would let him die rather than turn over a man she didn't know all that well. Unless ..." A thought came to her suddenly. "Unless she and the priest became unnaturally close during the siege. Has anyone determined for a certainty that her baby is in fact Kendryk's?"

"No one has," Countess Biaram said, a gleam in her eye. She always appreciated a good rumor and was helpful in spreading one, when necessary. "And even before the battle last year, there were rather scurrilous stories concerning her and Arian Orland. They said Orland wasn't there because Prince Kendryk sent him away after discovering an affair and that the princess was carrying a child that wasn't his."

"Why didn't I know this then?" Teodora demanded. "It might have been useful information. I could have killed Kendryk in battle and saved us all a great deal of trouble."

"It was one of many rumors." The countess seemed unworried by Teodora's anger. "At the time it seemed unimportant when we were more concerned with troop movements and the progress of plague in Prince Kendryk's army."

"Hm," Teodora said, fixing a withering stare on the countess. "Stop referring to him as 'Prince' Kendryk. He is no longer a prince. Let's continue." If she thought about Princess Gwynneth any more she was likely to rupture something.

Solteszy turned back to his document. "There is one fence-sitter right now. Prince Herryk Peloso of Tirilis is in a most uncomfortable position. His proximity to Olvisya makes him vulnerable to retaliation from us, but he is also friendly with Galladium and is working out a new treaty with King Gauvain. It seems he would prefer to stay neutral, but may well bend to the pressure of whoever exerts the most."

"Let it be us, then," Teodora said. "Send an envoy and let's have a treaty too, while he's at it. But surely, Arcius is still loyal to us?"

"Indeed, Princess Zelenka has been our most faithful partisan. She has even banned Landrus's teachings in her temples. Anyone found with copies of his work can be charged with heresy."

"At last, someone with sense. I suppose Lantura is a lost cause?"

"Yes, it seems so. Prince Eldrid has provided Arryk with everything he's asked for. Of course, it's hard to say no when the King of Norovaea has just garrisoned his twenty thousand troops on your land, but Benda was never the most resolute."

"True, though it makes him no less a traitor. What about Princess Martinek, in Podoska?"

"Bad news from there, too. She is also fielding her own army to support King Arryk. She's called in Seward Kurant to whip them into shape. I don't know where she's recruiting, but Kurant knows what he's about."

"Yes, he gave Barela a good run in Floradias a few years ago. Are there any more enemies to add to my tally?" She tried to sound casual, but having it laid out so methodically made the fear rise like bile in her throat. It was hard to see where it would stop.

"None at present." Solteszy sounded rather satisfied.

She stood. "I will make a decision about all of this soon. You can be sure I will not sit idly by while this threat builds." She walked out, hoping she looked more resolute than she felt.

When she returned to her private chambers, she sent for Livilla Maxima. The older woman arrived with no ceremony and came straight to Teodora, kissing her forehead. "How bad is it then?" she asked, sitting down across from her.

"Nearly intolerable. I had thought defeating Kendryk the way I did would put a stop to it all, but it only seems to have inflamed matters."

Livilla sighed. "It's impossible to see how these things will fall out, especially when there's unfinished business. And Princess Gwynneth reacted in a way we did not expect. But now my dear, it's time for you to react in a way no one expects."

"I'm sure it is, but I can't think of what I should do."

"I have an idea. You won't like it, but the gods sent me dreams about this person three nights in a row. There's no question this is their will."

Teodora was afraid to ask what Livilla might propose, so she waited in silence.

"Brynhild Mattila," Livilla said.

"No," Teodora replied before the name was out. "No. I can't bear it. Anyone but her."

"There isn't anyone else," Livilla said. "You know that. You must at least talk to her."

"I can't." Teodora was unable to stop the panic rising in her voice. "I won't."

"You must. There is no other way."

KENDRYK

Kendryk now saw the darkness as his friend and constant companion, so the light was an intrusion. Even worse was what followed: the empress, in as foul a mood as he'd ever seen her. But that gave him hope. Whatever was bad for her was good for him, at least in a general sense.

He sat up blinking, swung his legs over the side of the stone bench, stood up shakily and managed a somewhat proper bow. "Your Highness, this is a surprise."

She made a snorting noise, which didn't become her, then shouted something at the guards. He'd straightened up by the time they came in.

"The stench of this place, really," she said to the guards. "Take him to a better room where I can speak to him."

They grabbed him by both arms and half-dragged him out of the cell. He could walk now, but not as fast as they wanted him to. They hauled him into another room, already lit with a lamp, pushed him into a chair and asked, "Shall we chain him, Your Highness?"

Teodora gave Kendryk a long look. "It won't be necessary. You can stand outside the door. He was always on the puny side, but now I could overcome him with one finger."

Kendryk found that funny. "You're right." He smiled.

That was a mistake. "Don't mock me," she shouted, advancing on him, still holding the torch. Kendryk shrank back into the chair.

"I meant no offense," he said with all the calm he could muster. "And I give my word I will behave myself during your visit."

"Oh, you will." Teodora smiled her cold smile and handed the torch to a guard before sitting down across from him. She wore a court dress, which looked incongruous in the stone cell. For it was a cell, though a much nicer one than his.

Kendryk wondered what she wanted. Probably the same thing as always. Whenever something didn't go her way, she appeared sooner or later, trying to force him to abdicate. It seemed a ridiculous exercise, considering she had already removed him from his seat, but she seemed to want it badly. It made him suspect she'd suffered a setback in Terragand, or that the other Kronlanders were asking for his formal abdication before bending to her. He hoped that was true.

He didn't have to wait long. She leaned forward and looked at him intently. "You look awful. And you smell worse."

Kendryk believed it. He hadn't seen a mirror in some time, but he'd grown a patchy beard and his hair had grown out raggedly. He'd also lost several stone he couldn't afford to and was no doubt pasty pale from however many months he'd been down here. "I don't suppose I might have a bath?"

"Unlikely. Although, if you cooperate ..." She smiled sweetly, which was even more incongruous than her elaborate dress.

Kendryk sighed. "You can guess my answer, I'm sure."

"Shouldn't you listen to my proposal first?"

"Is it the same as always?"

"More or less. But I'm losing patience. If you don't comply, it might go badly for you."

"Worse than it already is?"

"Much worse."

"Will you kill me?"

"I might."

"I wouldn't mind that." Forcing a small smile wasn't as hard as he thought it might be.

"Not the way I plan to do it. If you imagine it'll go quickly or painlessly, think again."

"I've considered that."

"You can't have. Perhaps you should spend an afternoon in the lower cells where confessions are extracted from rebels."

Kendryk knew he should feel terror, but it was as though his heart refused to acknowledge what his head understood. He wondered if he was beyond fear. He sighed. "I'm completely at your mercy and you can do whatever you want, no matter what I do or don't do for you. Why do you hesitate?"

She shrugged. "I won't deny it would make my life easier if I received your abdication in writing."

"I'm sure it would. But I'll never do it. There is something else I'd consider however."

"Oh?" her smile was nasty.

"A public hearing. Put me on trial and invite all of the other rulers in the empire. Prove me guilty and I'll agree to give up everything."

"You've already lost everything."

"Not everything."

"You are a lunatic."

"Perhaps. But I still have my self-respect."

"I must admit your arrogance and stubbornness are astonishing. But I can hurt your family. You can spend an afternoon observing interrogations and then ponder how well your little girl would withstand that."

"You don't have my little girl." He said it with such confidence he could tell from the shock on her face she believed him.

"How do you know that? Which guard told you? I'll have him—"

"No guard told me. I received a message from the gods. I'm certain my family is safe, though I don't know exactly how."

"Don't be ridiculous. The gods don't send messages like that, and certainly not to heretics."

He shrugged. "They did. So there's nothing you can do to force me to give in to you. You can't hurt my family, and I can bear whatever you do to me. Ercos will give me strength."

"I do believe you have lost your mind."

"I've wondered that myself. But the gods sent me comfort, and haven't done so for you. So ..." He trailed off with a shrug, then almost pitied her, seeing the flash of pain that crossed her face and disappeared.

She stood up and slapped him hard. "How dare you preach to me, you little—" She slapped him again.

It stung just a little, though he felt a trickle of blood form at the corner of his mouth. He looked straight at her. "It's the simple truth, Your Highness. If you would but see it, we could end all of this."

She hit him harder. He saw stars this time, but through them, caught the twist of her mouth and pain in her eyes before she called to the guards and stormed out. It wasn't much, but he felt a small twinge of satisfaction. He'd once again held firm and perhaps even upset her. He would take the victory, however small.

ANTON

"It's annoying, but otherwise not so bad," Count Orland said. He and his officers sat around a table in his tent. It was still raining. Anton hovered in the background. He was there to bring drinks and anything else that might be needed, but he was also eavesdropping. No one seemed to mind as long as he didn't tell anyone what he'd heard.

"The Sanova Hussars going back to Atlona before we can take them on is annoying all right," Ossian Schurtz grumbled.

"They can't find forage for their horses during the winter and neither can we." The count studied the map spread out on the table. "It's time we picked the best place to spend the winter." They had hurried south once they'd received a message from Ruso Faris that the Sanova Hussars were operating in Lantura. Faris had taken a strong position in a walled city with his big guns, but it was a good opportunity for Orland to make a move. Anton was disappointed that they still hadn't been able to face the Sanova Hussars.

"Should we join King Arryk?" an officer asked.

"I doubt he'll want to see us. He'll have enough to do finding food and shelter for his own army. No, we should find a comfortable city, one well-situated to put us in position for a spring offensive. I'm sure once the king is certain of his western allies he'll want to take the fight straight into Olvisya. With any luck, Hohenwart and Kurant will join us by then. Arryk will move into Lantura while Falk and Faris will likely winter there. If we cross the river Lera here ..." the count pointed to a spot on the map, "... we can meet up with them and march to meet the king when he comes out of Fromenberg with more troops. Then we'll be straight on the road into Olvisya."

"I like the sound of wintering in Lerania," Schurtz said.

"So do I. It's a proper city so we shouldn't be too bored." The count smiled, as if imagining the fun he might have there. "Now, here's what we'll do." And there was a long discussion about sieges and deployments, and Anton was sent to bring food. By the time he returned with bread, cold meat and ale, talk had turned to money, which Anton found even less interesting than women, the other common topic.

Ossian Schurtz rode out the next morning with a force of two thousand. He was to secure Lerania which stood at the biggest bridge crossing the river Lera. The count would follow with the larger force, which had swelled to include several thousand infantry and a baggage train so long Anton had never seen the end of it.

Edric Maximus had been so successful in these western towns that all of the minor lords around them volunteered their militias to support the cause. The count added them to his force, but had little interest in infantry, so he let each lord command his own group. It was all very chaotic, but Anton supposed every soldier counted, when they planned to meet the empress on her home territory. He wasn't happy about spending a whole winter without fighting, but he would use the time to train Skandar and become a better shot. Maybe he could get the count to teach him how to fight with a sword, too. He was almost eleven and it was time he learned how to be a real soldier.

TEODORA

She came at last, weeks after Teodora sent for her, with an entourage to rival the empress herself. Teodora received her on her throne, with all the pomp of the empire. She told everyone she wanted to give Brynhild Mattila her due as a senior member of the loyal Moraltan nobility, and a potential savior of the realm. In reality, she wanted to make sure that Mattila understood who she was dealing with.

In contrast with her splendidly-robed entourage, all in fur-trimmed coats of dark velvet in the style of old Moralta, Mattila herself wore riding dress under a plain, somewhat battered suit of armor. It wasn't fitting for an audience with the empress, but it made her look very warlike. She approached the throne with her brisk, long stride and went down on one knee, her lips brushing Teodora's outstretched hand. Then she looked up, her gray eyes still hard and clear, though the rest of her looked quite faded.

"Your Highness," she said. "It has been many years."

"It has." Teodora forced a smile. Mattila had been Teodora's commanding officer when she first joined the military. She had made a point of showing everyone that the young archduchess would receive no special treatment because of her station. Teodora hadn't expected special treatment, but what she got from Mattila was nothing short of brutal bullying. She'd hated being on the receiving end, helpless to stop it.

But that was decades ago, and now Teodora was in charge.

She looked at Mattila a long time before speaking. "I worried something befell you on the road, you took so long. I hope your journey wasn't too difficult?" She nodded and Mattila stood up. She would have preferred to keep her kneeling longer, but didn't like having those cold eyes so close to hers.

"Not at all," Mattila said, her voice still unpleasantly harsh. It sounded as though she had grown used to shouting and could barely restrain herself. "The journey went well enough but I needed to see to some of my new estates along the way."

The Moraltan rebellion had not been a disaster for everyone. When Teodora arrested and executed the rebellious aristocrats, she sold their estates to raise cash to pay her army. Already-wealthy Moraltans like Mattila snapped them up at favorable prices. It was maddening. They were worth so much more, but Teodora had needed the money desperately at the time.

"I hope you found them to your satisfaction," Teodora said tightly.

"Some are in poor repair since your pet Daciana did rather more damage than was necessary." There was no question she remembered why Teodora and Daciana had become friends. Teodora would never forget it, or forgive it either.

"Daciana followed my orders perfectly," Teodora said. "The low prices reflected that they may not have been in perfect condition. I'm sure you will manage."

"Oh, I will." Mattila laughed, a rough cackle that echoed through the pillared room and would likely have embarrassed anyone else. But it was hard to put this woman at a disadvantage. Teodora reminded herself that it wouldn't help her cause to do so right now.

"Good," Teodora said. "I'll give you and your company time to refresh yourselves, and I will send for you later." She nodded a clear dismissal.

Mattila bowed and walked away, turning her back rather sooner than was proper.

Surely it was possible to be allies with someone so hateful.

Rather than meet Mattila in her private study, where she normally conducted such sensitive business, Teodora sent for her in the large council chamber. It was far more impressive and less intimate. She also surrounded herself with her ladies, Count Solteszy and Livilla. Uncomfortable as it was, she wanted witnesses to whatever transpired. Besides, it was easier to keep her temper with Livilla in her line of sight.

The Maxima had cautioned her against losing her temper. "It is upsetting, I know, but she is far too valuable to you right now. Get her to do your bidding, and use her as long as you can. When the time is right, and you no longer need her, do with her what you will. But right now, you must show restraint."

Teodora took deep breaths while she waited for her opponent to appear. No, she corrected herself, not an opponent; an ally.

146

Mattila came alone. She had changed into clean, though creased, clothing. Men's clothes, from the looks of them, but tailored to fit her lanky form. Her short gray hair was slicked back and she looked fresh, much fresher than Teodora felt. She also didn't seem the least bit intimidated by the people ranged on Teodora's side, giving them all courteous nods in turn.

"Let's not waste time on useless formalities," Teodora said. "You must know why I've sent for you."

Mattila nodded. "You need an army of some size, and someone who can command it to victory."

"Yes," Teodora said, "I do, and I've heard you can provide such a force."

"I certainly can. Not only can I supply one, but I can do so at no initial expense to you."

"None?" That was hard to believe.

"I have the resources to recruit, train and equip a large number. Once that's done, I intend to keep them supplied in the lands of your enemies."

"How many?"

"How many do you need?"

There was no use prevaricating. "My best estimates show that there are somewhere around thirty thousand enemy troops in Kronland, maybe as many as thirty-five, once the provincial militias are called. So I would say forty thousand unless you can succeed with less." Teodora thought she'd start high, hoping for at least thirty.

"I can field forty thousand, though it will take some months."

"What do I do in the meantime? Only the Sanova Hussars remain in the field. I need Demario Barela here to defend the city, should the worst happen."

"Ah yes." Mattila smirked. "Leaving the city undefended last year was ill-advised, even for you. Lucky that Beatryz was cooperative."

Teodora bit down on her tongue so hard it bled, aware of Livilla's insistent stare. A moment passed before she could speak in a normal tone again. "I intend to keep either Barela or Novitny close by until I have another force sufficient to keep Olvisya safe."

"In that case, you will be all right until spring. Winter is coming hard and early in the north and Orland and Falk have already gone into winter quarters. I'm sure Arryk will do the same. A force of his size will need to spread across several kingdoms unless he wants them to revolt."

Much as she hated the woman, her calm, professional assessment was a relief. "Very well then," Teodora said. "What do you want from me to put your recruitment in motion?"

"Supreme command," Mattila said, her eyes unblinking.

"What?" Teodora was supreme commander both by right and tradition.

"Supreme command over all of your forces."

"No," Teodora snapped, avoiding Livilla's imploring gaze.

"Then we are done here." Mattila stood.

"Wait, please," Livilla said, with an apologetic glance at Teodora. "This is an unexpected development and Her Highness needs time to consider your terms."

"There is nothing to negotiate," Mattila said. "If I am to repel a large invading army, I must control all imperial forces. I've operated under civilian authority before and I won't do it again. It's too difficult to command an operation like this from the capital."

"I won't be in the capital," Teodora said, finally finding her voice. "I'll be in the field."

"No, you won't," Mattila said calmly. "In moments like these it's important your subjects know where you are and that business is going on as usual. You cannot risk being shut out of Atlona again for any reason. It would be the end of your reign."

"It won't happen again." Teodora nearly choked on her anger.

"It could very well. Arryk will gather allies through the winter and without me in the spring, nothing stands between them and you. Barela and Novitny, able as they are, will not have a chance against a combined force of thirty thousand or more. If only one engagement goes against you, Arryk Roussay will be at your gates."

"Arryk is an idiot." Teodora snapped. "Perhaps even more stupid than Andor Korma."

"That may be." Mattila sat back down. "But for an idiot, he defeated Ensden rather easily. King Arryk may be a lightweight, but he's advised by experienced generals like Faris, Orland and Hohenwart. They all know how to besiege a city and take it. So you must decide if you will accept my terms. And perhaps I should be clearer so there's no confusion. Supreme command includes the Sanova Hussars and Demario Barela."

Teodora gasped. "Prince Novitny would never agree. He is sworn to me."

"No, he's sworn to your sister-in-law. I'm sure you can come to an arrangement with her. He'll do as he's told. Oh, Daciana Tomescu you can keep." Mattila stood again, but didn't back away from the table. "I'll leave you to discuss it. I have business here that will keep me three days. Shall we talk again at the end of the third?"

Outraged by her peremptory tone, Teodora began, "I'm no longer a cadet for you to—"

"That will do," Livilla interrupted, standing up as well. "We will discuss this and send for you in a few days. Thank you."

And before Teodora could say anything else, Mattila had left the room.

Teodora waited until the heavy door had closed behind her, then exploded. "There must be someone else. These are intolerable demands."

After a long, uncomfortable silence Count Solteszy said, "That woman is the height of arrogance. But her reputation is well-earned, and the situation desperate. The problem is that she knows this and feels she can make such demands."

"I could have her arrested," Teodora said, her mind whirling. With Mattila gone, her estates could be confiscated and Teodora could build her own army.

"On what grounds?" Livilla asked. "She has committed no crime except for that of rudeness. If you arrest her without cause, the nobility will abandon you, and you cannot afford that right now. In all of this, you must at least have the Olvisyan aristocracy behind you. As harsh as she sounds, I believe you can still negotiate. Give her the Sanova Hussars, but keep Barela. If she intends for you to stay here, it makes sense for you to be defended by troops under your direct command."

"But Beatryz could call Barela back at any time," Teodora said, panic rising.

"She might, but we can persuade her not to, just yet," Livilla said. "We can impress upon her the need to stop the Quadrene heresy before it spreads to Floradias and south. That will make an impression."

"All right," Teodora said. "But the rest? Must we give her everything else?"

"It can't be avoided right now," Solteszy said.

"I agree," Livilla said. "But once Arryk and the others have been defeated, you can take whatever measure you feel necessary to deal with Brynhild Mattila."

JANNA

"That can't be true," Janna said. "The Sanova Hussars would never let Arryk Roussay get so close to Atlona." She and Nisa sat in her little parlor on a blustery autumn day. Along with all of the other hussar's families, Nisa and her children had been left behind. She wasn't as fortunate as Janna and lived in a cramped apartment, so Janna invited her over often.

Two days ago, they had gone to the parade ground to watch General Barela and his forces march out. The Sanova Hussars were supposed to be on their way back to the capital and Barela was taking their place in the field.

Janna waited anxiously for Braeden to appear. The past few months had dragged by. She seldom heard from him and whenever much time went by between letters, worried that he'd been killed, his body lying in a ditch somewhere in Kronland.

"It makes sense though, doesn't it?" Nisa asked. "Our men might not return for a few more weeks and Barela is gone. The city is undefended, so it's the perfect chance for King Arryk to strike."

"Wasn't he supposed to be in western Kronland?"

"That's what he'd like everyone to believe," Nisa said. "That's what I would do if I were trying to surprise my enemies."

"But surely the city will hold if he comes." Janna remembered how well the city had withstood its last siege just over a year ago.

"Oh, the city will hold, I'm sure. But he'll draw in our fellows, won't he?"

"Oh gods." Janna didn't want to think of Braeden somewhere out there while she was trapped inside the walls here, no matter how safe. "But the empress is here. And didn't that General Mattila just arrive? Surely they can do something."

"Mattila has no troops and neither does the empress. It would be up to our lot and Barela to deal with Arryk."

"But they're not enough," Janna said, panic rising.

"No, they're not." Nisa's voice was grave.

The next few days were worse, as no one seemed able to discuss anything besides Arryk Roussay's imminent approach. Most of the city's inhabitants remembered Andor Korma's siege well and felt that King Arryk was much better organized, with larger numbers. Many seemed filled with an almost gleeful desire to see the city fall, which made no sense to Janna, since they would be the victims in a sacking.

Even though the weather grew cold, Janna took to pacing the ramparts of the outer wall. It swarmed with the soldiers of the imperial guard, but civilians could climb up in several spots and look out into the countryside. Janna bundled up Iryna and hired a carriage to take her there and bring her back. It was too cold to stay long, and though she didn't see the Sanova Hussars coming, there didn't seem to be any sign of Arryk Roussay either.

After a week had gone by, Janna hoped it had all been a figment of fearful imaginations. She decided to stay home and not worry, if she could. She was better off laying in supplies in case there was a siege. Food was still plentiful, but prices went up as people worried. So the next day, instead of going to the wall, she hired a small cart to take her to the market, where she bought as much food as she could load into it. It was nearly identical to the cart she'd had in Kaleva, the one she'd used to escape the city with the children, just days before Dimir's execution. It seemed like a lifetime ago, though it hadn't even been two years.

At home, she put a crying Iryna to bed, then set to work stowing everything in her spacious cellar and pantry. Her cook had the afternoon off and the house was quiet except for the rattle of an occasional wind gust against the windows.

Janna hummed to herself, tried to concentrate on her task and not worry about Braeden or Arryk Roussay. So she was unprepared when the front door burst open, blowing in a gust of frosty air, some brown dry leaves, and Braeden.

She hardly had time to register his presence when he shortened the distance to her and folded her into his arms. To her mortification, she started crying.

Braeden chuckled into her hair. "No need to cry, little mouse. I'm here now."

Janna tried to pull herself together. "I was so worried," she said, wiping her eyes. "There were rumors that Arryk Roussay was coming and you would have to fight him and you were outnumbered ..."

"Arryk Roussay? Are you joking?" Braeden pulled her close to him again.

"He's well away, in Fromenberg, last we heard. We even looked for him after Faris gave us the slip and he wasn't anywhere east of the river Lera."

"That's a relief." Janna sagged against him. "I was afraid of being stuck in here with you on the outside."

"Wasn't going to happen," Braeden said.

"Still," Janna said, looking up at him. "Promise me you won't leave me like this again. I want to be with you no matter what happens."

Braeden looked down at her, his eyes twinkling. "I promise. Now, where's my little girl? There's no way you missed me as much as I missed the two of you."

ARRYK

Arryk was having the most delightful dream involving Larisa and another girl who looked just like her. When he awoke suddenly, Larisa was shaking him.

"Up! Up!" she shouted, already up and pulling on her clothes before he could think. It took him another moment to recognize the noises outside.

"We're under attack," she said, more quietly now, strapping on what armor she could find, grabbing her sword, then ducking outside the tent.

It still hadn't registered, but he rummaged for pieces of clothing while shouting for a servant. He didn't have time for armor, but found a loaded brace of pistols. By the time he got out, everyone in camp was at the perimeter, firing into the trees. A few gave chase on horseback but most returned empty-handed, while a few didn't return at all.

The black sky was tinged with grey at its edges, when Arryk found Larisa. "What happened?"

She sheathed her sword scowling. "Hit and run."

"Brigands?"

"No. These were real, disciplined troops. Maladene, from the look of the helm one of them dropped after I cut off his head." She produced a silver helmet still dripping blood.

"Maladena hasn't entered this fight, has she?"

"Not officially. But last we heard, Demario Barela was still in the employ of the empress."

"But he only has a few thousand. Not enough to take us on."

"But he can attack us like this, it seems."

It wasn't until later that morning he got a list of casualties. There were only a few dozen, but far worse, several wagons holding powder and charges had been set ablaze and exploded, igniting other wagons nearby.

153

"It's not fatal," Arryk said, handing the list to Larisa, who crumpled it up. "But it's annoying, and we can't afford too many more attacks like it."

"Next time we'll be ready," she said. "Or even better, we take the fight to him."

When he talked to Gwynneth later, she tried to talk him out of it. "That's exactly what he wants. He wants to draw you out and distract you. You need to concentrate on recruitment and moving on Olvisya."

"I can't do that while he's attacking me."

"Of course you can. Set better guards and spread the munitions wagons out. Don't let him get so close again."

"I'm sure you're right," Arryk said, though he didn't want to sit and do nothing.

But Larisa took matters into her own hands. One day, while Arryk negotiated with Princess Keylinda for a few hundred of her ill-trained militia, Larisa took three hundred cavalry and fell upon an encampment.

"It wasn't all of them, by far," she said, unwinding her long braid from her helmet. "But we gave them something to think about, and we learned it's Barela."

"I wonder why," Arryk said. "I'd have thought Teodora would want to keep him close since she has no one besides the Sanova Hussars with her."

"She isn't someone who'll sit and let the fight come to her. I'll bet she has something up her sleeve." Larisa frowned.

"I wish Faris, Falk and Orland had moved faster," Arryk grumbled. "I wanted to get into Olvisya before winter. There's no way we'll do that now. I worry the empress will do something in the months ahead." Not to mention, the prospect of months of inaction filled him with gloom.

"Like what?"

"Raise another army."

"Pfft. She has no money."

"No, but the Floradias truce is holding so maybe she'll get more help from Maladena."

"I doubt it. Just in case, let's try to finish off Barela before he can run away."

"I like the sound of that." Arryk grinned at her. With Larisa around, he wouldn't be bored anytime soon.

TEODORA

Three days felt like weeks, but Teodora would rather have died than appear too eager. At the end of the fourth, she sent a message to Mattila, informing her the empress was busy and couldn't see her for at least a few more days. She had to make clear that even though the general might be doing her a favor, Teodora was still her sovereign.

After nearly a week, Teodora arranged the meeting, in the same chamber with the same attendants. Her agitation was so intense she needed Livilla's calming presence more than ever.

"We've considered your proposal, and have accepted it, with a few changes." Teodora was as nervous as a seventeen-year-old recruit standing in front of the illustrious general for the first time.

"Let's hear them then," Mattila said, in that rough way she had. Anyone else taking that tone with Teodora would have found themselves enjoying Kendryk's tedious company in the Arnfels. But not just anyone could raise forty thousand troops at no cost to the empire. She'd bring the Kronland kingdoms back into the empire, but they would pay, and they would pay so dearly no one would dream of rebellion for five hundred years.

"I have decided to give you supreme command of the army, but only for the duration of this campaign." This was a formality, but made it easier for Teodora to stomach. It seemed Mattila understood this as well, for she nodded with an ironical look on her face. "And this campaign ends when you've chased Arryk Roussay back into the sea and destroyed his allies."

"You don't wish to make a play for Norovaea? It's a unique opportunity."

"We'd need ships."

"I can get those, too."

155

Teodora didn't doubt it. "No, I don't wish for Norovaea. If you do your job, Arryk Roussay will be dead, or so completely defeated he will stay on his island for the rest of his life." Teodora had to admit she was tempted by Norovaea's riches, but she didn't want Mattila getting her hands on them. She could deal with a weakened Arryk later.

"All right then, I'll defeat Arryk, but let him get away if I must." She made it sound cowardly.

"But I want the rest of them, understood? Faris, Orland, Falk, Hohenwart and anyone else leading an army against me is to be killed or brought to Atlona in chains. No one else escapes."

"Easy enough," Mattila said.

"As to the Sanova Hussars, you can have them. I've spoken with Prince Novitny, and he has agreed to serve under you. I believe he's done so in the past, and it worked out well enough."

"Yes, he and I understand each other. Heavy cavalry will be useful against Orland."

"That brings me to the other matter. I must keep Demario Barela under my command. He is contracted to work for the Inferraras and no one else."

Mattila looked at her long, while Teodora's heart thudded and she hoped she appeared calm and detached. Under the table, she clenched her skirt with clammy palms. It was bad enough to be parted from Demario for so many months; that he might not return here on her command was intolerable. And if Mattila had even the slightest inkling of Teodora's feelings, she'd never see him again.

"All right." Mattila looked amused

Teodora was too shocked at the easy agreement to be relieved. "What else do you want?" Teodora knew the woman well enough to be cautious.

"Permission to quarter troops in the suburbs and outlying towns, and the use of your parade grounds for training."

"That won't be a problem." Teodora slowly unclenched her fists. "Do you plan to move out in the spring?"

"I do." Mattila stood, pushed her chair in, then fixed her hard stare on Teodora.

Teodora squirmed, but stared back. She wouldn't so much as blink.

"I know how you feel about me, Your Highness. On a personal level, I don't care. But I'm glad to find you've matured enough to behave professionally in this matter."

Teodora jumped up so quickly her chair fell backwards. "You forget yourself, general." The heat rose in her cheeks. "Your opinion is irrelevant. Just do your job," she snapped.

Mattila chuckled, sketched a slight bow and headed for the door. Before opening it, she turned back to Teodora. "I'll do my job, Your Highness. I hope you can do yours." And the door shut behind her before Teodora could say another word.

Teodora fell back into her chair, which Brytta had caught and put back into place. "I can't stand it," she said. "I'll kill her."

Livilla looked at her across the table. "Perhaps you should," she said. "But not yet."

ANTON

Anton liked being on the move, even if it ended in a boring city where he'd be stuck for months. But after two days of marching, Count Orland received word that Schurtz had failed to take Lerania. It seemed that Flavia Maxima had been booted out of the Kronfels temple and had taken refuge there. Supporters of the old faith filled the city and refused to open the gates to renegades and heretics.

As usual, the count shrugged at the news. "All right then," he said. "We'll give them something to look at when they peep out over those walls."

From then on, they flattened every village they saw as they neared Lerania. The baggage train swelled. With the villager's homes burned, those of fighting age could choose to change their religion and join Orland's army if they wanted to live.

The new faith had not taken hold here, and a fair number chose to die rather than join the enemy. Anton wouldn't have made the same choice, especially if it meant the death of his family. Still, several hundred ill-trained troops joined up and their families added to the horde following the army.

The rest were killed. A few of the prettier, younger women escaped death, though judging by the noises coming from various tents for days after, they were worse off now.

It was hard to watch and hear, so Anton looked away and closed his ears. If he let this get to him, he would become a helpless little boy, the way he'd been when his sister and mother had been killed. He would never be like that again. Only a little boy would cry over what couldn't be helped. He'd already learned enough about war to understand that this needed to be done if they wanted the city to surrender.

Schurtz had captured a few enemy soldiers during a sortie and marched them through the devastated villages, then sent them back into the city. They were told to spread the word that Lerania faced the same fate if it didn't surrender.

After about a week, it did. Most citizens survived if they didn't resist, but the count let everyone loot as long as they wanted. The recently added villagers were the greediest, whole families running into houses and back out with arms full of everything they could carry.

Anton didn't feel like looting. He had a lot of money and didn't need much, now he had a horse and armor. Besides, if he joined in, he would see things he'd have to ignore, and feel bad about it anyway.

That first evening, a priest led a service in the temple square. He was one of Edric Maximus's followers and told the people they must embrace the new faith or leave. If they left, there was no protection outside the walls, and they had seen what happened out there. Almost everyone stayed. Even Flavia Maxima decided she could see her way to making a few changes to keep her position.

Next, the count chose a place to stay for the winter, deciding on the burgomaster's house. It was one of the nicest in the city. He sent the family away, but called back the wife when he saw how pretty she was.

"You will be my guest, Madame," he said, flashing a smile at her. Upset as she was, the smile worked well enough she stopped crying as soon as her husband was out of sight. All the same, Anton had orders to lock her in the biggest bedroom in case she got any ideas and watch the door so no servants let her out.

That was boring, but after a few days, the count got her to like him so much she didn't want to run away. Anton was free to spend time with Skandar and explore the city.

JANNA

The happiest winter of Janna's life passed quickly. Braeden spent the days on the parade ground, exercising the horses and drilling his troops. On fine days, Janna sometimes went to watch and loved seeing how precisely the great horses could move. Though she knew little about the military, she began to understand why the Sanova Hussars were never defeated.

It made her feel better, knowing that when they took to the field, they would be well-prepared. Other troops might get soft in their winter quarters, but not these. Trisa had moved out of her father's tent and into one that Franca already shared with another girl. Braeden was training her to be his page and she worked harder and longer than everyone else, learning everything she needed to know to help him in battle. That comforted Janna too, knowing that Trisa would be right there with everything he needed. But she wondered about Trisa herself, still a little girl, in the heat of battle.

"Don't you worry about her?" she asked Braeden one evening as they sat over supper.

"No more than I worry about the others," he said. "She knows the life better than a lot of our recruits and her parents understand the risks. She's good at what she does and that's what's most important. That's what will keep her safe."

Janna looked over at Iryna, playing with some spoons on the floor. She seemed to enjoy the noises they made clanging together, or the dull thump when she hit the wood floor with them. "I wonder if she'll be a hussar?"

"I hope so, though she's not very fierce."

"She's not even a year old." Janna had to laugh. "I doubt you were fierce at that age."

It seemed he'd never considered that. "Probably not." He grinned. "We must teach her."

"You'll teach her," Janna said.

"Oh, I will. And a boy too, when we have him."

"I'd like a boy next." Janna smiled across the table at him, even though she felt a pang at missing Anton. She wasn't pregnant again, but it wasn't for lack of trying. "How's the rest of General Mattila's army shaping up?"

"Nearly ready, I've heard. She's a wonder. No one believed she could find forty thousand experienced soldiers in a year's time, and she's done it in just a few months. Now she's equipping them with the best of everything—new weapons, uniforms, everything. It must help she's so rich."

"Didn't she get most of her money from confiscated Moraltan estates?" Janna asked, remembering the house in Kaleva and wondering who it belonged to now.

"Some of it." Braeden nodded. "But she already had a bundle. She plundered Altus in Cesiano back in the day. It's said that city was made of gold and marble, at least until she took it apart, piece by piece. Carted it all the way back to Moralta, they say. Never looked the same since."

"She sounds terrifying." Janna shivered.

"Just tough and good at what she does," Braeden said. "At this rate, we'll be in Kronland by spring."

"I'm looking forward to it. I've enjoyed the house, but I don't mind being in the field again, either."

Braeden frowned. "I wanted to talk to you about that. Perhaps you and Iryna should stay here. Silbershmid says we can have the house as long as we like."

Janna gasped, surprised at the panic that surged up in her. "No."

"Why not?" Braeden was unruffled as always.

"It's hard to explain to you. You're never afraid of anything. But I am."

"There's a lot less to be afraid of here."

"But I felt safe in Kaleva until the day it fell. My husband left and never came back, and then terrible things didn't stop happening until you found me."

"Atlona won't fall."

"Maybe not, but no one knows. It was a near thing two years ago, and what if Mattila is defeated and Arryk Roussay comes? He has a much bigger army than Korma ever did and we already worried about it last autumn."

"That won't happen," Braeden said. "Mattila won't lose."

"Dimir didn't think the rebels would lose, either." Janna struggled to keep her voice even.

"Dimir was a brave fellow, but I doubt he knew much about military matters. You can believe me—there's almost no chance of Atlona falling."

161

"I don't care," Janna said. "As long as there's some chance, I'm safer with you. If you go without me, how long until I see you again? It could be years. I can't bear it. Besides, you promised." She didn't want to cry, but the tears welled up.

"It'll be different to be on campaign with a baby."

"Senta will be there and a lot of other women do it. Please don't leave us here," she ended with a whisper.

He was silent for a long time. She could tell he wasn't pleased, but for once, she didn't care.

"All right," he said after a while. "You'll come along if you're sure."

"I'm sure." She smiled. "I really want to."

"Don't get me wrong. I'd rather have you along, but I worry."

"You don't mind taking a thirteen-year-old girl into battle, but you worry about me living in a tent?"

"Something like that. I never claimed to be the smartest man."

TEODORA

"I must go somehow." Teodora didn't like shouting at Livilla, but no one else was there and she was angry. "It's the first time in my life I've sent an army on a major campaign without riding at its head. That of all people, she's doing it instead is intolerable." She paced the room, while Livilla sat in a chair by the fire, sipping steaming tea.

Teodora thought of something and returned to her own chair. "I'll go along in disguise."

Livilla raised her eyebrows and said nothing.

"I'll pretend to be an officer, cut my hair, take another name. She'll never even notice me."

Livilla smiled. "My dear, you overestimate your ability to blend in. Many of your subjects recognize you on sight, and those who don't, well, I'm not convinced you can easily put aside your regal bearing."

"True." Teodora frowned. She'd admit she was no actress, and being born to rule meant one carried oneself in a specific way from birth. "What shall I do then?"

Livilla set her mug on a small table. "The general is right in this—it is vital that people see you ruling here. When you leave your capital, your enemies think you are vulnerable. If you are here, it sends a message you have the resources to continue your business while sending servants to do your dirty work. And that's all General Mattila is—a servant. Keep that in mind when you feel discouraged. However," she went on, a twinkle in her eye, "You ought to be represented in some way."

"How in the world will I do that?"

"Send a family member along."

"Not my husband surely." Not that she considered him family, but he was the only adult nearby. Her cousin, her nearest competitor for the throne, had gone to ground somewhere and would no doubt cause trouble at the most inconvenient time.

"Oh heavens, no. He would be worse than useless. No, I was thinking it's time for Elektra to show herself as your heir."

"But she's only thirteen. What can she do?"

"Wear fetching armor and ride at the general's side. It will put to rest any mutterings you are not doing your part."

"Who's muttering that?" Teodora demanded. It was galling how difficult it was to get respect from those who should offer it without question.

"Oh, no one in particular. But if someone should think it, they'll be silenced when they see your own flesh and blood ride off to battle."

"But she can't fight. She hasn't done her military service. And besides, she shows no aptitude."

"Few do at that age. You were an exception in every way. In spite of what you think, Elektra is a bright girl and she will learn a great deal by observing. She can also report to you on what Mattila is doing with no one thinking twice about it. She can be well-guarded and won't take part in any action."

Teodora paced the room. "I don't dislike the idea. I've long been wondering what to do with her. She seems so dull."

"She's at an awkward stage," Livilla said. "Many girls go through it. She's growing and changing a great deal, but her mind is sound. I've found her a good pupil at the temple school. Maybe not the very best, but she is not destined to become a Maxima, so she needn't excel at theology. It will give her confidence to be given this task."

When Livilla had gone, Teodora sent for Elektra. With the whole capital in an uproar about the army moving out, Livilla's temple school was closed for a few days so the students could join in the excitement.

When Elektra entered the room, it was plain she was frightened.

Teodora looked her over critically. Short and dumpy, her face lacked definition and her hair was stringy and of some mousy hue. She was not empress material, but she would have to become one anyway, at some point.

"Sit." Teodora gestured to a chair.

Elektra sat down on the edge and fidgeted with the end of her braid.

"I have a job for you," Teodora said. "Your first official one as an archduchess and as my heir."

Her eyes widened at that, though Teodora saw fear rather than anticipation.

"I've decided to send you with General Mattila when she goes north."

Elektra's eyes grew wider still. "Doing what?" she asked, her voice small.

"You will ride next to her as my official representative. You needn't do anything except look good in armor and inspire the troops. Don't worry, we'll find something flattering."

"I don't know how to do that."

"It's easy. You appear every now and then, smile and wave. The general will do enough talking for everyone. But there's something else that's more important. I want you to pay attention to what the general is doing, who she talks to and what she said."

"You want me to spy on her?"

"Not in any devious fashion. You'll be present at a lot of meetings, many of them boring. Just listen to what is going on and write to me about it. You've learned the ciphers?"

Elektra nodded. "Some of them, at least."

"Are you any good at them?"

Her face brightened. "Yes, I am. Livilla Maxima says I'm one of the quickest she's seen in writing and deciphering the Ventophorm."

"Excellent. That's the one we'll use, then. Overlook nothing. Even remarks that seem unimportant, mentioned in passing, might matter."

"Do you suspect the general of treachery?" Elektra looked alarmed.

"Oh goodness, no. I just want to know what is going on since I can't come along."

"I was sure you would go." The girl still sounded uncertain, but not as frightened as before.

Teodora looked down her nose at Elektra. "Not that it's any of your business, but I've decided it's more important I stay here and show the people the strength and stability of the empire. And now you're old enough, you can represent me in the field. You needn't worry about going into battle, and I'll see you have a large contingent of your own guards."

Elektra swallowed hard and looked straight at Teodora.

"All right," she said. "I'll do it."

BRAEDEN

It was the largest force Braeden had been part of in at least a decade and one of the more impressive. The troops were seasoned veterans, which made training them easy, their weapons and armor the best.

Mattila could afford to spend money on that part because the campaign otherwise paid for itself. Once they left Atlona behind, it was a simple matter of living off the land and levying contributions from the town.

"We prefer to make the empress's enemies pay," she'd said. "But if allies must bear part of the burden, that's the price for our protection. Friend or enemy, we'll deal with anyone who complains the same way."

It only took a few examples to make everyone fall into line. When they entered Arcius, the only Kronland kingdom friendly to the empress, Mattila extracted large sums from every town they passed. The first few objected, but she wasted no time in sending her personal troops to sack the homes of every prominent citizen. A delegation laden with sacks of gold always appeared within hours.

Once they left Arcius, it was easy enough to get payment in exchange for protection from marauding Norovaeans, who presumably would be worse. Braeden didn't mind, because some of that gold flowed to Prince Novitny, and then to him.

Janna shook her head when he added another installment to the big chest in the corner of their tent. "It seems so unjust," she said. "They haven't even rebelled."

"No, and now they won't." Braeden couldn't feel too bad, especially when this gold meant security for Janna and Iryna if anything happened to him.

"Really? I would be far angrier with the empress now if I'd had any friendly feelings before."

"Yes, but you're already a rebel." Braeden gently poked her in the ribs.

Janna slapped his hand away and rolled her eyes. "True. But others must find it unjust as well."

Braeden sighed and pulled her closer. "It's different for soldiers. We've learned not to question these things. It would drive us mad otherwise."

"But you questioned Tomescu." Janna let herself sink into his arms.

"That was different."

"It was not."

"She was killing people who hadn't done anything."

"These people haven't done anything."

"No one's been killed."

"Not yet," Janna said.

Though late spring, it never stopped raining, so the going was cold, wet and unpleasant. Braeden had worried it would be hard for Janna to manage with a baby, but she got help from other women who'd had practice. Once, when he checked on her on a particularly nasty day, he found her riding Zoltan, covered in tent material, little Iryna dry and warm, cradled against her in a sling. They both looked far more comfortable than Braeden.

It was hard to keep everything dry all the same, and the tent was cold and drafty. The little brazier warmed a small area around it, but the wind blew in through every hole and seam.

"You can't be enjoying yourself." Braeden watched Janna rock Iryna in a little hammock she'd borrowed from another woman with four older children.

"Oh, but I am," she said, smiling at him. "I loved the house, but this is your life. I could tell you were getting restless in Atlona."

"I was." He sat down on the edge of the cot next to her and took over the rocking. Iryna was bundled up and sleeping soundly. She seemed to be a very good baby. He'd always heard they were more trouble. Might be he was lucky and the baby had inherited Janna's calm nature, or maybe she was just a good mother, or both. "But it was conditions like these that made me think twice about a permanent situation with a family. Everyone else seemed so miserable, with dirty, screaming brats. Someone always sick, with mud everywhere."

"It's bad for some," Janna said. "But we're well off compared to most. It makes a big difference to have a large tent and servants to set up, fetch water and build fires. If I had to do all of that myself while hauling the baby around, I'd be a lot less happy. Though I'd still be happy to be with you." She leaned against Braeden.

"I'm happy to be with you, too," he said, putting his free arm around her. "I'm just not used to worrying about someone. We're going up against multiple armies and King Arryk is a serious opponent. If we're defeated, and they get into the baggage train it could get ugly very quickly."

"Have you ever been defeated?" Janna asked.

"No, but I've seen it happen to the opposing forces. I've been part of it a time or two. We were chasing down the enemy, but there's always some who stop to plunder, or worse. Why, it was that Lermonov fellow, you know, the trooper with one eye? That's how he got his wife. He stopped to pick through some general's wagons, and found a servant girl hiding under a canvas. He threw her over his saddle and brought her back to camp."

"And she married him anyway?" Janna was aghast.

"Not like she had much choice, I suppose. Ugly fellow like him, though she wasn't much to look at herself. But they seemed happy enough."

"What happened to her? I didn't know he had a wife."

"She died having a baby. That was a few years ago."

"Oh," Janna said, and they were silent for a moment.

"I worry about that, too," Braeden said. "What if we have another baby while we're on campaign? That'll be much harder."

"But Doctor Toure is along; she'll take care of me." As bad as her experience having Iryna had been, Janna seemed unworried about repeating it. Braeden wished he could feel as confident.

ANTON

The winter had been long and cold, so Anton and Skandar were happy to leave Lerania when spring came.

But there was one problem. On the longest night of the year, a few citizens had revolted and during their brief rebellion, blown up the bridge across the river. Those people were dead, but there was still no bridge and with the river swollen from the spring rains, no way to ford.

"I won't wait any longer," the count said when he met with his officers to plan the spring campaign. "We must build our own bridge."

"But we have no Zeelund engineers with us," someone objected.

"How difficult can it be? The ancients built bridges like these, at this very spot." It wasn't easy to talk the count out of anything once he'd set his mind to it.

So they built a bridge. It was called a pontoon bridge and it floated. It took several days, but at least the weather had cleared and the water wasn't as fast as before. The count paced the riverbank anxiously. The most recent dispatches from King Arryk reported that General Mattila's huge army was moving west. King Arryk wanted the count to join him before she got between them.

Anton helped the bridge builders, shuttling pieces of wood from the carpenters to where engineers placed them across large empty boats. Some had been built for this, after they'd taken all the boats from fishing villages up and down the river. Anton had never seen anything like it, and he wasn't keen on crossing it.

"It'll be slow going," the count admitted, "But we must do it, so better slow than not at all."

When the bridge was ready, he was the first to cross, Anton right behind him. It wasn't as bad as he expected. The whole thing swayed, but it was wide enough to cross four abreast and Anton was in the middle, far from the edges, which was a good thing since he couldn't swim. He kept his eyes on Skandar's ears until they reached the other side.

It took all day for the troops to cross, and then the baggage started. They stopped at sunset and continued the next day. Almost everyone had crossed when a scout galloped up to the count. "It's Mattila." He gasped, trying to catch his breath. "She's right in front of you."

"How far?" The count's expression didn't change, even though Anton felt a surge of excitement.

"No more than half a day's march."

"By the Father's balls." The count swore. "We can't meet her here with our backs to the river. She'll demolish us." The land in front of them was flat, so there was no good place to put the guns, though the count ordered them deployed anyway. "We're falling back across the bridge," he said. "We'll go last," he told Anton. "I'll have to leave most of the baggage on this side."

That meant people. "What'll happen to them?" Anton asked.

"Who knows?" The count shrugged. "I can't get them back across the river in time, but I must save as many cavalry as I can. They're hardest to replace."

Bad as things were, Anton had to admire the count's calmness. He placed the few artillery pieces he had and a vanguard of pike to hold Mattila off as long as possible. Then troopers started crossing the bridge again, in the direction they had come only hours before.

The count paced some more. The scouts had reported no sign of Novitny or Barela with Mattila and he worried she'd sent them to outflank him. He sent more scouts in all directions to search for any movement across the burned land.

It started raining. The count cursed some more, and Anton got out of the way by leading spare horses across the bridge. By the fourth crossing, he was no longer afraid of the water. He was afraid of what was coming on the other side.

On his last trip, he escorted the burgomaster's wife back to her house. She'd followed the count across the river, but he made her leave now. "Go back to your husband," he said, kissing her on the forehead. "You don't want to be here when Mattila comes, trust me."

"I don't care about that," she wept. "I love you."

"No, you don't," the count said wearily. "I don't have time for this. Kronek, take her back."

"He's in love with someone else you know," Anton said as they returned to the city. She wouldn't stop crying, so it wasn't like he was making things worse.

She cried even harder, but didn't resist when he led her horse to the front door of the burgomaster's house and gave her a hand down. She went in without looking back.

Before leaving, Anton took a quick trip up the city walls, then wished he hadn't. He saw Mattila's forces already, wave upon wave of spear-tips, red and black flags, the beat of drums. He'd heard they outnumbered the count's forces four-to-one.

On the other side of the river, the drums were loud now, the screech of pipes above them. Anton's heart was in his mouth, but the count seemed unbothered.

"Guns!" he ordered, and the big pieces fired.

Mattila stopped, but only for a moment. Then the drumbeats and the rumble of thousands of marching feet continued. Anton didn't know what to do. He'd never retreated before. He saw the first square of pike advancing on them. Musketeers marched on either side. Soon they would be in range. Anton licked his parched lips and raised his pistol.

"Fall back," the count said. "Orderly now."

Most of the force was still on the wrong side of the river and they couldn't cross the bridge any faster. They would have to hold them off here.

"Go now," the count said to Anton. "I don't need you here."

"But," Anton said.

"Go. Save as many horses as you can. Swim them across."

Anton finally nodded and spurred Skandar back to the river. At the bank, he paused and shed his armor. If he fell off, he didn't want it pulling him under. He grabbed the leads of two spare horses, then mounted Skandar.

It was raining harder and the river rushed between the banks, muddy and foaming. Troops still crossed the bridge. Anton heard gunfire and screaming behind him, but didn't look back. Skandar waded into the water but it was flowing too fast and he couldn't swim straight across. "Into the water," Anton shouted at a few horse-boys nearby, riding spare mounts.

The current pulled Skandar so hard, he couldn't move forward at all. Anton tried not to panic. At this rate, they would end up a league downstream, not that it mattered right now. He'd be lucky to make it at all. The water was fast and wild and soldiers fell off the horses, screaming and flailing before being pulled under. Most hadn't taken off their armor, so they didn't have a chance. Far downstream, Anton saw some riderless horses struggle onto a steep muddy bank. He let the other two spares go and they floated downstream making slow progress to the other side.

He let Skandar swim and looked around. Next to him, a very small horse-boy clung to the neck of a huge charger, his face white and his eyes squeezed shut. "Come on." Though Anton felt just as scared, it helped to have someone else to worry about. "It's all right." He leaned over and grabbed the charger's reins.

The cold water rushed around his legs and Anton concentrated on the opposite bank. Fewer and fewer were making it. He had thought the worst was hearing the carnage behind him and watching people and horses go under around him. But that was like nothing when the bridge buckled, then disappeared.

By the time Anton noticed the strange creaking sound and turned toward it, the bridge had already come apart. A hideous wail rose from the crowds that had been on the bridge seconds ago, and were now in the water. Anton saw a groom he knew clutch at a board, miss, and go under. He didn't see him again.

Anton had to let go the other horse's reins and grab Skandar's neck as a flood of bodies rushed past. He held his breath as an entire wagon hurtled toward him, though it changed direction at the last second, sweeping two horses away right in front of him. He wasn't sure he could stay upright. "Come on Skandar," he whispered into the horse's ear and held on.

After the first rush it wasn't so bad as long as he didn't open his eyes. The gunfire sounded close now, but the opposite bank was near. Skandar struggled up it, sliding backward a few times, but finally reaching the grass. He fell to his knees and Anton slid off his back, his legs numb, and collapsed beside him.

For a while, Anton and Skandar both lay on the bank, breathing hard. The sounds of the guns were closer now—Mattila must have moved hers down the road. Anton couldn't bear thinking about the carnage on the other bank. The river had seemed so wide while he was crossing it, but now it wasn't wide enough. He saw and heard everything.

Most of the cuirassiers never made it back to the bridge, and even though they fought hard, they were outnumbered and cut down by the dozens. At one point, Anton thought he'd spotted the count's purple plume, but it got dark and he didn't see it again.

Once Mattila's army killed all of the soldiers, they turned their attention to the wagons and the soldier's families. That was much worse. Anton wondered if Mattila was taking revenge for what the count had done to the villages around Lerania, or if she was just as bad.

Anton put his hands over his ears, but that didn't help. Finally, exhausted as he was, he pulled Skandar to his feet and walked him toward the city. On the side of the road not far away, he spotted a small group of the count's officers rounding up soldiers and horses.

Anton walked up to one he knew. "Any sign of Count Orland?" he asked.

The man shook his head. "Say, you're his page, aren't you? Why weren't you with him?"

"He sent me back with the horses," Anton said miserably.

"Good thinking," the man said. "We have a few, more than we have troopers."

"What do we do now?" Anton asked.

"We have a day or two before Mattila throws up a bridge. Those of us who want to will wait until morning for Count Orland and anyone else who makes it. After that, I plan to ride north and find Emilya Hohenwart's army."

"Can I come too?" Anton asked. He didn't see how the count could have survived between Mattila on the other shore and the mess in the river.

"Don't see why not, as long as you can make yourself useful."

The screams and shooting died down at some point and the rain let up a little. Anton fell asleep in the wet grass, propped against Skandar, who lay on his side, still exhausted.

In the middle of the night, there was a commotion, and Anton jumped up, drawing his knife from his belt. It was the only weapon he had. Someone lit a torch and there was a familiar laugh. Anton ran toward the light, then had to laugh too. It was the count. He was soaking wet and his armor was gone, but Cid stood next to him. Anton raced over and put his arms around Cid's neck. "I knew you'd make it," he murmured.

The count noticed him then. "You really are a scrappy little bugger, aren't you? Almost as lucky as I am."

Anton grinned, surprised at how glad he was to see him. "I'll give Cid a good rubdown," he said, noticing the horse's quivering legs.

The count nodded. "He had quite a swim. That water is still high, and I started out several leagues upstream where I wouldn't be spotted. I hope he can get enough rest. We have to leave at first light."

Anton looked around. No more than a few dozen troopers had made it here, some still soaking wet, like Anton, and a few wounded. They were a sorry-looking bunch, and in a hurry since they wanted to be far away by the time Mattila made it across.

"She might not bother following us," the count said. "There's hardly enough to make it worthwhile. She got the baggage after all," he added bitterly.

It was then Anton realized that all of their supplies were in the baggage train and so was most of the money. Aside from what the count carried on his person, they had nothing. No spare clothes, no tents, no food, no armor, no weapons.

Anton wondered what they'd do if someone attacked.

The count spent the morning in a black mood, and Anton stayed clear. But by afternoon, he seemed to have a plan. He gathered the officers around him and said, "We make for Floradias. I have contacts there and will be able to raise money. The truce still holds, so maybe we can recruit as well."

"You want back in the fight after this?" one officer asked incredulously.

"Why not? As long as I live, I won't abandon Princess Gwynneth."

Fire burned in the count's dark eyes and Anton shivered. The count might be a little crazy, but his loyalty to the princess impressed Anton. It was the way heroes in the stories behaved. He decided right then he'd go to Floradias with him.

BRAEDEN

"She plans to pick 'em off, one at a time, and it seems they'll let her," Prince Novitny said to the officers gathered in his tent. The rain drummed on the canvas. Novitny had just returned from a staff meeting with General Mattila. He unrolled a large map on a table. "Now she's finished off Orland, we'll take on Faris and this time we'll get him. Our scouts say he's here." He pointed at a spot somewhat to the east. "It takes us off our path toward Arryk, but it's a good chance to neutralize Faris first."

"I thought he'd linked up with Arryk by now," Braeden said.

"I think that was his plan, but he got hung up in this godsawful weather. All those big artillery pieces are bogged down in the mud. They're moving, but slowly. If we can get there fast, he won't have time to set them up, like he did at Birkenfels."

It was almost summer, but the rains continued. Miserable as it was for men and horses, Janna never let Braeden forget that it would be far worse for the people trying to plant crops. Bad enough that war had come, now there was no food either.

But Braeden knew feeling bad didn't make the corn grow. The sooner they defeated King Arryk and his allies, the sooner everyone could get back to their regular lives.

Mattila managed the affair efficiently. Once she'd spotted Faris, she surrounded him. He knew she was there, but it didn't matter. He set up his guns where he could, and placed his infantry. They put up a good fight, but it wasn't enough. Mattila didn't even bother placing her own guns. The weather made moving them difficult, so she had left them in Lantura, closer to where she planned to meet King Arryk.

The Sanova Hussars took on Faris from the front. They waited until his guns fired a few times, ineffectively, then they came down on the main body of badly placed infantry. They had been marching down the Podoska road, trying to link up with Seward Kurant's army, and were strung out for leagues. The guns got bogged down in the low places on the road, which meant they were placed where they could do the least damage.

Aware of his poor position, Count Faris ranged his pike in the van as the hussars bore down on them, but like everyone else faced with the long lances and disciplined charges, they broke soon enough. Then Braeden went to work with saber and axe. It was nastier than usual, since the road there ran between two stone outcroppings and few could get away. They fought hard, but at the end of a few hours, many of Faris's Zeelund mercenaries were dead or wounded and even more surrendered. Faris himself had been shot three times and, though he survived, was taken prisoner.

Mattila had put it about the countryside that she would offer three months' pay up front to any soldier who came over to her. This worked well, since the allies were constantly strapped for cash. The terrible weather had made it difficult for them to get even the most basic supplies, so a fair number of the prisoners were happy to get a square meal, let alone a pay increase.

"So, she steals from the people here and uses that money to pay the soldiers who'll steal even more from them." Janna was carefully stitching up a long gash on Braeden's arm. "I don't understand how that got through your armor," she said, her brow furrowed in concentration and her tongue sticking out just the slightest bit.

Braeden wasn't sure where she'd learned field medicine, but he preferred her clumsy stitches to those of any doctor.

"You must really love me to let me do this to you," she said, reading his mind.

"I do," he said. "It was a halberd that got through; a nice sharp one. Caught me right under the vambraces and sliced right through the mail. Doesn't happen often."

Braeden winced as she pulled another stitch through.

She frowned. "I'm sorry. I'd do it more quickly if I could."

"Just takes practice," Braeden said through clenched teeth. He should have had some of that brandy first.

ARRYK

"You can't afford to wait any longer," Gwynneth said, flinging the message on the desk in front of Arryk. "She's picking your allies off one at a time. Barela isn't with her so you have a better chance."

Arryk read the message, then put his head in his hands. The news of Ruso Faris's defeat and capture on the heels of Arian Orland's obliteration at Lerania made him sick. "No, we need more allies, better ones. I just don't know how to get them." It was summer now, but here he sat, waiting for Mattila to defeat him next. It had come as a considerable shock to learn that Teodora had a new general, one who had conjured up a formidable army in a matter of months. Now he was angry he hadn't attacked Teodora a year ago. He wished he'd been strong enough to override Gwynneth when she'd advised waiting to build up a stronger alliance, but it was too late for that now.

"We'll think of something." Gwynneth sat back down across from him. "But in the meantime I'm worried. Kendryk has been a captive for nearly two years and I don't even know if he's still alive. And I had good reason to believe that Arian Orland could help. Now I'm not sure if he's alive either, and if he is, if we'll ever hear from him again."

"I'm worried, too," Arryk admitted. "I never intended to be away from home so long. Things there can't be going as well as Classen claims in his letters."

"What do your own sources say?" Gwynneth asked

"Don't have any," Arryk said, looking down.

"What? You don't have your own people at court?"

"I told you. I had no interest in being there. All of my friends are military." For the hundredth time, Arryk felt completely inadequate.

"Well, what about your Larisa? Isn't she a duchess? Surely she has connections who can help you."

"She's a duchess because I made her one," Arryk said, squirming in his seat, wishing he were anywhere but here. "She's originally a farmer's daughter from the Helmen Islands." He'd forgotten about undoing the duchess thing, but Larisa no longer bothered him about it so perhaps she'd come around to the idea.

"Oh Arryk." Gwynneth laughed, though he detected sympathy in her eyes.

"She's worth a hundred courtiers."

"I'm sure she is," Gwynneth said. "I wasn't being critical. I like her and I'm glad you have her. It's just a shame your position isn't more secure. What does Aksel say?"

"The usual. He writes all about his scientific experiments. He's building a telescope he means to take out to sea."

"In other words, he's no help at all. But there's no point in worrying about that right now. Let's think about what we must to defeat Mattila as quickly as possible so you can go home. I see no alternative except to get help from Galladium. You must avoid fighting Mattila in the meantime."

"Will Galladium help? And even if they do, I'm sure they'll end up taking all of the credit," Arryk grumbled.

"If you beat Mattila there will be plenty of credit for everyone." Gwynneth stood. "I'll take Maryna along. It's time she met Natalya."

"But I need you here," Arryk said, standing as well. It was true. He relied on Gwynneth for just about everything. She had little interest in military matters, but was excellent at keeping up the troops' spirits and there was no better negotiator. She also had a knack for turning reluctant potential allies into real, sometimes mildly enthusiastic ones.

Gwynneth took him by the hand. "I know, and I hate to leave you. I'll do this as fast as I can and with any luck, I'll bring good news when I return."

KENDRYK

Kendryk wore rags and his hair had grown to hang far down his back. No visitors had come since his last audience with Teodora months ago. The only light came from the flicker of the torch when a guard passed his cell. His cell was surprisingly warm, but also damp and he'd often awaken from sleep drenched in sweat. He slept a great deal, but seldom dreamed. And when dreams came, they were nightmares.

He recited over and over to himself everything he'd ever learned. Songs and poems and grammar in four languages, and the parts of the Holy Scrolls he'd pored over so often. He reconstructed the Bernotas family tree in his head, then Sebesta—his mother's side—as far back as he remembered, and then Roussay. Then he recited the royal lineages of Inferrara, Brevard, Sikora and Ostberg.

He supposed that kept him sane, though his mind wandered often enough he wasn't sure. He wondered about his family and what they were doing. The children must have grown a great deal by now. Did any of them remember him? Though he believed that Gwynneth had kept her word about the castle, he wondered about everything else. Was she true to him now?

He wondered if Arian Orland had helped rescue her and if they were together now. At first, the idea gave him a great deal of pain, which he welcomed, since anything was better than the flat dullness of feeling nothing. But now, he didn't even have that. Kendryk still loved his wife, but was sure he'd never see her again, so what she did without him didn't matter. He wished her well, like he'd wish a friend or distant family member well. He hoped she could be happy.

There was nothing for him now, not even faith. For a long time, he expected another message from the gods, but after dreaming of Gwynneth, they sent nothing more. He'd spent all of his waking hours in prayer, but still nothing. At some point, he'd given up. The gods had abandoned him because he'd failed them and was of no more use to them. He didn't blame them for that.

It occurred to him that the black which surrounded him now might have been the black of the dream that came to him after his first meeting Edric. He didn't like to remember, but if he closed his eyes, sometimes it returned far too vividly:

A great shadow moved over the land, covering first the army of the enemy, then rolling toward Kendryk. Blacker than ink, it coated everyone and everything like hot tar. Kendryk tried to run, to fly, but the shadow caught him, black tendrils clutching at him, pulling him to the ground. He reached for something to hold onto but found nothing.

The shadow covered everything, and Kendryk still had one eye open to see it. When he opened his mouth to scream, it filled with black. He fought the shadow with everything in him, but he was slipping into it. If there was something he should do or should have done, he couldn't remember it. A voice shrieked at him in a language he didn't understand, but it was too late. His eye closed, and his breath stopped ...

He opened his eyes, shivering and shaking just like that first time. Even though that dream hadn't come true, Kendryk knew dreams were representations—they didn't foretell events exactly. And wasn't he now covered in blackness? Perhaps that battle below Birkenfels had been the last one. He had failed and all was lost.

And perhaps the end of the world wasn't so literal either. His world had ended, along with the worlds of thousands of others—those who died in battle, or as an indirect result of the war. And if the war dragged on, as he suspected it did, the world ended every day for thousands more. In that case, he had failed utterly, though he'd tried hard to do the right thing.

It gave him hope to wonder if Edric had been wrong and Kendryk wasn't the ruler foretold in the Scrolls. If that was true, then all wasn't lost and perhaps someone else would succeed in his stead. He'd never seen his brother-in-law Arryk as a religious sort, or very thoughtful at all, but he was still young and might have changed a great deal.

Kendryk thought about King Lennart in Estenor; he seemed a more likely candidate. He was tough, resolute, and many said, a military genius. If anyone could succeed where Kendryk had failed, it was Lennart Ostberg.

He lay on his back on the dirty, damp straw and pictured Lennart conquering and utterly humiliating Teodora. He doubted he'd live to see it, but thinking about it comforted him anyway.

GWYNNETH

As her carriage pulled into the ornate courtyard of the Maxima's palace in Allaux, Gwynneth made sure she and Maryna at least looked tidy. They had no time to change, but it didn't matter.

Natalya Maxima stood at the door, waiting for them. "I worried when you weren't here by noon." She kissed Gwynneth on both cheeks, then gave Maryna her hand in response to her curtsy.

"Muddy roads," Gwynneth said by way of explanation. Clearly, Natalya's sources were good since Gwynneth had told no one where she was going. "This is Maryna Bernotas," she added.

"She's perfect," Natalya said. "I can't decide if she's more like you or like Kendryk."

"She looks more like me." Gwynneth smiled. "But in everything else, she's her father's child, through and through."

"So she really is perfect," Natalya said, leading them into a cool, marble-lined parlor that matched the grandeur of her entryway. A maid came in right after with a tray of goblets and a flagon of cold, crisp white wine. Gwynneth breathed in deep and took a long drink. It was nice to sit down with a friend.

"The king will see you, of course," Natalya said. "Naturally, he's heartbroken about Kendryk, but I'll let him tell you himself what the problems are."

"I expected problems." Gwynneth tried to conceal her disappointment. "But I was hoping—"

"I know," Natalya sat down next to her and took both hands in her own. "It's a dreadful situation. I'd hoped Arryk could manage things, but that was too much to expect, I suppose."

"It's my fault." Gwynneth knew Natalya had never been impressed with Arryk's abilities. "I should have concentrated on rescuing Kendryk, but instead I spent far too much time seeing that the Edric's teachings were spread through Kronland."

"I'm surprised at you," Natalya said. "You were always disturbingly impious."

"I was," Gwynneth said. "Until I read the Scrolls myself."

"Ah." Natalya nodded, her green eyes understanding. She had changed little since Gwynneth had seen her a few years before. Then, she'd been the priestess at an Allaux temple, but after Kendryk arranged an introduction, she caught the eye of the young king, and understandably so. She was not quite beautiful, but had an arresting, cat-like face, with luminous intelligent eyes. King Gauvain was so smitten he would have given her his kingdom had she asked for it. She hadn't, but he gave her the Maxima position, which was even better.

"I agree; Edric's work is extraordinary. We are experiencing a similar reformation here."

"I'm sure you don't approve," Gwynneth said, her heart sinking. It hadn't occurred to her she was promoting something her friend would certainly oppose.

"Oh, but I do." Natalya smiled. "Terragand might have been first to break with the Imperata, but Galladium is not far behind. I've already commissioned a group of scholars to translate the Scrolls into our tongue. Once that work is complete, I expect great changes here as well."

Then it dawned on Gwynneth. Natalya had never made a secret of her ambition and having complete control over the Galladium temples would make her answerable to no one. "So it makes sense you would want to help us."

"In theory, it does," Natalya said, "though there are as always, complications. But we'll speak of that soon. Why don't you and Maryna get some rest and a hot bath? I have a suite ready for you right next to my quarters. We'll dine with the king tonight, and you can discuss everything with him then." She turned to Maryna. "And you'll go to the nursery, if that's all right with you."

Maryna looked at Gwynneth uncertainly and Gwynneth nodded, wondering why Natalya needed a nursery.

"Did you know I have a little girl, too?" Natalya asked. Gwynneth could barely hold back her gasp. "You'll have supper with her. She's littler than you, but she'll like making a new friend."

When Gwynneth turned to her, the unasked question in her eyes, Natalya nodded. "He can't claim her openly until he has an official heir, but we're working on that."

"You amaze me." Gwynneth smiled. "I had no idea you felt that way about the king."

"To be honest, he caught me by surprise." Natalya looked uncomfortable. "It's a complication I don't like, but the heart can be stupid, eh?"

"Indeed," Gwynneth said.

After months in a military camp or quartered in houses given up grudgingly, Gwynneth enjoyed the luxury of her rooms. And the Maxima's palace in Allaux was one of the most beautiful in a city known for its fabulous dwellings. After a long bath and careful attention from two maids who dressed her hair and helped her into her best dress, she felt quite new.

Before meeting the king, she asked to be taken to the nursery. A clean Maryna wore a lacy nightdress and was playing with a fat little girl with a shock of dark hair.

"I'm just going to supper, darling," Gwynneth said. "You'll be good and go to bed when you're told?"

Maryna nodded. "Nurse said I can stay up later than Joslyn because she's little and I'm big."

"All right. Have fun and do as nurse tells you." Gwynneth kissed Maryna on the head and smiled at little Joslyn who stared at her with gooseberry-green eyes. If the little girl was going to be as striking as her mother, she showed no sign of it yet. Perhaps she took after her father.

BRAEDEN

Count Faris was in no condition to travel, but he was going anyway. General Mattila made all of the arrangements for an exchange of prisoners and Braeden was to take four hundred troopers to the designated place. They headed for Terragand's border where they'd be met by a group coming from Birkenfels.

The rainy summer had finally turned hot, which did little to improve the prisoner's condition. The worst of his wounds had healed, but he was far from complete recovery. Still, Ruso Faris was no pushover and bore the pain and discomfort without a word. It no doubt helped that he knew he was about to be freed.

Braeden didn't like to be involved in such a clear violation of the empress's orders, but since Mattila was supreme commander, he didn't have much choice.

"Terragand needs a leader," she'd said flatly, when she explained her plan to Novitny and his officers. "Her highness thinks to rule directly, but it's not practical in time of war. And besides, they are more likely to accept a Kronlander than an Inferrara ruling from a distance. The girl doesn't know what she's doing."

This brought a stifled giggle from the Archduchess Elektra, standing at Mattila's elbow. A plain girl who didn't resemble Teodora in any way Braeden could see, Elektra didn't seem to mind having her mother put in her place.

In Braeden's opinion, Count Faris was far too valuable to be exchanged for Evard Bernotas, but no one asked him. And he hadn't forgotten being thwarted by the duke at the Garsten Gap, though he told himself that was more a feature of the terrain than any military genius on Evard's part.

They arrived at the border late in the day and made camp. Braeden had left his girls behind with Mattila so they could move faster. Besides, this area wasn't secure. Although both Faris and Orland were defeated, renegade soldiers still roamed these lands. Worse, the local population were converts to the Quadrene heresy and took it upon themselves to wage war upon supporters of the old faith. Those included anyone in the pay of Teodora.

These days, no one went out in parties smaller than forty, and a hundred was preferable. In most cases, the peasants knew better than to attack large armed groups, but there had been incidents of smaller foraging parties being set upon and horrible atrocities committed.

The group from Birkenfels arrived at the border before midday. Their path was longer, though through friendlier territory. Or maybe they wanted to make Braeden sweat. Which he did, wearing all his armor in the heat. The exchange took place on a bridge over the River Lera, and while they waited he looked longingly at the rushing waters.

They finally saw horsemen bearing the Bernotas standard appearing from the woods. Count Faris insisted on riding a horse, though he could barely sit upright. Still, Braeden helped hoist him up, and from a distance, he doubted anyone would notice how he barely clung to the saddle.

"You can't keep the horse," Braeden said.

"That's all right." Faris grimaced. "Just so I look better than the duke."

That wasn't hard. Evard Bernotas was in his fifties and had been imprisoned in the Birkenfels dungeon for over a year. Having experienced a dungeon himself, Braeden wasn't surprised the old fellow looked like a corpse.

Evard insisted on riding as well, and he and Faris exchanged hard stares as they passed each other. Braeden had to catch the duke from falling off his horse once he reached them, and had him put into the wagon that had been carrying Faris. That done, he turned to the commander of Birkenfels.

The young man grinned broadly. "I'm Merton," he said. "Count Faris is my uncle and I'm glad to see him alive. Thank you for bringing him."

"Can't say I'm pleased about the exchange," Braeden said, "But I wasn't asked. Your uncle is a general of quality and I'm not looking forward to meeting him in the field again. One of these days, his luck is bound to turn."

"I hope so," Merton said. "I don't suppose you could be persuaded to join us."

"I'm afraid not. Nothing personal against your lot. Contracts and such."

"Of course," Merton said, still friendly. His manner reminded Braeden a bit of Prince Kendryk. Perhaps they'd been friends. "Still, if you ever find yourself at loose ends, we'd be happy to have you and as many of your people as you can bring."

"I'll keep it in mind," Braeden said. He'd love to work for anyone but Teodora, though in the end, he preferred to stay on the winning side. And as long as Brynhild Mattila led the imperial armies, they were likely to be the winners.

Duke Evard wasn't so pleasant. He was extremely angry that Mattila hadn't also demanded the release of his son, who'd been imprisoned by Princess Gwynneth nearly two years earlier.

"How can I be expected to rule Terragand?" he ranted, after reading the letter Braeden handed him containing Mattila's instructions. "I have no castle and my heir is imprisoned. Where does she expect me to rule from?"

"She's got a few places in mind," Braeden said, riding alongside the cart. That had offended the duke's dignity as well. Did he expect a gilded carriage?

The duke snorted. "Probably some derelict manor house or pig-sty of a fortress."

"Don't know," Braeden said. "It's got to be in lands she controls. Otherwise, with your luck, you're likely to get locked up again." After that, he left the man to his own devices. Let him complain to the general.

ANTON

Zeelund was the strangest place Anton had ever seen. The houses were tall, narrow and painted in bright colors, and the people looked very odd. The women wore enormous white hats with what looked like wings on them. He expected them to fly away with the next gust of wind. The men wore strange hats as well, both tall and slouchy, and everyone had round, red faces. They clomped around in huge wooden shoes, though Anton reckoned he might wear those soon enough since his boots had nearly fallen apart.

Anton and the count had left Floradias after the count found he couldn't raise another army on promises of plunder alone. Word of the disaster at Lerania had traveled faster than they had, and people acted like the count had the plague, from the way they looked at him. Even the few fellows who'd come along from Kronland had melted away over the past months.

Though the count swore and drank more than usual, he was in good spirits and still seemed to think there was a way to get back into the fight.

"If you want to leave, you can," he'd said to Anton as they made their way north. "I can raise money in Zeelund, but it'll take time. You can take Skandar and find King Arryk. I'm sure he'll take care of you."

"I don't want to," Anton said, though he wasn't sure why. He liked it that the count refused to give up and wanted to help him get back into the fight.

Besides, he was having fun on this new adventure. Zeelund's capital city of Bonnenruck was the most crowded place Anton had ever seen. Maybe it was because canals replaced most of the streets, so all of the people were jammed onto little bits of dry ground. The canals were just as crowded with boats of all sizes, packed so close that Anton could have walked right across them like a bridge. Not that he ever would. Not anymore.

After Lerania, he wasn't so keen on bridges either, but he couldn't avoid them here. At first he hung back whenever they came up to one, but they were made of sturdy stone and the crowds pulled him along when he wanted to hesitate. After a while, he got used to them.

After they got kicked out of one lodging house because they weren't able to pay, they moved into a tavern. Or rather, the count moved in with the tavern's owner, and she stuck Anton into a little room behind the kitchen. He thought it might have been a pantry once, since it smelled like ham and flour, which meant he was always hungry.

They had no money, but they still had their horses. When they were turfed out of the lodging house, Anton worried the count would try to sell them. But he was as attached to Cid as Anton was.

"I'll starve before I sell him," the count said. "I'll just have to find some woman who'll take us in and feed them too."

Much as Anton wanted to keep the horses, he felt bad for the count. He acted cheerful most of the time, but Vrouw Belsen, the tavern owner, was not a fun woman to be around. She might have been pretty once, but she was old and fat now, and missing most of her teeth. Probably her hair too, since Anton never saw a wisp of it, even though her yellow wig slid all over her head when she laughed.

She was wild for the count, and couldn't keep her hands off him. Anton could tell it was awful for him, though he pretended to like it.

"It's only for a short time," he told Anton. "I have an appointment with my banker soon, and when he gives me money, we'll move out."

"Good," Anton said. "I don't like her." He didn't want to make it worse for the count, so he didn't tell him that Vrouw Belsen never fed Anton and boxed his ears if she caught him sneaking something from the kitchen. He was on good terms with the cook, but that didn't save him when the tavern owner had it in for him.

The count shuddered. "I don't like her either. And I don't enjoy feeling like a whore, though I suppose that's what I am now."

"At least you don't look like one," Anton said, ducking away from the half-hearted blow the count threw at him.

He worried, because the count was drinking an awful lot. More than usual. "It's the only way I can stand it," he said, polishing off another tankard of strong Zeelund beer. "Wish me luck Kronek. One more night." And he got up from the table, swaying a little, then snatched Vrouw Belsen by the hand and dragged her upstairs with him. She giggled all the way.

TEODORA

"Call a carriage," Teodora said, after reading the letter. Elyse hurried out the study door while Teodora paced, fuming.

Teodora couldn't remember the last time she had visited Livilla in the private laboratory inside the Maxima's palace. It had been one of the favorite haunts of her girlhood, but now that she ruled, she never had time to leave her own palace. Today though, she had to go before the weight of her problems crushed her.

Livilla wasn't expecting her, but looked up from her work and said, "Good morning my dear. Could you hand me that bunch of yarrow?" as if Teodora was still her student. She didn't mind.

"What are you doing?" Teodora asked, handing the flower to Livilla, who tore it into pieces into a small dish.

"I'm looking for a better cure for that fever. A few girls in the temple school have it and the old remedy is too slow for my liking. I will mix this with foxglove."

"Isn't that dangerous?" Teodora shivered happily. She always liked it when they talked of poison.

"Not particularly, as long as it's administered correctly. What's Mattila done now?" Livilla kept working, but her voice was soft.

"How did you know?"

Livilla shook her head. "I've had dreams. Nothing specific, but tales of trouble and they all surround Brynhild Mattila. I realize you need her, but the cost is high."

"It just got higher." Teodora handed the letter to Livilla. "She's traded Ruso Faris for Evard Bernotas. Have you ever heard of such stupidity?" Teodora went back to pacing. She had worn a path in the heavy Zastwar carpet in her study, and now her feet tapped out a similar though louder rhythm on Livilla's stone floor.

"What a terrible bargain," Livilla said, after reading the letter. "And her tone is nothing short of insolent. It seems she's forgotten she is no longer your commanding officer."

"She hasn't been in twenty years," Teodora screeched. It had taken all her self-control to hold her temper this long. "I should have let Daciana kill her when she had the chance."

"It's better she's alive, troublesome as she is. It's true that Faris is a great loss, though it will take time for him to raise another army. On the other hand, it won't hurt Terragand to have a ruler again, especially one beholden to you." Livilla put cork stoppers in a few bottles, then placed them on a shelf behind her, neatly written labels facing out.

"What good does it do? Half the country is in ruins and Evard can't control the other. Everyone follows Edric Landrus. Oh, I regret the moment I offered to bring that heretic here. If he'd been executed in Kronfels, none of this would have happened."

"I disagree." Livilla's calm seemed unshakable. She walked to a bench in front of a large window and sat down, the afternoon sunlight casting a halo around her head. "You acted as you did to avert open rebellion. Events were already in motion before the trial. But you must look forward, not back."

"I must do something." Teodora forced herself to stop pacing and sat down beside Livilla. "Why didn't I hear from Elektra about this?"

"Hasn't she written to you? I've received several letters from her."

"She's sent me several as well. Full of the most boring talk of staff meetings and logistics and maps. It seems the child has developed a fascination for infantry tactics. I would be proud, except I need her to become more interested in Mattila's other activities."

"Don't be too angry with her," Livilla said. "If Mattila has any sense, she makes sure that Elektra is not privy to discussions of interest to you. She'll fill her ears with military trivia, which she'll dutifully report back to you, while she makes her other plans secretly."

"Elektra must gain her trust somehow."

"She will. She looks unremarkable, but that can work to her advantage. In time, Mattila will see she's not a threat and let down her guard. You don't see it, but Elektra has a way about her, a gift for making friends. She will win Mattila over before long."

"I hope so," Teodora grumbled. "I must learn Mattila's plans before she can act on them. I agreed to let her command my army, not make unilateral decisions on prisoner exchanges. She must obey me."

"Perhaps I can help," Livilla said. "I've developed a plan to put a stop to the Quadrene heresy. While the Kronland cities are rife with it, it's also been spreading in the armies. I've received worrisome reports from chaplains assigned to Mattila's troops."

"How is the heresy taking hold there?" Was there no end to the problems Kendryk and his horrid priest had caused?

"Soldiers are questioning their chaplains and showing them pamphlets and copies of the Holy Scrolls."

"How did they receive those? We must stop them now." Teodora couldn't imagine how and felt the blood roaring in her ears again.

"I believe I've found a way."

"Tell me." Teodora tried to calm herself.

"Quadrene fanatics fill the ranks of the allied armies. Since Faris's defeat, many of them fight for Mattila, but they brought their heretical faith with them."

"Unacceptable."

"I agree. Especially since Mattila has done nothing to stop this. I asked Elektra about it, and she in turn asked Mattila what she plans to do about these heretical practices."

"And what did she say?"

"She laughed and said she's a soldier, not a priestess, and doesn't care what gods her troops pray to as long as they fight well."

"I cannot allow this."

"Neither can I. As Maxima of Olvisya, I am responsible for the spiritual well-being of the Olvisyan soldiers. Since they're being threatened by heretical teachings, I must stop those teachings. I have already trained a group of clerics to send to the army. They will replace all current chaplains, with the exceptions of a few proven to be solid in their faith. They will convert all the Quadrene soldiers and correct the errors of those infected by heresy. All who refuse will be disciplined."

"Mattila won't like that."

"No, she won't. But she will comply or become herself suspected of heresy. I won't ask her to dismiss or execute soldiers who don't comply—that would play into the hands of the enemy. But she will need to fine officers and imprison enlisted troops."

"Much as I want to inconvenience her, I still need her to win," Teodora said, though she felt considerable glee picturing Mattila's frustration.

"Oh, she'll win anyway, and I'm sure she'll soon learn to deal with this as well. She's resourceful. But in the meantime, it will show her she's not the only one with power over her people."

"How soon can you start this?"

"Right away. I started special training for this group shortly after Kendryk rescued Edric Landrus. I knew we would need to counter this new heresy."

"Why did it take so long? I wish we had stopped it at the beginning."

"So do I. But Landrus makes a compelling argument, based on the actual words in the Scrolls. The best way to counter him is to put forth arguments even more persuasive than his that are also based in the study of the Scrolls."

"Isn't that dangerous? So many people reading the original words, it makes me nervous."

"I worried too, at first. But it's easy to manipulate the interpretation in our favor. That's all Landrus and his followers do. People can read the words, but he tells them how they are to understand them. We can do the same thing, but on a larger scale. There is just one Landrus, but we can offer great numbers of those teaching our truth."

"How many do you have?"

"Two hundred."

Teodora gasped. "And you'll send all of them to the army?"

"Yes, and two hundred more are in training. Best of all, Elektra is already well-versed in these teachings. I'll ask her to offer unconditional support to these clerics and Mattila can't say a word against it."

"You're a wonder," Teodora said. "I never thought of taking that approach."

Livilla smiled. "It's my job to consider the religious possibilities. And someone has just arrived who might help you with military options. An old friend of yours, who hates Brynhild Mattila even more than you do."

GWYNNETH

Natalya had done better than get Gwynneth a private audience with the king; they were to have supper, just the three of them. It was a far more intimate setting than the usual small council chamber and having Natalya there gave her confidence.

When Gwynneth reached the small dining room, exquisitely appointed as the rest of the palace, the king was already there. Perhaps she was predisposed because of Kendryk's affection for him, but she liked Gauvain Brevard at once.

His looks were unprepossessing. He was short and scrawny, with a head too large for his body. His features were ungainly and topped by a mop of sandy hair. But his crooked smile was generous and unlike most Galladian courtiers, he was completely unaffected.

He greeted Gwynneth like a long-lost sister, taking both her hands and kissing her cheeks in the Galladian manner. He kept her hands in his while regarding her with a friendly grin. "I've heard so much about you from both Kendryk and Natalya, I feel like we already know each other well."

"It's the same for me." Gwynneth returned his smile. "And I'm so pleased to find you good friends with Natalya."

He flushed crimson and Gwynneth nearly loved him at that moment. "I had no choice," he said with a shy smile. "She's quite irresistible."

"Now we've all established how much we love each other," Natalya said wryly, "let's go in to supper before it's cold. "

They sat around a tiny table, served by an elaborately liveried footman. Once their glasses were filled with a dark red wine, the king raised his and said, "To Kendryk, who is missed more than words can say "

Caught off guard, Gwynneth quickly took several sips to cover her emotion. It wouldn't do to dissolve into tears just yet. But the other two were infinitely tactful, and while they ate, kept the conversation on neutral topics, such as their children and the general state of affairs in Galladium. Once the seven-course meal was finished, they moved into a small adjoining parlor.

When they were seated again, the king asked, "So tell me Gwynneth, what news do you have of Kendryk, if any?"

"I have none," Gwynneth said. "In the early months of the siege, I received a letter from the empress, asking me to turn over Edric Maximus and the castle in exchange for Kendryk. Then I heard he had been deposed in favor of Evard, and that was the last of it. "

"I don't wish to accuse you in any way," Gauvain said, clearly choosing his words with care. "But I have to wonder why you didn't give in to the empress's demands."

"I wonder at it myself." Gwynneth met his eyes without flinching. "It would have been so easy, but Kendryk made me swear I wouldn't before he went into battle. He had guessed what Teodora would demand should he lose and he made me promise not to surrender the castle or the priest."

Natalya looked at her searchingly. "It seems that in such a situation disobedience might be forgiven."

"Usually, it might," Gwynneth said. "But the circumstances were different. I don't want to go into detail, but I had to prove myself to him."

"Of course," the king said. "You did what you thought was best and I'm sure Kendryk appreciates your loyalty. Now the problem remains how we spring him. I'm sure he is still alive. The empress gains nothing at this point by concealing his death and word of it would deal a terrible blow to you and your brother's hopes. I've made overtures to the empress myself, but the conditions she required were impossible."

"I still appreciate it. Kendryk prizes your friendship above all others."

"I wish I could do more."

"Perhaps you can, but in a military, rather than diplomatic way." Gwynneth didn't see any point in pretending she wanted anything less.

Gauvain smiled ruefully. "If things were different, I'd put all of my armies at your disposal until Kendryk is returned to you. But I find myself beset on all sides. Tell her, Natalya."

Natalya came from the window where she'd been standing and perched on the arm of the king's chair. Unconsciously, his hand caressed the small of her back. Gwynneth smiled at the intimate gesture. It caused her less pain than she had expected to see a happy couple.

"Things are better than when Gauvain first gained the throne," Natalya said. "But not much. With the truce in Floradias, Maladena threatens our borders again. Thanks to the late king's efforts, we have a strong military, but its commanders are difficult to control. Most are dukes and princes who think they must be consulted at every turn. Many still question Gauvain's authority, feeling he came to power too young."

"I will help," the king said. "I swear it. It will just take time before I can use the military. But I don't wish to leave Kendryk imprisoned any longer, so Natalya has conceived a plan that might secure his release."

Gwynneth's heart leapt in unexpected hope, but once Natalya explained what they would offer Teodora, it sank again. "I hope it works. But if it does, she will insist on exile," Gwynneth said. "There's no way she'll release him just to allow him back into the field against her."

"No, she will not." Natalya's eyes were full of sympathy. "But exile is not the end of the world. And it would mean an end to this dreadful war, before anyone else gets involved."

"But what about the Faith and Edric Maximus? I don't think Kendryk could accept the end of that."

"Edric continues as he is and the Faith continues to change. He will not be part of the deal although Kendryk will have to agree to not help him."

"He might not agree to that," Gwynneth whispered. "I'm not sure I want him to."

"I will speak with Kendryk myself," Natalya said. "The new faith has taken on its own momentum now and neither Kendryk nor you are needed to see it continue. Since I know you wish to stay involved, what I propose is this: Kendryk goes into exile, but instead of Norovaea, the two of you and your children will come here. I am just beginning to make the necessary changes to the Faith, and I can use the help of knowledgeable people like you. You will be among friends, in a place where you can do some good. And I believe Teodora will overreach herself before long. Much can change in a few years and exile need not be forever."

"I suppose you're right." Gwynneth's mind was at war. On the one hand, she would give anything to see Kendryk back with her and safe. On the other, she didn't wish to abandon Kronland to Teodora's retribution. "But what if Teodora takes measures to act against Kronland?"

"That will be part of the deal," Natalya said. "She may not intervene in Kronland's religious affairs. I will make her understand it was her interference that caused the problem in the first place. Kronland must be given independence in this matter."

"Who will guarantee it?" Gwynneth asked. "Since Galladium is not in a position to force Teodora to behave."

"We cannot do it," Natalya said. "Not right now, at least. But that's where you can help."

JANNA

While Braeden was still gone on the prisoner exchange, Janna started feeling sick again. Before he had returned, she was certain she was pregnant. This worried her, not because of the discomfort and risk, but because she was sure he would send her away.

Braeden had caught up to them before they engaged Seward Kurant's army in Terragand. Kurant had marched from Podoska with several thousand mercenaries, many of them hired from Briansk, far to the east.

"He'll lead us on a merry chase, if he's smart," Braeden said, sitting on the cot, and bouncing Iryna on his knee. Little as she was, she remembered him and smiled when she saw him, which Janna could tell pleased him. "You'll see even more of Terragand than you did last time."

"I'm glad you're back. I try to believe that you'll be safe no matter what, but I can't help but picture the most awful things."

"I know," Braeden said. "Come here." He pulled Janna onto his other knee. "Prince Novitny won't let us go out unless we're prepared. No one bothered us, not even the remnants of Orland's army."

Janna shuddered. "Are they very desperate?"

"Yes, though by now most are gone. Those that survived joined Emilya Hohenwart up north, or went to Floradias. There's a rumor that Arian Orland is there trying to raise more troops."

"Why doesn't he give up?" Janna wondered. "Didn't he lose everything?"

Braeden shrugged. "Now he has to get it back. He doesn't strike me as the sort to give up easy. Besides, what else would he do? Some of us are cut out for fighting and nothing else."

"Is that what you'd do? If you lost everything?" Janna leaned against his shoulder.

"Sure. Nothing for it but to keep trying. It's what you'd do too. It's what you did, even though you didn't see it that way."

"I gave up," Janna said. "Long before you found me, I'd given up."

"Well, you weren't doing a good job of it, seeing's you were still alive. And now with Iryna, it's even more important to keep going."

Janna nodded. They were quiet for a moment, then she burst out. "I'm pregnant."

He looked at her, clearly delighted. "You sure?"

"Yes. I didn't want to tell you right away."

"Why not? You had to know I'd be happy."

"Oh yes. But also worried you'd start thinking about sending me away again."

Braeden's smile faded. "Oh, that. Well, I won't send you away if you don't want to go. I'd rather see you safe, but I hate making you cry." He snorted. "Never thought I'd get so soft in my old age."

Janna snuggled up against him, smiling. "It will be fine. Doctor Toure is here and she's excellent. I've already spoken with her and she'll keep an especially close eye on me this time to make sure there aren't any problems. Besides, we might be in winter quarters by the time I'm due."

"Very likely," Braeden said. "Mattila wants to engage Arryk before then, but if she can't manage it, I doubt she'll chase him when the weather gets bad."

Janna was pleased he'd reacted so well. "I'm sure it will be a boy," she said.

"I hope so. Though I wouldn't mind another like this one." Braeden planted a kiss on Iryna's curly head. "She's as sweet as her mother, and no trouble at all."

"I've found the oldest are often easy." Janna smiled. "So you'll have more. Then the second ones are dreadful."

"I suppose we'll find out," Braeden said, his eyes twinkling. "I can't wait to meet him."

They had to travel far to catch up with Kurant. Janna was sick more often and Braeden insisted she not ride Zoltan, so she had to walk, or ride in a wagon. It wasn't so bad. Nisa Retter was pregnant with her fourth, and Janna rode with her. Iryna could play with her little ones and Janna had someone to talk to.

"It's best if we're in winter quarters," Nisa said, "but you'll manage either way. It's always hardest, getting used to the first baby, but now you've done it, it'll be easier. Ask your husband about hiring another servant or two—it's nice to have the extra help."

Money was no problem for the officers in this army. With all the gold and plunder, it was easy to find people to hire. The bad times in the countryside meant that many left the land and followed the army instead, doing what they could to make a living.

Janna decided to wait before asking for more servants. She wanted to complain as little as possible so Braeden would have no cause to send her back to Atlona.

ARRYK

"Prince Bronson, it's good to see you." Arryk forced a friendly smile, though he had little use for the crusty old fellow. "What brings you to Fromenberg?" He didn't mention that Bronson was supposed to be very far away, helping Emilya Hohenwart build up her forces.

"It's that woman." Prince Bronson ground his teeth, after taking his place at a table where a servant had cleared a space. Arryk kept it covered with maps and papers. Even when he didn't know what to do, the mess made him feel like he was working very hard.

"Which woman?" Arryk waved over a page who poured wine for both of them. The Fromenberg varieties were uncommonly good. He and his officers had taken over an entire wing of Princess Keylinda's palace and were putting a large dent in her excellent cellar. "Mattila?"

"No." Bronson took a long swig, draining his cup, and banged it down on the table. "No, it's Emilya Hohenwart. I refuse to work with her."

Arryk sighed. He had hoped this wouldn't be a problem. Prince Bronson seemed unable to get along with anyone. But his force was too small to operate independently, so it made sense to combine it with Hohenwart's larger infantry and artillery.

"Why? She has a good record. Experienced. What's wrong?"

"I won't take orders from a jumped-up country squire's daughter."

"You're not taking orders, really. You're joint commanders, and she's the senior. She still has to consult you on everything."

"But she doesn't. She acts like I don't exist and does exactly as she pleases."

"Well, it's true she's used to working on her own and I've heard her manners are rough."

"Lack of breeding." Prince Bronson sniffed, though he hardly personified good manners himself.

Arryk swallowed down that observation. He needed a deft touch here and he regretted Gwynneth's absence for the thousandth time. "Breeding doesn't matter in the military, but results do, and hers have been good."

Not perfect, but good. Hohenwart had suffered a few defeats in her ten years as a commander, but she'd always come back from them quickly. She had the type of experience Arryk needed around him, now with Faris and Orland gone. "And I was wondering what was keeping her. I need her here. What if I send for her and we'll all sit down over some ale and discuss it?" That could end in a brawl, but might sort things out.

"She won't come. It's money that's keeping her there. She needs more before traveling across Kronland. And she can't get down here before winter. Besides, you don't want to feed and quarter a force that size. No, she'll sit in Brandana for at least a few months more, living off the untouched parts of the land. And I don't intend to keep her company."

"Well, maybe you needn't." Arryk waved for another glass of wine. "Why don't you spend the winter with me and we'll work out everything else in the meantime? Did you bring many troops?"

"A few. I sent most of them home for the winter."

Arryk pushed down his anger, something he'd learned to do well of late. He wondered what it would take to make his few remaining allies do as they were told and join him when he needed them.

ANTON

Anton went to the banker's with the count since they were taking the horses and didn't plan to return. Not that they had told Vrouw Belsen anything.

"She'd just carry on," the count said. "I can't stand women who carry on, though most of them do."

Anton wondered if that was why he liked Princess Gwynneth. She didn't seem like the sort who'd carry on much at all.

They had to walk far, to a better part of the city. Here the streets were wider and the tall houses decorated with bright paintings and beautiful dark woodwork. "Most of the money for the whole continent comes from here," the count said, stopping in front of a heavy door with a small window in it.

Anton nodded, though he didn't understand how all the money came from here. He thought if it did, more people would carry bags of it around. The count had tried explaining to him that most of the money was on paper, but that didn't make any sense.

The count handed Cid's reins to Anton, already holding Skandar, and said, "Wait here. It might be a while."

Then he used a heavy brass knocker to pound on the door. Almost right away, the tiny window opened and closed again, and then the enormous door swung open. Anton tried to look inside, but caught only a glimpse of a shiny dark floor before the door closed again.

The horses were restless from being cooped up in the stable for the past several days, so Anton walked them up and down the street. It seemed that fine warhorses weren't often seen inside the city, so several people stopped to admire them. One man wearing a tall black hat came out of a nearby house and offered to buy both of them on the spot.

"They're not for sale." Anton was surprised at how easy it was to turn down the huge amount of money the man offered.

"If you change your mind, I work there," the man said, pointing to a house down the street. "Just knock and ask for Kornelyus. It's not often I see horseflesh this fine."

Anton gave him a friendly nod, even though he didn't like how he'd referred to Cid and Skandar as "horseflesh." As far as Anton was concerned, these two were better than most people.

The count returned quickly. That wasn't good. Anton knew him well enough to know that he shouldn't ask how it went.

They walked to the end of the street in silence, when the count stopped. "I can't do it," he said. "I can't go back to that woman."

Anton didn't think they had much choice, but was silent.

"I'll have to sell Cid," the count said.

Anton thought maybe he should offer to sell Skandar too, but he didn't want to.

"I know what to do," the count went on, "But I need money to do it."

Anton took a deep breath and told him about the man who'd offered to buy the horses.

"He offered you how much?"

'That was for both," Anton admitted.

"You can't sell Skandar," the count said. "He was a gift from a king. "

Anton was glad he saw it that way, though the thought of selling Cid made him want to cry. But he showed the count the door and told him to ask for Kornelyus. He was still wearing his tall hat and was very happy to buy Cid. Even though Skandar wasn't part of the deal, he handed over a large purse. Anton hoped it would be enough for whatever the count was planning.

When they left the man after handing Cid over to him, Anton couldn't stop the tears sliding down his cheeks.

When he glanced up at the count, his eyes blazed and his mouth was set. "He said I could buy him back if I can come up with the money in a week's time."

"Can you?" Anton couldn't imagine how.

"I will try. But first, we're going to get really, really drunk."

Getting drunk and getting over it took the rest of the day and night, but by morning the count was ready. He and Anton found a room in a nice lodging house with a stable for Skandar. Then they went to a tailor down the street where the count spent a huge part of the money he got from Cid on several fine suits of clothes, including one for Anton. "We have to appear rich for a few days," he said.

They walked out a few hours later in matching red doublets and hats. The count looked Anton over approvingly. "You could almost be my little brother," he said. "Though I doubt you'll turn out as good-looking as me."

Anton doubted it too. He had to admit that in the fine clothes, he at least didn't seem like such a ragamuffin. He had shiny new black boots that actually fit and when they returned to the lodging house, the count insisted he have a bath.

"But I got a good soaking the other day when it rained so hard," Anton protested.

"It's not the same," the count said. "Now get in that tub and don't come out until all the dirt is gone. I'll check behind your ears to be sure."

It was worse than having a mother, Anton grumbled to himself as he lowered himself into the steaming water. Once he got used to the heat, he had to admit it felt good, and he almost fell asleep after scrubbing himself raw. Thankfully, the count didn't check behind his ears since he came out looking pink and scalded.

The count had had a bath too and once they put on their finery they looked completely different.

"We don't want anyone thinking we're soldiers," the count said.

Anton was happy the count thought he had looked like one in the first place.

"And I will use a different name for the rest of our stay in Bonnenruck," the count went on. "From now on, I'll be known as Eberhard, Count of Winterberg."

"Why?"

The count scowled. "After Lerania, anyone who hears my real name thinks of failure. Better if their first impression is this." He pulled his fine, feathered hat down over one eye and smiled the way he always did when he was making a woman fall in love with him.

Next, they got Skandar from the stable. The groom had cleaned his bridle and saddle, also gifts from King Anyk, and now they looked shiny and new, much like Anton. He could tell Skandar was sad about Cid, but he was also happy to get out of the stable again.

As they walked down a narrow street, Anton leading Skandar, the count explained that they were going to a grand party. "The key is to act like you belong there," he said.

"But I don't speak the language very well."

"That's all right. I'll say I picked you up on my travels, which is true enough. You must take Skandar to the stable, see he's looked after, then find me in the big house."

"And then what?"

"Stand around until I wave at you to come. I'll send you on little errands to make you seem useful."

"I don't see why."

"I need to appear rich and important. I don't have an invitation to this party, but if I show up riding a fine horse like Skandar with a nicely dressed page, I'll look like I belong there."

"Why do you need to go to this party?"

"Rich women will be there. I need to find one for myself."

"One that looks better than Vrouw Belsen, hopefully."

"Hopefully. Though piles of gold will make up for quite a bit of ugliness."

The count, Anton and Skandar made their way to a nice neighborhood and joined a string of fine carriages all going in the same direction. The count jumped onto Skandar and Anton walked alongside, trying to look dignified. Ahead of them, the carriages lined up at the front door of an enormous house with light blazing from rows of windows. Finely-dressed people climbed out of each carriage before it moved on.

Anton was nervous because they were the only ones without a carriage, but the count acted like he didn't care. When it was their turn, he jumped down, tossed the reins to Anton like usual, then looked down his nose at the footman standing in front of the door. Anton tried to act bored and casual.

The footman looked both of them over. "Your invitation?" he asked, holding out his hand.

"I'm afraid my wife has it," the count said. "I'm sure she's already here. Oh yes, there she is." He waved at a young woman who had turned to have her cloak taken by another footman inside. The count beamed at her. "Darling! You didn't wait for me."

"Oh, I," she said, flustered. "I'm sorry. I didn't. I mean ..."

"Is this gentleman with you?" the footman asked.

"Oh yes!" she said.

Anton looked sideways at the count and almost laughed. He was using his best intense stare on her, the one that worked on every woman but the princess. He put out his hand and she took it and they swept past both footmen.

The footman looked down his nose at Anton and talked for a long time. He talked so fast, it was hard to figure out what he was saying, but Anton caught the word "stables," and since the footman pointed to the right, figured he should take

Skandar that way. Anton nodded as if he understood, then hurried off since he didn't want to miss the show. He didn't know what the count had planned, exactly, but it was sure to be good.

It took a long time to get Skandar in his stall and find his way through the enormous house. Large as it looked from the front, the rest of it covered an entire block. Anton paused in the kitchen to stare at the vast trays of food being readied. When no one was looking, he snatched a flaky piece of pastry from one of them and walked off. When he bit into it, he almost moaned with pleasure. It was warm and filled with nuts, butter, dark sugar and some kind of spice he didn't recognize. He considered going back to get another, except he needed to find the count.

He followed haughty servants dressed up in fancy liveries bearing trays laden with food and carrying crystal decanters filled with drinks of all kinds. Now he was especially glad for his fine suit.

The house was about ten times the size of the one he'd grown up in and twenty times as luxurious. His feet sank deep into soft carpets and it was hard not to stop and stare at the beautiful paintings hanging on the walls or the brightly colored glass that made patterns in lampshades and windows. He wondered who lived here, but knew it wouldn't be smart to ask. Perhaps it was the home of the Zeelund king, though he remembered the count explaining to him that Zeelund didn't have a king, exactly.

Crowds of richly-dressed people spilled from every room and jewelry glittered in the light of thousands of candles. Anton was glad he didn't have to light them all. He finally spotted the count in one of the largest rooms, laughing and surrounded by women. Anton worked his way in until he was in his line of sight. The count saw him right away and waved him over. It was like being in battle, but without the pistols. "I'll need you to stand behind me at dinner," he said, "but that's still an hour away. In the meantime, go fetch wine for these ladies."

Anton ran off, glad he'd paid attention to where the servants put the drinks. When he returned, carefully balancing four fine crystal glasses, the women tittered and pinched his cheeks.

Anton looked them over. There were just two left. He reckoned they'd frightened the others off. One was younger, tall and skinny, and not bad-looking until she opened her mouth. The other was old, but so heavily painted and powdered she didn't look too bad, especially in the candlelight.

Though Anton couldn't follow their conversation very well, he could see the count was laying it on extra thick with the old one, though it was the younger one who grabbed him when it was time for dinner. That made the old one mad, and she put up a fuss until a man with large red whiskers came over and made loud angry noises at the younger woman. Anton wondered if she was his daughter, or maybe his wife. The old woman ended up going in with the count, and acted like she'd bagged a prize wildfowl. The count looked pleased too, and Anton had a feeling they would have money again soon.

TEODORA

"It's been too long." Teodora took Daciana into her arms.

"You should have called me back sooner," Daciana said, pulling away with a smile. "There's nothing left to burn up north."

"So you've done your work well, as always." Teodora sat down and Daciana sprawled across a nearby chair. She'd come straight from the road, her hair a wild tangle and her boots muddy. Knowing her, she wouldn't bother to pretty up for court. Teodora couldn't recall ever seeing her in a dress.

"I shouldn't call it work; I enjoy it so."

"You really are a monster as they say." Teodora smiled.

Daciana shrugged. "Could be. The reputation makes me more frightening in any case."

"Eat." Teodora gestured toward a heavily laden tray, while she poured two glasses of wine. She'd had everything brought in ahead so there'd be no eavesdroppers. "I take it your raiders are in the city, drinking themselves silly and causing all kinds of trouble?"

"Most likely." Daciana's mouth was full of cheese. Her manners had always been atrocious. "I told them not to get too drunk in case we have to ride out again soon."

"Good. It will be soon, but you can take a few days to rest and resupply."

"What's next?" Daciana drank down her glass of wine in one long swig.

Teodora refilled it. "I think it's time for you to go east again. Princess Martinek has fielded an army led by Seward Kurant and he's marching them out of Podoska."

"You need him stopped?"

"Oh, Mattila will do that."

"So it's true. I'm sure you had a good reason for what you did." Daciana put the glass—empty again—down hard and her eyes flashed yellow, though her tone remained even.

"I hope so." Now Teodora needed more wine too. "Believe me, I didn't want to. I always hoped that neither one of us would have to see her again."

Daciana sighed and leaned back. "So did I. It will be hard for me to ride in her direction without at least trying—"

"No." Teodora's tone was sharp. "Not now. I need her alive right now. She's the only person who can lead a large force to victory against just about anyone. Once she's finished off Arryk Roussay and his allies and I no longer have a use for her, she's all yours."

"Good." Daciana pulled out a long curved knife to slice off a piece of sausage. The blade looked rusty. Or maybe bloody. "But I still can't promise I will leave her completely unharmed. It's so unfair. Why does she always have the advantage of us?"

"It's only temporary. I can't stop you from harassing her, but try to remember that her force needs to stay intact if she's going to win."

"Hmph," Daciana said, her mouth full again.

While she ate, Teodora told her more about the progress of the war and of Mattila's latest outrage.

"I can get Count Faris back for you," Daciana said.

"Don't bother. He's safe inside Birkenfels for now and it's too difficult to get in there. He won't be a threat until spring at the earliest, and Mattila might be able to defeat Arryk before then. No, I need you elsewhere. Arryk has had far too easy a time getting the Kronlanders over to his cause. I'm glad you punished Brandana, but now I want you to do the same in Podoska."

"Podoska?" Daciana wiped her mouth on her sleeve and frowned. "Even with Kurant gone, they'll be harder to intimidate."

"Yes, and that's why you must do it. It takes a lot to shock Princess Martinek, but you should try."

Daciana grinned, her fangs showing. "That should be fun. Martinek—aren't they the ones who grind their enemy's bodies into a pulp which they plow into their fields? It's said they grow the most delicious peaches there because of it."

"That's the story," Teodora said. "And it might be true. They're known for being strange and barbaric. Still, with most of their army gone, they'll have a hard time resisting you. And I would think you'd enjoy it if the peasantry was fiercer than usual."

"I do, but it's hard on the regular recruits who go foraging and end up with their guts pulled out through their necks, or worse. Though I don't mind seeing the common-folk stand up for themselves like that. I realize you don't agree, but you know what I'm like."

"I do," Teodora said, with a fond smile. "And I don't fault you. I imagine if I were a peasant I wouldn't take kindly to enemy troops plundering my home and raping my daughters, though I doubt they'd want mine. She's such an unattractive girl."

"Who, Elektra? She's likely just in an awkward stage."

"That's what Livilla says, but I worry. It's ever so much easier to get what you want from people if you're good-looking."

"Only if you don't like using force." Daciana laughed and poured the last of the wine into her glass. "But I know what you mean. I still don't think you should worry. Remember what a sight I was when we first met? And I wasn't much older than your Elektra."

"Of course I remember. But your life had been very different. Elektra has had it so easy; always had enough of everything. Perhaps too much."

"Most children have too little. I'm sure it doesn't hurt her to be a little spoiled. Far better she learn to keep what she has than have to claw it away from others. Though I imagine she'll have plenty of that to do."

"Not if I can help it. By the time I die—which please Vica, will not be for many years—I plan to leave Elektra with a powerful, well-run empire. She needs only the wit to manage it."

"I'm sure she will have it. She's your daughter, after all. Now, let's open another bottle of wine and you can tell me if these rumors about you and General Barela are true."

BRAEDEN

"Do you have a moment, Doctor?" Braeden asked, ducking into the largest medical tent.

"Braeden!" Ashia Toure turned from the basin where she was scrubbing her hands. "Are you well?"

"Well enough." He'd known Doctor Toure since she'd dug a big chunk of shot out of his calf several years before. She'd also delivered Iryna, her knowledge and quick thinking saving both Janna and the baby's life. Braeden had given her a large bag of silver for that.

He wasn't certain where she was from. He'd never seen anyone with such dark skin and had heard she came from the southern lands of Neviar, where they mixed medicine with magic. Braeden didn't know about the magic and didn't want to ask, but there was no question Toure was better at medicine than most doctors he'd met.

His face must have given away more than he realized. "Something's bothering you," she said. "Why don't we sit? I could use a break after that amputation."

"I'm sure Janna's told you she's pregnant again."

The doctor nodded. "She came to me right away, for which I was glad. I hope this time there will be no complications."

"Is it likely, because she had them last time?"

"Not necessarily. Each pregnancy is different. Still, she's so small, and I understand has been through some difficulties in the past few years. I should like to keep a close eye on her health in general."

"I agree." It was a relief to talk about it with someone he didn't need to risk upsetting. "I worry too. I've already asked her to ride in a cart instead of on horseback, but even that can be difficult. The army is no place for a pregnant woman."

"It's not. But babies don't stop being born because there's a war."

"They should know better," Braeden joked. "I've tried to persuade her to go live in a town somewhere."

"That would certainly be best. I suppose she doesn't want to?"

"No, she doesn't. I don't like to leave her either, but I'm worried, even with you here. Could you persuade her?"

Doctor Toure sighed. "I can try. She ought to be in a warm, dry house with servants to do the hard work and look after Iryna. I should like to see her rest and gain some weight. She was sick while you were away and lost too much."

"She's worried about being trapped someplace unsafe. It's happened to her before."

"I see. Atlona would be best, but it's too far for her to travel. Have you considered Kersenstadt?"

"I haven't, but maybe I should. Mattila seems to think it's important. She wants to fill it with arms and supplies, and use it as one of her biggest depots. I imagine she'll keep it well-guarded."

"I'm sure she will. It's also a larger town so it's easy to find good lodging and servants. Even better, I have a colleague there who is something of a specialist in delivering babies. He would be ideal to check on her and be there when her time comes."

Hope swelled up inside him. "I'd pay him well to give Janna extra attention. Could you tell me his name?"

The doctor turned and scribbled something, then handed Braeden the note. "You can write to him or call on him. I'm sure we'll stop in Kersenstadt on our way east. You can at least speak with him and make preparations for later, if she doesn't want to go now. I suspect that once she becomes more uncomfortable and the weather worsens, it will be easier to convince her."

"I hope so." Braeden decided to write to the doctor that day. No need to say anything to Janna just yet.

KENDRYK

By now Kendryk was so lethargic even the sudden light and noise took too long to rouse him. Hope flickered, quickly replaced by dread, since no good had ever come of an unexpected visit. As long as he ate most of his food and didn't make loud noises, no one bothered him. Ever. He had lost track of time altogether and hadn't spoken to another person in months. Or maybe it had been years. It didn't matter.

He almost hoped this would be the end. There was no point in going on like this. Two guards strode into his cell and grabbed him by each arm. Kendryk wobbled. Of late, he hadn't even tried to exercise. He crawled on the floor, like an animal. He probably looked like one too.

They dragged him stumbling into the dark corridor. Nothing but torchlight flickered, but it was still brighter than anything Kendryk had seen since he'd been force-fed so long ago.

"What's this about?" he croaked.

The guards didn't answer. They dragged him down a long corridor and up several flights of stairs. By then, Kendryk was gasping for air. To his surprise, it was daylight. The deep slits in the stone showed blue sky and fluffy clouds coasting across it. As they passed one, a slight breeze blew over him. He grinned.

He was about to collapse when they shoved him into a small room with one window. It provided just enough light that he saw who awaited him. He tried to force himself to smile, but failed.

"Your Highness," he croaked.

"Darling." Teodora seemed to have no trouble smiling that nasty one she had. "You look terrible."

"You look lovely as always," Kendryk gasped, collapsing into a chair. She sat across the room from him, which wasn't far. He calculated the distance, but reckoned he couldn't reach her in one step. With the guards standing right there,

213

he didn't have a chance. Not that he would try it. He was unarmed and weaker than he'd ever been. Still, it would be a way to get it over with quickly.

"There's no need to play nice with me," she said, still smiling.

"It comes naturally," he said, tired already.

Her smile disappeared. "Good. I need you to be nice enough to cooperate. I've had enough of your stubbornness and it's not doing anyone any good."

"It's not doing you any good," Kendryk said. "You wouldn't be here if things were going your way."

"Oh, they're going my way, just not as quickly as I'd like. You have the power to speed them up."

"By doing what? Abdicating? You already took care of that for me."

"I want you to do it formally and publicly. You might beg my forgiveness and I might even grant it. I can imagine the most charming ceremony. We'd get you fit again first, and presentable. It would make a pretty picture, the two of us embracing as friends after you admit your youthful errors."

Kendryk's anger surprised him. He hadn't felt any emotion for so long. "That will never happen. I will never beg forgiveness from you for anything. Ever."

"I've been too lenient with you." Teodora's voice was flat. "I treat you better than my own children."

"I doubt that's true, though I don't envy the poor things, having you for a mother."

She was on him like a flash, her slap stinging his cheek, and then he fell out of the chair, her weight crushing him. Her fist crashed into his eye, and she pinned his arms to the floor with her knees. Kendryk couldn't move.

He closed his eyes and the next punch hit his jaw. The power of her blows shouldn't have surprised him. By the time she was through with him, both eyes were swelling shut, blood dripped from his nose and ran from his lip. A few teeth had loosened. It was a relief as her weight lifted, but before he could enjoy it, she delivered a sharp kick to his ribs. He heard the crunch and the pain was sharper than anything he'd felt since the battle.

He couldn't see her, but she grabbed him by the hair and whispered in his ear. "Think about it. Next time I'll bring a professional, and that will be much worse."

BRAEDEN

Braeden wondered if they'd ever find Seward Kurant. He and his army seemed to have marched out of Podoska and disappeared.

"Think he got around us and linked up with King Arryk?" Novitny wondered.

"No," Mattila snapped. "We would have heard. I have reliable sources in the king's camp. No, Kurant is out there, but his force isn't large and the population will be friendly toward him. They won't tell us anything." She tapped a finger on the map laying in front of her. "We'll do this instead. I must stop at Kersenstadt and make sure it's well stocked as a base for me to march on Arryk. We won't bother going any further east from there, though. We'll fortify it, supply it and head west."

"At our current strength, we can easily take on Arryk. I'd rather not face Emilya Hohenwart, but she's far to the north and I doubt she'll join Arryk before winter. Arian Orland is out of play for now, but might be back by spring, along with Faris. I want to strike the king, and strike him hard before that happens."

Then followed a lengthy discussion of armaments and wagons and troop dispositions. Braeden tried to pay attention, but General Mattila's tent was packed with all of her staff and it was warm. He found it hard to stay awake. Iryna had a tooth coming in and had cried much of the night, so he was hoping for a nap if the meeting ended soon.

Mattila droned on while Archduchess Elektra scribbled notes. Braeden wondered if she was reporting all of this to her mother. After awhile, another general spoke; some old fellow with an unpronounceable Marjatyan name and long white hair. Braeden had to make considerable effort to keep his eyes open.

There was a sudden commotion and a young man burst into the tent. "We're under attack," he said, skidding to a stop.

Everyone jumped up at once. Braeden realized there'd been no sound of guns or other noise. "Where?" Mattila asked calmly.

"The camp."

Braeden's heart jumped into his throat, though he knew the camp was vast.

"What part of the camp, you idiot?" Mattila snapped.

"Sanova's. They're trying to make off with the horses."

"Raiders then," Mattila said, still calm, as Braeden and Novitny shot out of the tent and ran. Braeden tried not to panic.

Novitny read his thoughts. "They'll leave the tents alone, most likely. Probably gone already with some excellent horseflesh, the cursed devils."

Braeden hoped he was right.

Their part of the camp seemed far away. By now others had heard of the attack and milled about in some excitement, although no one seemed inclined to act. "We're under attack," Braeden shouted, not caring if he started a panic. "Anyone bearing arms, follow me now!"

As they neared the Sanovan encampment, they made a well-armed crowd. It was hard to tell how many raiders there were. Several tents were on fire and people ran around screaming while riders chased them down.

Braeden pulled a short sword from his belt and waded in. He'd prefer to be on horseback with an ax, but he didn't know where the horses were and he had to stop the raiders now.

A woman holding a baby ran toward Braeden, a raider bearing down on her fast. Braeden pushed the woman behind him and stood in the pony's path. The woman on its back didn't have time to slow down, but lifted her curved blade and shifted slightly to meet Braeden. His blade was much shorter, but he waited for her swing, then darted underneath, grabbing her leg and pulling her to the ground.

It wasn't until after Braeden had cut her throat that he realized he needed to take someone alive for questioning. Though he had a good idea of who was behind this, it made little sense and there were others who operated in the same fashion. Mattila would want specific information.

Now that they faced armed opposition, the raiders melted away. A few had been stopped, but except for one, they were all dead. Much as he wanted to make sure that Janna and Iryna were all right, Braeden forced himself to see the prisoner first.

The man's face was filthy and covered with blood, but he laughed at Braeden while spitting out broken teeth. "Didn't think to ever see you again. Can't say I'm glad to."

Braeden recognized the fellow as one he'd arrested years ago during his first run-in with the empress's favorite marauder. He grabbed him by the jacket and hauled him to his feet. "What is Tomescu doing here? These are the empress's troops."

The man laughed harder. "Doubt very much your general would call them that."

"We'll see about that. You'll be talking to her shortly." Braeden handed him off to another trooper with instructions to take him straight to Mattila. He needed to find Janna.

It took a few minutes to orient himself since the camp was in such confusion. To his relief, only a few tents had been pulled down or set on fire. By the time he reached his, all was quiet and dark. He ducked his head inside. It was dark, cold and silent. He wondered if Janna had gone to take refuge with one of her friends. "Janna," he called, then listened. "Janna?" a little louder this time. There was a rustle and a whimper.

"Stay where you are," he said, "I'm coming." He fumbled for a tinder and lit a lamp. As soon as Iryna let out a small cry, he saw them. Janna had climbed behind a pile of saddles and blankets and pulled another blanket over her head. She was peeking out from under it. Braeden set the lamp down and picked both of them up and pulled them onto the floor with him. "It's all right," he said. "It's safe now."

He could feel Janna trembling as he held her close. Iryna made a noise of protest at being squeezed and pushed away. Braeden took her into his other arm. "Are you all right? Are you hurt?"

Janna shook her head. She still trembled all over.

"Hold on." He put Iryna on the cot, then picked Janna up and put her down next to her. He grabbed a blanket and wrapped her up tight. "I'll start a fire in a moment. Where's that good-for-nothing Gergo, anyway?"

"He went to check on the horses," Janna said in a small voice. "I hope they didn't get him."

"I hope not, too. Though we don't know how much damage they did."

"It was her," Janna whispered. "I saw her riding at their head, though she didn't see me. But why did she attack us? I thought she was on our side."

"It was Tomescu, all right. I recognized one of her men. He's being questioned by the general so I doubt he'll be with us much longer. Why she did this, I don't know. I don't care either, but Janna ..." He pulled her into his arms, "... this is too dangerous. This is why I want you in a city, in a house, behind walls."

To his surprise, she nodded, though her tears wet the front of his shirt.

TEODORA

"How dare she take that tone with me!" Teodora fumed.

"She's used to dealing with subordinates," Livilla said, appearing calm, though Teodora couldn't help but think the harshness of Mattila's letter had affected her too.

Teodora paced the length of the room. "She's doing it to test me. She thinks she can walk all over me. I'll show her."

"No." Livilla stood and crossed the room to Teodora. "That's exactly what she wants. She's trying to provoke you. She knows of your hot temper from experience and wishes to exploit it. Don't let her."

"I can't let her get away with this."

"What Daciana did was wrong, but I can't blame her, considering their history. You must curb her, however, at least for now. Perhaps you can use her later."

"I don't want to wait. I want to punish that bitch Mattila right now."

"You need her. Once she's finished off Arryk Roussay, it will be different. With this attitude, she's sure to overreach herself. In time, she'll alienate everyone and others will beg you to intervene. But at the moment she's seen as the Empire's possible savior."

"Once she defeats Arryk, that will only get worse," Teodora said bitterly. "She'll receive all of the credit."

"She'll be so ungracious about it, she'll make far more enemies than friends."

"Pfft. A successful general is never short on sycophants."

"No, she will always have supporters. But if those supporters hate her, they will abandon her at the first sign that things are going against her. And that will be your moment."

"I don't know if I can wait that long."

"You must. It's one of many unpleasant things an effective ruler must be able to do. You must wait."

"Perhaps. But she wants me to send Demario to her," Teodora wailed. That had been the part of the letter that hit her hardest: Mattila demanding that Barela be put under her direct command.

"I cannot operate freely throughout Kronland knowing you cannot control your troops. Demario Barela must be under my command by month end, or I will resign and dissolve this army," the letter had said.

"That's a problem," Livilla said. "You cannot deny her, but you must not allow it to happen. I'm sure he will help you."

"He would never take orders from her."

"He will, if he must. Oh, child." Livilla came closer and took both of Teodora's hands in hers. "Of course it's all right to show them in front of me, but you must learn to hide your emotions. If others see how you feel about him, it gives them power over you."

"It gives him power over me, too." Teodora wanted to cry on Livilla's shoulder, as she had when she was a girl, but it wasn't possible. She might not have complete self-control, but she had some.

"Yes, it's unfortunate. But I don't think he'll take advantage. He doesn't appear to want anything from you aside from your company. But let it be a lesson to you—you might not be so lucky next time."

"There won't be a next time. Falling in love is the most ridiculous thing, and so inconvenient."

"Yes, but it's already happened. I'm sure you'll get over him. With any luck you'll do it before he gets over you."

Panic struck Teodora. "Will he?"

"Of course he will, sooner or later. Men always do. Even the best ones. The difference is that the best ones stay with you anyway. But in the general's case, it won't be possible."

"I don't think I will be able to bear it."

"You will have to, but not yet. At least, not for a long time. At any rate, you can't worry about it now. You must keep him from Mattila without denying her outright."

Teodora paced some more. After a time she said, "What if I send him after Daciana?"

That was the other part of the letter. Mattila had taken matters into her own hands and declared Daciana and her riders outlaws, to be killed on sight. "I must warn her to stay away from any imperial troops. He can deliver the message."

"That's an excellent idea. Tell Mattila that Barela will join her soon. Unfortunately, you had already heard of what Daciana did and sent him after her.

Right now he's gods-knows-where between here and Podoska."

"He'll get the message to Daciana and then we'll find another way to occupy him. It will buy us time at the least." Teodora started to feel a tiny bit hopeful.

"And time is all we need. My new military clerics should arrive at Kersenstadt any day now and once they are operational, Mattila will be distracted for quite a while."

"I'll talk to him now." Teodora hated to send him away, but she had no choice if she wanted to keep him out of Mattila's clutches.

ANTON

After the party, Anton learned the old woman's name was Kamyla Melchor.

"She's not really that old," the count said.

"She looks old to me."

"Everyone looks old to you. Truth is, it could be a lot worse. And it doesn't matter anyway because she's swimming in gold. She was rich to start with, then married a fellow who made another fortune in the spice trade. He died a few years ago, and she's had her pick of suitors."

"But she hasn't picked anyone."

"That's because she hadn't met me." The count grinned.

"Will she give you money?" That was the key thing.

"She doesn't have to. I only need her to stand surety for a loan. A large loan, but I'm sure she'll do it."

The widow wasn't so easy to persuade. After three days, the count was getting the same expression he had while pretending to like Vrouw Belsen. He'd been spending a lot of time at the Melchor mansion—Anton was already familiar with the stables and had made friends with the cook, who fed him pastries and was teaching him how to talk like a Zeelunder. It wasn't so different from Olvisyan, which Anton had picked up easily enough.

"The woman is much too suspicious," the count grumbled as they headed back to the lodging house one evening. "She's been flattered by so many men for so long and they're all after her money, so she thinks I'm just like them."

"She's right," Anton said.

The count thwacked him on the head for that, but not very hard.

"What if I'm losing my touch?" the count asked. "First the princess; now this old woman. Where will it end?"

"What does she want?" Anton asked. "What does she want from you so she'll help you with your loan?"

"That's the problem," the count said heavily. "Marriage."

"But you're already married."

"Yes. Though that needn't stop me, since I'm not using my real name. You'll keep your mouth shut, won't you?" He glared at Anton.

"I won't say a word."

"On the bright side, if I marry her, I won't need a loan."

"She'll let you have her money?"

"I'm sure she will."

Anton hoped it would be soon enough to get Cid back. That was all he thought about right now.

It was all the count thought about too. As soon as the widow Melchor accepted his proposal of marriage, she gave him enough money to get his horse back as a kind of engagement gift.

Anton was overjoyed, and spent the next few days in the stables grooming Cid and talking to him and enjoying the feeling of all being together again. The count didn't feel quite like family, but the horses sure did.

After that, it didn't take long to arrange the marriage. The count wasn't entirely happy. "She's got her money all tied up in trusts," he groused. "She wants to give me an allowance, and it won't be enough to do anything."

"What about her businesses?" Anton wondered. "Won't she want your help with those? You can make your own money that way."

"I don't know anything about business." The count frowned. Then his face brightened. "But wait. You're right. You're a genius, Kronek."

And he was off, leaving Anton wondering what was so great about his idea. He didn't know much about business either, except his father had done well enough at it.

So the count and the widow were married. The best part was that Anton got to move into her mansion too. The stables were full of beautiful horses, and the cook was trying to fatten him up. It wasn't really working, since Anton kept getting taller, but that was a good thing. He decided he wouldn't mind staying in Zeelund a little longer. Hopefully the war wouldn't be over before he and the count could get back to Kronland.

BRAEDEN

There was no argument when Braeden decided to find a place for Janna and Iryna to live until after the baby was born. Once they neared Kersenstadt, he asked for and received permission to ride ahead of the army, leaving Janna under Senta's and Dr. Toure's watchful eyes.

Janna was poorly after Tomescu's attack, and Doctor Toure had been firm with Braeden. "She cannot have another shock like this," she said. "As it is, she was lucky not to lose this one. She must have rest and quiet. Soon it will be cold, and that will do her no good either."

Braeden liked what he saw. Though not a capital city, Kersenstadt was large and important. As he rode up to the main gate, Braeden cast a critical eye at the fortifications. They appeared to be in excellent repair and of the latest design. Mattila had already taken care to garrison the city, so the walls were manned by troops accustomed to Zastwar border duty. In other words, they knew what they were about and Braeden could feel certain that Janna and Iryna would be safe here.

Located where the borders of Tirilis, Lantura and Arcius met, Kersenstadt stood comfortingly near Olvisya and far from Arryk Roussay's armies. It was unlikely in the extreme that this city would be threatened by the enemy. And even if it was, there was almost no chance of it being taken. By the time Mattila left, all cellars and warehouses would be filled to bursting. Braeden would see that Janna had plenty of money so she could get the best of everything, no matter what happened.

He followed Doctor Toure's instructions and found the practice of the doctor she'd recommended. A pale, serious-looking young man, Alen Marsel had already received Braeden's letter and said he'd heard from Doctor Toure as well. Marsel seemed to be a bit in awe of her. "She's an extraordinary doctor. I'm honored that she'd trust me with your wife's care. Will she live nearby? Most of my patients are in this part of the city so I can reach them within minutes if needed."

So Braeden had Doctor Marsel direct him to the offices of a wealthy property owner. When he explained what he needed, she smiled. "I have a place in mind, if you can afford it."

"Let's take a look then," Braeden said, and followed her out. It wasn't far, just down a street or two from the prosperous commercial district. "Will it be noisy?' he wondered.

The landlady shook her head. "Most traffic stays on the main road. It's all homes here, and they are all occupied by quiet, well-established people. No young rowdies or students."

She unlocked a heavy oak door and Braeden followed her in. It belonged to a tall stone house with mullioned windows. Janna would like this. Very pretty.

The interior was even better. "The house is old," the landlady explained. "But I modernized it when I bought it ten years ago. I put in new floors, glass in all the windows, fireplaces or stoves in the main rooms and installed a water pump directly inside the kitchen. You'll want three or four servants to help run it."

"Do you know where I might find a good cook and a few maids? Oh, and a big ugly fellow for the front door," Braeden asked. "We'll also need a nurse for our little girl."

"Certainly. Just give me a few days. Quite the proper little family you've got," the woman said, looking Braeden over as if she didn't expect that from him.

"Quite." He smiled wistfully, wishing he didn't have to leave them here.

The house was comfortably furnished with modern furniture and thick carpets. It would be warm and dry here, even during the worst winter storms. He expected it to be expensive, but the high rent took him aback. Still, he would feel good about leaving his girls here, in comfort and behind a stout door.

In the end, he negotiated a lower price by agreeing to lease it for two years. It would be at least six months before the baby was born and he wanted it to be a bit bigger before going back on campaign. And besides, at this rate, there might be another baby before the lease was up. Leaving the landlady to hire help, he hurried back to Janna.

The weather had turned bad and the city wasn't big enough to quarter the whole army. Most of Mattila's vast host had to camp outside the city and conditions in the tents were miserable. It was a relief to bring Janna and Iryna back inside the walls.

Janna was as pleased as he'd hoped she'd be. "It's beautiful," she said. "I wish you could stay here with us."

"We might be close by for a while. I'll come visit when I can." He took Iryna up to the well-equipped nursery and handed her off to the nurse who was already there. Birgid was a kindly-looking older woman and Janna didn't seem to mind leaving Iryna with her. Braeden was pleased; the landlady had done well.

After showing her the rest of the house, he sat her down in the little front parlor where someone had lit a fire in the grate. Rain drummed against the windows and wind rattled the panes, but it was warm in there.

"Now to business," he said. "I don't want you to have to worry about much and I'll take care of what I can, but I still want you to know what to do in case I can't come as often as I'd like. Tomorrow, we'll visit my factor here. The house is paid for and he'll pay the servants every month. You'll get an allowance for expenses, though you can always ask for more if you want anything special. I'm sure I haven't thought of everything you might need. You'll meet the doctor too, before I go, and he'll stop in often. He seems reliable enough and Doctor Toure speaks highly of him."

"It all sounds so expensive," Janna said.

"It is, but I don't want you to worry. I've done well on this campaign, and before I met you, I wasn't spending that much. I've got some tucked away in Zeelund too, just in case."

"Thank you for taking such marvelous care of me." She stood up smiling, and pulled him to his feet. "Do you suppose we have time to inspect the bedroom once more before supper?"

TEODORA

It was annoying that Natalya had left Galladium, traveled across all of Kronland and entered Atlona with none of Teodora's agents knowing about it, but it wasn't unexpected. Teodora sent for Livilla as soon as she heard.

They had both known Natalya since she first came to study with Livilla and were on friendly terms with her. Teodora didn't begrudge Natalya her early success overmuch. Rumor said her appointment as Maxima came about because she had seduced that horrid Gauvain Brevard, but Teodora appreciated a woman who knew how to get what she wanted.

"Your Highness." Natalya sank into a graceful curtsy. "Thank you for your kind invitation. Of course I'll stay with you."

The moment Teodora had heard that Natalya was in the city, she'd sent an official invitation to be her guest at the Palais Arden. The messenger said she was staying at a plain but respectable inn, arriving in a hired coach with very little baggage.

All the same, she looked perfect. Her Maxima's robes were spotlessly white, uncreased, and somehow appeared more stylish than the usual. Instead of the long braid most Maximas affected, Natalya wore her straight chestnut hair unbound, so it fell to her knees in a shimmering ripple. Teodora felt a pang of envy and was glad that Demario wasn't here. She had a feeling that Natalya was just the type he'd like, and she was so much younger than Teodora.

"You should have let me know you were coming," Teodora said, taking Natalya by the hand and leading her to a group of chairs in the corner of her library. "You should enter Atlona with all the pomp befitting your station."

"I'm sorry to surprise you like this, but I come on a mission of considerable delicacy. It's better that no one knows I'm here."

"Goodness, that sounds ominous." Teodora hoped she wasn't bringing awful tidings of some sort.

226

"Nothing ominous for you." Natalya smiled. "But several people in the Maladene court would be unhappy with this visit."

"Fools, the lot of them." Teodora sniffed. "Still, I suppose you need to keep them sweet." She didn't mind if Maladena occupied Galladium on its southern borders to keep it distracted from Kronland, but of course she would never say so. "Isn't King Gauvain on the verge of marriage to the Enfanta Johanna?"

"He was. But the Enfanta is ill and not expected to recover."

"Poor Beatryz. Her only daughter."

"Yes, it's quite a blow for her personally, but also for the hopes of peace between our countries. We must come to some other arrangement. But the Enfanta's imminent death creates a different opportunity."

Teodora cocked her head and said nothing, though she felt a thrill of expectation. She could think of an excellent solution.

"King Gauvain would like to make a formal offer for the hand of the Archduchess Zofya."

"Zofya? She's just twelve." Teodora hid her disappointment. "Why not Elektra? She's nearly old enough and my heir."

"That's why it can't be Elektra." Natalya's tone was sympathetic but firm. She no doubt understood Teodora's hopes. "The Queen of Galladium cannot also be the Olvisyan Empress. It would create the same entanglement that caused the break with Maladena in the first place."

"I'm sure that might have been avoided, had it been handled properly." Teodora would not let this go easily.

"Perhaps." Natalya shrugged. "But I won't put it to the test just now. And you must admit it's an excellent opportunity for a second daughter."

"Oh, it is." Teodora settled back into her chair. "You just caught me a bit off guard. King Gauvain would still benefit from a match with some other Maladene princess. Why is he looking to us instead?"

"Only one reason." Natalya's eyes narrowed and her tone intensified. "Kendryk Bernotas. If the king marries your daughter, you will release Kendryk into the protection of Galladium."

Teodora was stunned speechless for a moment. It had never occurred to her that Kendryk would be part of any deal. She tried to slow her breathing and consider the proposal, all the while making sure her face didn't change expression.

It would be an excellent arrangement for Zofya, though it was annoying that Elektra remained on the table. And Kendryk had turned out to be a worthless hostage. The best she could do now was use him to make another deal that might

227

help her. But she feared squandering some future, better opportunity. "I'll have to consider this carefully," she finally ventured, hoping Livilla got here soon.

Natalya smiled. "That's all right. I expected the offer would be a surprise. King Gauvain and Prince Kendryk have been close since they were little boys. He considers him his dearest friend and would do anything to see him released. We realize of course that Zofya is still too young, but we can arrange a formal betrothal now and she will come to Galladium in four or five years."

Teodora nodded and smiled, trying to remember what her youngest daughter looked like. With any luck, she'd be more promising than Elektra. But it would still be hard to compete with Natalya.

"She will be young," Natalya went on. "But King Gauvain is kind and will make a good husband. You needn't worry about that. Besides, I will take a personal interest in her to make sure she settles in well."

Teodora didn't care what kind of husband the king made, but Natalya seemed to think it should matter to her as a mother, so she nodded again. Mercifully, Livilla arrived at last.

After the greetings were over, Natalya repeated the offer.

Livilla looked thoughtful. "How touching," she said. "The king must care for Kendryk a great deal."

"Oh, he does."

"I'm afraid it's impossible my dear. Though I'm sure Teodora has already told you."

"We didn't get quite that far," Natalya said, looking calm in the face of this categorical refusal of her offer.

"I hate to see Zofya not get this opportunity," Teodora said. She had to confess that the idea of being mother to the Galladian queen was a thrilling one.

"I agree," Livilla said. "And we can still come to an agreement. This is what I propose. It is impossible for us to exchange Kendryk Bernotas for anyone less than the heretic Edric Landrus. In addition, Kendryk's brother-in-law threatens our borders. We would require Duchess Larisa Karsten to join us in Atlona as our honored guest, held as surety for King Arryk's good behavior. Once he and his armies have returned to Norovaea, his allies have disbanded and Norovaea signs a peace treaty with the empire, Duchess Karsten will return home. Edric will of course need to submit to the sentence he has so far avoided."

"Both of those are beyond my ability to grant, though I can assure you that Princess Gwynneth would never turn over Edric in exchange for her husband." Natalya's voice was calm, though her eyes hardened.

"I find that very curious," Teodora said. "They seemed devoted to each other when I saw them."

"Oh, they are," Natalya said. "It's because of that devotion the princess has refused to turn Edric over. Prince Kendryk made her swear not to do so under any circumstances, and the princess takes her oaths very seriously."

"Gods, he's such a tiresome little fanatic," Teodora burst out, annoyed that Kendryk had been a step ahead of her in this.

Natalya smiled. "Perhaps. But I'm afraid if you cannot release him then a marriage between your daughter and the king will be impossible."

"I was thinking of a compromise," Livilla said, shooting Teodora a glance she knew meant she should hold her tongue. "What if the conditions under which Kendryk is imprisoned were drastically improved?"

"I assume he currently resides in the Arnfels dungeon," Natalya said, her eyes grave.

"He does. And he would have to stay within the bounds of the fortress. But he can be made much more comfortable, given his own rooms, servants, books. He could even receive visitors, within reason."

Teodora's hands clenched the arms of her chair. She wasn't sure she could bear to see Kendryk live in comfort after all he had put her through.

"That's a start, but not enough. I can't counter with a smaller part of the king than I first offered," Natalya said.

"Of course." Livilla nodded. "But we haven't yet discussed the matter of the Archduchess Zofya's dowry. In light of the circumstances, it might be considerably augmented."

Natalya leaned forward. "What do you have in mind?"

"The Dallmaring Provinces."

Teodora couldn't hold back a gasp, and Natalya was unable to hide her shock either. "All four of them?"

Livilla nodded.

"Granted to Galladium in perpetuity?"

Livilla nodded again and shot Teodora another glance before she could protest. "Just consider it my dear," she said quickly. "They are tiny, their people have never embraced the rule of the empire and they've created trouble with Galladium for a hundred years. Just think of how popular Zofya will be, bringing them with her."

Teodora had once visited the Dallmarings and was impressed only by their forbidding mountains and brutish peasant population. Those peasants revolted regularly and even though Teodora had ordered thousands executed after the last uprising, there were already rumors of more trouble. Turning them into Gauvain and Natalya's headache while Zofya became Galladian queen seemed a reasonable proposition. "All right," she said.

"Devolution must begin at once," Natalya said. "It will be finalized upon consummation of the marriage. But yes, this is something I can agree to. The king will be displeased that I haven't returned with his friend, but he will be happy about Dallmaring. I have authority to sign on the king's behalf and will want this drawn up formally before I go. And there's one more thing."

"What?" Teodora asked, hoping she wasn't making a terrible mistake.

"I want Prince Kendryk moved out of the dungeon today. Then I wish to see him in his new quarters and speak to him alone."

KENDRYK

Kendryk squinted against the light as it flooded his cell. He sat up on the stone bench, but didn't stand. He wasn't sure he could.

"Come along now," a guard said, hauling him to his feet. "Your life's about to get better, lucky sod."

Kendryk wondered if that meant he was finally being beheaded. At this point, he considered that an improvement in his circumstances. He swayed and took a small step. Someone grabbed him by the other arm and he stumbled out of the cell. If he was to go to the scaffold, he'd need some of his strength back. It would be too humiliating to have to be carried to the executioner.

He was dragged up a few flights of stairs, deposited in a room, then left alone. He looked around. The room was light and clean with several sturdy pieces of furniture. A chilly breeze blew in between the bars of the window and the sky outside was gray. The door opened again and a skinny young woman carrying a tray scurried in.

She stared at Kendryk like he was some sort of monster, dropped the tray on the table beside him with a clatter and said, "You're to eat this before the doctor arrives." Then she scurried back out, the door falling shut behind her.

Kendryk waited to hear the sound of the lock turning, but there was nothing but the wind. If he walked out right now he wondered how far he would get before collapsing. Not far enough. And then what? He was inside the Arnfels, inside Atlona's massive walls, deep in the Empire. No friends for hundreds of leagues around.

The tray held a steaming bowl of broth, a few slices of fine white bread and a glass of very watery red wine. Perhaps they meant for him to mount the block on his own strength. He sipped the hot broth carefully. It tasted marvelous. He hadn't had real food in so long. He devoured the bread and wine and wanted more, but only until the nausea hit. Then he felt so weak he had to lay his head on the table.

He stayed that way for a while until the nausea subsided. When he lifted his head, the door was opening.

Sybila came in, beaming. "Good, you could eat."

Kendryk tried to smile back but wasn't sure he'd succeeded. He hadn't smiled in a long time.

She sat down across from him. "I suppose no one has told you anything."

He shook his head.

"For once I get to bring you some good news. A powerful friend of yours is with the empress right now and has secured a great improvement in your circumstances. As we speak, rooms in the castle proper are being prepared for you and you will move into them shortly."

"Rooms?" This made no sense at all.

"Yes. You will receive an apartment of your own, and several servants. You will have access to the garden and castle library and be able to receive visitors."

"I don't understand," Kendryk said, his mind whirling. He had only one friend powerful enough to manage this, but try as he might, he couldn't picture Gauvain Brevard having tea with the empress.

Sybila was no help. "I don't know who changed the empress's mind, though you'll find out soon enough. Your friend wishes to visit you and I must make you presentable."

"That ought to take a while."

"It's not as bad as you think. I want to make sure your health is good, and then I'll help you with a bath. We'll get someone in to shave you and I've already arranged for some suitable clothes to be sent up here."

Kendryk let Sybila take care of everything. He felt like a little boy whose nurse was getting him ready for bed. It was nice. A guard bearing clothes arrived before he was out of the bath. Right after that came a barber, who scraped off the patchy beard he'd grown and cut off all of his by now very long, lice-infested hair.

Somehow, Sybila had found a suit that fit him reasonably well. It was about a generation out of date, but looked better than anything he'd worn since he got here.

"You'll have nicer clothes soon," she said. "A tailor will visit you tomorrow. I imagine you can order some warm things, since winter is coming."

"How long have I been here?" Kendryk had given up keeping track of days and months long ago.

"Nearly two years." Sybila's voice softened.

"Gods. I'm almost twenty-four then." Thinking of how much older his children were by now made him want to cry.

Sybila laid a comforting hand on his shoulder. "Goodness. You really were as young as you looked. When I first saw you, I worried that Teodora got the wrong fellow and almost murdered a child."

"Not a child. But not old enough to know better."

"Her Highness is hard enough on you. Be kind to yourself at least. Now come, we must get you upstairs."

That took some doing. Even though Kendryk's new rooms were on the second floor of the castle, it took many flights of stairs to reach them from the dungeon. Sybila made him drink another bowl of broth before starting, but he still thought he would collapse before reaching his destination. He was so tired he barely registered the pleasant surroundings.

Sybila bundled him into a soft chair facing a warm fire. "You're sweating right now, but it's cold. I can't have you catching a chill after all of this."

She sat on a footstool and rubbed his icy hands between hers. "Rest here for a few hours and I'll tell them down at the palace that you can receive your visitor tonight. It will take a while to get your strength up, but I've ordered light meals sent up often and I want you to eat everything, even if you don't feel like it. If there's something you want they can't get from the castle kitchen, send a servant to the inn at the bottom of the hill. They have an excellent cook. In fact, you'll probably want to get most of your meals from there once your appetite returns."

"I can't pay for all of this," Kendryk said weakly.

"Yes, you can. Your friend has arranged an allowance for you so you can buy whatever you need. Get some warm clothes, order whatever books you want and can't find in the castle library and treat yourself to some good wine. You might be here a while longer so you might as well make things pleasant for yourself. I'll check on you every few days."

"Thank you," Kendryk said, still not able to absorb all of the changes. Until he knew who was behind this, he remained uneasy. "Not just for today. But for keeping me alive and helping me not lose hope."

"I don't think I quite succeeded in that."

"Not all the time. But if I hadn't known my family was safe, I may well have given in to Teodora at a weak moment. I hope you don't get in trouble for that."

"Only if you tell her." Sybila patted his knee and stood. "I'll see you soon."

ANTON

Ice-skating was harder than it looked. All of the other children flew past him as if they had wings on their heels, even the little ones. Anton gritted his teeth and put one foot in front of the other. It had never taken him so long to learn anything. He stayed close to the edge of the canal and took tiny steps. It had looked like fun and he needed to get out of the house or the count's new wife would make him go to school. She didn't think a boy his age should spend all his time with horses.

"Why can't you skate?" someone asked and Anton looked up. A pretty girl with gold braids and apple-red cheeks was skating backwards in front of him.

"Not from here," Anton said, his teeth still clenched. He thought he might fall over if he relaxed. "No skating where I'm from."

"Where are you from?" The girl had cornflower blue eyes and kept skating backwards like it was nothing. She put both hands out. "Here, hold on to me. It's easier." She wore bright red mittens.

"Moralta," Anton said, grabbing onto her. "Though I've been in Kronland the last few years."

"How exciting. Why do you travel so much? Is your father a merchant?"

Anton could hardly breathe and talk and skate at the same time, but he gasped out, "War. Long story."

"War? That's even more exciting. Is it very dreadful? Have you killed anyone?" Then she laughed. "I'm sorry. My manners are terrible. I remember it's hard trying to talk while you're learning to skate. Let's go sit over here." And she dragged Anton off the ice and onto a bench next to the canal. "Take your skates off." Hers came off in a flash. "We'll get something warm to drink. Then you can tell me about the war."

Anton nodded. A hot drink sounded good. His nose was cold and starting to drip. He got his skates off, tied them together and threw them over his shoulder like he saw the others doing. The girl grabbed him by the hand again and pulled him along with her. "Do you like chocolate?"

"I do," Anton said.

"Have you ever had it hot?"

"No. Is it good?"

"Divine. I'll get you some. My treat. Oh, there's Peter!" She waved at a tall good-looking boy with a friendly face and gold curls. Anton hated him until the girl said, "This is my brother Peter, and I'm Gretel. What's your name?"

Peter laughed and said, "Slow down Gretel. Let's get the man a hot chocolate before you question him some more."

Anton liked him very much for calling him a man, so he smiled at Peter. "I'm Anton. Anton Kronek."

"Ooh, you even have a Moraltan name." Gretel stood at the counter of a brightly painted market stall next to them and somehow stopped talking long enough to order three hot chocolates. "He's going to tell us all about being in the wars in Kronland."

That brought Peter up short. "You've been in the war? Like a soldier?"

Anton nodded. "I'm not a real soldier yet. But I'm a page to a cavalry general and I have my own horse."

"You have a horse?" Gretel handed him a large blue mug full of steaming liquid with what looked like cream on top. "Be careful, it's hot."

Anton let the mug warm his hands. "King Arryk of Norovaea gave me the horse." He couldn't help bragging just a little, with Gretel's bright blue eyes fixed on him. "But that's a long story too."

"I want to hear it," Peter said.

"I want to see this horse," Gretel said.

"Why don't we do both? I'll tell you the story while we drink our chocolate and then I'll take you to see my horse. You can meet the general's battle charger too."

"That sounds much better than ice-skating," Peter said, yelping as he tried to drink his chocolate too fast and burned his tongue.

Anton let his cool off more and told about how he helped with the big guns before the second battle of Birkenfels. When he took a few sips of his chocolate, he nearly forgot what he was talking about. He'd never tasted anything so good.

Gretel poked Anton's arm. "So what happened to the girl? The one who was supposed to be helping the general?"

"She died," Anton said, finishing his drink. "She got scared, hung back and the rank she was in got hit by the other side's big guns and that was it."

"How dreadful. Were you very sad?" Gretel's eyes were like saucers.

Anton shrugged. "Didn't really know her. A little bit sad, I suppose."

"What do your parents think about all of this?" Peter asked. "I would love to go soldiering, but my father would never allow it."

"My parents are dead."

"Oh, how dreadful!" Gretel looked like she was about to cry. "What happened?"

Anton didn't want to talk about it, but also didn't want to be rude. "My father was hanged for a rebel in Kaleva."

"Was he a rebel?" Peter wanted to know.

"He was just a Moraltan patriot. He was only called a rebel because the Moraltans lost the war."

"It's always bad to lose a war," Gretel said, looking wise.

"Yes, it is."

"What about your mother?" Gretel grabbed Anton and Peter's empty mugs and put them back on the counter of the stall, all without ever taking her eyes off Anton.

"My real mother died when I was little, and then I got another. But Marjatyan soldiers killed her a few years back."

"Oh, how dreadful," Gretel whispered. "But you survived and now you work for a general and got a horse from a king."

"I'll tell you about that while we walk," Anton said. He was getting cold. It wasn't too far to the Melchor mansion and Peter and Gretel were impressed by the size of the stables. They lived nearby, in the same nice neighborhood, but it sounded like their house wasn't as big and didn't have a stable. "We won't be here long," Anton said, though now he wished that wasn't true. "As soon as the count raises enough money to buy another army, we'll leave."

"I hope that won't be too soon," Gretel said, while Skandar nuzzled her cheek.

GWYNNETH

"Your Grace, please understand. I can't think of anything more important for Norovaea right now than having you here." Norvel Classen mopped his forehead. He'd lost a considerable amount of weight since Gwynneth last saw him, and it didn't suit him. She worried this job would kill him. "The work you've already done in captivating the members of the council is beyond price. Can you not give us a few more months?"

Gwynneth shook her head. "I am sorry. I know that things need attending to here, but I must go to Estenor, and soon. Arryk must assume his responsibilities here and he can do that only if he's freed up in Kronland. The fastest way to do that is to get Estenor involved."

"If you can. Estenor is so tied up in Sanova, Lennart will need years to extricate himself."

"If he wants to keep fighting." Gwynneth leaned back in her chair. "But there is another way. Raysa Sikora is old enough to marry. Why shouldn't she marry Lennart? It would end the war at once."

"You make it sound simple. It's anything but. Lennart is always looking to the west while the Sikoras look east. I'm sure he'd prefer a princess of Anglana."

"He hasn't been able to get one though, has he? And he's got to be at least thirty and in need of an heir, with his cousins practically slavering at the mouth whenever they see the throne. I know the Sikoras are hoping for a match with Briansk, but that hasn't materialized either. Why should they waste all of this time and money fighting each other when there's such an easy solution in sight?"

"Why indeed?" Classen chuckled. "Well, there's no better person for persuading them all to come to their senses than you. I do wish you luck, even though I don't want you to go."

"I'll ask Aksel to help you once I'm gone," Gwynneth said. "Perhaps he'll see reason."

"It's the opposite of reason, Gwynn." Aksel was in full protest mode. She'd waylaid him as he left his laboratory so he wouldn't still be distracted by his work. "I can't do this sort of thing."

"Only because you keep telling yourself that." She took his arm and walked him to a bench at a window overlooking the gardens. With snow covering all of the great evergreen trees and hedges, she'd always thought they were most beautiful in winter. She pulled Aksel down on the bench next to her. "You are perfectly capable of doing this. You're not interested, I know. This isn't how you want to spend your time. But neither does Arryk."

"Arryk is doing what he's always loved," Aksel huffed.

"It appears that way, but in reality, he spends his days at a desk, checking requisition forms, mediating disputes between squabbling officers and writing letters. Battles are few and far between. We all do what we have to."

"So you feel I'm not pulling my weight?" Aksel turned his best wounded look on her. It had sometimes worked when he was a little boy, but it didn't work now.

"You're not. You're a Roussay prince, second in line to the throne. The king is fighting overseas and I'm helping him. You must do your part. You aren't the only person who doesn't get the vocation he'd like. Do you think Kendryk wanted to be a ruler? He never did. But it was his duty and he took it on and did well."

Aksel rolled his eyes. "I rather think of Kendryk as a cautionary tale, not someone I should emulate."

Gwynneth wanted to slap him for that, but that wouldn't improve matters. "Kendryk's situation has nothing to do with his abilities. The fact remains that we need your help. Please. The nobles of the council won't listen to Norvel Classen. He's not one of them. But they will listen to you."

"They'll never take me seriously."

"They will if you're serious. Everyone knows you're intelligent and if you apply that intelligence to matters of state no one will be surprised to find you capable. Try it, please? If my mission to Estenor succeeds, Arryk will be home within months. Can you at least try that long?"

Aksel drummed his fingers on his leg and stared out the window. "I don't have the slightest clue how to get started," he finally said.

"I'll help you. I'll put my departure off for a few more weeks though I hate to miss this window of fine weather to sail. But I'll do it if it means you'll help."

"What must I do?"

"We'll start tomorrow. We'll meet with Classen and he can show you what he's working on. There are a number of things he hasn't been able to deal with because he needs someone from the family to do them. I've done what I can, but I'm leaving. You needn't worry. He's very capable and organized, so you'll just have to decide on matters he's already looked into. Oh, and you should spend time with the council."

"They don't need the king to help them conduct their business."

"No, they don't. But it's encouraging to them if you take an interest. And you must continue to lobby for support for Arryk. The nobility no longer want to pay taxes to fund the war. You must make them change their minds."

"I don't know how to do any of that."

"I've already softened them up, so I'll take you along and show you what I do. It's quite simple. They'll be very grateful for any bit of attention from you. You mustn't forget that the king's favor is all some of these people live for. If you show them that favor, you can make a lot of friends."

"Will they expect something from me?"

"Nothing but a smile and a bit of conversation."

"Ugh," Aksel said. "I hate the idea. But I'll try."

ARRYK

Arryk received Gwynneth's letter with a sense of foreboding. She had sent it before leaving Norovaea for Estenor.

"The nobles refuse to pay further taxes," Gwynneth wrote. *"They are tired of funding an army they say brings no benefit to Norovaea itself. While I was in Arenberg, I threw several parties and invited everyone of note. I thanked them for their help with our cause and assured them they will benefit when the empress's power is checked, once and for all. Aksel has promised to take a more active role, but he can't take your place.*

"We must wrap this matter up as quickly as possible so you can come home and put things in order. Which brings me to an interesting bit of information I recently received. Brynhild Mattila has just left Kersenstadt and is marching north, probably to winter in Isenwald so she is in a better position to face you in the spring. Mattila has turned Kersenstadt into an enormous materiel depot to support her rear. She's packed the city with all manner of foodstuffs along with vast amounts of powder, shot and weapons of all kinds.

"I didn't receive details, though I'm sure she left it well-guarded. Still, perhaps you can find a way to get your hands on it. I'd love to help, but I doubt I'll return before spring. The weather is terrible and I'm having trouble getting a ship to take me to Estenor. I won't be able to return to Kronland until the weather improves."

Arryk was on his own. He tried to push the troublesome news about Norovaea to the back of his mind. He was grateful for whatever Gwynneth accomplished while she was there and hoped it would be enough. For the thousandth time he wondered how he might persuade her to take the throne. It was obvious she had a much better understanding of what needed to be done.

He turned his thoughts back to Kersenstadt. He needed what was inside that city and needed it badly. So far he'd been able to keep the goodwill of his allies by spending large amounts of coin. It was bad enough for the people here that soldiers lived in their houses through the winter, but much grumbling was averted when all was paid for. He couldn't keep it up and didn't need Norovaean aristocrats to tell him that. He needed to survive the winter and defeat Mattila in the spring. That would be much easier if he got most of her supplies.

But the last part of the letter was the worst.

"I realize you don't want to," Gwynneth continued. *"But you must consider marriage. With Aksel so uninterested in politics, it's important you have an heir. Equally important, you need a consort who will be of help to you. The younger daughter of the King of Anglana is of marriageable age and by all accounts, has a good head on her shoulders. Classen is putting out feelers, though of course nothing will happen without your consent. Just start thinking about it. It's important."*

Arryk laid the letter down and stared at the wall. He wouldn't do it. He'd always understood that someone in his position would have to make a politically advantageous match, but he'd never faced the reality of it.

"Why the long face?" Larisa came in, rosy-cheeked from the cold and sprawled in a chair across from him.

There was no point in pretending. "Gwynneth and Classen think I should marry."

"They're probably right."

"Not you too. You know I can't even consider it."

"Do they have someone in mind?"

"Some little princess from Anglana. I'm sure I'll hate her."

"You might not love her, but you don't have to hate her."

"But what happens to us if I marry?" He had to force the words out.

Larisa looked grave. "I've tried not to think about it."

"I don't suppose you'd settle for being an official mistress of sorts?" Arryk felt bad asking, but he had to know. A political marriage might be tolerable if he had Larisa anyway.

"I can't." Larisa's voice shook a little. She stopped and took a deep breath. "I've always known you can't marry me, but I hoped when the time came, I could let you go. I must, but I don't want to. The only thing worse though, is being your mistress. What I am now is tolerable, but I believe that marriage is sacred and I won't do that to another woman, no matter how much you dislike her. Right now, away from court, we can be quiet and informal about it. But in Arenberg, it will be different. I'm sorry."

This was worse than anything he'd imagined and it took Arryk a moment to find his voice. "But surely, we could work something out. It's bad enough I have to marry a stranger, but I can't bear losing you too."

"I would do anything to make it easier for you, but not at the cost of my self-respect. I can't do it."

They were both silent for a moment.

Then Arryk said. "So marry me. Marry me now before anyone arranges something else."

"I can't. You know we can't."

"Of course we can. I'm the king and if I can't do what I want in this matter, what can I do?"

"Be reasonable?"

"Never." Arryk smiled at her until she smiled back. "What do you say? We'll do it soon and keep it quiet for now."

"It will cause a lot of trouble."

"Not as much trouble as forcing me to marry some princess I don't like."

"I feel like I should say no."

"Please say yes," Arryk said. "Please. I want this more than anything." To his surprise, he realized it was true.

BRAEDEN

They spent a few happy weeks in Kersenstadt. Braeden had little to do, since the weather was too wet for much drilling, and Mattila was busy filling the city with everything she needed for a long campaign against Arryk. If numbers were roughly equal, the better-supplied army would come out ahead, and she intended to be better-supplied.

Arryk had an advantage, with most of Kronland behind him, and much of it as yet untouched by fighting. Through the Kronland rulers, he would have access to nearly unlimited funds, arms and soldiers. All of that meant nothing if he didn't deploy them efficiently and that was where Mattila would outdo him. She took her time and Braeden took advantage of that time.

Now that Janna wasn't jolting along in a wagon every day, she felt much better. She and Braeden went out most days to explore the city. Braeden made sure she became well-acquainted with his factor and paid a social call on the landlady, who served them coffee in a house about half as big and fine as theirs. He would have liked for her to have friends her own age, but she got on well with Iryna's nurse Birgid, and seemed quite content.

"I don't need to spend a lot of time with people, except for you," Janna said, leaning back in a stuffed leather chair, her feet on Braeden's lap. They had taken advantage of a dry day to climb the city wall so he could point out how well-built it was.

"You're right, " she had said, though he suspected she was humoring him. "I feel very safe. I can't imagine any Norovaeans ever getting in here."

"If we do our jobs, they won't come within a hundred leagues," Braeden said.

The day of Braeden's departure came too soon. It was clear Janna was trying to be brave, but it did no good. "I'm being ridiculous." She was fighting tears, and losing the battle. "But I'm so afraid. Not so much that something will happen to you, but that we won't see each other again."

"It might be a few months," Braeden said, feeling uneasy. He hated it when she said things like that.

"No, I mean ever. Something will happen and after you leave this house, you will never come back."

"Sweetheart," he said, sitting on the bed and pulling her onto his lap. "This isn't Kaleva and I'm not Dimir. I'm with an army that will win and you're inside one of the safest cities in the empire. It's normal to be frightened."

She nodded, wiping tears away with her sleeve. "I don't mean to carry on. I'll miss you dreadfully."

"I'll miss you too. But you'll write."

"I will. But you won't." She smiled through her tears.

"I'll try, but it won't be pretty." He read well enough, but his writing had never been good, especially not in Moraltan. He needed Franca to double-check his work.

"You don't have to. I'll know you're thinking of me."

"Oh, I will be. No question. But it'll be easier for me knowing you and the little ones are safe." He'd also made the doctor promise to send word if anything changed for the worse but didn't tell her that. He hoped to visit again before the baby was born. "Now I'd better say goodbye to my little mouse." He scooped Iryna off the floor and held her close. She put her chubby arms around his neck and planted a sloppy wet kiss on his cheek.

"Say goodbye to Papa," Janna said, her voice quavering.

"Bye-bye Papa," Iryna said. That was about half her vocabulary.

To Braeden's surprise, his voice failed him, so he kissed the little girl and handed her back to Janna while he swallowed hard and blinked a few times.

Janna gave Iryna to the nurse, then went downstairs with Braeden. Kazmir was saddled and waiting at the front door. Janna stroked Kazmir's nose then turned suddenly and clung to Braeden. "I know you have to go, but I don't want you to," she said, nearly choking on tears.

"I don't want to," he murmured into her hair. "I love you. I'll be back soon."

She walked with him to the end of the street where he mounted Kazmir and reached down to squeeze her hand one more time. He turned again before he was out of sight. She still stood in the street, looking small and fragile between the towering houses.

KENDRYK

Kendryk dozed in the cushioned chair, waking up once when a round-faced freckled girl brought him more of the white bread, some soft cheese and more watery wine.

"Wait," he said, before she darted out of the room. "What's your name?"

"Ulla," she said, a flush spreading over her face.

"Thank you, Ulla. Will you be working for me?"

"Yes, sir. Me and my brother Dolf."

"How nice. You can go now." He noticed she seemed frozen in place. He wondered if Atlona mothers were frightening their children with stories of the evil Prince Kendryk these days.

Ulla hurried out and Kendryk fell asleep after his meal. When he awoke again, it was dark outside and someone had drawn the heavy drapes and built up the fire again. A soft wool blanket covered his legs and he was warm and comfortable. He wondered if he should stand up and explore his new home, but didn't want to move.

From his chair, he saw the room's furnishings were cozy and luxurious, like those in an expensive inn. Right now, it felt more magnificent than Birkenhof. He just hoped he would be able to stay and that this wasn't some ploy of Teodora's.

There was a rustling at the door behind him and he heard Ulla's voice. Then the door opened. Kendryk stood up slowly and turned around. The light was dim and at first all he saw was a sweep of white robes and long dark hair. Then she stood before him.

"Natalya?" He went weak in the knees.

"Yes," she said, a laugh in her voice. "Sit, sit." And she quickly put an arm around his shoulder and pushed him back into his chair. She smelled heavenly.

There was more rustling and she pulled a chair close and sat down right across from him.

"You're even more beautiful than last time we met." He couldn't think of anything else to say. "No wonder Gauvain lost his mind."

"I'd return the compliment." She chuckled and took his hand. "But I'm afraid you look dreadful."

"You should have seen me earlier today. You have no idea."

Her eyes clouded over. "Was it terrible? Is your health all right?"

"Yes, and yes. I lost all hope and track of time. But I'm so disgustingly healthy I wasn't able to waste away at all like I'd hoped." He tried to keep his tone light, but a wobble still crept into his voice.

"Thank Ercos for that. Gwynneth was wild with fear that you'd catch some dreadful disease and just be gone."

That sounded promising. "So Gwynneth is well then? And the children?"

"All well. You have another little girl, Stella. She was born right after the siege ended. I've spent a great deal of time with Maryna who is a completely delightful child. It's too bad she'll inherit Terragand since she'd make a marvelous Maxima."

"How strange. I had a dream long ago about Gwynn being pregnant and knowing she was safe. What happened?"

Natalya told him all about his father-in-law's death and Arryk's belated invasion. When she told him about Gwynneth's new-found faith and her support for Edric Maximus, Kendryk nearly came out of his chair. "Now that's something I never expected. There was something about that in the dream too, but I didn't understand."

"I was surprised too. Gwynneth has always been so practical. But she sent one of your generals, Arian Orland, to take Edric all across Kronland to spread the new faith. Nearly every city in northern Kronland converted peacefully and Orland encouraged the others with a bit of violence. He's been defeated in the meantime and I'm not sure where he is now. But it no longer matters. The new faith has its own momentum. It's even infiltrated Brynhild Mattila's army to the point that Livilla Maxima has had to intervene."

Kendryk's head swam. All was not lost. In fact, it seemed things had carried on well without him. "This is wonderful news," he said. "Though I understand if you don't agree. I was so worried I'd ruined everything."

"On the contrary." Natalya smiled. "You set something very important in motion. I had the chance to spend time with Edric Maximus and he's full of regret for what's happened to you. He explained about the prophecy and worried he'd made some terrible mistake in interpretation, which caused you to lose everything. But I read over it with him, and I'm sure he's right. I think it likely you are the ruler that was foreseen. There's a possibility it's King Lennart of Estenor, but I don't know enough about him. Gwynneth is going to see him right now so perhaps we'll know more soon."

"Wait. What? What is Gwynneth doing?"

"She's gone to Estenor to treat with Lennart and bring him into the fight on your side. That's why I spent so much time with Maryna. She and Gwynneth came to Allaux, and from there, Gwynneth left for Zeelund where she took ship for Estenor. I took Maryna back with me and returned her to her Uncle Arryk who's settling into winter quarters in Fromenberg. It gave me a chance to meet with Edric Maximus on the way. It seems he and Maryna are already great friends."

"Yes, she's always loved him." Kendryk smiled. "And it seems the lot of you have been very busy. It's annoying not to be able to help."

"I understand. I came here intending to free you, but Teodora and Livilla are too stubborn. Unfortunately, this was the best I could do for now."

"It's enough," Kendryk said. "I don't know how to thank you and Gauvain. I hope he didn't have to give up to much."

"He must marry Teodora's youngest daughter in a few years, but it doesn't matter to him. It was always going to be a princess he didn't know. And she's coming with the Dallmaring Provinces, so Gauvain will be pleased. He'll be disappointed that I didn't free you, though I swear to you I tried."

"You did brilliantly. I'm amazed Teodora gave up Dallmaring."

"It was Livilla. She rather walked all over Teodora, much to my surprise. Something seems to have knocked the stuffing out of her."

"Perhaps it's Arryk sitting so close to her borders."

"Maybe. If it were any other woman, I'd say she's troubled over a man. In any event, she's not quite herself."

"Can't say I'm sorry."

"Well, she might come visit you and take out her bad mood on you. Don't let her discourage you. She can't send you back to the dungeon."

"She can't? I confess I'm a little worried she'll do just that the minute you leave."

"Oh no. I'll be checking on you. You can expect to see someone from the Galladian court or military every few months. They will visit you and make sure all is well. Teodora won't know who they are or when they're coming, so she can't play any games."

"You really don't trust her, do you?" Relief washed over Kendryk.

"I don't trust anyone." Natalya's beautiful eyes hardened. "It's bad enough she won't let you go when there's no chance she'll get her hands on Edric now. I refuse to allow her to go back on our deal in the tiniest way."

"You are more than a match for her it seems."

"I try."

ANTON

"This is taking much too long. I must be back in the field before spring, or the war will be over." Count Orland finished off the tankard and slammed it on the table. He and Anton sat in the kitchen of the Melchor mansion after everyone else had gone to bed. Anton poured more beer for the count and topped off his own mug.

Anton said nothing and sipped his drink. When the count was in one of these moods, he just wanted to talk.

"I must get some of that money. It's maddening. Thousands of gulden pass through the ledgers every day and I can't get my hands on a single one. There are two more ships coming in this week, weighed down with silk and spices. A fortune right there and I can't touch it. Their cargo is sold and the money already tucked away in Kamyla's trusts."

"How can the cargo be sold already? I'd want to see what I was buying."

"They get letters from the ship's captains when they first set sail from Indium. It takes months for the ships to arrive and in the meantime everyone here has already decided what they want to buy."

"What if the ship sinks? Or pirates attack?"

"That's what insurance is for."

Anton didn't understand that. But he thought of something else. "What keeps the captains from just selling everything on the ships before they get here and taking the money for themselves?"

The count stared at Anton. "It's a crime, for one thing. They could never come back here again. And I suppose honest sorts wouldn't even dream of it in the first place.

Anton wondered if the fact he'd thought of it meant he wasn't an honest sort.

"Kronek, I knew you were a genius. You've given me the most splendid idea." The count stood up, swaying a little. "We're leaving. We'll take the horses and everything we can carry. I'll wrap up my affairs, such as they are, and we'll head out this time tomorrow night. Say your goodbyes to your friends, but don't tell them where we're going."

"I can't. I don't know where we're going," Anton said, bewildered, then thought of Gretel and Peter.

"So much the better. Hey, what's this? Why the long face?" The count threw back his head and laughed. "It's that little blonde I've seen around the stables, isn't it? I don't blame you. At your age, I would have been wild about her too. Well, there'll be plenty others."

"I don't want any others," Anton said sullenly. He was excited at the idea of adventure, but leaving Peter and Gretel made his heart hurt just a little. They'd been having so much fun together. Anton had even won a short ice-skating race and Gretel had learned to ride Skandar. He didn't want all that to end.

"Of course you don't. The girl in front of you is always the best one in the world. Until you meet the next one. You'll see."

Anton didn't believe him. He'd met quite a few girls already and knew for a fact that none were as pretty, or as nice or as funny as Gretel.

Early the next afternoon, Anton waited near Peter and Gretel's school. He saw Gretel right after the doors opened. She broke away from a cluster of other blond girls and ran to him.

"It's so nice today. Can I ride Skandar again?" she asked. "Peter will come a bit later. He's helping a friend with his sums. They were learning something dreadfully difficult today."

"You can ride Skandar." Anton tried to keep his tone casual. "But it will be the last time. We're leaving tonight."

Gretel stopped short. "What do you mean? Leaving? Where are you going?"

"I'm not sure. But the count is ready to get back into the war and I must go with him. He needs to recruit an army and get them ready to go to Kronland by spring."

"Why can't he do that here?"

"He needs to get horses in Floradias, or even Galladium."

"That's so far away." Gretel grabbed his hand, her eyes brimming with tears. Anton couldn't bear to look at her.

"Do you have to go? Why don't you just stay here? Surely you can stay with Vrouw Melchor? Or stay with us. I'm sure my parents wouldn't mind. We'll go to school together and you can be a soldier when you're older."

Anton almost gave in. The prospect of being a normal boy, living in a house like the one he grew up in with a family, going to school, being friends with Gretel and Peter stretched ahead of him like a glittering dream. But something inside him poked at him, insisting that would never be his life, much as he might want it. He swallowed it down and said, "I would love that; really, I would. But I can't. I have to be a soldier."

"I don't understand," Gretel said, tears running down her plump cheeks. "You don't have to be a soldier. You can be a merchant. When Peter grows up he'll take over Papa's business and you can marry me and become his partner. It would be perfect."

"It would." Anton took one of Gretel's hands and pulled off the red mitten. Her hand was small, and soft and warm between his. "It would be wonderful. But I don't know how to explain it. I have to fight. It's what I was meant to do."

"But fight for what? Those princes over there, they're fighting about the most ridiculous things. Why should you?"

"Did I ever tell you why the count fights?"

Gretel shook her head.

"He fights for love. There's a beautiful princess he loves and she needs his help. He's doing all of this for her."

That was the right thing to say. Gretel's eyes lit up. "Oh, and when he wins, will she marry him?"

"She's already married to someone else."

"Oh, how tragic." Gretel took her hand back and put it over her heart. "Lovely and hopeless."

"It's not so lovely for the count."

"No, I suppose it isn't. Oh, the poor man. I suppose you must go with him then."

Anton was relieved. The crisis had passed. "Let's go see Skandar. After your ride we'll meet Peter and you can treat me to one more of those hot chocolates."

At the end of the afternoon, Anton wandered slowly with Gretel and Peter back to their house.

"Wait here," Gretel said, running inside.

"You know you're welcome here anytime, if you want to come back," Peter said.

"Thank you." It was nice to think he might have a safe place to return to.

"I wish I could come along. It sounds like such excellent fun."

"It is, sometimes. But it can be pretty bad too. And boring."

"I suppose you're right."

Gretel was back. "Here, take this." She took Anton's hand and slid something into his palm. It was a locket on a fine gold chain. The locket was of cream porcelain with a "G" in a fancy blue script. "Open it," Gretel said. "Give me your pocket knife, Peter."

Anton hoped she wasn't going to cut herself, but she took the little knife and sawed a bit of hair from the end of her braid. She laid it into the locket, where it curled, soft and golden. Anton bit his lip. Crying in front of her would be the worst.

"Please don't forget about me," she whispered, tears running out of her eyes.

"I couldn't. Never," Anton managed, without his voice shaking too much.

Peter shook his hand and then Gretel threw her arms around his neck and cried all over the front of his doublet. Anton supposed that was what the count meant when he talked about women carrying on and he couldn't see anything bad about it. Maybe it only was bad with the wrong woman.

But once he'd said goodbye, Anton turned his mind to the adventure ahead. He didn't know what the count had in mind, except that it would be illegal. It was hard to sit through dinner and pretend like everything was normal. Fortunately, the count was good at just that kind of thing; talking, laughing, and winking at his wife until she blushed. Her red face looked funny under the paint and powder, but Anton felt a little sorry for her.

At bedtime, Anton went to his room and put on all of his warmest clothes in layers. Then he packed the rest in fine leather saddlebags that Vrouw Melchor had given him for his twelfth birthday.

The count had laughed. "I thought you'd be at least fourteen by now. Lied about your age, did you?"

Anton shrugged. "Didn't want anyone to stop me from fighting because I was too young."

"Quite right. Some folk have the strangest ideas about how old you should be to fight. I say you're old enough when you feel like it, and are big enough to manage a weapon. And you've done well so far." The count had added a little bag of silver as a birthday present. If he'd had more time Anton would have bought Gretel a trinket to remember him by.

After Anton finished packing, he looked at the locket in his hand for a long time, opened it and ran his fingers over the lock of hair. After closing it, he hung it around his neck. He didn't care who saw.

The count spotted it right away. Anton thought he would make a joke, but his face turned serious. "I'm sorry to take you away from your friends. But it would have ended in tears sooner or later. I wasn't much older than you the first time I really liked a girl and I hated leaving her. But these little romances never work out, especially at your age. Don't worry, we'll be so busy you won't have to think about her for long. Here, fill your pockets with these." He tossed some small velvet bags at Anton. When he peeked inside, he saw the glitter of jewels.

"Just a few souvenirs. She can always get more," the count said.

"Isn't that stealing?"

"Not really. I'm her husband. And what we're about to do is far worse. We can't get caught."

"What are we going to do?"

"Let's get out of the city and onto the road. Then I'll tell you."

JANNA

Even though Janna's life was easier, this pregnancy was harder. Perhaps it was because she had a little one to look after as well. Or maybe it was the awful weather. Or that she missed Braeden so much it hurt. She couldn't fault the accommodations. She'd never lived anywhere so comfortable with so many servants.

Perhaps she was bored. There wasn't much to do by way of work, and with the army she had been used to seeing new places almost every day. Here, she rarely went out.

In her first weeks here, she'd taken the time to explore the area around her house. It was pleasant enough, reminding her a great deal of Kaleva. She even went to the market a few times and helped the cook pick out the day's food. But now it rained every day and when it didn't she felt too large and cumbersome to waddle up and down stairs and streets.

Doctor Marsel looked in on her every fortnight. She didn't like him quite like she did Doctor Toure, but he knew his business and his dry competence somehow always put her at ease.

So she couldn't explain her unease. Iryna was thriving, though she must have asked for her father at least ten times a day. Janna hoped her own anxieties would lessen after a while, but they never did.

She occupied herself in sewing and knitting things for the baby and writing to Braeden. There just wasn't much to write about. She supposed it was good that not much happened, and she'd be busy enough once the baby was born.

Braeden wrote back from time to time, though it was clear it wasn't something he was comfortable with. None of his personality and bluff wit came through at all, and it didn't help that his letters, short as they were, were littered with Franca's corrections. Those at least made Janna laugh. Franca wrote no better than Braeden, but clearly thought she did. He clearly thought she did too.

"Here she is."

Janna looked up as the study door opened and Birgid came in, carrying Iryna. Iryna could walk well by now, but both Janna and Birgid were terrified of her falling down the house's steep stairs, so they still carried her much of the time.

"Early, isn't it?" Janna reached for Iryna and Birgid handed her over. "Stay, if you can. We can have a cup of tea." She was probably too informal with the servants, but she like Birgid in particular and was dying for someone to talk to.

"The little one slept well, but once she woke up, she was awake. And then nothing would do but we'd come see Mama."

"I don't mind." Janna cuddled Iryna close, who was already squirming to be put down. "Oh, all right." She put her on the floor and Iryna ran to get a rag doll she had left behind a table. She rang the bell for the maid and ordered tea and some cakes.

"How are you doing today, ma'am?" Birgid asked.

"Well enough. Mostly bored."

"It's good for you to get some rest. We're all tired of this weather I daresay, and now that all the soldiers have gone the whole town seems dull."

"I don't mind that kind of dull." Janna had never even hinted at her disastrous time after the fall of Kaleva. "I just wish I had more to do."

"You need a few friends your own age," Birgid said wisely. "Other young women with babies you can talk to."

"That was one of the nice things about camp." Janna thought of Nisa Retter and wondered how she was doing. "There were so many other women with small children."

"Hmph," Birgid said. "I can't think that's a good place for a fine young lady like you to spend time. Not the right kind of people at all." Birgid made no secret of the fact she found a military camp an appalling place and terrible for a family.

Janna smiled. "Oh, you'd be surprised. Some of the officers are quite cultured and their wives come from good families."

"If you say so, though I can't imagine those families approving of that life, if they knew what it was like."

"I'm sure some wouldn't. But a great many do. Until I met my husband I would never have dreamed of it either."

"Well, your husband is a good enough sort." Birgid paused as a maid brought tea in and poured a cup for Janna and one for herself. Then she gave Iryna a hard biscuit to chew on and settled back into her chair. "Though I must confess he frightened me terribly the first time I saw him. Such a rough-looking fellow.

But he's mannerly enough and so gentle with you and the little one. It's a pleasure to watch."

"He frightened me the first time I saw him too." Janna smiled at the memory, wishing she could keep the emotion from welling up. "But he really is kind. I miss him terribly."

"Oh come now, ma'am. There's no need to cry. I'm sure he'll return soon enough."

"I hope so."

ARRYK

Arryk's relief that Larisa had finally agreed was intense. He'd decided not to tell Gwynneth until she returned and otherwise informed only those who needed to know.

"I realize I can't tell your highness what to do, but I beg you, please think about it longer," Magnus said, appalled.

"I have," Arryk said. "A lot. I know it would be smart to make a political marriage, but it's even more important to have Larisa by my side. She knows me and she knows Norovaea. She'll be a great help to me."

"If you say so." Magnus looked unconvinced.

"You'll still be a witness, won't you?"

"Of course I will," Magnus said somewhat impatiently. "It's not like I can say no."

"You can. I'm not ordering you to."

"You don't need to. And I suppose you'll want to keep it quiet for the time being."

"Yes," Arryk said. "Definitely."

The priest was easier to convince. He looked at Larisa and a broad smile spread over his face. "She is certainly the one," he said.

Larisa scowled. Probably because she was wearing a dress and a wreath of winter lilies on her head. "I thought King Arryk was the one," she said.

"Oh he is." The priest beamed. "But I've done my own studying and it's my belief that the Holy Scrolls mention a consort to the chosen ruler."

"Hmph," Larisa said. "I hope they don't mean some princess or other. We don't want to run afoul of any prophecy, do we?"

Seeing she was becoming belligerent, Arryk cleared his throat, then took her by the arm. "We must get started." He was still worried she'd back out at the last minute, or that something would happen to prevent it.

"Of course," the priest said. "And you needn't worry about the prophecy. It's quite clear to me that the prince's consort will come from the same country as he does."

"Well thank the gods for that." Larisa allowed Arryk to drag her to the altar.

The temple was small, dark and drafty, but to Arryk it was the loveliest place in the world. Candles flickered, turning Larisa's beautiful skin to gold and casting fiery red highlights from her hair hanging loose past her waist.

Arryk had never minded that she didn't care about looking pretty like many girls. But he wished there were a way to capture how she looked right now. He was sure she'd never do it again. Although maybe ... there would have to be a coronation at some point. He wouldn't rest until she became queen, even if no one else approved. Surely she would have to wear finery for that.

"What are you grinning at?" Larisa snapped.

"You." Arryk tucked her hand under his arm. "You look so beautiful and I'm very happy to be marrying you."

Larisa made an unladylike noise, but when Arryk looked at her sideways, she smiled.

"I hope marrying me is not too awful for you," he said, glad now she was coming around.

"Not too bad. Just don't expect me to dress up like this every day."

"I don't. I love you just the way you are."

"Idiot."

The priest cleared his throat. "Shall we start?"

The vows were short and in the new Quadrene style. They walked around to each icon of the Holy Family and said the words. Arryk couldn't stop smiling and when he looked at Larisa at the end, her smile was almost as broad as his. It was a relief when the priest pronounced them man and wife and Arryk pulled her into his arms. He swore he'd never let her go.

ANTON

Even though Anton still felt sad at leaving his friends behind, it was nice to be out of the tight confines of the city. Skandar seemed to like the crisp, cold air, tossed his head so his harness jingled and settled into a canter down the road leading straight south.

Once they were well away from the city, the count said,"We're going to Kleeren. I just pray we make it in time and those ships aren't early."

"Why there?" Kleeren was one of the largest western port cities. "I thought all of Kamyla's ships came to Bonnenruck first."

"I found out these two are stopping in Kleeren to unload some of the cargo already sold there. I liked your idea of selling it myself."

"Who will you sell it to?"

"I know a few people and I've already sent a message to them. We won't get what it's worth, but the proceeds of two ships will be enough for me to fund a small army."

"Isn't it stealing? What if they catch us?"

"They'll kill us. Well, maybe not you. Though you'll probably go to the galleys. But they won't catch us."

Anton hoped he was right.

The count explained that he'd left his wife a message with some excuse why he had to leave so suddenly in the middle of the night. He reckoned they would get a good head start before she found out it was a lie.

They rode all night and were in Kleeren by mid-afternoon the next day. Anton had never seen such a busy place. The long waterfront teemed with people and he lost count of the many ships in the large harbor. He wondered how they would find the right ones. At the docks, the count made a few inquiries, then returned looking satisfied. "They're not here yet. They met up off Galladium and are sailing together. Very convenient for us."

They got a room in an inn and Anton tried to get some rest even though he was both worried and excited.

The count seemed nervous and couldn't so much as sit down. "Once this happens, we must move fast," he said, pacing the length of the little room, his boots thumping on the wooden floor.

"What's happening? What do I need to do?"

"Take the horses out of the city tomorrow and meet me at a secret place. Do you think you can manage that?"

Anton's mouth felt dry. "What is this place?"

The count pulled out a map. "Can you read a map?"

"I don't know." Anton remembered looking at maps of Moralta and Marjatya with his father, who tried to explain to him where the goods he sold came from.

"It's easy." The count unrolled the map and laid it across the bed. "Hold that corner down. All right. Here's Kleeren. See?" He pointed at a large circle on what looked like the edge of the land.

Anton nodded.

"I will meet the ships at the docks here with some friends and we'll sail them here." The count's finger slid along the line of the shore until it came to a spot where it curved. "People who can sell the goods quickly and in secret will meet us there and that's where I'll get paid. You'll wait there with the horses because we must head south as fast as we can. We have to get across the border with Floradias and into territory held by Maladena. They can't do anything to us there."

"Why Maladena?"

"They'll be pleased that I did a bit of harm to Zeelund shipping. Besides, I'll make it worth their while."

It seemed dangerous. "Who are these people? Will you be safe?"

"They're not good people. That's why I'll need you to be waiting with the horses. Make sure all of the blades are sharpened tonight and all pistols loaded. It'll be hard for them to chase us since they won't have horses as good as ours. It's very important you be there two nights from now. Do you think you can find the spot?"

Anton thought he could. He was a little bit scared, but also excited at being trusted with such an important mission all by himself.

TEODORA

"You sent for me, Your Highness?" A tiny, dark-haired girl stood before Teodora.

She looked up from her desk. "Yes. Please sit." She recognized Zofya, her second daughter. Waving at Brytta and Elyse, she said, "Bring me another light and then leave us." She needed to inspect the girl more closely.

"What are you now, twelve?"

"Yes. Though everyone says I'm mature for my age."

Teodora hid a smile. Naturally an archduchess would be constantly flattered by those around her. Now there was more light, she fixed a critical stare upon her daughter. Not bad. Better than Elektra. "That's good. I have news for you that means you are now an adult."

Zofya looked interested, but stayed composed.

"I've just signed an agreement with Natalya Maxima of Allaux. The major part of it concerns your marriage to King Gauvain of Galladium."

"What?" Zofya jumped out of her seat. "I'm to be married? Now?"

"Not right now. You will be officially engaged, once I deal with a few minor matters. Upon your fifteenth birthday, you will travel to Galladium and be married."

"But I don't want to." Zofya stamped a little foot, then stood in front of Teodora's desk, her arms crossed, a fierce glare on her face.

Teodora didn't bother to hide her amusement. At least this one had spirit. "What you want has no bearing on the matter, my dear. I had no choice about marrying your father either. Believe me, I was less than thrilled, and that never changed. Those of lower station might marry for sentiment, but we must think of our family's power. Which will be considerable once you are queen of Galladium and your sister is empress."

"I'll be a queen?" Zofya sat back down. It seemed that hadn't occurred to her.

"Yes, of a large, wealthy, powerful country. Everything I know about Gauvain indicates he can be easily influenced, if you know what you're doing. And by the time you meet him in person, you will."

"So, all I have to do is marry this Gauvain fellow and I can rule Galladium?" There was a noticeable spark in Zofya's dark eyes.

"More or less. Much will depend on you; how well you get on with him, as well as your political abilities. But we will step up your education in the next few years and I'm sure you will learn everything you need. How is your Galladian?" All of Teodora's children learned at least six of the languages spoken on the continent, and more if required.

"It's all right. My Moraltan is better."

"Well, forget about Moraltan for now. Spend extra time on Galladian." Teodora paused and looked at Zofya, who looked straight back. Now she was glad it wasn't Elektra doing this. She'd no doubt be whining and sniveling. "I will also speak with Livilla and have you transferred to the temple school at once."

Zofya bounced with glee. "I can leave the palace?"

"Don't be so happy yet. It's just one prison to another. But if you do well in school, Livilla will give you greater responsibility and privileges. Be ready to go tomorrow."

"I don't know what to say, Your Highness."

"Say thank you. You will be a queen with a pliable husband. You are a fortunate girl."

"Thank you mother." To Teodora's surprise, Zofya ran to her, threw her arms around her neck and kissed her rather sloppily on the cheek. "Might I write to the king? Since we are to be married?"

"What a charming idea. Natalya Maxima is still here and can take it along with her. I would like for you to meet her since she will be a great help to you once you reach Allaux."

"Goodness, I'm excited." Zofya put her hands to her cheeks that were glowing pink in a rather becoming way. It looked well with her black hair. With a few years of proper training, perhaps she could distract King Gauvain from Natalya after all.

ARRYK

"We should move out now," Prince Bronson said upon entering the room.

"What? Where? Have a seat." Arryk waved at a chair. His head ached and his eyes blurred from looking at papers. The quartermaster had given him forms to sign and he started out feeling he should understand what he was signing. But after a good quarter hour of trying to decipher the crabbed numbers in the tiny lines, it seemed hopeless. Arryk had to trust the man knew what he was doing, which was likely, and honest, which was unlikely. He sighed and pushed the papers away, then waved for a drink. Once he and Prince Falk each had theirs he said, "All right, start again. What do you want?"

"I think we should attack Kersenstadt right now." Arryk had shared Gwynneth's information with his staff in hopes of getting ideas on how to take the city.

"I'd love to, but I doubt it's possible. Mattila has left the place well-defended."

"We have more than enough troops to take it."

"I need artillery for a frontal assault. Specifically, I need Hohenwart's artillery and her sappers. She's an expert in siege-craft, as you know." For the thousandth time, he wished Falk and Hohenwart hadn't fallen out, or that Hohenwart had come here instead. There was an excellent chance she'd be better company.

"Pfft. We don't need that girl. She's got a reputation because of her looks, that's all."

Arryk chuckled. "I doubt it was her looks that brought her victory at Redden."

"Oh, she had plenty of help, but she gets all the credit from men trying to get into her bed."

"I doubt that's all it is. And I don't care; I need her guns and her mines. I have another idea for getting into Kersenstadt but it involves Edric Maximus."

Bronson frowned. "He's not here right now."

"I've sent for him and I'm sure he'll be here soon."

"It might be weeks before he comes."

"It doesn't matter. The Duchess Karsten believes that once Edric Maximus is inside the city, it can be ours in only a matter of days."

"That makes no sense at all." Bronson looked suspicious.

"It makes plenty of sense. So far, every city in Kronland has become friendly toward us when Edric starts preaching. If we can get him into Kersenstadt, it's likely to go the same way."

"Kersenstadt is firmly in the imperial camp."

"The city government is." Arryk had already hashed this out with Larisa several times. "But if the populace can be swayed, they will overthrow the government. We've seen it before."

"I don't like that." Bronson sniffed. "Sneaky. Where 's the glory in it?"

"I don't care about glory." To his surprise, Arryk realized that was true. He wondered when it had happened. Maybe because he finally understood that nothing but winning mattered and how you did it mattered even less. "I care about results. Whatever gets me Kersenstadt the fastest is all I want."

"Let me get it for you," Bronson said eagerly. "I'm rotting away here, with nothing to do all winter. Let me try."

"No, you must wait along with the rest of us. Once Edric arrives, I can ensure you become part of the force to take the city. There might still be fighting once inside."

"That's well enough. But I don't see the point of delay. Every day we wait are days of those wonderful supplies being used by the enemy."

"I doubt they'll use much. Mattila will want them in the spring. We have time."

"I don't agree." Prince Bronson was annoyingly stubborn. Arryk found that true of most Kronlanders and it made them very hard to deal with.

Arryk shrugged. "I understand. But my order remains: we wait for Edric Maximus. Once he's here, you'll be part of the attack, understood?"

Bronson pulled a face, but nodded in what Arryk hoped was agreement.

BRAEDEN

Now Braeden remembered why marriage had never appealed to him before. The good parts of it were very good. But now he felt awful. He kept telling himself that keeping the girls safe in the city was the right decision. Conditions were terrible out here in midwinter, and they had to range far every day to find forage for their horses. But living in his tent without them left him with a dull ache.

Reno rode up next to him. "That's the worst part of having a family," he said. "When you have to leave them behind."

"I was just thinking that," Braeden said. "I understand they're safer there, but I worry more, for some reason."

"You did the right thing. It will be easier once the children get older. You can take them along all the time."

"True." The thought made Braeden brighten. He pictured Iryna riding on Kazmir in front of him, and soon after that, a little boy. They'd of course get their own ponies as soon as they were big enough. He felt better already.

He pulled ahead to find Prince Novitny. "Where do we rendezvous with Mattila?"

"Have to find her first, though I doubt she'll want us around. We use too much fodder. We'll go see her, but I reckon she'll order us into Lantura for the rest of the winter. I'd love to take the fight to Faris while he's still regrouping in Terragand, but she won't send us that far afield."

"I wish she would. Could use some action right now."

"Me too. But first let's find the old girl. I've sent scouts ahead to locate her."

Mattila had marched out of Kersenstadt a week ahead of the Sanova Hussars. Her plan was to locate Arryk Roussay while the hussars made sure the city and its environs were secure. That didn't take much, since she'd left it well-fortified. And Braeden welcomed the extra time with his family.

To Braeden's surprise, Novitny called him to his command tent that evening. "The scouts didn't find Mattila, but they found hostiles ahead."

"Who?" Reno wondered.

"Kronlanders of some sort, though it's hard to say who. It might be Hohenwart though I didn't expect to see her down here before spring. Mattila was hoping to cut her off before she got here. Anyway, this lot is headed straight for Kersenstadt. No doubt word has gotten out about what Mattila has there and someone reckons they'll get their hands on it."

"Not likely," Braeden said.

"Exactly. Let's stop them in the morning. They've made camp for the night and we'll deploy now, jump on them before it gets light."

"I like the sound of that." Braeden was happy to get his regiment ready.

It was a foggy, frosty night and the horses' hooves crunched on the frozen mud of the road. They went as quickly as they could, with scouts well ahead to make sure the enemy hadn't moved. When they were close, Braeden rode up with Novitny to take a look.

"How many do you reckon?" Novitny asked.

"Only one or two thousand foot, maybe a hundred cavalry. Don't know what they hope to do with that."

"Wonder if they're waiting for someone else."

"Hard to say. Best to take them out now if that's the case."

"I agree."

Braeden held the glass and looked over the camp carefully. He stood on a small hill and torchlight flickered between the tents. He laughed. "It's Bronson Falk, I'm sure of it."

"Falk? Of Helvundala? Isn't he supposed to be up north somewhere?"

"Yes, but I'd know his banner anywhere. I saw a bit of him back during the Landrus trial. He was one of the troublemakers at the time."

"I hate to trouble someone who might have given the empress a headache. That seems a poor reward." Novitny chuckled.

"It does. We should ride in and offer him a drink instead." That was just talk. Braeden knew what they had to do.

The hussars deployed near the camp and silently took out the pickets. This wouldn't take long.

ANTON

Anton left Kleeren early the next morning, riding Skandar and leading Cid, saddled and ready to go. He loaded two pistols and put them in his belt. His cloak covered them and it felt good to know they were there.

Count Orland gave him a purse. "You'll need to take a room at the inn in Mierzeck. If anyone gives you trouble, tell them your master is joining you in a few hours. Make sure the horses are fed, watered and rested."

Anton nodded, tension creating a knot in his stomach.

"One more thing," the count said.

"What's that?"

"You'll be able to see what's going on in that cove from the spot I told you about. If anything happens to me, or if the ships don't appear tomorrow night, take the horses to Floradias. They'll let you into a garrison there. You can wait for me in case the ships are delayed, but you don't have to. There'll be enough money to get you back to Kronland or wherever you want to go."

"You'll make it though, won't you?" It was hard to hide how worried he was, since he was sure the count was doing something terribly dangerous.

The count laughed his familiar laugh. "I plan to. Now off you go, and I'll see you tomorrow night."

The weather along the coast was cold and rainy. Anton's cloak was thick and warm, but he was still chilled and wet when he reached the fishing village of Mierzeck. He quickly found the inn, a weathered-looking building of gray clapboard. He didn't like the look of the innkeep, so he told the man he was waiting for a party of four and let him catch a glimpse of the pistols at his belt.

The fellow was rude anyway. "How do I know a scrap like you is good for the room and the feed for the horses? How do I know you ain't stole fine beasts like that?"

267

Anton narrowed his eyes. "Do I look like a horse-thief?" he said in a haughty tone he had learned from the count. "Perhaps this will put your mind at ease." He spoke the Zeelund tongue well by now and could imitate the crisp, clipped accent of the Bonnenruck quality while laying a silver coin on the table.

"That'll do nicely, sir." The innkeep snatched up the coin and it disappeared down a sleeve.

"Good." Anton hoped he sounded bored. "Now bring me something to eat and some beer. I'll check on the horses later to make sure those incompetent louts of yours take proper care of them."

By the time he finished speaking, the innkeep was bowing and scraping and Anton had to hide a grin as he swept into the dining room. It was empty at this hour, but a grubby-looking serving girl brought him a pewter plate piled high with steaming meat and potatoes. She quickly returned with a tall tankard of dark beer. Anton had become accustomed to much better at Vrouw Melchor's fine table in Bonnenruck, but he was hungry enough not to care.

He made sure to leave the dining room before the regulars arrived since he didn't want to answer too many questions. The fewer people who noticed him the better. He checked on the horses, doing his best to intimidate the stable lad, who was probably several years older than Anton, and went to his room early. It was amazing what fine clothes, a pile of coin, a brace of pistols and a bit of attitude could do.

Anton worried he might not sleep well, anxious as he felt about the next day's operation, but the journey had tired him. The bedding was warm and comfortable, if perhaps not entirely clean. Anton reckoned the slight musty scent wasn't as bad as the smell of the horse blankets he used to sleep in. He hoped living in Bonnenruck hadn't made him too soft and fell asleep with the count's instructions running through his head.

He visited the stables again the next morning, then had breakfast in the dining room. There was only one other guest eating the runny porridge and she was even less interested in talking to Anton than he was in talking to her. He knew from the stable-boy she was a courier working for a consortium of Bonnenruck merchants. She'd come in late last night, bearing dispatches from further down the coast, headed for Kleeren. Anton had noticed her fine horse.

"That's how they find out where their ships are," the stable-boy said. "The couriers collect messages from the ship's captains and relay them up the coast. Most of our out-of-town custom comes from them." That was probably how the count had learned where the ships were.

Anton kept to his room for the rest of the day, coming out again for one solitary meal in the late afternoon. As evening fell, he collected the horses. "It's time for me to meet my master," he told the stable-boy. "I doubt I'll be back." He gave him a handful of coppers. "If anyone asks, I was never here, and neither were these horses." He'd gotten a similar agreement from the innkeep for a lot more coin.

As darkness fell, the wind turned sharper, driving a cold drizzle straight into Anton's face. He wondered how he would ever find his way. But after a while, his eyes adjusted and he noticed the overcast sky was quite light, the wind blowing clouds across an almost-full moon that peeked out from time to time.

When he reached the bluffs overlooking the cove, he had a good view of the beach below, and the still-empty sea. He had wrapped the horse's harnesses with rags so they didn't jingle and he had a pocket full of sugar lumps to keep them happy.

It was cold. Anton paced along the bluff, holding his cloak tight around him. After what felt like hours, there was noise and movement on the beach below. Four small boats were drawing up. He hadn't seen them until they were close. Once on the beach, someone lit torches and built a small driftwood fire. Not long after that, Anton saw the ships. In spite of the stiff wind they were running at nearly full sail, although they began furling them as they came near the beach.

Anton's heart thudded in his dry mouth. He prayed the count was on one of those ships. It took a while longer, but a boat launched from the ship finally reached the beach. Several people climbed out and pulled it ashore and then someone else got out. Anton was sure he recognized the count's hat and was even more certain when Cid nickered. "Shh," Anton said, giving Cid another sugar lump and petting his nose.

Anton got as close to the edge of the bluff as he dared and looked down. The wind carried snatches of conversation and made the torches flicker. If anyone had looked up they might have seen Anton silhouetted against the sky, but no one did.

The talking seemed to go on forever, but Anton wasn't cold anymore. He sweated under his wool doublet and heavy cloak. After a long time all of the boats pushed back into the water and the count started along the beach. He headed to a path winding up the bluff to where Anton stood. Anton watched the boats row out toward the ships. The count disappeared under the bluff.

Suddenly, one of the boats turned around and started back toward the beach. Anton fell to his stomach, flattened to the ground, then pulled out both pistols.

He shouted over the edge, "Sir, watch the beach."

An instant later, light exploded from the boat.

ARRYK

"Wait, what?" Arryk was still groggy. Magnus stood in his dark bedroom, a faint light coming through the open door. "It's Bronson Falk, Your Highness. He's dead."

Arryk rubbed his eyes, stumbled out of bed and into a dressing gown. Larisa stirred on the other side and a moment later, a lamp flared up as she came up beside him.

"All right," he said, "Tell me from the beginning. Has an accident befallen him?"

"Not exactly." Magnus looked grim. "We're not sure of what he intended, but he had marched his entire force toward Kersenstadt. The Sanova Hussars fell upon their camp and utterly destroyed them. If there are any survivors, they haven't come here."

"How did you find out?" Arryk hadn't seen Prince Bronson in several days but that wasn't unusual. He had quartered his troops some distance from the rest, so he wouldn't have missed them when they marched out.

"Someone in a nearby village saw what happened and thought we should know."

Arryk dropped into a chair. How could the only ally near him do this? Falk had few enough troops he had no hope of success at taking the city and should have known the Sanova Hussars would roam the countryside. Of course he'd be no match for them.

"What are your orders, Your Highness?" Magnus shifted to another foot.

"I want to see my staff at daybreak. In the meantime, see what other news can be gathered from the farms and villages. I need an exact account of what happened and the numbers involved. We must search for survivors, if there are any."

After Magnus left, Arryk slumped forward.

Larisa stroked his hair. "You didn't need him," she said.

"Yes, I did." Arryk lifted his head and leaned into her hand. "He was an ass, but at least he had experience. I must gather the rest of my allies before they all disintegrate."

His staff was waiting for him when he reached the dining hall of the mansion he was staying in. From the look on everyone's faces, they'd heard the news.

Arryk tried to keep his face neutral, as if this weren't a disaster. "First of all," he said, sounding stern. "Were any of you aware that Prince Bronson might try such a feat? Did he speak with anyone?"

A colonel spoke up. "Not to us, he didn't. Falk's Kronlanders kept to themselves. Not the friendliest. So we let them be. Never thought the old fellow would be such a fool. I wouldn't want to take our whole cavalry against the Sanovans, let alone his few thousand ragtags."

Arryk wanted to think his horse were able to handle the hussars, but he also realized that probably wasn't true. He needed to face Mattila before the hussars joined her, but it wasn't wise to try it until he had more allies. Gwynneth had written that no immediate help would be forthcoming from Galladium, though there was another plan afoot. But that would take time and Arryk was running out of it.

He swallowed, surprised at the dryness of his mouth. "Send messengers," he said. "I need Seward Kurant to join us at once. I understand he's trying to subdue Daciana Tomescu in the Podoska marches, but I don't care about that. He's needed here. I want Ruso Faris to garrison Birkenfels and bring every remaining soldier here. And I want Emilya Hohenwart here now."

"I'll write up the orders," Magnus said.

"That's all for now." Arryk rose. "We'll meet again when I have more information." He left, feeling defeated already. Faris had written to him, stating he didn't want to leave Terragand while Kersenstadt lay in enemy hands. Since it dominated the crossroads, Mattila could march across the border unopposed. Kurant couldn't or wouldn't get past Tomescu. And even if Emilya Hohenwart left Brandana today, it would take weeks for her to haul her guns down the muddy roads. Too much could happen in weeks, and none of it good.

GWYNNETH

Gwynneth was glad the journey was over. She was a good sailor, but the Northern Sea in late winter was an unpleasant place for anyone. It was a relief to see the harbor of Tharvik appear out of the mist, all gold and white. Her appearance on the dock went unnoticed, since she traveled with no escort aside from her maid, Catrin. With her salt-stained cloak drawn close around her she looked like just another weary traveler.

Catrin hailed the closest hired carriage and Gwynneth instructed the driver to take her to the nearest comfortable inn. She wanted to repair her looks as much as possible before appearing at the palace. It had been ten years since the king had last seen her, and she had been a fresh-faced young girl then. She didn't want the contrast between then and now to appear too harsh.

The coachman obliged by bringing her to a pretty inn well away from the harbor and its biting winds. The innkeep was a tall woman with blonde braids wrapped around her head and a bright red apron. She needed only a glance at Gwynneth to detect quality, taking her straight to the best suite of rooms in the house. Money wasn't a problem since Natalya had slipped a purse full of gold into Gwynneth's baggage when she left Galladium.

Aksel had made her an even larger present in Norovaea. "I'd give you everything I have if you can end the war somehow," he'd said, smiling down at her. She made sure he and Norvel Classen reached an understanding before she left. Aksel finally agreed to attend to affairs of state for at least six hours each day. He could spend the remaining time in his laboratory.

Classen was pleased at his aptitude. "I always thought it a shame he didn't turn some of that prodigious brain toward the problems of the kingdom." He looked livelier than he had in some time. Perhaps he would gain some of his weight back.

Settled in front of a blazing fire, a warm quilt wrapped around her shoulders and sipping a hot drink while sleet lashed the windows, Gwynneth considered her next move. First, she needed to assess the limited wardrobe she'd brought to find something appropriate for court. She wanted something more dazzling than the dress she'd worn in Allaux and Arenberg on formal occasions. Perhaps she should arrange for a dressmaker before letting the king know she was here.

Behind her, Catrin sighed loudly over an ironing board. "I don't know, Your Grace. Everything got so damp; I'm not sure I can get the creases out."

"Do your best," Gwynneth said, feeling relaxed. She wondered exactly what was in her drink. "I think I'll need something new."

"Oh yes, I agree." Catrin suddenly sounded much happier. She loved dress fittings because she often received Gwynneth's cast-offs.

"When you're done there, ask the innkeep about good dressmakers; someone who understands the latest styles. I don't want to be mistaken for a jumped-up Estenor peasant."

"Oh, you never could." Catrin giggled at the idea.

Gwynneth smiled to herself. She wondered if Lennart would find it amusing if she tried a rustic look. No, better to look grand and dignified. The last thing she wanted was to appear in need of charity. "Next, I must learn how the king spends his days. I want a private audience and need to know who can get me one."

"I'll find out," Catrin said.

Gwynneth didn't know how she would, since she barely spoke the language, but that had never seemed to keep Catrin from communicating before. "Oh, and be discreet. I'd prefer to not have this be an official visit, at least not until I've spoken with the king."

After a delicious early dinner, Gwynneth fell asleep in a bed with fluffy down-filled quilts above and below her. By the time she awoke and breakfasted, Catrin had arranged an appointment with a dressmaker and gone off to get the court gossip. Gwynneth was getting ready to go out, when she returned, bundled up in Gwynneth's plain traveling cloak.

"Bad news, Your Grace," she said without preamble.

Gwynneth stopped pulling on her gloves. "What is it?"

"The king isn't here."

"What? Has he gone hunting?"

"No. He's gone to Sanova on a winter campaign."

"Unbelievable." Gwynneth sank into a chair. "Fighting in this horrid weather? What is he thinking?"

"That the Sanovans will like it even less." Catrin smiled.

"I suppose we must chase after him. Did you find out where in Sanova he is?"

"He sailed for the Prinova Islands about a fortnight ago. They've received messages here that he landed successfully and secured a base there."

"How dreadful. That will be an unpleasant voyage and even worse once we get there. At least, we'll be near Sanova should I need to go."

"When will we go? Should I book a passage?" Catrin never seemed to miss a beat.

"I still need a dress. Nothing formal, but I want to look nice. We'll plan to leave in three days. Ride with me to the dressmaker, and from there you can go to the harbor and find a ship for us. Something sturdy, with an experienced captain, one who knows how to find the king."

ARRYK

Arryk thought he would be less worried now that Larisa was his wife, but he felt worse. Maybe it was because he'd been unable to talk her out of leading the assault on Kersenstadt. After Prince Bronson's failure, Arryk decided that getting Edric Maximus to infiltrate the city was the only way.

"I won't be in any danger," Larisa said, laughing at him as she always did. "I won't go in unless Edric Maximus sways the population and once I'm in, I'll be safe behind those huge walls forever."

"I won't let you stay there forever," Arryk said. The need to get her out of Kersenstadt would give him the resolve to face Mattila, no matter how badly his allies behaved.

"I know." She smiled at him, kissed him and fell asleep in his arms.

But sleep didn't come for him. He stared into the dark until he thought he was imagining moving shapes against the black wall. A lamp flickered in an alcove, but the black was so all-consuming, Arryk wondered that he still saw its light.

The blackness closed in on him. Arryk tried to sit up, to reach for another light, but a great weight pressed him down. He still felt his arms around Larisa, heard her even breathing, but she seemed very far away. He struggled to move, but his limbs felt tied to the bed. This had to be a dream.

Out of the black, a figure advanced on him. In spite of the dark, he saw her clearly. She was tall and pale, her face framed by hair as black as the night around her. She wore armor of gold that should have caught the light, but it was flat, as though it reflected the surrounding blackness. Now she stood in front of him.

"You know who I am," she said, her voice harsh and grating. "I will destroy you."

Arryk tried to choke out a "Why?" but no words came.

She understood him anyway. "Why? Because you dared defy me. Because you left your home, where you belong, and invaded my lands. Wasn't what I did to Kendryk enough?"

"What have you done to Kendryk?" He gasped.

She laughed, a horrid cackle. "Imagine the worst, then understand I'm capable of much more. What I have planned for you will hurt so badly you'll never be the same after."

Arryk couldn't speak.

"I know you're dying to find out, so I'll give you a hint." She moved closer, so close that Arryk might have touched her, if he'd been able to move. She pulled a long sword from a scabbard at her waist. The metal screeched, much like her voice.

Arryk shivered and tried to move, but the blackness pinned him down.

She raised the sword high, brought it straight down, and Arryk braced for the cut. But it went into Larisa instead. She lay motionless in his arms as the sword plunged in again and again.

Arryk tried to scream, tried to grab the sword but he was paralyzed. Blood sprang from Larisa like a fountain, washing over Arryk. He needed to lift his head if he wasn't to drown, but still couldn't move. Now the woman was laughing again, still plunging the blade into Larisa's limp body. Arryk opened his mouth to scream, but it filled with blood. He gasped for air, but now the blood filled his nose. Just before it covered his eyes he saw the woman stop and look down at him, a triumphant smile on her face.

Then Larisa was shaking him, her voice frantic. "Wake up, Arryk. Please, please wake up."

When he could finally open his eyes, a lamp flickered nearby and Larisa was still shaking him.

"Oh gods," he said, grabbing onto her. "You're alive."

"Of course I'm alive. I was wondering about you, though. You were shaking and screaming and I couldn't wake you up. Must have been quite a nightmare."

Arryk sat up slowly, still holding onto Larisa. "Not a nightmare," he said. "I'm certain of it. I'm also certain you must not go to Kersenstadt."

ANTON

Someone jumped out of the boat and waded to shore. They had fired the pistol, and likely had another. Anton knew he was too far away for an accurate shot, so he waited, his tongue glued to the dry roof of his mouth. Now a second person ran for the beach. A blast came from somewhere below Anton and one of the figures fell into the surf. The other one came faster. He was on the beach now, running straight toward Anton. The count was probably right below him on the path. Anton waited until he could make out the man's shape and fired.

He missed and the man shot back. The ball hit the dirt a few feet below Anton, a few clods springing into his face. The man was even closer now. Anton fired again and another blast came from right below him. The man fell and didn't get up again. After a moment, the boat rowed back toward the ships.

Anton held his breath and didn't move. A few seconds later, the count burst out of a cluster of grass and threw himself onto the ground next to Anton. "Stay down a moment longer. Where are the horses?"

"Behind those rocks." Anton had left them on the downslope of the bluff so they wouldn't be silhouetted.

"Let's crawl that way. Once they get back to the ships I wouldn't be surprised if they blast at us with the big guns. We want to be well away by then."

That was all Anton needed to get him to scramble down the hillside. The horses stood where he left them, inspecting the long, tough and apparently tasteless grass. Cid nickered again when he saw the count.

"Let's go. We must leave the coast road as soon as possible so they can't intercept us further south."

They rode hard until they reached the main road linking Kleeren with a Floradias border town. "Slow down," the count said. "We don't want to blow the horses. We'll ride until morning and find a place to stay. If we leave out again in the evening, we can make Floradias by the next morning."

"What happened back there?" Anton asked after a while.

"Bastards tried to double-cross me, as I half expected. I insisted on payment in coin, which they weren't happy about. They thought they'd pay me, take the ships, then come back to kill and rob me. You did well back there. I'm sure I missed that last fellow."

"Did I kill him then?" Anton asked in a small voice.

"Likely. If he's wounded, his friends won't come back for him, so in this weather he'll be dead by morning."

Anton felt bad, but would have felt worse if the man had gotten the count. "What will they do with the ships?"

"If they're not stupid enough to fire the guns and make a commotion, they'll unload the goods onto those boats and take everything into caves below those cliffs. From there, they'll sell everything off in smaller batches. Smugglers come to that spot all the time so they should make about twice what they paid me."

"What happened to the captains of those ships?"

"I put 'em ashore on a beach outside Kleeren. They ought to make it back to town by morning, another reason we'll want to lay low tomorrow."

"How did you get them to hand over the ships?"

"I came aboard and told them I was the owner's husband, which is true. I brought along a few toughs I knew from before—unemployed soldiers—and convinced the captains it would be smart to cooperate. Once I spread a bit of silver around the crew they behaved well enough."

"What'll happen to them?"

"As long as they don't cause trouble, they'll be turned loose once the ship is empty. I wouldn't be surprised if some join the smugglers. The rest will probably sail to Bonnenruck where Kamyla can make her insurance claim."

"Did you get as much as you were hoping?"

"Almost. I'll have a smaller force than before, but it should be enough. Once we get to Floradias, we'll stay in Maladene territory, then I'll set to recruiting and get supplies ordered. You'll see first-hand how an army is put together."

KENDRYK

First, Kendryk slept. He'd slept a great deal while in the dungeon, but this was different. He wasn't on a hard stone bench, covered in musty, louse-ridden straw in a place that was just a little too cold and damp. He lay on top of and underneath marvelously soft feather beds, with a fire burning in the hearth when he fell asleep and when he awakened.

And when he woke up, he ate. He was unbelievably hungry and had forgotten how much he missed good food. He started with simple meals cooked in the fortress kitchen, but once his regular appetite returned, found he wanted more.

"Ulla," he said the next time the maid came into the little room he'd turned into a study. "Please send your brother into the city for food. Sybila said there's an excellent inn nearby."

"Yes, sir." Ulla ran off. She still seemed a little frightened. It was also odd to not be addressed as Your Grace, but the fact remained that no one here considered him a prince. Since it might take a while for the food to arrive, he decided to explore a bit more. He'd acquainted himself with his little suite of rooms and stepped into the garden once or twice, though the bitter cold soon drove him back indoors.

Dolf, his other servant, had told him he was allowed to go wherever he wished on the fortress ground floor, except for the guardroom, behind which was the gate. Kendryk knew there'd be other gates beyond that, and more guards, and then the impressive city walls. He wanted to escape, but he also knew he could never manage that on his own. Gauvain and Natalya had already accomplished this much. Surely, given time, they would get a chance to do more.

Kendryk turned down a corridor running along the other side of the courtyard. Dolf had said there'd be a library here. It was time he looked at it. The door was open, revealing walls lined with old-looking books. It was chilly in here and the hearth stood black and empty. Kendryk hadn't bothered to bring a cloak, but resolved to ask for a fire later. Enough light came in through the windows that he could read the titles. It appeared every book in this library was at least fifty years old. He sighed. It would have to do until he ordered something better.

There was a cough behind him. Kendryk turned, wondering if Dolf was already back. To his surprise, a boy sat at a table, reading by the light coming in from an opposite window.

"Who are you?" Kendryk asked.

"Who are you?" the boy asked, closing his book and looking surly.

Kendryk smiled, walked over and sat down across from him. "I'm Kendryk Bernotas. Recently of the dungeon."

"I've heard of you. How did you get here?"

"It's a long story. What about you? You look too young to be guilty of any crime."

"I'm a hostage." The boy looked glum. "I've been here for almost three years. My family are Marjatyan rebels and I can't go home until they obey the empress. I'm surprised she hasn't killed me yet."

Kendryk was surprised as well, but he didn't say so. "What's your name?" he asked gently. "Tell me what happened."

"I'm Karil Andarosz, heir to Count Andarosz. The Sanova Hussars brought me here during the siege. I think they've forgotten about me."

"Maybe," Kendryk said. "But you're probably right about your family. And even if they're behaving, the empress might keep you here to make sure they continue. Are you very bored?"

Karil nodded.

"Well, I'll get more books. Tell me what you like to read and I'll order some for you as well. And I need to get some exercise. Do you enjoy swordplay?"

"The guards would never let us."

"We won't have swords. But sticks will serve well enough. I doubt the guards will mind if we knock each other about the head with fallen branches."

That coaxed a smile from the boy.

"We'll practice every day," Kendryk said. "Just in case we get a chance to fight our way out of here." He knew that was optimism beyond foolishness, but it felt good to have hope, and it was even nicer to have a friend.

GWYNNETH

A storm was coming in as Gwynneth boarded the sturdy little ship. "Will we wait for it to blow over?" she asked the captain, a stocky, black-haired woman with cheeks chapped red by the wind.

"Don't see the point." The captain shrugged, the ear-flaps of her cap smacking the sides of her head. Gwynneth wondered she could hear anything at all. "It'll just start up again, sooner rather than later this time of year. You needn't worry your ladyship. I make this crossing at least once a week and now I'm trying to do it more often since the king's gone there. They need a lot of supplies. Your husband based out there?"

"No. I'm on personal business."

"Understood." The captain didn't seem offended. "I'm Kelsi Brun. You can call me either, or both. I don't stand much on ceremony on a ship the size of the *Rusa*. You're welcome to join me in my cabin for dinner. Nothing fancy, but I find it nice to have the company."

"I'd like that." Gwynneth smiled. There was something about this woman she liked. Or maybe it was that as a girl she'd imagined she would have enjoyed the life of a sea captain. She nearly envied this Kelsi Brun her little ship and her freedom.

For the most part, Gwynneth wore her obligations lightly, but of late they were so many she felt crushed. She worried about Terragand and Norovaea and the progress of the war. She worried about her brothers, her children, and Kendryk most of all. She worried that if she didn't untangle all of these problems soon, she'd never see her husband again, and her daughter would never come into her birthright.

To her surprise, she found herself telling Captain Brun who she was and what her plans were. The captain looked shocked. "I wish you'd let me know your ladyship—I mean Your Grace. You should be better guarded."

"I feel quite safe, as long as no one knows who I am."

"If you say so, though I'm surprised. I never dreamed a princess would travel all over by herself with no baggage to speak of and a slip of a girl as companion."

"We've kept to ourselves and no one's bothered us. It's very different from Kronland, where I have to go everywhere with at least a hundred guards. I've rather enjoyed it."

"I expect you have. I'm glad you've told me what you're up to. That way I can land you close to the king. Otherwise I would have headed for another island and you would have had a time getting back."

"Isn't it easy to take small boats between islands?"

"It is during good weather, but it's almost impossible right now. No, I'll sail you right into the harbor at the fortress. I've got a pass so there won't be a problem. But if you want my advice, from there it's best if we let the commander know who you are straight away. It's a rough bunch who's garrisoned there and I'd worry about you and your maid finding the king on your own."

"That seems sensible. I've known the king since I was a girl and I'm sure he remembers me. I hope once he hears I'm there he'll grant me an audience right away."

"I'm sure he will. In fact, if I might be so bold, I wonder he never married you. He knew you some time ago, before you married the prince, I take it?"

Gwynneth smiled and took a sip from the fine cut-glass tumbler. Her meal had been surprisingly good and the ship's motion seemed less bothersome in the cozy well-appointed cabin. The only other officer, a young man who looked so like the captain he could only be a relative, took watch while the captain dined. "The fact is, he paid court to me before I met my husband."

"He did? And you turned him down?" Captain Brun looked at Gwynneth as if she were mad. Perhaps she had been.

"Not quite. He never made an offer. I'm sure he liked me, and I liked him, too. But he told me I was likely to be too much trouble. We argued quite a bit, over all kinds of ridiculous things. I enjoyed it, but looking back, I suppose he imagined me turning into a nagging shrew who questioned his every decision. He wasn't interested in having a true consort who would help him rule. And frankly, I wouldn't settle for less than that."

"Nor should you," Brun said with an approving nod.

"So, King Lennart returned to Estenor to think about it, and Kendryk appeared shortly after that. Once I met him, there was no question of who I wanted to marry, and he never seemed to have second thoughts about letting me help him. My great concern now is that Raysa Sikora will be too strong-willed for the king. Though perhaps he's changed, and of course, I don't know her at all."

"We don't hear much about her, just that Queen Ottilya would dearly love a match with Briansk, and they seem to love the idea much less."

"Raysa is still young. Perhaps Lennart will find her easier to control."

"I wouldn't count on that. Were you easier to control at seventeen?"

"Good point." Gwynneth smiled. "Well, I can do nothing but make the proposal and see what he thinks."

"If he's sensible he'll see it's a good one. It's high time we had peace with Sanova."

"I agree. Though it might mean war in Kronland."

"True. But with any luck, it'll be a short one."

"That's what I hope for as well."

JANNA

Occupying herself became increasingly difficult as her pregnancy progressed, so Janna turned to reading. She had never cared much for books, but then she'd always been busy with other tasks. And it was a good way to improve her Olvisyan.

Doctor Marsel was happy to bring her books from his personal library. He was interested in history and politics, so that was what Janna read. She learned why this war was unlikely to end soon. It was about much more than a rebellious priest and prince. If it hadn't been Edric Landrus and Kendryk Bernotas, it would have been someone else. As Moralta had tried and failed, so had Terragand, but both their defeats didn't seem to mean anything to those who wanted change.

"So the Kronland rulers won't be satisfied unless they receive complete independence from the empire. But the empire won't let them go. Is there no way to settle it without a war?" Janna asked Doctor Marsel when he came by to bring her more books.

The doctor put down his cup. They always had tea together when he visited and discussed what Janna had been reading. "They've been trying to find a diplomatic solution for the past fifty years. Teodora's predecessors were more tractable and allowed greater freedoms. They would give the Kronlanders enough independence to avert rebellion. Of course doing so meant weakening the empire over time and that's something Teodora won't stand for."

Janna sighed. "I don't blame her for that. If I were empress I wouldn't be keen on seeing my empire splinter into little pieces."

The doctor smiled. "But it's been in little pieces for several hundred years. Aside from the imperial courts, the empire has had no direct authority over Kronland since signing the Treaty of Veben." He rummaged in the bag of books he'd brought and pulled out a slim volume, handing it to Janna. "It's rather dry reading I'm afraid, but this explains all about that treaty and what it means for Kronland today."

Janna took the book and placed it on the pile next to her chair. "I'll read it. Though I don't see what good it does me to know any of this. I doubt Teodora would change her mind, even if every person in Kronland argued about this with her, quoting from the treaty directly."

"Teodora won't change her mind. But it's useful if we Kronlanders understand what we're fighting for." He paused and smiled. "I forget you are not one of us, Madame Terris, and that your husband is in the empress's employ. I hope you're not offended."

Janna had to laugh at that, then told him a little about Dimir's part in the Moraltan revolt and her official status as a rebel.

Doctor Marsel looked mildly horrified. "Commander Terris was aware of this and still took you into the empress's presence? That seems very risky." Janna had already told him about meeting Teodora.

"I worried as well, but we were careful and I don't think it ever occurred to her that anyone on her list would set foot in her palace voluntarily." Janna doubted she'd ever forget the mingled feeling of fear and excitement when Teodora first spoke to her.

The doctor shook his head. "That was brave of you; you don't look the type to be considered a rebel, let alone face the empress directly."

"I'm not the type." Janna paused to pour more tea for both of them. "But my husband hoped it would help me get over my fear of the empress and he was right. I still fear what she might do, but I also understand that she's a person who can be hurt or killed, like any of us, rather than some invincible monster."

"Many still believe her a monster," the doctor said. "But it's true she is mortal, and that is a good thing. Since she's unlikely to ever let Kronland go peacefully, someone will have to kill her before it ends."

Janna thought of Braeden. He was one of the few people who could get close to the empress without being questioned. She wondered if he'd kill her. But doing it would mean his death, and Janna didn't care if the war went on for a hundred years as long as Braeden lived and came back to her.

"How are you feeling?" the doctor asked, no doubt noticing her mood turn melancholy.

"Well enough. Bored. Tired. I want to have this baby and recover so I can get back to my husband."

"So life in the field agrees with you?"

"Yes, surprisingly. I became so used to comfort in Kaleva, but when I lost all of that, living in a tent wasn't so bad. And there's always something new to see."

"Isn't it boring, being in camp?"

"Only if the weather is too bad to go out. But I had a lot of friends and there was always someone stopping by, or someone to visit." Janna trailed off, realizing that was what she missed here. In Atlona, she had the Torresia clan close by and they were there on campaign as well, besides friends like Nisa. She'd met no one here and she didn't see how she could, so she was grateful to Iryna's nurse and to Doctor Marsel. She smiled at him. "I'm so glad you come by; otherwise it's much too quiet, I find."

"Quiet is good for you," he said gently. "Doctor Toure told me about the difficulties you had with Iryna. This is the best place for you, even though you might not like it much. Your husband did right setting you up here."

"I know," Janna said. "I just wish it could be different."

GWYNNETH

The Prinova Islands were shockingly small. As Captain Brun threaded the *Rusa* into a tiny, rocky harbor, Gwynneth glimpsed the ocean on the other side of the land. It couldn't be more than a league across, and this was the largest of the six islands. That was probably why it had the fortress, though calling it a fortress was generous. Rising straight from a rocky outcropping, the fort looked more like a tall stone house with a high wooden fence around it. Any attackers would have to fight their way up the rocks.

A tiny village clung to the cliffside, and as they drew near, Gwynneth spotted a little staircase with many switchbacks going up the cliff's face. She wondered if that was the only route to the fort. "What do they call the fort and the village?" she asked the captain.

"Strutka, after the old pirate. It's said he once had his base here, before King Lennart's father rooted him out."

"Rooting anyone out of here seems difficult."

"It is, though King Lennart managed it well enough. Some Sanovan troops were garrisoned here, but he got rid of them. Don't know how."

"I'll ask." Now they were coming up on the docks. "I might need a few days here," Gwynneth said. "But then I'll either need a ship to take me back to Kronland, or on to Sanova. Can you do that? I'll pay double."

"I can. And no need for extra pay. I have to make a few stops on other islands, but I'll be back in four days. Will that be long enough?"

"More than enough. If I can't convince him in a day or two, I'll give up. I don't even know where I'll stay while I'm here."

"I imagine the king will put you up in the fortress. It won't be comfortable, since he's never stood on luxury. His soldiers love him for that. He lives just like they do."

"The poor man. I suppose I can bear it for a few days. Is this where I get off?"

"Yes. But let me come along. I'm not leaving the two of you alone on this dock. Once the king sends someone for you, I'll go, but not before."

"Thank you." Gwynneth looked around as she walked down the gangplank, Catrin on her heels. This was a rough-looking place. A dusting of snow covered gray rock and the sky and sea matched the drab landscape. Even the tiny houses of the village were of the same gray stone with slate roofs just a shade darker.

Captain Brun yelled "Hey!" at a guard lounging against the wall of what looked like a very small tavern. The man jumped to attention. "Go get the king," Brun said.

"Why?" The man looked Gwynneth over with a leer, then winked at Catrin. "What if I don't feel like sharing?"

"What you feel like doesn't enter into it," Brun said. "This here's Princess Gwynneth of Norovaea and she needs a word with the king. He'll want to see her right away, so best go get him right quick."

Gwynneth was grateful to the captain and glad she'd left a small stack of silver coins on her table in the cabin. She would not have enjoyed dealing with this lot alone. And she was also glad that the good captain had brought her here in one bedraggled piece after some nasty squalls.

It was freezing on the quay, so the captain led them into the tavern. A peat fire barely warmed the place, but at least the wind didn't reach them and Gwynneth could warm her hands. It was only a quarter hour before there was a small commotion at the door. Gwynneth turned around quickly, but he was already inside.

"Is it ..." He began, and then "By Ercos, it really is you, Gwynn. I didn't believe them when they told me. What in the name of all the gods are you doing here?"

"I'm sorry to bother you on campaign." Gwynneth curtsied, finding herself every bit as awkward before him as she had at fifteen.

"Not at all, not at all. And what are you doing? Stand up straight and let me take a look at you. By the Father, you're as beautiful as ever."

Gwynneth blushed in spite of herself. King Lennart was just as loud, and as large as she remembered. She steeled herself to look him in the eye, cursing herself for her lack of composure. Even Arian Orland had never caught her off guard like this.

His dark hazel eyes were as large and clear as ever, though she detected a faint weariness and lines that weren't from laughter alone. He wore his light brown hair shorter than before, though the wind had blown it into a tousled mess. If he didn't frighten the poor Sanovan princess half to death first, she might find him attractive.

Gwynneth recalled being rather frightened herself. She had never met anyone so loud, with such an imposing physical presence to match. But it had soon become clear that Lennart Ostberg was entirely good-natured and quick to laugh, although he boomed alarmingly when he did so. Everyone who met him liked him and Gwynneth was no different.

She stood up straighter and said, "I see you're as charming as ever. But I'm afraid I'm not here to exchange compliments. I come on a rather urgent mission. I hope you can spare a few hours so we might discuss it."

"Of course, of course," Lennart said. "I'm afraid I can't put you up in style, though you shouldn't freeze to death. You and your young lady here." He winked at Catrin, who stiffened up, uncharacteristically. "Now, come along. It's a bit of a hike up to the fort and we haven't got horses. Hope you're up for it."

"I'm sure I can manage," Gwynneth said, praying she could.

The climb was brutal, but short. She reached the top of the cliff just in time to watch the *Rusa* sail out of the harbor. Gwynneth hoped when she returned, it would be to take her to Sanova.

ANTON

As soon as the count and Anton reached Floradias the count put out word that he was recruiting cavalry and paying three month's wages upfront. The troopers came streaming in. The truce had been hard on soldiers. Those who were able had gone to join the fighting in Kronland, but a fair number had lost, sold, or gambled away their equipment. They almost all had their horses, though. Most were Maladene cavalry with the most splendid mounts on the continent. Some of the men were half-starved, but they kept their horses fed. Anton liked these fellows right away.

It was a bit difficult to get all of the armor and weaponry needed on short notice, but this force was much smaller than the count's last, so they didn't need as much either.

"I can't field more than three thousand," the count said with a sigh. "But it's still a useful enough force. We ride for Kronland tomorrow. I'll have the rest of the equipment come after."

To Anton's dismay, they had to cross another frozen river into Kronland. There was a bridge further north, but that would have meant crossing the border back into Zeelund and the count wasn't taking a chance. Worst of all, Anton was expected to go first, right behind the count leading the whole troop.

The riverbanks here were flat, so getting to the river was easy, but the ice itself seemed endlessly wide. "Just like ice-skating," Anton muttered to himself. He'd become at home on the ice of Bonnenruck's canals. This was no different. Just bigger, and a horse was so much heavier. Still, he'd rather die than show fear in front of anyone here. So he pushed down the nausea he felt and urged Skandar onto the ice, right on Cid's heels.

It seemed to take forever, but finally they climbed the opposite bank. Anton realized he'd been holding his breath for much of the time.

291

The count glanced back at him and laughed. "The ice is nice and thick this year, even though it's almost spring. No need to worry."

"It's just, after Lerania ..." Anton trailed off. They never talked about that awful day.

The count's face turned sober. "I know. I don't like to remember it either and an experience like that stays with you awhile. But look. We made it and everyone will be across within the next hour or two. Nothing to worry about."

And somehow, it was true. No matter how hair-raising the scheme, the count always seemed to come out ahead.

Now they were in Aquianus, in friendly territory. "Emilya Hohenwart should be here somewhere in winter quarters," the count said. "I want to find her and see what's going on."

He sent scouts out, and by the end of the day, they had found her. She was living in a small castle belonging to Prince Fabrey with her troops quartered on the villages for leagues around.

"I'm sure the peasants love that." The count laughed. "They're crammed into those cottages as it is. They'll hate having a few soldiers thrown into the mix."

"So the soldiers just live in the people's houses?" Anton didn't think he'd like that much, if he had a house.

The count nodded. "It's not popular, especially if there are young girls about. Though I must say, I had such fun in those situations, in my early days of soldiering. Ah, this one farmer's daughter. She had the blackest hair and eyes. Ercos, how they sparkled. I wasn't much older than you and she was the most magnificent thing I'd ever seen.

"I left her pregnant, so I likely have a little bastard running around that village. Or maybe not so little. He'd be your age." The count sighed like it was a lovely thing. Anton shook his head. "Oh, just you wait, Kronek. It's already started for you with that little bit back in Bonnenruck. Next time you won't get off so easy."

Anton fingered the locket under his shirt. He did that a hundred times a day and each time he saw Gretel's twinkling eyes and heard her merry laugh, her endless breathless questions. He was sure there wouldn't be a next time. No other girl could ever come close.

"You can bunk here, if you're staying for a night or two, but your troopers will need to shift for themselves." Emilya Hohenwart wasn't exactly friendly, but she wasn't quite hostile either. And she didn't seem to care at all when the count smiled or looked at her from under his lashes. "We're packed into this place like herring in a barrel and it's worse since Edric Maximus got here."

"He's here?" the count asked. "I heard he was up in Brandana."

"He was." Hohenwart shrugged. "But he got a message from King Arryk that he's needed in Fromenberg right away. Don't know why."

"I'll take him. I have to find the king anyway. Is Princess Gwynneth with him?" Anton could tell the count was trying to sound casual, but it wasn't working.

Hohenwart laughed, a short, sharp bark. "Rumor has it she's in Estenor or on her way there. She took ship from Zeelund so you probably just missed her."

The count went pale. "I didn't realize she was there. Why is she going to Estenor?"

"Not sure, though I suspect she will try to talk King Lennart into entering the fight. Don't know how she proposes to do that with him tied up in Sanova."

"If anyone can do it, she can."

Hohenwart greeted this with a raised eyebrow. Anton found it funny that the count couldn't get anywhere with her. He could tell he thought she was attractive. She was as tall as the count with short blond hair and cold gray eyes, broad-shouldered from swinging a sword. She was good—Anton had watched her practice in the castle courtyard and reckoned she would give the count a good run if she had a mind to. But she responded to the count with blank neutrality and just a hint of condescension, as if he were a slightly stupid child.

"I'd appreciate it if you'd take Edric Maximus off my hands. His escort is much too large and people come from leagues around to see him."

"Send his escort back to Brandana," the count said. "I'll take him to Fromenberg."

GWYNNETH

Gwynneth was given a small room inside the tiny fortress of Strutka and an hour or two to prepare before meeting with the king. She did her best to freshen up, though her hair was dry and windblown and her cheeks chapped to an alarming red. This was so far removed from how she had pictured an audience with Lennart. She had hoped for a quiet meeting in a luxurious room in his palace, while she lounged in a dainty chair, elegant and well-groomed.

A guard came to get her and led her down the twisting narrow staircase to another little room. It had a small fireplace and was just big enough to hold a map-strewn table and two wooden chairs.

Lennart took Gwynneth by the hand and asked her to sit. "I hope you don't mind if it's just us," he said, standing with his back to the fire. "I sent old Meldahl out on a raid, or he'd be here."

Ludvik Meldahl was Lennart's chief adviser and only a few years older than the king. "He's on a raid? I thought he'd be keeping your court in Tharvik."

"Eh, I need him here more. There's none better with a little boat loaded with soldiers, stealing onto a Sanovan beach at night and hitting 'em where it hurts."

"I suppose not. So that's why you're in this ungodly place at this ungodly time of year. Raiding?"

"It's just to soften them up before spring. Then I'll hit 'em hard. Finish this thing once and for all."

"I wanted to talk to you about that."

"About Sanova?"

"Yes."

"All right then. But you've got me flummoxed. I reckoned you came to tell me how it's in my best interests to invade Kronland. I don't dislike the idea, but as you can see, they've had me tied up here for years."

"I know. And yes, I want you to invade Kronland and I have an idea of how you can end this fight with Sanova."

"You're a smart girl, Gwynn, but I'd be surprised if you've come up with something old Ludvik and I haven't chewed over a thousand times."

"Perhaps not. But there is one thing you should consider more carefully because I can help you with it. And that's marriage to Raysa Sikora."

"That's one of the thousand things we can't do."

"Won't do."

"Not that simple. I won't lie—I'm not keen on wedding a little girl who's grown up under that hag Ottilya's thumb. I feel sorry for the poor thing even though I've never met her. But I'd do it if it meant peace. Thing is, Queen Ottilya won't do it. I'm sure of it."

"Have you asked? Since I remember from personal experience you tend not to?" She couldn't resist the barb, though it was at least as embarrassing to her.

His laugh boomed out. "Oh, you got me there, you little vixen. See, that's why I never asked for you. Can't be married to a girl who'll get the better of me, no matter how pretty. But you're right, I haven't asked because I know what the answer will be."

"If I do the asking for you, you might get a different answer."

"What are you saying?" Lennart frowned and sat down at the table across from her.

"I'm saying I'll go to Sanova and negotiate a marriage on your behalf. It's the perfect solution. Ottilya will have no reason to harp on her claim to the Estenor crown if she can be assured her own grandchild will inherit it one day."

"Think so?"

"Yes, I do. I doubt she likes this war any more than you do. You hate her, and no doubt the feeling is mutual, but I'm sure she'd like to find a diplomatic solution. And if I do the talking, she won't have to swallow her pride to speak with you directly. At least not until you're her son-in-law."

"That's one theory, but it's as good as any. Let's lay it all out right now then. Let's say you pull this off, and I marry Raysa Sikora, which will end the war with Sanova. What do you want in exchange for that? Don't get me wrong, I can guess. But I want to hear it from you straight."

"Very well then." All unease had left her. Gwynneth was in her element now and sure of what she was doing. "I want you to enter the war in Kronland. Not on the side of my brother, but on behalf of Kendryk."

Lennart smiled. "Interesting. How does your brother feel about this?"

"I haven't asked. But I'm sure he won't like it. Still, he needs the help. More than that, he needs to get home. He never consolidated his rule in Norovaea and I don't like Norvel Classen running everything."

"True, Arryk blundered off to Terragand pretty fast after being crowned. Not that I blame him. I was about ready to come rescue you myself."

Gwynneth was glad that hadn't happened. This level of obligation was bad enough. "In any event, I'd like you to invade Kronland on behalf of Terragand with the goal of restoring Kendryk to the throne."

"How do you propose to get Kendryk?"

"I'm working on it. Gauvain Brevard is trying but hasn't yet succeeded and I have ideas of my own."

"All right. I can leave that part to you. There's something else. We haven't talked in a long time so you probably don't know how things stand with me. I've heard about the changes in the faith sweeping Kronland right now and I'd like to see those changes become permanent."

Gwynneth couldn't keep the smile from spreading across her face. "I would like nothing more."

"Really? I hadn't taken you for a religious sort."

"I wasn't." She told him about Edric Maximus and the Scrolls.

His face lit up as she spoke. "Same thing happened to me. It was well over a year ago when I got the first copy of the Scrolls, one of your Edric's translations. I'd never been very devout, but those words I read, they spoke to me. It was like the gods themselves touched me, if you can picture that."

"I know what you mean," Gwynneth said eagerly. "And that's why I've spent far too much time making sure Edric spreads the truth everywhere when I should have tried to attack Teodora directly."

"No, you did right. Teodora will fall that much easier with the groundwork laid in Kronland."

"I hadn't thought of it that way. I hope you're right. "

"I hope so too. Teodora needs to go. For a while, I wondered if we could negotiate a peace that guarantees religious freedom for the Kronland rulers, but now I don't think that's good enough. The Empire is a corrupt relic of the old faith and must be wiped out."

There was a passion in his voice that Gwynneth had never noticed before, and she found herself swept up in it. He went on. "The only way to do it is to gather all of the Kronland rulers into one big army, along with your brother, if he can. If we all stand together, we'll easily defeat Brynhild Mattila and the rest.

Then it's only a matter of time before we're at the gates of Atlona. I know I can take it."

Gwynneth was certain he could too. He was no Andor Korma. She had heard glowing praise of Lennart's military theories and innovations for several years now. No doubt he couldn't wait to try them out. "I must get you out of Sanova so you can do this."

"Good. Like I said, I'm not keen on the Sikora girl. I'm twice her age, and I'm sure she'll be less thrilled about it than I am. But you're right. If there's an easy way to end this, it's that one. When can you sail?"

"I thought I'd wait for Captain Brun to return in a few days. She said she could take me."

"Excellent. I hope you're not too uncomfortable here, but I wouldn't mind talking over a few things with you while you wait. This might be a good time to discuss some invasion plans so you can lay the groundwork with the northerners when you get back to Kronland."

Gwynneth didn't bother hiding her excitement. Now she just needed to get the agreement of Queen Ottilya.

ANTON

Anton and the count didn't spend long in Aquianus because Edric Maximus had been ordered by King Arryk to join him in all haste.

"Any idea what it's about?" the count had asked Edric.

The Maximus shook his head. "He said it was urgent and critical to the war effort. Of course I'll help where I can."

It took several days to get to Fromenberg and they rode straight to the king. It was hard to say if he was happier to welcome Edric Maximus, or the count with his three thousand fresh troops.

"Barela's attacks decimated our horse, so we are in sore need of cavalry," King Arryk said, clapping the count on the shoulder. "And I have a mission you can help with."

Anton went to the stables while the count was in meetings with the king and Maximus. He'd hear what it was about soon enough.

He got the horses settled in when there was a small commotion. Someone important was riding into the stable-yard. Anton dusted his hands off on his breeches and went out to see what was going on. It was the Duchess Maryna and her little brother—Anton didn't remember his name. It seemed they had been out for a ride with a large group of grooms and bodyguards.

Though Maryna couldn't have been over eight, she rode a full-grown Zastwarian mare. Not much taller than a large pony, the mare had the glossiest chestnut coat, a black mane and tail, and the finest bones Anton had seen on a horse. He couldn't stop himself. "What a beautiful horse," he said, as a groom helped the duchess down.

"Mind your place, boy," a guard snapped at him. "This here's the Duchess of Terragand and the likes of her don't speak to the likes of you."

Anton didn't back up, and smiled at the duchess.

"Oh, it's you!" she said. "You're the boy who helped my uncle in the battle. I will speak with him." She nodded at the guard and walked up to Anton, extending a tiny hand encased in a white leather glove. He wasn't sure what to do, so he took it and bowed.

"I didn't know you were here," she said. "Come, let's go to the stables. Do you still have the horse Uncle Arryk gave you?"

"Oh yes," Anton said. "Would you like to meet him?"

"Come, Devyn," Maryna said to the little boy who had also dismounted by now. "You need to see this horse. This is my brother, Duke Devyn Bernotas. Devyn, this is—oh dear, I'm afraid I've forgotten your name."

Anton doubted she'd ever known it. "Anton Kronek, at your service," he said, sketching a small bow toward the little duke.

"Oh yes. Anton. Kronek is Moraltan, isn't it?"

"It is," Anton said. "Here's Skandar." They came to Skandar's stall and went inside.

Even though she was much smaller, Anton couldn't help comparing the little duchess to Gretel. Maryna was far more serious, but Anton liked her directness. Though he hated to admit it, she was even prettier than Gretel, looking like a miniature version of her mother, the beautiful princess.

"Is it safe?" A groom was tagging along, no doubt to serve as a guard.

"He's as gentle as can be." Anton watched as Maryna petted Skandar's nose. "He loves girls especially."

"He's beautiful." Maryna sounded almost reverent. Maybe she loved horses as much as Anton did. "Just look at that shaggy winter coat, Devyn. This is a fine Norovaean stallion. Uncle Arryk must have been very pleased."

"I want one." Devyn rested his cheek against Skandar's flank.

"I'm sure your uncle, the king, will give you one," Anton said.

"He probably will," Maryna said. "Though he must wait until Devyn is older. This horse is much too big for him."

"Is not," Devyn said.

"Hmph. We'll see," Maryna said.

"I love your pony, too," Anton said, seeing that Devyn wanted to argue.

"He's all right," Devyn said. "I want a real horse."

Maryna rolled her eyes and Anton hid a smile.

"Perhaps you can go riding with us next time, Anton," she said.

Anton thrilled at the idea, but then remembered. "I'll be leaving soon."

"Didn't you just get here?"

"Yes. But I'm with Count Orland and the king said he's sending him on a mission. Something to do with Edric Maximus."

Maryna's face fell. "I heard Edric Maximus was here. I like him so much. And now we've made friends and you're leaving with him. Everyone always leaves me.'"

"Me too." Anton was surprised at the rush of sadness he felt.

"Are your parents dead?" Maryna wanted to know.

"Yes, and my sister."

"That's dreadful," she said softly. "I shouldn't be ungrateful. I think my papa is still alive and Mama is just away for a while, though I miss them both. And I've missed Edric Maximus so."

"I'll take you to see him," Anton said. "I know where he's lodged."

He felt bad, making friends, only to leave again right away.

ARRYK

"Let someone else do it," Arryk said. He didn't want to beg. He shouldn't have to. Kings never begged. But now he had what he wanted, which was for Larisa to treat him the same as ever. Edric Maximus had arrived with Count Orland's new army and Larisa was leaving for Kersenstadt the next day.

"No one else will do it as well." She came over and sat on his lap, wrapping her arms around his neck and pulling him close. They were in their bedchamber and this was their last night together. They hadn't been separated since the invasion.

Arryk breathed her in. It was ridiculous, that he couldn't explain why he didn't want to let her go. Dreams and superstitions. She would laugh. He wished Gwynneth were here because she might believe him, now she'd gone all religious. Not to mention Larisa had considerable respect for his sister and might actually listen to what she said.

"It shouldn't be that hard." He pulled back so he could look her in the eye. "Olsen can do it."

"I'm sure he can get the Maximus in, but preparing for a siege? I doubt it." Even though it seemed unlikely that Mattila would try to take the city back with Arryk at her rear, they had decided to prepare for the possibility.

"Do you know how to get ready for a siege?"

"I do. I wrote to General Hohenwart and she sent me a few books. She's the best at that sort of thing."

"Wish I could send her instead," Arryk grumbled.

"She's too far away. And besides, Count Orland said her army is scattered across the countryside for leagues around. She'd have to round them up, bring them here, and you'd have to put them up somehow since she won't need them all for Kersenstadt. No, I know what I'm doing. And there's more."

"Isn't there always?" He kissed the tip of her ear.

"I'm serious, Arryk. This is the chance I've been waiting for, to prove myself. Listen, I don't want you to think I regret meeting you, ever. I don't. But ever since we became lovers, everyone else is certain that my only value is because of what I mean to you. It doesn't occur to anyone that I might be a rather competent soldier all on my own."

"Oh come now. The way you fought at Birkenfels should end all doubts about that."

"It should, but I didn't command there. I did well enough as your bodyguard, but we only survived because Orland broke through at the last minute. The fact remains, no one thinks I'm capable of commanding my own operation."

"Who cares what anyone else thinks?"

"I care. I want to be taken seriously and I can be a greater help to you if I am. Please let me do this?"

"You'll be gone so long."

"Just until summer. I'll get the city garrisoned and fortified, build up outerworks like no one has ever seen. In the meantime, I'll send you all of the guns and other equipment I can spare. While I hold the city, you'll march on Mattila as soon as the weather clears and Hohenwart gets here. Once you've defeated Mattila, Kersenstadt will be secure and I'll come join you."

"You make it sound so easy."

"It won't be. My part will be straightforward, though I'll have to work hard. Now that you have Orland back and Hohenwart and maybe even Faris in the spring, you should be able to defeat Mattila. Just choose a good spot—Hohenwart can help with that."

"I suppose you're right. But I hate doing this by myself, especially with Gwynneth gone."

"I don't like to leave you. But Gwynneth is doing you a good turn up in Estenor. Can you imagine how quickly this will be over if she gets Lennart to invade?"

"I don't see how she can." That made Arryk grumpy, too. Everything he'd heard about the Estenorian king showed that he was the kind of ruler that Arryk could only wish he was. Arryk had met Lennart when he was courting Gwynneth and had been both impressed and intimidated, even though Lennart had been nothing but friendly and generous. He was intelligent, an excellent soldier, well-educated, and many found him good-looking in a rough, manly sort of way. It didn't suit Arryk to have Lennart breeze in and succeed where he so far was only making the slowest progress.

"You don't like him, I know." Larisa looked into his eyes.

"But I do like him. That's the problem. You'll like him too, perhaps better than me." That was his biggest worry. He hadn't meant to say it, but there it was.

"That's what you're worried about?" Larisa laughed, then nuzzled Arryk's chin. "Believe me, I've heard the stories, and to be honest, he sounds very dull. Your sister must have written pages about their religious conversations and I've told you before how I feel about scholars. I don't care how great a warrior he is. If

he wants to talk about Edric's sermons, or even worse, the Holy Scrolls, I'll be tempted to kill him. You won't get rid of me that easily."

"Thank the gods for that," Arryk said, relieved. He pulled her close once more. "You're right and I must let you do this. I'll just miss you so terribly."

"I'll miss you too. I'll write to you all the time. So often in fact, you'll be most annoyed."

"I doubt that."

"I know how you feel about letters."

"Yes, but I'll love yours."

"Just wait until you see my writing skills before you say that." She laughed and kissed him. "Now stop making me sad and take me to bed one more time."

GWYNNETH

Gwynneth was ready when Captain Brun returned. Her time with Lennart had been productive, but it was all for nothing if she couldn't make this marriage happen within the next few months.

Brun sailed straight into the harbor at Novuk, Sanova's principal city.

"Is it safe to fly the Estenor flag here?" Gwynneth asked, more than a little nervous.

"Oh sure. We're not officially at war, and here, I'll run up a little white flag underneath if it'll put your mind at ease."

"That helps; thank you." Gwynneth eyed the guns sticking out from the ramparts that lined the harbor approach. They resembled the bristles of a hedgehog. No wonder Lennart was raiding elsewhere.

Somewhere ahead of them, a gun boomed. "I think they want us to stop," Gwynneth said.

"Seems like it." For all her casual tone, Brun's face was set. Surely she found this at least a little bit nerve-wracking. "Oh look; here they come."

A small boat, rowed by a crew of eight, approached rapidly. Gwynneth pulled back the hood of her cloak, even though the wind was icy and stepped to the rail as the boat drew near. She looked for the person in charge and spotted him right away, his arrogant manner as obvious as his red and gold uniform. "State your name and rank," she called out before he could speak.

He had opened his mouth to ask hers, then closed it again.

Gwynneth raised an eyebrow, hoping she appeared haughtier than she felt.

"Count Bendik Tarka, lieutenant of the guard of her majesty Queen Ottilya Sikora." He doffed his hat, though he didn't quite bow, understandable since the little boat was pitching rather alarmingly.

Gwynneth decided not to draw things out. "Good day, Count. I am Gwynneth Roussay, Princess of Norovaea and Terragand, here on a diplomatic mission. I would speak with the queen as soon as possible."

Tarka almost fell out of the boat but recovered, and his hat came off in a wide sweep. "Princess, forgive me. We did not expect you. Especially not on such a vessel." He eyed the stout little *Rusa* with some condescension and Gwynneth felt the captain bristle beside her.

"This is not an official visit." Gwynneth kept her tone cool. "My mission requires delicacy and I'd prefer to remain anonymous until I have spoken with the queen. Can you manage that?"

"I believe I can." The count nearly swept off his hat again, but appeared to change his mind as another swell hit his boat. "You may follow us into the harbor if you please."

Gwynneth inclined her head, then smiled at Captain Brun as soon as Tarka's back was turned. "Better now, I think."

"I hope so," the captain muttered under her breath. "Though I don't trust these Sanovans for a second."

"Now they know who I am, I'm sure we're safe. Whatever its opinion on Terragand, I know Sanova does not care for trouble with Norovaea."

"I hope you're right." The *Rusa* bumped up against a dock.

"Wait for word from me," Gwynneth said as she prepared to disembark. "If I succeed, I'll return to Kronland overland, but I'll need you to take a message back to Lennart." She pressed a small purse into the captain's hand. "Find a nice inn for a few days. I'll see you soon and thank you."

"No, thank you." Captain Brun grinned at Gwynneth, hefting the weight of the purse. "Best of luck to you Princess."

"I'll need it," Gwynneth said, and joined Count Tarka on the dock. Tall and slender, with long hair so blond it was nearly white and piercing blue eyes in a narrow face, he was a perfect specimen of Sanovan nobility.

He had already called for a hired carriage and took her straight to the palace. "I apologize for the conveyance, Your Grace," he said, still flustered by her unconventional arrival and appreciative gaze. "But it's best not to use one of the royal coaches if you don't wish to attract attention."

"Quite right, I hope Queen Ottilya is in residence."

"She is. You're in luck. She just returned from touring the north coast. That bastard—begging your pardon—I mean King Lennart, has been raiding all up and down it. To be honest, it's shocking to see a ship flying the Estenor flag approach our harbor under the circumstances."

"I wondered about that. I hope the situation can soon be remedied." Gwynneth could tell the count was dying to ask her how, but she contented herself with a mysterious smile.

The count had sent word ahead to the palace, so a tall, dour-looking woman met her carriage at the main entrance and whisked her off to a luxurious suite. "I am Zytka, Duchess Hylek," she said. "I am in charge of Her Highness's household. I will let the queen know you are here and arrange an audience. Be prepared to see her as soon as morning."

Gwynneth hadn't expected a friendly reception and perhaps it was just the duchess's manner, but she detected distinct undertones of hostility.

By the time she settled into her rooms, it was evening. Exotic but delicious food materialized from somewhere, and Gwynneth found herself sleepy before long. After making sure her best dress was in good repair, she went to bed and slept until morning. She hadn't had such comfortable accommodation since Norovaea.

Gwynneth was still breakfasting when Duchess Hylek came for her. Fortunately, she was already dressed and Catrin had arranged her hair.

The duchess led Gwynneth down endless vast corridors until they reached a crowded antechamber. "Her Highness is hearing petitioners, but due to your rank, you should be next."

Gwynneth swallowed down her indignation. This was not appropriate treatment for someone who was nearly a fellow head of state. She had no time to stew as the duchess opened a door. "You may approach her majesty," she said.

A throne in a throne room. It seemed so pretentious. As far as Gwynneth knew, only Teodora bothered to receive petitioners in such formal conditions. Still, Ottilya Sikora was Teodora's sister-in-law, so perhaps she thought herself equal.

Gwynneth approached the throne with firm, measured steps. She would not be intimidated. The room was empty, save for a few people standing near the queen, all staring at her curiously. Gwynneth ignored them and swept into a curtsy. "Your Highness. Thank you for seeing me on such short notice."

"You may rise, Princess." Ottilya's voice was rough and deep. It matched her face, which couldn't be called anything but hatchet-like. "What brings you to Novuk, stealing into the harbor like a smuggler, and under an Estenor flag of all things?"

"I'm here on behalf of King Lennart Ostberg." Gwynneth let her voice echo through the vast room to show she wasn't cowed.

"Why in the world would you do such a thing?"

"The king wishes to request the hand of your daughter, Princess Raysa Sikora in marriage."

The queen burst out laughing.

ANTON

The count was excited when Anton found him later. "We're to be part of a force that will take Kersenstadt," he said.

"Isn't that a big city?"

"Pretty big. Heavily fortified and manned by veteran garrison troops."

"How will we get in?"

"The gates ought to open from the inside. With any luck, we won't have to fight much. Make sure the horses are well-rested. We ride out tomorrow."

A sizable force left the castle where King Arryk stayed. Orland's three thousand cuirassiers joined two hundred horse and another thousand pike and musket, commanded by Larisa Karsten. Anton could tell the king didn't want her to go, but didn't want to show it in front of everyone.

"We must move quickly," the count told Anton. "There won't be much forage along the way. It's been a hard winter and the snow took long to melt. Still, the country around here should be untouched and there ought to be barns full of hay. Once we get within a day or two of the city, I expect the Sanova Hussars will have already picked the area clean."

It was cold, but Anton didn't mind. The mornings were foggy, but when it lifted the trees and grass were covered in white frost and sparkled in the sun. It looked like a fairy kingdom.

About ten leagues from Kersenstadt, they stopped. From here, Edric Maximus would continue with a small escort. "It might take a few days," he said, pulling on a borrowed cloak. He wore different clothes from normal in hopes he wouldn't be recognized right away. "The temples ought to be easy enough, but if the town council is sympathetic to the empire, changing the government might take longer. Look for a light above the main gate. When it appears, the gate will open at midnight. When that happens it means most people in the city support the true faith. Please be gentle with them." He gave the count a stern look.

308

Larisa Karsten sent patrols to keep an eye on the city and then they waited. Anton wondered how they would get the gates open from the inside. He was getting sick of being cold and bored when the message came, just after dark on the sixth day.

"We take the city tonight," the count said, grinning as he put on his armor. Anton helped with some of the trickier buckles. "If the Maximus has done his work, it will be easy."

Late that night, all the troops moved out in quiet and orderly fashion. Anton made sure he and the count were ready to fight just in case. They walked through the open gate without a soul to oppose them at first. A mob of armed citizens had overcome most of Mattila's garrison. Those who remained barricaded themselves into the castle, but Karsten turned her big guns on them, while the count got his troops ready to attack.

Anton had never experienced cannon-fire inside city walls. It was so loud he was deaf for a long time after. But the guns did their work, turning the flimsy old castle gate into kindling with just one barrage. Even though Anton couldn't hear, he saw the count raise his saber and charge through the broken gate. He followed, spurring Skandar to a gallop, holding one of his pistols ready. Those inside didn't have much by way of weapons, since they'd already fought and lost at the city gate. A few of Mattila's soldiers fired their pistols, then drew swords, but were quickly overrun by the cavalry.

Anton fired at a woman charging the count with a drawn sword, but missed. The count didn't though, and by the time Anton had drawn his own saber, it was over. Bodies lay everywhere, and everyone else surrendered. There was a small commotion as Larisa Karsten rode into the castle courtyard, on a horse that looked a lot like Skandar. The flickering torchlight revealed grime on her face and Anton wondered if she'd fired one of the cannon herself.

The count smiled his special smile at her. "Congratulations, Duchess. The city is yours."

She stared back, unsmiling. "Thank you. Now we must find a way to keep it."

After that one fight, they had no more trouble, since most people seemed happy to see them. Not quite so happy once they realized they'd have to feed and quarter the troops, but everyone cooperated well enough.

The count found a pleasant townhouse and they stayed for a few days. "I want to leave once the city is secure," he told Anton. "Karsten has plenty of troops to hold the place and she'll work on building up the outerworks. I don't want my cavalry used for that kind of labor, so we'll move out as soon as we can. In the meantime, go have fun in the city."

Anton had money, so he found the nearest stall selling hot chocolate and a pastry shop nearby. It had been cold and he was growing, so he was always hungry. Kersenstadt was an interesting place—so different from Bonnenruck, though it reminded Anton of Kaleva. He visited several of the temples, which were famous for their beauty. These were usually packed. Edric Maximus moved around, preaching at each one in turn, making sure the priest or priestess there had a copy of the Holy Scrolls and was teaching from them correctly. He wouldn't stay here long.

Anton listened to some of the sermons, though he'd heard it all before. But the people of Kersenstadt were excited. This was probably all new to them.

The count spent a lot of time at various warehouses. Brynhild Mattila had left the city well-stocked with all kinds of military equipment and Larisa Karsten was sending most of it to King Arryk. After a bit of shouting, it was decided that the count would take a convoy back to the king. He had wanted to go north to harass Mattila, but Karsten insisted.

"Stubborn bitch," the count swore, coming home one evening. "She's much too used to getting her way. She's got the king wrapped around her little finger and thinks she can do as she likes."

"You've met your match then," Anton said, and ducked, not completely missing the blow aimed at his head. The count was sour whenever he couldn't make a woman do what he wanted. Especially when she was as attractive as the Duchess Karsten. But it seemed the duchess had eyes only for the king and Anton saw why. Not only was he at least as good-looking as the count, he was also a king. Anton didn't blame her for being so loyal.

JANNA

The bombardment though short, was terrifying. For Janna, the worst was not knowing what had happened. She heard some of the news from Klaus the footman, but it made little sense. "Didn't General Mattila leave a whole garrison?" she asked. Braeden had been so sure the city was impregnable.

"Seems so," Klaus said, his broad face bewildered, though he seemed to always wear that expression. Braeden had hired him for his size, not his wit.

"So why couldn't they stop this?"

"I believe they tried, ma'am. That's what all the shooting was about. The people of the city raided the armory and told the garrison to surrender. They put up a fight, but there weren't enough of them. Those that could ran to the castle, but then that duchess and Count Orland turned the big guns on them and that was that."

"So what happens now?" Janna tried to push down the dread welling up inside her.

"Soldiers. Foreign soldiers and plenty of 'em. Looks like they'll stay awhile."

"Oh Holy Mother," Janna whispered, pulling Iryna close. "What will become of us?"

"With any luck, not much." Birgid spoke up. "We might have to put up some officers here, but beyond that, who knows?"

"Some say they'll leave as soon as they get all the weapons they want."

"I hope so." Janna tried not to cry, since everyone else seemed to be bearing up quite well.

She didn't stay in suspense too long. That evening, there was a pounding on the door and Klaus ran up the stairs and burst into the parlor. "Norovacans," he gasped. "What should I do?"

"Best let them in," Birgid said.

Janna nodded. It was unlikely her door would keep them out for long in any case. She struggled to stand and keep her knees from shaking. She had just pulled herself together when they walked into her parlor.

"Good evening, Madame," a tall blond man swept his plumed hat in a bow. "I am Major Holgar Ellert of King Arryk Roussay's army." He spoke strongly accented Olvisyan but it was no worse than Janna's.

Her throat was so dry. "Good evening," she croaked.

Major Ellert introduced two other men and a woman, all of them officers with names that made no sense to Janna. At least Ellert had a name she could pronounce. "We are sorry to inconvenience you, but we require lodging for the near future, and you have ample space. Who lives here?"

Janna found her voice. "Just me and my daughter, and the servants." Iryna had taken one look at all of the tall blond people and hidden behind Janna's skirts.

"Your husband?"

"He's away." She hoped they wouldn't ask for details. She didn't want to be considered one of the enemy, even though she supposed she was.

"Well, if he's outside the city, he won't be back for a while. Duchess Karsten has ordered the gates shut and no one allowed to enter."

Janna nodded. She didn't suppose she could expect Braeden to just walk into the midst of a nest of Norovaeans, though she wished he would.

All was well until the woman insisted on her own room and Janna felt obligated to give up hers. She could sleep in the nursery.

"We will of course pay for all of our own food," Ellert said. "I imagine we'll stay out of your way as much as we can."

Janna nodded, relieved. The less she saw of them the better, even though none looked particularly threatening. She and Birgid got all of her things from her bedroom, the bedroom she'd shared with Braeden when he was here, she thought sadly. No matter. These people would be gone by the time Braeden returned, and hopefully soon.

For the first few days, she seldom saw them. She went from the nursery to her little parlor while the servants took care of the rest of the house, and the Norovaeans stayed out all day and most of the night.

"No doubt they have much work at the walls," Birgid said.

And they did. One evening, Ellert strode into the parlor, again giving her a courteous bow. "I am sorry to trouble you again Madame, but I'm afraid I have a requirement."

312

Janna indicated that he take a seat. It only seemed polite, and he was so very tall, looming over her.

"The Duchess Karsten is working to build up the fortifications around the city and requires one able-bodied person from each household until the work is done. Your large footman should do nicely."

"Klaus? Oh dear. I can't order him to ..."

"You needn't do any such thing. If you prefer, I have the authority to draft him into the duchess's service."

"I'd rather he didn't."

"I am very sorry, but someone must, and he would be most able to bear the work."

"Is it very hard?"

"There is a great deal of digging and hauling dirt and stone. The ground is frozen, which makes it more difficult."

"Will he be able to come back here when it's done?" It seemed she wasn't being given much choice in the matter.

"Certainly. It shouldn't take more than a week or two and the Norovaean army will feed and house him during that time."

"I see. I have another question," Janna asked in a small voice.

"I can try to answer." Major Ellert seemed to have a constantly pleasant expression on his rosy face which looked strangely boyish on someone his size.

"I realize you cannot tell me all of your plans, but I thought perhaps you would take what you wanted from the city and go?"

Ellert smiled, and didn't look offended. "We considered that at one point, but the duchess determined the city has immense strategic value and should be held. She will send Count Orland's force back to King Arryk with all of the supplies he needs along with Edric Maximus."

Janna tried to stave off her rising panic. "Will there be a siege?"

"I think not. King Arryk will defeat Mattila long before she can get back here. But don't worry. We are keeping the city well-supplied just in case. There will be no starvation."

"Oh, good," Janna said weakly.

GWYNNETH

Gwynneth kept her composure and waited for the queen to stop laughing. Since the laughter wasn't the least bit sincere, it didn't take long.

Queen Ottilya wiped non-existent tears, then said, "That's the most ridiculous thing I've ever heard. Why would I marry my darling daughter off to that horrid oaf?"

"So your grandchild can sit on the throne of Estenor someday."

"A lovely thought, but not quite what I had in mind. Do you realize I personally have a claim to that throne?"

"I do. But you have yet to succeed in pressing it, I'm afraid."

The queen frowned. "Don't be insolent, Princess. My patience with anyone who claims to be a friend to Lennart is very thin."

"I don't claim to be his friend. I'm merely an envoy."

"Why are you putting yourself through this?"

"I have reason for directing Lennart's attention away from Sanova. I care little for your dynastic disputes, but I need Estenor to invade Kronland." Gwynneth realized she was taking a risk in matching her tone to the queen's, but if her guess was correct, Ottilya liked a good argument and had no respect for doormats.

"Oh-ho. I'll bet you do," the queen cackled. "Quite a mess you and your husband have made of things there."

Gwynneth narrowed her eyes, but kept her tone even. "In addition, it seems to me that you don't wish for Teodora Inferrara's unchecked success."

That hit home. Someone behind the throne gasped and the queen frowned. Everyone held their breaths.

"Hmm. You're right; I don't. My husband in particular would love to see Teodora laid low."

The rumors were true then. Atinos Inferrara hated his sister.

"I can hardly blame him," Gwynneth said with a wry smile. "And if you wish to press a dynastic claim, the imperial throne holds a great deal more weight than that of Estenor."

"Yes, quite right. Still, I don't wish to speak of these things here, though I'd like to discuss this further. Now don't get your hopes up, Princess. I still think your errand ridiculous. But it's not every day I get to speak with someone who refuses to snivel and simper. It's refreshing. You'll hear from me soon. You are dismissed."

It was rude and it was abrupt, but it wasn't a flat no.

Gwynneth was left to stew for a good long while. She dined with the queen every evening, but avoided bringing up her petition. She worried Ottilya would use the opportunity to turn her down flat in front of everyone. After nearly a fortnight, Gwynneth felt frantic, though she would rather die than show it.

So she came to dinner, was witty and charming. She spent her days with the dressmaker, so she wore something new and pretty every time the queen saw her. The last thing she wanted was to appear drab or desperate. To all appearances, Princess Gwynneth was having a marvelous time in Novuk, flirting with all of the men and charming their wives.

She was careful to be friendly with Atinos Inferrara, despite his resemblance to Teodora. He was just as unpleasant but lacked his sister's intelligence and wit. Much as Gwynneth hated Teodora, she had to admit that she was by far the better choice for the imperial throne.

Gwynneth also took the opportunity to cultivate some new contacts. She had always found it difficult to keep abreast of the doings of Ottilya's court, but now she had several friends who assured her they would write to her often with all of the news.

Her stamina paid off. One evening after dinner, the queen rose and said, "Roussay, you'll come with me," and swept out of the dining room.

Gwynneth wasted no time in following her. The queen glided down a broad, tapestry-lined corridor unaccompanied. She turned suddenly, and Gwynneth almost missed the door falling shut. She knocked, then opened it without waiting for a reply.

Ottilya sat before a crackling fire that smelled of juniper. For someone of her bulk, she had moved swiftly. "Come in and have a seat," she said, as if Gwynneth were an old friend.

Gwynneth sat down and tried to relax. She'd come this far; it wouldn't do to appear overeager now.

"You are ..." Ottilya trailed off and stared into the fire. "You are most persistent, without being annoying. I must confess I'm impressed." She drew a deep sigh. "In fact, I wish my daughter were more like you. Raysa is such a weakling, I can't imagine where she got such thin blood. I thank Vica every day she isn't my heir."

"She is still young," Gwynneth said, her head swimming at the compliment. She must find a way to take advantage of this. "I'm far more resolute today than I was at seventeen." That wasn't true, but Gwynneth felt a need to defend the hapless Raysa.

"Hmph. I hope you're right. I'd hoped to marry her off to Briansk, but they won't give me anyone important enough. I'd considered your brother too, though he hasn't put himself on the market."

"He will, and soon," Gwynneth said. "The Norovaean council will require it. But he needs a strong woman. Lennart on the other hand, wants someone more docile. He'd courted me at one time, before my marriage, and decided I was too much for him."

The queen barked a laugh. "I'm sure you were. Well, if he's looking for docile, Raysa is that. Tell me; do you think he'll be a good husband?"

The question caught Gwynneth off guard. "I do," she said, after giving it a moment's thought. "It's true he's loud and rough, but at heart, he's a decent fellow. I know he's worried that Raysa is too young and that he'll frighten her."

"Interesting. In my experience, someone truly frightening would never worry about that."

"I doubt they'd see each other much in any case. If he marries Raysa and there is peace between you as a result, he will soon make for Kronland. He's a warrior through and through, and if he's not on campaign, he's recruiting and drilling. He won't be underfoot."

"There's something to be said for that. Nothing worse than a husband always in the way. In fact, you have mine to thank for this meeting. He wouldn't give me a moment's peace until I spoke with you."

The queen shifted in her chair and sighed. She seemed tired, perhaps somewhat deflated. "To be honest, Princess, I'm sick to death of this war. I can't afford it and never stop worrying that Briansk will take advantage of the situation. If a marriage with my daughter will make a treaty with Lennart possible, I'm inclined to agree. But I have a condition before we go further."

"What is that?" Gwynneth did her best to keep her elation from showing.

"I want you to broker the marriage and resulting treaty personally."

Gwynneth's heart sank. She wanted to return to Kronland without delay.

The queen turned to face her. "It's a requirement. I don't trust Lennart and don't want the negotiations to drag on for months or years."

"I don't want that either."

"Good. I'll draft a preliminary treaty for you to deliver to Lennart. If he agrees, you can come back here and we'll finalize matters."

It wasn't perfect, but she couldn't say no.

TEODORA

Teodora laughed and handed the letter to Livilla. "Your plan is working. Your League of Aeternos clerics are performing as planned and Mattila is livid."

Livilla looked over the letter and smiled. "I didn't think she'd like it, but there's not much she can do except complain, is there? Oh, and the same for Barela. She asks you to call him back, but that's all she can do."

"It's the way things should be. She shouldn't be allowed to have everything her own way all the time. And she was in winter quarters where disciplinary problems aren't unusual. Though I'm not happy with Elektra. Her letters are nothing but an echo of Mattila's. I swear I don't know who's side she's on."

Livilla shrugged. "She's likely to be influenced by the person she spends the most time with. I've arranged to have one of the League priestesses serve as Elektra's personal chaplain. It will take a little while, but I don't see how she can follow the faith strictly without seeing Mattila's many flaws. It's just a matter of time."

"I hope so. I suppose it was too much to expect loyalty from a fourteen-year-old. How I wish I could have foisted her off on Gauvain Brevard!"

"Elektra will show her value soon enough. She is still young and has much to learn. No one can spend much time with Brynhild Mattila and remain fond of her."

"True." Teodora smiled. Waiting like this was hard but spring was here and once Arryk Roussay was gone she could deal with Mattila.

Her good mood didn't last. Sometime the next afternoon, Elyse came running with a dirty messenger pouch. "Your Highness," she gasped. "Urgent news from Kronland." Elyse handed over the pouch. "It came from Prince Novitny."

"Oh gods, now what?" Teodora opened the pouch and pulled out the hastily scrawled letter. Novitny, the dolt, hadn't even bothered to encrypt it. Of course what he had written wouldn't remain secret for long, if it ever was a secret. Teo-

318

dora sprang out of her chair as she read. "How could this happen?" she shrieked. "How? I've never seen such incompetence. It was for this she wanted supreme command?" She needed to scream at someone, but there was only Elyse and she was unlikely to dissolve into tears the way Teodora would have liked.

"Is there something I can do, Your Highness?" Elyse looked alarmed.

"No." Teodora paced the room. "Get out but don't go far. I need to think." She concentrated on taking deep breaths until she heard the door close. She picked up a cushion from a chair and punched it. Unhelpful. She scanned the room until she spotted a lovely, heavy vase from Neviar. Perfect. She felt its smooth weight in her hand, then hurled it with all her strength at the glass of the tall garden doors. It took out a satisfying half-dozen panes before shattering against a low stone wall outside.

Still not good enough. She wondered if she could kill someone. Go to the dungeons, find a deserving criminal and do the deed herself. That was it. She ran into the corridor, shouting for her coach.

Elyse materialized from around a corner, Count Solteszy in tow. Teodora should have known the girl was up to something.

"Your Highness, where are you going?" Solteszy asked.

"To the Arnfels."

"But why?"

"Come with me and I'll tell you on the way."

Her coach pulled into the courtyard with a few frazzled-looking guards hanging on. No doubt the useless sods had been prodded out of a nap. Teodora peered at one of them. "Is that halberd sharp?"

"Yes, Your Highness," the young woman said, bewildered. Teodora hadn't seen her before, so she was most likely new and hadn't yet experienced an imperial tantrum.

"Good. You can come along."

Settled in the coach with Solteszy, flying down the cobblestones, she said. "Do you know about Kersenstadt?"

He looked puzzled. "General Mattila is using it as a depot for her supplies when she takes on Roussay."

"Was. She's lost it and is doing nothing about it."

"Lost it? How?"

"That strumpet of Arryk's smuggled the heretic Landrus into the city and within a few days he'd turned everyone against Mattila's garrison. It also seems that Arian Orland has returned from Floradias with a significant force. He and

Karsten secured the city and killed most of the garrison. As we speak, all of Mattila's precious supplies are on their way to Arryk Roussay."

"This is a disaster," Solteszy said. "What does Mattila propose to do about it?"

"No idea. I haven't heard a word about it from her. The letter came from Novitny. For all I know, Mattila hasn't a clue. And it's too late in any case. Karsten holds the city and is building up the fortifications. I can't imagine why Mattila neglected to do the same."

"How many?" Solteszy's tone was much like the one he would have used to inquire about the number of guests coming to dinner.

"How many what?"

"How many troops does Karsten have? How many guns? How many people inside the city?"

"How should I know?" Teodora snapped. "It's not my job anymore. And Mattila is too far away to do anything. Even if she marched on the city right now she'd have to get past Roussay and Orland, since Novitny says she's gone north. I don't understand what she's doing."

Solteszy looked thoughtful. "She might be chasing down Emilya Hohenwart. In which case you ought to take matters into your own hands."

"Yes, I suppose I should. But how? And with what army?"

"Isn't that why you're going to the Arnfels?"

"What in the world are you on about? I'm going to the Arnfels to kill Kendryk Bernotas."

BRAEDEN

Braeden didn't believe what he was hearing. "She did what? How? Mattila left the place well-defended; we saw it."

"Not well enough," Novitny said, his face sympathetic. "At least, not well enough to stand up to the whole citizenry turned into a mob." He had ordered the hussars to make camp on the spot upon receiving the news of Larisa Karsten's conquest of Kersenstadt.

"But there were armed guards. Hundreds of them." He still couldn't piece it all together. After Atlona, Kersenstadt was the safest place in the empire. It had to be. He never would have left his girls there otherwise.

"Were." Novitny's face was grim. "Those that survived the first onslaught took refuge in the fortress, but Karsten and Orland turned Mattila's biggest guns on it, and they surrendered within hours. Seems the thing was blown to bits. A few civilians were in there along with clergy from temples that Landrus took over and those of their congregations that refused to convert. A lot of them didn't make it, though I'm sure Janna wasn't among them."

"Gods. Those culverins Mattila left throw twenty-pound balls." Braeden didn't want to face the wrong end of those cannon, but he might have to. "How do I get in?"

"You don't. I'm sorry. First we need to find out what General Mattila wants to do."

"She'll want it back, I'm sure. She'll attack and it'll be a bloodbath." Braeden paced, getting angry now. "Best case, there'll be a long siege." Long sieges meant children always died first, followed by the sick. Hunger wouldn't be a worry for some time, but plague often took hold much earlier. Braeden remembered how pale Janna had looked when he left her.

"We can't be sure of that," Novitny said. "I wonder if Karsten's plan is to hold the city, or just to clean out the supplies and get them to Arryk."

"That would make sense." A flicker of hope sprang up in Braeden's chest.

"That's our opportunity," Novitny said. They had split off from Mattila's main force and had made camp in Tirilis, with a view toward flanking Arryk from the south now that spring had come. "We can't assault the city on our own, but we can attack any convoys that Karsten sends out."

"We don't want Arryk getting those supplies." Braeden agreed, remembering the vast warehouses full of food and equipment. He hoped Karsten would keep a lot of food in the city in case of a siege. Janna had money and could buy everything she needed for some time.

"My thoughts exactly." Novitny clapped a hand on Braeden's shoulder. "The best thing for you is to keep busy. I understand all you want to do right now is head straight for Kersenstadt, but that's not the way. From what I've heard the city is shut up tight. It was Mattila's mistake she didn't do that before Landrus got in."

"Why would they let in a known troublemaker? Was he in disguise?"

"Could be. No one realized he was inside the city until he caused trouble in the temples. By then it was too late. Don't know what the man says, but he knows how to get folks fired up."

"I wish he'd never been born." Braeden left the prince and went to his tent. Without Janna, it had deteriorated to its former condition. Clothing, armor and horse blankets lay strewn everywhere and there was no fire in the brazier. Gergo was probably snuggled up under his laundress's blankets, and even when he was here, he was useless. He'd become far too accustomed to Janna's specific instructions and didn't seem to know what to do when she wasn't there.

Braeden built a small fire outside, then sat on the ground in front of it, warming his hands. The spring sunshine was welcome but still too weak to do much good. He wondered if there was a way for Janna to leave the city. If Karsten and Orland were preparing for a siege, they might be happy to get rid of any extra mouths to feed. But by now Janna would be heavily pregnant, making travel difficult. He wondered if he could get a message to her somehow.

He went in search of Franca. From the look on her face, he could tell she had already heard.

"I'm so sorry, sir," she said. "Think we can go get her? I'll come along."

"Seems no one's getting in without an army," Braeden said, trying to keep his tone light. "But some might get out. "

"Right. Women who can't fight and children, useless mouths."

322

"I don't know if she'll think of it herself, or if she can travel if she does. I haven't had a message from the doctor in some weeks. She always says she's fine, but I'm sure she's humoring me."

"How do we get her a message? Surely they're still letting in people with supplies they need."

"I'll find someone. Help me with a letter. It'll feel better to do something."

"You're right." Franca found a quill and some paper. "We'll make it short but specific. We must tell her where to go and how to reach you."

"It sounds dangerous when you put it that way." Braeden thought of the last time Janna had been alone on the road with two small children.

"It is dangerous. A young pregnant woman with a little girl."

"She's done it before and it didn't work out well for her. I can't ask her to do it again."

Franca put down the quill. "What's worse? Being on the road for a few days until you can get to her, or the chance of a siege and maybe a sacking?"

"It's all worse. I can't stand it."

"Sir, you have to. Let's think about it a bit longer. She's safe for now, in a sturdy house with plenty of money. With any luck, Karsten will clear the place out and leave. Then you can go get her first thing."

And he would. He didn't care what Janna's condition was, he'd get her and keep her by his side and never leave her anywhere again.

TEODORA

Count Solteszy blanched. "Your Highness, you can't be serious."

"I'm completely serious." Teodora smiled. "I feel like killing someone, and Kendryk is long overdue."

"Please, Your Highness. It would be a dreadful mistake."

"No, my mistake was in keeping him alive all this time. I don't know what I was thinking."

"But King Gauvain intervened personally. You can't think that Archduchess Zofya's marriage would still go forward, should you execute the king's close friend."

"Vica's tits. I'd forgotten all about that." Teodora leaned back against the cushions, deflated.

Solteszy looked at her as if she had lost her mind, which she had, but just for a moment. She was feeling like herself again. "It's a good thing Baroness Rastell found me. This could have been a disaster." He still wore a disapproving frown.

"Oh, I'm sure it would have worked out," Teodora snapped, irritated that she'd been so impulsive and that someone had to stop her. Killing Kendryk, while enjoyable, would have had serious political repercussions. "Such a shame I didn't get rid of him ages ago. It would have been so satisfying."

"No doubt. But that time has passed." Solteszy cleared his throat. "To be honest, I was sure you had a different purpose in visiting the Arnfels."

"What other reason could I have?"

Solteszy shook his head and smiled. "Hear me out, Your Highness. You can win back Kersenstadt without Mattila's help."

Teodora leaned forward. "Do tell."

When they reached the Arnfels, Teodora had her carriage take Solteszy straight back to the palace where he could start planning. He insisted on taking the guard with the sharp halberd, too. Teodora ordered the prisoner brought to her, and waited for him in a little anteroom. She ought to pay Kendryk a visit while she was here, though she still didn't trust herself to leave him unharmed. If it wasn't for him and his ridiculous ideas she wouldn't be having any of this trouble right now.

So she waited until the prisoner was ready and brought to her.

"Count Ensden." She walked up to him, taking both of his hands in hers. "It's good to see you again. I trust you are well?"

"Well enough, Your Highness," he said, though her old general looked even more corpse-like than the last time she saw him. She'd thrown him in here months ago after all, and if the dungeon could destroy the looks of a pretty boy like Kendryk, it did much worse on a fellow who was already a dried-out old husk. "Is it time for my court martial?"

She had forgotten about that. "No, I've decided to dispense with that altogether." She smiled brightly.

He paled. "So it's straight to the block then?"

"Oh heavens, no." She had to laugh. The poor man really expected the worst. "No, no. I'm here to set you free and to reinstate you."

"I'm afraid I don't understand."

"Your replacement has proved a disappointment. She has made a frightful mess in Kronland and I will need your help to clean it up."

"Brynhild Mattila? That's a surprise. She's not known for making mistakes."

"No. But there's a first time for everything. She's lost Kersenstadt."

"Oh dear."

"Yes. And what's worse, she'd filled it with the bulk of her supplies she'll need for a spring campaign. Supplies now on their way to Arryk Roussay while his whore Larisa Karsten builds up the fortifications and turns our own guns on us."

Ensden stood up straight and his eyes cleared. "Unbelievable. We must go there straightaway."

"Unfortunately, I have no army of my own. Demario Barela is under my command, but he's gone east. In any case, I will need more than that to besiege a city the size of Kersenstadt."

"Yes, though it can be managed." Right before her eyes, her pathetic prisoner had turned into the resolute warrior she'd known for so long. Ensden's voice strengthened and all he lacked now was weapons and armor. "With my contacts in Cesiano, and sufficient incentive, I should be able to gather a suitable force within a month or two."

"That long?"

"At least that long, especially with the mountains still difficult to pass."

"Can't you get troops from anywhere else?"

"I'm sure Mattila has picked the area clean. I'll send to Floradias as well, but the armies in Kronland drew heavily from there."

"Oh, it's frustrating!"

"Yes, it is. But please be assured, Kersenstadt will be yours before long and Mattila will receive no credit for it."

"That would be most gratifying." She had to admit, it was nice to have her old general back. They had always worked well together. "I'll tell you what. Give me Kersenstadt by summer and I'll make you a duke."

"Your Highness, I am very honored. But it's unnecessary. I only wish to do my duty."

"Oh, I know, but the offer stands. You are released at once and all of your property returned to you and so on. I'm sure your family will be pleased."

His smile was broad. "Is my wife well? And my daughters?"

She had no idea. "I'm sure they are. I believe they left the capital after ..."

"Yes, of course. They ought to be with my brother-in-law in Moralta. I will write to them right away."

"Certainly. Though don't take too long. I will expect you at the palace tomorrow morning so we can make plans."

"I would like nothing better. Please don't worry, Your Highness. It will all come right. I can't imagine what Mattila is doing, but we will correct whatever damage has been done."

"And when it has," Teodora allowed herself to dream a little, "I won't have much use for her and you can take your rightful place at the head of all my armies."

"As you wish. Let's get Kersenstadt first."

KENDRYK

Kendryk was reading in his little study when the door burst open and Teodora swept in.

"Darling!" she said, coming in and putting her wrap on a chair.

"Your Highness," he said, standing up rather abruptly. "How good of you to visit." He bowed and motioned toward an empty chair with soft velvet cushions.

She sat, then said, "I was here anyway." She paused. "Well, to be honest, I was coming to kill you."

He found it hard to take her seriously, though he probably should. "What stopped you?"

"Someone reminded me of my stupid agreement with your stupid friend, and I decided it would be unwise."

"That's never stopped you before."

"Careful, brat. I can still put you back in the dungeon."

"No, you can't. Natalya will check on me."

"I can keep you in the dungeon until she sends someone."

"Oh? When will that be?"

"I'll be notified of an official visitor from Galladium."

"But they won't always be official. It might be anyone."

"She said that?"

"Yes. I can expect visitors from Galladium of virtually any occupation or position." The look of surprise on her face was priceless.

She stamped her foot. "I'll find another way to make you miserable, then."

"I'm sure you will." He smiled softly and closed his book. "I apologize, Your Highness. I don't wish to have a difficult relationship with you. Even if you had no power over me, I'd rather we were on better terms."

"I don't."

"Just know for my part, I wish we were friends."

"Whatever for?"

He sighed. "Shouldn't we find a way to end this terrible war? Hasn't it gone on long enough?"

"No, absolutely not. It will be long enough once I've driven your brother-in-law back into the sea and have at last executed that horrid priest of yours. When I have a ruler of my choosing installed in Terragand and all of Kronland

acknowledges that neither you nor your children will ever live or rule there again, it will be long enough."

Her words struck Kendryk at his core, but he also knew she was trying to upset him. He did his best not to rise to the bait. "What if my brother-in-law could be persuaded to return home in exchange for something else?"

"If it involves you getting your country back and your pet priest running around unhindered, then no."

"You wouldn't discuss the possibility? What if I abdicated in favor of my uncle, while he acts as regent until Maryna comes of age? I'll even do a public ceremony so you look good in front of the Kronlanders." He would forgo ruling Terragand if it gave Maryna a chance in the future.

She shook her head. "You want to sit here and negotiate?"

"Why not? I don't know what's happening right now, but surely an agreement would make your life easier."

"There can be no possible deal unless Edric Landrus is part of it." Her face took on that stubborn cast he knew all too well.

"I'm afraid Edric Maximus has passed out of my jurisdiction altogether. And you realize that what you do to him makes no difference at this point, don't you? The new faith has taken hold and it's too late to undo that. Executing Edric would only inflame matters."

"I don't have to listen to this." She stood abruptly.

Kendryk rose more slowly. "I'm sorry if I've offended you. But when you're not angry anymore, please think about it. Arryk Roussay returns to Norovaea, the armies of his allies are dissolved, and I abdicate in favor of my uncle and daughter. It could all be over within weeks."

Teodora took a step closer and looked into his eyes. "I think not. You are mistaken if you believe I would negotiate with you as an equal in any way. You are no longer Prince of Terragand. You are a nobody. I would never negotiate with a nobody."

Anger rose inside him, but he did his best to keep his face impassive.

She took a few steps until she stood uncomfortably close to him. "If you think I would make any agreement that would let your heresy run unchecked through my empire, you are also mistaken. There can be no compromise. I will defeat Arryk Roussay and his allies, and then I will wipe Kronland clean of all heresy. I don't care how long it takes. And you will sit here and watch me do it. And when I am done, you will watch me finally, finally execute your priest, and then you will confess to the error of your ways, or follow him to the stake. Is that clear?" Her voice rose to a shriek, bouncing off the stone walls of the little room.

Kendryk stepped back. His jaw trembled, but he stopped it somehow. He took a deep breath. "That is unacceptable, Your Highness. I'm afraid my friends will have to defeat you on the field to show you the error of your ways. And I am sure they will."

Teodora stared at him for a long moment, breathing hard. He wondered if she really would try to kill him. Then she took a deep breath and without another word, turned on her heel and left the room.

Kendryk took a shaky step back and sank into his chair.

TEODORA

Teodora found it marvelous to be outside the city again with no fear of attack from another quarter. Andor Korma hadn't made a peep in three years and the Zastwar border remained secure since a renewal of the temporary truce a year ago. Once she neutralized Kronland she would be in a position of strength and could negotiate a permanent treaty.

Already, Teodora was in a much stronger position than the last time she had left Atlona to attend the Landrus trial. She left a strong garrison from troops Ensden felt he could spare while Solteszy headed the civilian government.

Livilla accompanied the army. "I will send another hundred of the League of Aeternos with you, but I want to move on to Mattila's army and see how that group is faring."

"I'm sure Ensden's army is most devout," Teodora insisted, not wanting to be hampered with too many priests on her march. "Most of his recruits are from Cesiano and Maladena and surely uninfected with heresy."

"I'm sure that's true. No, it's the people of Kersenstadt who will need instruction. Several priests and priestesses fled the city after Landrus came." Livilla pulled a face as if mentioning him left a bad taste. Teodora understood. Just saying the name made her want to spit. "They bring the most alarming tidings. Many of the temple acolytes were too easily swayed by heresy and now preach it in all the temples of the city. Their congregations eat up every false word. When you take the city, the heretic clergy will be removed and punished, but their congregations must be returned to the faith."

"They will be." Teodora still couldn't quite grasp how much trouble one man had caused. If someone had told her three years ago that all of Kronland would turn from the true faith, she would not have believed it.

Still, it was obvious the gods had not blessed the Quadrene heresy. In spite of Arryk Roussay's vast resources he had failed to attack Teodora when she was vulnerable and now it was too late. Mattila would meet him in battle soon and

Teodora was sure there was no chance a lightweight like Arryk could prevail against the seasoned general. Mattila might have miscalculated with Kersenstadt, but she wouldn't make the same mistake twice.

As Teodora's army moved north through Tirilis, she received letters from all directions. First and most frequent were messages from Mattila. She wasn't the least bit apologetic for losing Kersenstadt and in fact acted as though it didn't matter at all. She was most displeased at Teodora and Ensden taking the field. "This clearly violates our earlier agreement," she wrote. "I'm afraid we will need to revisit terms the next time we speak."

"Indeed we shall," Teodora sniffed, dropping the letter on the road and smiling as it crunched under her horse's hooves.

"Do you think she'll refuse to engage Arryk, just out of spite?" Ensden looked worried.

"Never. Now she's in the field, she won't be able to let it go. I hate the woman, but I must admit she's never shied from a fight. And if Arryk can gather his allies soon, she'll have a good one on her hands."

More civil, if less literate, correspondence came from Prince Novitny. Mattila had sent him south to harass Arian Orland's cavalry and prevent him from meeting up with Arryk. Fodder was scarce in Fromenberg, so Orland had struck out for southern Lantura, where grass grew plentifully. If Novitny did his work well, Arryk would have to face Mattila without Orland's support.

Novitny also grudgingly noted that Daciana Tomescu was doing her part by harassing Seward Kurant as he moved out of his Oltena winter quarters. "Daciana will keep him out of the fight, I'm sure." Teodora was pleased. "Kurant is a decent soldier, but he's old and unable to manage anything unconventional."

"Daciana is unconventional enough." Livilla smiled.

Novitny went on to say that as far as he knew, Count Faris had assembled a force of indeterminate size in Terragand, but wasn't budging from Birkenfels and the surrounding area. "It appears he plans keep himself apart from Arryk's activity, which is prudent of him and good for us," Novitny wrote.

"Faris will be easy enough to mop up when we've dealt with the others," Teodora said, though it rankled that Birkenfels was still not hers.

Mattila had split her force, and neglected to inform Teodora. This intelligence came from Elektra. "Finally, something of use." Teodora hoped it wasn't misdirection, but Elektra's letter was full of her new spiritual adviser, Mother Luca. "It's Luca this and Luca that." Teodora rolled her eyes and handed the note to Livilla.

"Good." Livilla smiled. "Luca is clever and subtle; she will see that Elektra is drawn away from Mattila so slowly she will scarcely notice it."

"I hope you're right. Since Mattila neglected to inform me she sent four thousand foot and two thousand horse north to face Emilya Hohenwart, I assume she didn't want me to know. In which case, Elektra has done well."

"Do not let on to Mattila that you know," Livilla warned. "Or she might find out it came from Elektra and will no longer speak so freely in front of her."

"Of course," Teodora said, not mentioning that her first impulse had been to send Mattila an angry missive, ordering her to include such vital information in all future correspondences. Much as she hated to admit it to herself, it was a good idea to have an adviser or two keeping her from being too impulsive.

GWYNNETH

Gwynneth was sick, exhausted and terrified by the time Captain Brun sailed into the tiny harbor at Strutka. Though it was spring now, the storms in the Northern Sea didn't abate. The *Rusa* had pitched and rolled endlessly on its slow progress to the Prinova Islands. Both the village and the fortress looked as forbidding as before. The snow had disappeared, but Gwynneth couldn't imagine greenery ever covering this rocky bit of ground.

"Damn." Lennart struck the table with his fist, making Gwynneth jump. "I should have married you when I had the chance. We might have fought like a couple of terriers, but I would have sent you off on embassies to keep you out of my hair and conjure up treaties everywhere. You're a sight more useful than any Sanovan princess."

Gwynneth rolled her eyes. "In this case, there's no substitute for a Sanovan princess. Without her, there's no treaty."

"There might not be one anyway." Lennart had already attacked the documents she brought with a quill and great splotches of ink. "Ottilya wants these islands back."

"You won't scuttle your chance at peace arguing over this bit of rock, will you?"

"Likely not." Lennart sighed and kept reading.

Gwynneth felt the Sanovan terms were more than fair. "Ottilya is giving up all direct claim to the throne of Estenor. The least you can do is throw a sop to her pride."

"Is that what they're calling it?" Lennart looked up. "So, what can you tell me about Princess Raysa?"

Gwynneth frowned. "She's terribly unhappy, I'm afraid. She's spent her life being told you represented all the evil in the world and now she has to marry you."

"Poor girl. Please tell me you lied to her about how wonderful I am."

333

"I tried to console her, but I think she's nearly as frightened of me. She's quite timid."

"I suppose I'll try to not be so loud around her. I'm having a go at not swearing so much since my priest reckons I should set a better example. Maybe that will help. Do you think I ought to get rid of the beard too?" He looked distressed at the prospect of so much domestication.

Gwynneth smiled. "The beard isn't too alarming, as long as you keep it trimmed." It looked like he'd let it grow while he was on Strutka, likely in a vain attempt to keep his face warm.

"I can do that. In any case, I won't frighten her for long. I plan to leave for Kronland within a year or so."

"That long?" Gwynneth couldn't hide her dismay.

"I must bring in all the troops scattered along the border with Sanova, and recruit more before I sail south."

"I thought you already had a rather large army."

"Hardly." He barked a laugh. "Estenor is a small country, and we've been at war for years. I'll need to levy a second round of militia troops from the countryside, and that's unlikely to go over well. I imagine I'll spend some time in Tharvik, drumming up support since I'll have to raise taxes as well." His face brightened. "You might help with that."

"I must return to Sanova first. I was hoping to leave for Kronland from there, as soon as this treaty is finalized."

"I suppose you have other fish to fry. Well, let's get this thing done. I'm making a mess here, trying to write in the margins."

"Why don't I take notes." Gwynneth offered. "We'll read down the list and you can tell me which items can stand and which ones you'll change."

"Good enough." Lennart turned his attention back to the draft treaty. "Write this down. I'll give up these islands, but I want a bigger dowry in return. Twenty thousand is paltry for a princess."

"I agree. I came with fifty."

"See? Another reason I should have married you. Let's ask for fifty, but I'll settle for forty if I must. My army will eat that up in a month or two."

"War is an expensive business."

"In every way. I'll be glad to see the end of this one. I hope I can do things differently in Kronland so there's a faster resolution."

"Teodora won't give up easily."

"I don't expect her to. In fact, I expect her to die before the end. I might too, but if I can take her down with me, it might be worth it."

Gwynneth looked at him, appalled. "What a horrid thing to say. You mustn't die."

"I'd rather not. But I also understand that what I'm proposing for Kronland and the Empire goes beyond what most folk might think reasonable. I expect to win, but I expect the cost to be high."

"It's already high."

"I know, Gwynn." He put the paper down and leaned across the table. "I know you're the last person I can complain to about cost."

"I'm not sure I can bear much more." Gwynneth could hardly meet his eyes.

"You can. You're a tough girl, and I reckon that husband of yours is tougher than he looks. Teodora has dealt you a big blow, but you didn't break down. You're fighting back and fighting hard. What's more, you're fighting on the side of truth. The gods are with us, Gwynn, and soon they'll lead us to victory."

TEODORA

It had been so long since Teodora had last seen him, but when they finally met, it was in broad daylight in front of both armies. Teodora kept her face impassive, but Demario's dark eyes twinkled at her. Just for her, although she thought Livilla noticed, judging by the smirk she failed to hide.

He'd led his force south from Oltena to meet her before she reached Kersenstadt. "I was unable to apprehend your villainous friend." He flashed her a maddening grin.

"Oh, that's all right." Teodora looked at him out of the corner of her eye. She hardly trusted herself to look at him directly. "It seems she's keeping Seward Kurant busy in Oltena."

"Yes, between the two of us, we had him hemmed in. Naturally, Princess Sebesta has done everything she can to support Kurant and thwart us. It made for a hard winter for everyone."

"You don't appear to be much worse for the wear." It was true, he looked marvelous, if perhaps a bit more gaunt than normal. Teodora decided it suited him.

"No worse than usual." He flashed her a smile. "Though I'm much better now. If I'm not too bold, I must say you look uncommonly fine, even for an empress."

"Sweet words will get you nowhere, General." Teodora's insides jumped with glee, and something else.

"I don't mind. I am a man of action, after all."

"Thank the gods for that."

The Tirilis foothills rolling out from the Galwend mountains were lush and green with spring. Winter had stayed long and the snow had been deep, but now that it was gone, new life bloomed in rare intensity. Teodora felt the sap flowing through her veins.

336

She gave no specific orders as to where her tent was to be pitched that night. But she noticed that General Barela insisted on placing his nearby. "Should Her Highness and I need to consult before morning," he said with a straight face.

Teodora wondered if they were fooling anyone, then decided she didn't care. For the hundredth time, she was glad she had left her husband in Atlona. His uselessness was less grating at a distance and now she had one less appearance to keep up.

She cut dinner a bit early that evening, forgoing the usual entertainment so there was time for a bath. The road was dirty and bathing was a rare luxury. But tonight they camped near a rushing river and it was no great matter for hordes of servants to bring endless buckets to the cook-fires.

Teodora had changed into a loose dressing gown and was drying her hair at the little brazier in her tent. The nights were cold, but she would be warm. She stared into the dancing flames, wishing she could discern her fate from them, as Livillia sometimes did.

There was a rustling in the tent's outer chamber and Brytta cleared her throat. "Your Highness, General Barela is here to see you."

"Show him in. And leave us."

She remained seated until she felt his hand on her shoulder. "I hoped you would see me." His voice was husky.

"Of course I would. I've missed you." She was doing everything wrong. If she were wise, she would keep him guessing, not let him realize that she had thought of him a hundred times a day in the past months.

"Good. I've also missed you." He sat down on the bench next to her, picked up her hand and kissed it. "It's been so long I thought it possible you had moved on. Taken a lover who was more convenient."

"It's true, you are most inconvenient." She leaned against him, just a little. It was nice to feel someone solid holding her up. "But I don't mind."

He put his arm around her shoulder, drawing her close, and kissed the top of her damp head. "I hope Kersenstadt falls quickly, but not too quickly. I should like to see more of you, even under appalling conditions."

"Do you think it will be very bad?"

"If it goes on for any length of time. Mattila first and then Orland have already picked the area clean, I'm sure. We will struggle to find food, although at least the grass is growing. But I don't want to talk about sieges. We can do that tomorrow. Come here."

Teodora's pulse pounded in her head. She wished she had the strength to pull away even for a second, if only to prove to herself and to him that she didn't need him. Want, yes. But need was a matter of dependency and she could not, must not depend on anyone for anything. It wasn't safe.

Demario kissed her, then pulled back and looked down at her. "What is it, love?"

That he could read her so well was worrisome.

"You make me feel weak. I don't like being weak."

He chuckled. "You are not weak. Not at all. You are simply experiencing a small side effect of desire. It can momentarily turn one's limbs to jelly. I'm feeling less than sturdy myself. Perhaps I should get you into bed before one of us slides off this bench."

GWYNNETH

Over the next few days, Gwynneth, Lennart and Ludvik Meldahl pored over the treaty and finally had a draft Lennart could live with. Meldahl then took it to read over once more with a lawyer's eye, leaving Gwynneth to discuss the coming invasion with Lennart.

"How will you pay for a Kronland campaign?" Gwynneth asked. "It sounds like Raysa's dowry won't go far, no matter how much you get."

"It won't. But I've been thinking about it while you were gone. You know who has a fair amount of coin and would love to put a bee in Teodora's bonnet?"

"Queen Ottilya, or rather Archduke Atinos."

"Well, yes. But I'll be lucky to squeeze that fifty thousand out of them. No, I was thinking of your good friend Natalya Maxima. If she's as cozy with Gauvain Brevard as you say, I reckon she can come up with some funding for me."

Gwynneth's first impulse was to say Lennart was being ridiculous, but she held her tongue and considered it. "It's not quite that simple," she said, finally. "It's true that Galladium is rich, but Gauvain must contend with a rather fractious noble council. He rules by their courtesy and they must approve all large expenditures."

"What's new? I must do the same, though I've got my council well in hand."

"Gauvain doesn't. At least not yet. I'm sure Natalya is working on it."

"No doubt she is. You've also said that she approves of the changes in the faith. That could be another reason for her to help me."

"I'm sure it is, though she must tread carefully. Maladena menaces their border, and Queen Beatryz is a staunch ally of the Imperata. She's already taken brutal measures to deal with heresy in her own country. If Natalya moves too quickly, Beatryz might justify an invasion on grounds of preventing heresy from bleeding over her border, or some such nonsense."

"Which is why it makes sense for her to act indirectly. You're good at these discreet operations. When you leave Sanova, travel back to Galladium and ar-

339

range me some kind of subsidy. No doubt it can be funneled through Zeelund. In the meantime, I'll marry little Raysa and soften up my aristocracy. They won't object to another war quite so much if someone else is paying for it."

"I should hope not." Gwynneth couldn't deny that he was making a great deal of sense, and hoped she, Natalya and Gauvain could come to an agreement. "But I have a problem of a more personal nature. Arryk will go into the field against Mattila anytime now and I don't want my children going with him. I must get back to them soon."

"Take them to Galladium with you, then. You can stay there until I come and once Terragand is secure you can return."

"That's a good solution. I want the children safe in Allaux. I should have left them there a long time ago,but I imagined they would be more useful to the cause in Kronland. Maryna adores Natalya who's the perfect person to teach her statecraft."

"I'll bet she is. I would very much like to meet this Natalya." Lennart leaned back in his chair, a dreamy look in his eyes.

"You'd like her. She's lovely, though rather forceful for your tastes."

"I'm changing my mind about forceful women." Lennart straightened up and looked right at Gwynneth.

"It's a little late for that. Though it's possible Raysa might be trained up, given time away from her mother."

"Don't know. I won't care much for her in any case. You on the other hand—"

"Oh, stop teasing." It was clear he was serious, but Gwynneth couldn't so much as entertain the thought.

"I'm not teasing, Gwynn. Please don't laugh at me." He came around the table and took the chair next to hers. "All this time we've spent together, plotting and planning, I've fallen in love with you."

"I doubt it." She slid her chair a bit farther away. "You just haven't seen any other women in some time, and we get on rather well. Once I'm gone, I'm sure you'll forget all about it." She tried to keep her tone light, but her heart banged against her ribs. It would be so easy. He was so close, and so very attractive. And unlike Arian Orland, she liked him as a person. She appreciated his good nature, his blunt intelligence and supreme confidence. And here they were, alone on this godsforsaken rock. She had to admit she was tempted.

"No, I don't think so Gwynn." His voice was husky. "I'll say it right now: I really am sorry I didn't marry you. I know it sounded like I was joking earlier, but it's the truth. You would have been the perfect wife for me and a magnificent queen for Estenor."

"Perhaps." She turned to face him. "But that ship sailed long ago, don't you agree? I'm married now, with children and the fact my husband is imprisoned doesn't change that. And you are about to marry as well. There's no point in regretting anything now."

"I was thinking more along the lines of, well, I don't wish to be crude, but we could have some fun while you're here, don't you think? Maybe we can get it out of our systems. I understand if you're not interested, naturally." His eyes were wide and hopeful.

He'd put his cards on the table and Gwynneth felt he'd earned a measure of honesty from her. "I'm tempted; I won't lie."

A hopeful smile spread across his face.

"But. I can't do it, Lennart."

The smile fled. "I know. I shouldn't have asked. You're an honorable woman and would never do such a thing. I apologize if I've insulted you. I got carried away."

Now she smiled. "You haven't insulted me. In fact, I'm flattered. But you're wrong about me being too honorable to do it. It's exactly why I can't. I made a dreadful mistake a few years ago and I must never do anything like it again."

"You made a mistake?" He raised an eyebrow. "I find that hard to believe."

"It was a bad time. I had a moment of weakness and someone was there to take advantage of it."

"Who was it? I'll kill him if you like."

"That's not necessary. He's rather sorry as well, and I'm making use of him in another way. In fact, I've made him swear to rescue Kendryk."

Lennart threw back his head and laughed his hearty booming laugh. "Of course you did. You are an amazing woman." Then he sobered. "I have to say, I'm a bit jealous of the fellow, but I wouldn't want to be in his shoes now. Do you reckon he can rescue Kendryk without losing his own life?"

"I have no idea. And I don't care. From what I've heard, Kendryk is shut up in the empress's largest, most secure fortress. I doubt anyone can get him out. That's why I was so hopeful Gauvain could arrange something."

"You don't care, eh?" Funny he'd latched onto that.

"No. I have no interest in the man. Like I said, it was a moment of weakness, he was attractive and knew exactly what to do. But once it was over, I hated him for nearly destroying my marriage."

"Kendryk found out?"

Gwynneth nodded, feeling rather sick. She had pushed the episode far back in her mind and did her best to never think about it.

"Well if that doesn't beat all. But the two of you are all right now?"

"We reconciled before the battle, but just. So you see why I can't even entertain the idea?"

"Of course. I'm sorry I brought it up."

"It's all right. Let's just forget about it, shall we?" She stood and started rolling up the documents on the table. "I'll leave for Sanova tomorrow and when I next see you, it might well be in Terragand. Perhaps by then you will have fallen in love with your lovely young wife."

The look on Lennart's face indicated that was unlikely.

TEODORA

Demario had been right about the state of affairs around Kersenstadt. There was no food for miles around. As Teodora's armies drew near, both generals sent large bodies of troops back to the areas that had still appeared prosperous as they marched through. They wouldn't stay prosperous for long.

Ensden had raised only fifteen thousand with the short time he had and the little money Teodora could borrow from her cousin, Queen Beatryz, but Barela brought another three thousand. His force was diminished since he had first brought it to relieve Atlona, but he had been in the field almost constantly since then. Teodora decided that once she was through with Mattila, she'd give those troops to Barela. Perhaps she could get him away from her cousin's service in the end.

Still, with all of the animals, camp followers and baggage train, the army snaked over tens of leagues of countryside, devouring everything in its path. Until Teodora needed them at Kersenstadt, it was best to keep as many troops as possible quartered on surrounding towns and villages. Teodora sent a curt message to Prince Herryk, letting him know she appreciated his cooperation in this matter. He had claimed loyalty to her while allowing King Arryk to march all over his land, aiding and abetting him. He could pay for that now.

Teodora was shocked at the size of the earthworks surrounding Kersenstadt's already formidable wall. A river wound around one side and then turned north, but it was full and would be difficult to cross. A great wall of earth with a tall wooden stockade on top stood wherever there was no river. When Teodora looked at it through a glass, she could catch the glint of large guns positioned all along the top.

Her first task was to ride around the city, at least to the river on the east side. She took Barela, Ensden, and all of their various staff. "Do you think we can undermine that?" She asked the colonel in charge of Barela's engineers.

"Perhaps." He shrugged. "It will take time, but we can start immediately. I am short on manpower, so that will slow me down. Most of my sappers died in the winter." Digging was hard work and those who did it were often first to succumb when food was short or disease struck.

"Can you use regular troops?" Teodora didn't mind bringing in infantry, though feeding them would be another matter.

"They must be strong enough to dig for long periods of time."

"They will be. Let me know how many you need."

She turned to an artillery captain and handed him her glass. "What size are those guns? I know that Mattila had several demi-cannon, but would she have left them here?"

The captain peered through the glass. "These don't appear to be quite so large. Culverins perhaps. We can still expect a considerable range, though quite how far, I don't know. We should consider provoking a barrage so we can find out."

"Do we have anything to counter those?"

"I should think so. I've brought some mortars, though we will need entrenchments to make them the most effective. We also have a few culverins. They're on the small side, but if we concentrate fire, we can take down that stockade, perhaps even the walls."

"That's what I need. You said you have a few. How many is that exactly?"

"Eight."

"Gods." She couldn't believe Mattila had walked off with all those armaments just so she could lose them here. The idea of Arryk Roussay now in possession of all those guns made her feel sick.

She wanted to blast away at the earthworks at once, but both Ensden and Barela counseled patience. "Let them wait. They will expect an attack soon and will be alert. Once time has passed and nothing happens, they will relax. That's when we strike," Ensden said.

"Let the engineers do their work," Barela added. "Then we launch a coordinated attack. With so many troops quartered several leagues away, Karsten will think our force is much smaller than it is. We'll position our mortars and what larger guns we have. We'll build entrenchments so we can get foot soldiers closer and build ladders so we can scale the walls when we reach them. When all of that is ready, we'll soften them up with the guns, then follow with a frontal assault."

Ensden nodded in agreement, so Teodora tried to curb her impatience. "How long?"

Barela and Ensden looked at each other. "Three or four weeks?" Ensden finally said.

"I suppose I can wait that long." She forced herself to sound reasonable, even though she wanted to shout and hit something. She didn't want Demario to see her like that.

It wasn't quite that simple. Karsten's earthworks were much wider than expected. "It will take much longer to get in deep enough to mine them." The engineering colonel was not nearly as apologetic as he should have been, though Teodora supposed it wasn't his fault Larisa Karsten had been unexpectedly diligent. "How can you do it faster?"

He shrugged. "Only so many people can work on this at once. It's the nature of a siege. Karsten must have studied with Hohenwart. Her fortifications are textbook. They can still be overcome, it will simply take longer."

The delay was maddening, but Teodora didn't mind every additional night she got with Demario, although the camp was unpleasant and became more so with every passing day. The weather warmed and the stench rose. Teodora had sweet-smelling herbs burned in her tent around the clock, but it was barely enough.

"Is it always like this?" she asked Demario, her nose wrinkling as they walked between the tents. The days alternated rain and sunshine, so steam rose from the mud, left after every blade of grass for leagues around had been eaten. With so many feet trampling it, it seemed unlikely that anything new would grow there.

"It's often worse." He grinned at her. "This is a rather small camp and therefore not as awful. We certainly don't want to bring the rest in until we're ready."

"I imagine that will be unbearable."

"You can get used to anything."

"I can't. I won't."

JANNA

"Madame?" Holgar Ellert knocked on the parlor's open door.

"What is it?" Janna asked. The Norovaeans seldom bothered her, but she worried he might have bad news.

"I'm afraid the city is besieged," Ellert said, sitting down across from her.

Janna made a small noise of consternation. "Mattila?"

"No, Empress Teodora is leading this army herself. Our sources tell us that Count Ensden and General Barela are with her."

"What about the Sanova Hussars?" Janna thought she might be sick.

"Oh dear," Ellert said, with a sympathetic look. "Your husband?"

"Yes," Janna said, heedless of the tears that leaked from her eyes. She'd already been crying so much. She still had nearly two months before the baby was due and her emotions were out of control as it was. "Yes, he might be out there with that army."

"We have heard nothing of the hussars, but that he's on the other side is very bad luck. You have my sympathies."

Janna was unsure of what to say to that.

"In any event, I wished to tell you what is happening. The city will not fall. Duchess Karsten has fortified it well and there are no weak spots. With the provisions in the city, we can hold out for months. Still, it would be wise to stock up if you can. Food is still likely to become expensive and the army will receive priority rations."

"I see," Janna said, though she really didn't. She didn't know what she was supposed to do now.

Doctor Marsel came to visit the following afternoon with more specific advice. "You must get as much money as you can," he said, taking Janna up on her offer of tea. "Buy as much food as you can; things like flour and dried or cured

346

meat that will keep for a while. Fill your cellar and put that fearsome footman back at your door. He hasn't been there lately."

"I don't know what's become of him. He was sent to work on the fortifications and never returned."

"Ran off, most likely. They worked a few poor souls to death, but that fellow looked like a sturdier sort. I'm sure he's all right," he added, seeing Janna was about to cry. "Keep the door locked in any case. How do you get on with the quartered troops? Those at my house are civil enough."

"They're fine," Janna said. "I don't see them much."

"You might ask them to keep an eye on the house. I know this is a difficult situation, but you must try to relax and rest. From what I can tell, the baby is doing well, but it's very large and you'll have a difficult delivery. The stronger and healthier you are when the time comes, the better."

Janna told him about Braeden possibly being among the besiegers.

Dr. Marsel looked grim. "I realize it must be upsetting for you, but try not to worry. There is simply nothing that can be done. It seems unlikely that the city will fall soon, and in most cases, the besiegers are drawn away when they run out of food. There's also a possibility if it goes on a long time, that some agreement will be reached and your husband will enter the city peacefully."

"That would be best."

"Yes it would, and it's a real possibility. Please, try not to worry."

She would try.

The next morning, Janna made a supreme effort and struggled into her best dress that still fit.

"Oh ma'am, you shouldn't go out on your own," Birgid said, alarmed, as Janna put on her hat.

"I must go while I still can," Janna said, tying on her cloak. Spring had come, but a cold wind still blew around the house corners. "I needn't go far, just down the street to the factor's."

Birgid looked as dubious as Janna felt, but she knew she had to go.

The factor was very busy, the front room of his house crowded with merchants and other well-dressed folk. No one spoke, but anxiety pervaded the room. When Janna finally got in to see him, the factor looked sad and exhausted. "I can give you two thousand, and no more." He slid a stack of coins across the shiny wood of his desk.

"I think that will be enough." It was an enormous amount of money for food, though far from the whole amount Braeden had put on deposit.

"The problem is that food prices have already tripled. If you can, do your shopping today before things get scarcer. If you need more, come back next week. I'm trying to get everyone what they want, but they all want it now. The other factors are as pressed for coin as I am, but I'll do my best."

"Thank you." Janna took the purse. She'd never had so much money in her life.

When she got back to the house, she went straight to the kitchen. "We must go to market now," she told Hilda, her cook.

"Shall we take the cart?" Hilda reached for her shawl.

"Yes. Is there much room in the cellar?"

"Quite a bit. We should stock up if we can. I survived a short siege when I was a girl and whatever amount of food you have, it won't be enough. If it looks like it's too much, get more."

"I hope we can."

They wasted no time getting to the market, but Janna was appalled to find nearly all of the stalls picked clean and it wasn't yet noon. She bought everything she could, except for fresh vegetables, but a few hams, a wheel of cheese and two sacks of flour hardly took up any space in the cart.

"We need to find more," Hilda said.

"How?"

"Leave it to me. With your permission, I'll go out this afternoon and talk to some people. Be ready to go see them anytime."

ARRYK

"But she can't!" Arryk realized he was spluttering but couldn't quite stop himself. "Where did she get the troops?"

"It's unclear, but it doesn't matter," Magnus said. "Teodora besieges Kersenstadt with at least ten thousand on top of what Barela can bring. At least they won't be reinforcing Mattila right now."

"How can we be sure of that? The hussars could be anywhere, so we need to go now." Arryk stood. He was certain Larisa would never surrender, but worry clawed at his insides.

His officers looked at each other uncertainly but no one said anything.

"What?" Arryk asked. "What is it?"

"We can't just go marching off to Kersenstadt, Your Highness," Magnus said. He seemed to be the only one unafraid to speak his mind.

"Why not? If we go now we can get there before Teodora can make much progress."

"Have you considered it might be a trap? You leave Fromenberg with Mattila sitting to your north, between you and Hohenwart. While you attack Teodora, Mattila attacks you. You'd be caught between two armies of some size."

Arryk slumped back into his chair. "You're right. But we can't just let her get away with it."

"She won't get in," an engineering officer said confidently. "The duchess showed me her plans for fortifications and she had time to put them in place. Teodora has little artillery. I doubt any attempts to storm the walls will succeed. In fact, I'd be surprised if Barela and Ensden even so much as try."

"I hope you're right." Arryk tried to calm himself. "But we can't take too long. What if they run out of food?"

"They won't," said the quartermaster. "The place was stuffed with supplies."

"But there must be at least twenty thousand souls inside. How long could any supplies last?"

"Long. If the administrators understand what they're doing, and what I've gathered from these Kronlanders is that they're good at organizing that sort of thing."

"Your Highness," said a colonel. "I realize this is very alarming. But it mustn't distract us from our real mission, which is to defeat Brynhild Mattila as soon as possible. As soon as she is dispatched, we can turn our attention to Teodora."

"I can't beat Mattila without allies."

"Call in Arian Orland. With any luck he can reach you before the Sanova Hussars join Mattila and you'll have a chance with him."

"We'll still be outnumbered."

"A bit. Let's give Hohenwart another week to get here. Send messengers telling her to hurry. In the meantime, let's plan the artillery dispositions. We have all of those lovely guns Mattila left in Kersenstadt. Let's use them."

Arryk stood up again, feeling heavy. Still, he saw sense in what the colonel said. "Let's do that. The sooner the better." He still didn't see how he was supposed to win. "Have we heard from Ruso Faris?" he asked. His artillery expertise would be welcome.

"We only know our messenger reached Birkenfels. He's not back yet."

Arryk didn't understand what reason Faris had for delay, but it seemed he had one. It didn't matter. He would have to do with what he had.

JANNA

Hilda was as good as her word. She returned before supper and came straight to Janna. "I hope you don't mind eating cold tonight. We must hurry out again later."

"I don't mind. What have you found?"

"I know your landlady's cook. Her brother works at a warehouse down by the river. The merchant who owns it is trying to hold back the food and wait for prices to rise."

"That's horrid. How can he take advantage of people like that?"

Hilda shrugged. "It's just business. But we're in luck. He'll let a few acquaintances—those with good coin at least—buy as much as they can. We want to do it after dark, and we'll need an armed escort."

"Goodness, why?"

"Folks are already panicking and if they see a cart they think might be filled with food, there's no telling what they'll do."

"How in the world am I supposed to find an armed escort?"

"Ask our Norovaeans. They can help, or find someone who can."

"I can't see Major Ellert approving of something like this."

"In this situation, what's yours is theirs, so they have an interest in having the house well-stocked, don't you think?"

"I suppose." Janna was afraid to ask Ellert, or anyone else. She would have to do it anyway. She asked the maid to send the captain to her when he returned from whatever it was he did all day.

Ellert appeared in her parlor, courteous as always. He listened to Janna's idea, then said, "Why don't we all go? I imagine four of us will be enough, well-armed."

"There's one more thing. I know about this because someone is doing me a personal favor and I don't wish them betrayed to the authorities because of me."

351

"So the operation isn't legal?" Ellert looked amused.

"I doubt it."

He shrugged. "I don't mind if people in the city are making the best of the situation. Perhaps we can make it work to our advantage."

"I don't see how."

"Leave it to me. When do we go?"

Everyone met in the kitchen after supper. Hilda raised her eyebrows at the sight of four Norovaean officers, all laden with swords and pistols, then said, "I was thinking more like a few fellows with clubs, but this ought to be better."

"I should hope so," Ellert said.

Janna wished she didn't have to go, but she didn't trust anyone else with her money.

It was not quite dark when they left the house, but the streets were quiet. Now they were besieged, folk kept to themselves, venturing out only to market or attend the temples, which according to Birgid, were packed every day.

Hilda led the donkey hitched to the little cart, and Janna remembered how she had left Kaleva. She would have given all of her coin and then some to leave now. She knew she would be able to find Braeden if only she could get outside the city.

They trooped down to the river, lined with docks and warehouses. It was quiet here, though most of the warehouses had guards posted, private employees of the merchants who owned them. They looked none too pleased to see the Norovaeans, but no one bothered them.

Hilda finally stopped in front of a nondescript building. Janna didn't know how she could tell it apart from the rest. She knocked and a small window opened. She turned to Janna. "They say just the two of us can come in. The armed escort has to stay outside."

"Unacceptable," Ellert said. "It is impossible that Madame enter this place unattended."

Janna felt he was right, since she had no idea what awaited her inside. Anyone engaged in illegal activities might be desperate.

Hilda shook her head. "No one armed may enter, they said."

"I'll leave my weapons here with the other three. Is that acceptable?" Ellert handed his pistols to the woman, then removed at least four blades from his person and gave them to the others.

The door opened.

The warehouse was a hive of activity. A red-faced, sweating clerk sat at a table near the front, collecting coin and handing scraps of paper out in return. There was a short line, so Janna and her companions waited.

When they reached the clerk, he asked "How much?"

Janna must have looked as confused as she felt. "How much what?"

"How much money have you got? You tell me, and then I tell you what you can get for it."

That seemed like a strange way of doing things. "Oh, er, I have five hundred." There was no way Janna wanted anyone to know how much she had.

The clerk ran a dirty finger down a list on the table. "That'll get you four hams, ten wheels of cheese, and six sacks of flour."

That would scarcely fill a corner of the cellar. "What about a thousand?"

Before the clerk could speak again, Ellert said, "My good man, remember it's in your best interest to keep this operation from the attention of the authorities. Surely our discretion is worth some consideration?"

The clerk looked Ellert up and down. "If you don't mind my saying so, you're not in a good position to make demands."

"Oh, but I am," Ellert said cheerfully, his good nature unflagging. "If you can't see your way to giving Madame here a substantial discount, Duchess Karsten's troops will be all over this operation before morning."

"And if someone in here cuts your throat, how is Duchess Karsten supposed to find out you were here?"

Ellert laughed. "My comrades are just outside, and they're armed to the teeth. If I, and these ladies don't appear within the hour, they will go straight to the duchess."

The clerk narrowed his eyes and Ellert stared back, frank, pleasant, blue-eyed. The clerk finally said. "All right. But you ain't coming back. Now, you said you had a thousand? I reckon we can load you up well enough for that amount. Have your cart brought to that side door."

Hilda ducked out to get the cart and Janna said, "Thank you sir. Though that seemed rather risky."

"Not very. My officers out there would have gone for help if we hadn't come out soon."

Janna was relieved they had come, and even more so when they accompanied her cart, piled high with food, through Kersenstadt's dark streets.

Back at the house, Hilda and the other three officers put everything in the cellar while Janna went upstairs, pulling off her cloak as she went. She paused in the parlor to hang it up, since she no longer had her own room and there wasn't space in the nursery for her things. Ellert was on her heels and followed her into the room, closing the door behind him.

Birgid had left a lamp burning, but Janna felt very uneasy. "What is it, sir?" she asked, trying to keep her voice even.

"I'm very sorry to do this, Madame," he said in his bland, pleasant tone. "But you will please hand over the rest of your money."

"I don't have any more." Janna was acutely aware of the purse hanging under her apron. She had split all of the coin into three separate purses and had given over two at the warehouse.

"I know you do. Now please give it to me. Your house is well-supplied, thanks to our help, and the Norovaean army needs it more than you do."

Janna shook her head. She wondered what about her made everyone think they could take what they wanted.

"Madame, I do apologize." Ellert gripped her firmly by the upper arm and pulled her close. "But if you don't hand it over I will be forced to do it myself." He grabbed a fistful of Janna's skirt and she shrieked. "Madame, please stop making such a fuss."

"All right, all right." Janna's hands shook so, she could scarcely grip the strings of the purse and unwind them from her apron. Ellert dropped her arm and stood by as if he were waiting to start a dance. At last she untangled the purse and threw it at Ellert, before running out of the room and to the nursery, where she sobbed into her pillow until an uneasy sleep finally came.

ANTON

Anton and the count spent the spring chasing the Sanova Hussars all over the green countryside. "They're trying to keep us from meeting up with King Arryk," the count explained. "And we're trying to keep them away from Brynhild Mattila."

They were both doing a good job, since neither force could reach their allies. This was better than being with the king, anyway. Even though it would have been fun to spend time with Duchess Maryna and her brother, sitting in camp was boring. Out here, troopers chased each other, exchanging pistol shots when they could. So far, no one had been hurt much, although they'd once shot up several houses in a village when two scouting parties stumbled upon each other.

King Arryk's messenger found them when it was time. The count read the letter and frowned. "It seems he's decided to take on Mattila. I wish he wouldn't try it without Hohenwart, and I'd like to know what's keeping Seward Kurant. We're very under strength right now."

"So he'll need us," Anton said, thrilling at the prospect of a big battle.

"Yes, we must go soon, and somehow slip past the Sanovans. It's likely they'll try to join Mattila's army."

"Shouldn't we stop them first?"

"I don't see how we can. If the king fights in a place of his choosing, we'll be more help there. He might be able to engage Mattila before the hussars get to her. We'll leave tonight."

Scouts were sent in all directions while the count pored over a map. Once everyone had reported in, he made his decision. "We'll cross the Lera river on the Fromenberg bridge, then blow it behind us. If the hussars want to chase us, they'll have to travel twenty leagues to the next ford. "

Anton was glad they weren't fording. The rivers were raging torrents, even in shallow places. It didn't help that there'd been so much rain earlier in the spring.

He preferred a sturdy stone bridge, and so did Skandar.

It took the hussars a little time to figure out which way the count's troops had gone, but less than a league from the bridge, they were upon them.

"Get across the bridge with the spare mounts," the count told Anton. "Then round up as many boys as you can to help the engineers lay the explosives."

Anton hesitated. He hated leaving the count on the wrong side of the river again.

"Go," the count said, holding back Cid, who was eager to charge toward gunfire where the hussars had already engaged the rear guard.

Anton swallowed his fear and spurred Skandar toward the bridge. Most of the baggage was already on it or on the other side. Anton pushed his way through, shouting at boys to bring the spares behind him. Drovers cursed when Skandar reared up, forcing them to draw their wagons to the side, but Anton didn't care. The horses were more important than baggage. Sounds of fighting were close now.

By the time he'd struggled to the other side, and secured the horses, the engineers were nearly done. Two of them hung on ropes from the arch of the bridge so they could place charges on the underside. "When do you blow it?" Anton asked one standing on the bank, holding at bit of lit match.

"When the count's across. A few hussars might get across too, so be ready."

Anton was ready. He'd loaded his pistols and his sword was sharp. The count had given him most of his old weapons when he re-outfitted in Floradias. He rode Skandar as close to the bridge as the engineers would allow. The last wagons were crossing, followed by the thundering hoofbeats of several hundred of Orland's cuirassiers. They spread out along the banks and fired at the hussars on the other side. Anton was sure they were out of range, but wished he could do something. He wanted to keep his pistols loaded in case some hussars made it across. If he got close enough, he might hit one.

The fighting was fierce now. For the first time, Anton could see the hussars in force, their black wings fluttering like a dark cloud. A number of Orland's troops had fallen and Anton couldn't see the count. More and more horsemen crossed the bridge and the engineers stood ready.

Finally, Anton saw the purple plume of the count's helmet. He was using his saber to fight off a huge hussar with a long black plume rippling from his gold helm. The hussar had an axe, but Cid danced every which way and the axe narrowly missed him twice. The hussar was pushing the count hard and Anton realized he was holding his breath. Skandar danced around almost as much as Cid. Maybe he was worried too.

When the axe swung down once more, Cid spun, then made for the bridge. The big hussar thundered after him, axe held high. Anton raised his pistol.

Suddenly, there was shouting from the other hussars, and another one galloped onto the bridge, yelling at the big one, who was nearly on the count now. The two hussars halted on the bridge, then galloped in the other direction.

When the count cleared the bridge, the engineers blew it.

Anton had never heard a noise like it before. Too late he realized he was standing too close to the charges at the corner. Skandar shrieked and reared up, then ran away from the river. Anton barely held on and only reined him in after scattering a group of children gathered at the edge of the baggage train to watch the fight.

"Whoa, whoa," Anton said, breathless, petting Skandar's neck. Skandar snorted and rolled his eyes. "I know, I know. Sorry old boy. Let's go look for Cid."

Skandar knew that name and turned back towards the bridge a bit reluctantly. Or rather, where the bridge had been. The engineers had only set charges to the middle, so half of the stone still hung out over the river. Anton spotted Cid and the count standing near the engineers. The count was laughing.

Anton looked across the river and saw the big hussar. He had made it back just in time. Anton was sorry he hadn't followed the count. He would have made a marvelously large target for Anton's pistols.

JANNA

For several nights after Ellert took her money, Janna had nightmares of drunken soldiers laughing in her face, dirty hands grabbing her, while Anton and Anyezka screamed somewhere far away.

Doctor Marsel came on one of his regular visits. "You must try to get more rest," he said, looking concerned. "You look like you aren't sleeping well."

"I've been having bad dreams. I suppose I'm terribly frightened."

"You mustn't be. You must pray, and trust in the gods. They always look after their children."

"I know that's not true," Janna said. "The gods allowed the most dreadful things to happen to me. They let bad people kill my children and get away with it."

Doctor Marsel looked sympathetic. "The gods took your children to live with them in paradise. They no longer suffer in this world. And they let you suffer so you could learn how to properly respect them. All of this trouble has come because we allowed empress and Imperata to lead us to damnation. For that we are punished, the guilty and the innocent alike."

He looked so eager and certain she hated to contradict him, but she simply didn't agree. "That seems so harsh and unfair. I always believed, I always went to temple and prayed like I was supposed to and all I got for it was my family killed."

"It's not up to us to question the ways of the gods. And it was not your fault, but all of your temple visits and prayers meant nothing if they were delivered in error. We are fortunate that we live in a time that has given us Edric Maximus and the priests who follow his teachings. We are climbing out of the mire of sin and corruption, on our way to a new world free of war and suffering."

"I don't really understand that." Janna had heard bits of talk about the teachings of Edric, but didn't understand what was so different from what she'd been taught.

"Oh, but you should." Doctor Marsel's eyes glowed. "I am sure if you learn more about the truth, you would worry less and see why these things are happening. When I return, I will bring a few books for you to read, if that's all right."

"Of course." Janna was tired of reading about politics and didn't mind learning something new. "I've never been much good at understanding theology, though."

"Oh, that's not necessary. Edric Maximus writes simply and clearly. He tells us priests are not needed to interpret the word of the gods. All of his writings are meant for the common person to understand."

It seemed the teachings of Edric Maximus were all anyone thought about these days. Before Doctor Marsel returned, Birgid came in from an afternoon out. Her eyes sparkled and her cheeks were flushed from the cold that persisted, even though it was nearly summer.

"We were just sitting down to some tea," Janna said, although Iryna ran off to get a toy as soon as Janna let her off her lap. "Won't you have some?"

Birgid grabbed Iryna and put her in a chair. "You must learn how to sit quietly, young lady. Here." She handed Iryna a sweet biscuit, just as she looked like she was about to cry. "Oh, Madame, I do wish you could get out more. I've just been to the most wonderful service at the East Temple."

"But it's the middle of the week. I'm afraid I don't understand why there are so many services these days."

"It's that everyone is so excited at finally receiving the word of the gods. Those who can read get their own copy of the Holy Scrolls in Olvisyan and for those who can't, why the priestess reads direct from them. It's thrilling."

"How is that different from before? My priestess always told us what the Scrolls said about everything important."

"But it might not have been true," Birgid said, dipping a biscuit into her cup. They were getting stale and Hilda would bake no more since flour was reserved for bread. "There was no way to know. Even most priests and priestesses didn't have the learning to read the Scrolls for themselves and the Imperata would never allow them to be translated out of the ancient tongue. But Edric Maximus did it, and now we can all read what they say for ourselves."

"And you understand them?"

"Oh yes, they're quite straightforward. There's no mention of many things we were taught to believe were important. We don't need big temple ceremonies, we don't need to give money to the temple so the gods will hear our prayers, and there's no mention of an Imperata anywhere."

"How strange." Janna sipped her tea. "Why wouldn't they just tell us the truth?"

"So they could keep us as slaves, I suppose. So we'd give them money and do whatever they said. Here ..." Birgid rummaged in the pockets of her cloak, thrown over the back of her chair. "I brought you some pamphlets. These are some of Edric Maximus's most famous sermons." She handed Janna a stack of papers.

Doctor Marsel came the next day, even though he wasn't due for a visit. "I brought you this." He handed Janna a small book. It was bound in cloth and plainly made. "The Holy Scrolls in Olvisyan," he said, looking at the pile of pamphlets on Janna's table and seeming pleased. "So you are already familiar with Edric's sermons?"

"No. One of the servants just brought me these yesterday. She was at the East Temple and very excited about what was taught there."

"Oh yes, I attend the East Temple as well. Mother Ilsa is a compelling speaker and so compassionate toward her congregation. It would do you much good if you could attend a service."

"I'd like to go out, but can't walk that far."

"I'll come check on you again in three days. There will be a special afternoon service and I'll take you there myself. I'll bring my little carriage so you needn't walk."

Janna was beginning to feel like she would be given little choice in the matter.

BRAEDEN

After failing to stop Arian Orland, the Sanova Hussars joined Mattila's army, and then waited to find out whether she planned to move on Arryk or on Kersenstadt first.

"This can't be good news," Prince Novitny said as he and Braeden hurried to a meeting Mattila had called on short notice. "You know how she likes to schedule everything."

Braeden said nothing, but had a bad feeling as well. He couldn't imagine Mattila allowing the Norovaeans to take Kersenstadt with no repercussions and imagined the weeks of delay were due to the general making plans to take back the city.

By the time they reached the inn that Mattila used for her headquarters, most of her senior officers had assembled in the main dining room. Braeden and Novitny chose a spot at the long table near the foot, as far away from the general's place as they could get.

Filled with officers who usually chattered like sparrows, the room was awkwardly quiet. Just like Braeden and Novitny, the rest seemed to think the news wouldn't be good, and no one enjoyed being on the receiving end of Mattila's temper.

The general herself strode into the room moments later, slamming the door behind her. Two crimson spots bloomed on her pale cheeks, her mouth was set in a thin line and her eyes blazed. She threw herself into a chair, pulling it up to the table with a loud screech.

There was complete silence for a moment as she stared down, breathing hard, arms spread so her fists clenched the table's corners. No one moved a muscle. Braeden noticed that the Archduchess Elektra was not there, which seemed odd, considering the girl followed Mattila around like a shadow.

The silence dragged on, but Mattila spoke at last. "I have received the most extraordinary correspondence from one of my agents in the imperial court." Her voice was harsh and loud, as though she were shouting at troops on the parade ground. A young Moraltan officer sitting across from Braeden flinched.

Mattila went on. "It appears Her Imperial Highness has besieged Kersenstadt." She paused, appearing to take some satisfaction from the shocked gasp that went up.

It took an instant for her words to sink in, but when they did, they hit Braeden in the stomach like a shot. He grabbed the table's edge, barely conscious of Novitny's hand on his shoulder.

Mattila kept talking. "Somehow, Count Ensden hired an army from Cesiano, and General Barela has joined the empress as well, in direct violation of our agreement."

Braeden didn't know what their agreement was, and didn't care, but he felt the tiniest bit of hope since Barela was there too. Perhaps his friend would be of some help, though he didn't see how.

Far up the table, someone asked, "Is that not a good thing? The empress dealing with Kersenstadt means we don't have to, and can concentrate all of our resources on defeating Arryk."

Mattila whirled on him. "I'll say what's good and what isn't, and I'll thank you to keep your mouth shut. I had a plan for dealing with both Arryk and Kersenstadt, which is now unworkable. And Her Highness is likely to make a muddle of things, as usual."

Another gasp went up at such blatant disrespect toward the empress, but Braeden was no longer listening. He kept holding on to the edge of the table, tried to quiet his spinning head and waited for the meeting to end.

When it finally did, he stood up, Novitny's steadying hand on his elbow. "I'm all right," he muttered, but Novitny didn't let go.

"We'll go back to my quarters," the prince said. "I'll call the others and we'll think of something."

Even though Braeden's mind wasn't working well, he couldn't imagine what might be done. His family was still inside Kersenstadt, at the mercy of enemy troops. Now Teodora sat outside, and would be ruthless in dealing with that enemy. Braeden knew her well enough to be certain she wouldn't hesitate to destroy as many innocents as she needed to defeat the Norovaeans. Thinking about it made him sick.

Novitny steered Braeden to the house where he'd headquartered the Sanova Hussars, dragged him to the room he'd taken as a study, and shoved him into a chair. "Wait here," he said, as if Braeden could have moved at all, then disappeared.

Braeden didn't know how much time had gone by, but when the prince reappeared, he had Reno, Franca and Miro in tow. They pulled up chairs in a semicircle around Novitny's desk. No one said a word, though Franca gave Braeden's shoulder a squeeze as she went by.

"I've already told them what's going on," Novitny said, once he'd taken a seat. "I'm sure there's something we can do."

"I can't think of anything." Braeden's mouth felt full of cotton.

"General Barela is a friend of yours, isn't he?" Franca asked.

Braeden nodded, though he didn't see how that helped right now. It had occurred to him that Barela was even better friends with Teodora.

"You can write to him," Franca went on.

Novitny frowned. "Not sure what Barela can do."

"Maybe nothing right now." Franca's tone was patient, her voice softer than usual. "But if Teodora takes the city, he can look for Janna and make sure she's unharmed." She turned to look at Braeden. "Write to him, tell him where your house is, and if the city should fall, he can send someone to protect your family."

It was as though a light pierced through the fog in Braeden's head. "That's a great idea," he said. He didn't even want to think of what a sacking would be like with Teodora present, but this was more hope than he'd had a moment ago.

"It is." Novitny looked pleased. "Dura, why don't you help with the letter? I'll send a messenger to Kersenstadt as soon as it's written."

They decided not to use an official messenger, since Mattila might not be keen on communications with Teodora's camp, so they sent a young trooper with the fastest horse in Braeden's banner. The boy returned four days later with a message from Barela.

Braeden had been overseeing a drill, but Miro hurried to bring him a camp chair so he sat down before reading it. It started with a rather long, flowery passage in which the general expressed his regrets at the terrible situation. Braeden skimmed over that, then gave a great sigh, handing it off to Franca, who by now hovered over his shoulder.

"I suppose it makes sense he can do nothing right now, since they can't get into the city," he said, when she'd finished reading.

"Looks like they're not ready to attack soon." Franca frowned, folded up the paper and handed it back to Braeden. "But it sounds like he still hopes they might negotiate with Karsten."

"Teodora won't negotiate with anyone." Braeden was certain of that. "Mattila would have, but it's too late for that."

"Now Barela knows how to find Janna, I'm sure he'll make sure she's safe if the city falls," Franca said, looking resolute.

Braeden wished he could believe her.

GWYNNETH

"And now the water's smooth as glass." Kelsi Brun looked at the blue sky with some suspicion. Gwynneth didn't blame her. This was the first time in months they'd crossed into Sanova without fearing for their lives. It was also a nice change to sail into Novuk harbor, Estenor flag flying, without a worry about the big guns. If all went well, the two countries would be allies, if not friends, within a matter of days.

Someone had been keeping an eye out for the *Rusa*, and Count Tarka waited for her at the docks with a fine carriage. Once at the palace, Gwynneth was shown into a small study in the residential wing.

The queen sat behind an enormous desk carved from ebony and studded with amber. "Well?" she asked. "What did he say?"

Gwynneth dropped into a seat without bothering to curtsy. If no one was around, Ottilya didn't stand on ceremony. "He says yes, mostly. Naturally, there were a few quibbles."

"Naturally. Well then, what are they?"

Gwynneth handed over the original documents and read from her notes. Most of the changes were technicalities. Ludvik Meldahl had gone over every word and changed anything objectionable.

"What a tedious fellow." The queen huffed. "Please tell me Lennart isn't the lawyerly type."

"Oh not at all. But it makes sense to keep an adviser who knows his way around these things."

"I suppose you're right. What else?"

Gwynneth brought up the paltry dowry.

"I was sure he wouldn't like that, but reckoned I'd start low. How much does he want?"

"Fifty thousand."

"Hmph. But he'll hand over Prinova right away?"

"Yes."

"All right then, I'll give him fifty. I won't have it said I'm cheap."

Gwynneth could hardly conceal her relief. After shuttling back and forth, she wasn't keen on haggling any more. It was bad enough she would need to go to Galladium next and she wasn't at all certain that funding could be arranged as Lennart hoped. She prayed she could persuade him to invade anyway.

"I'll sign this thing as soon as I have a copy made." The queen leaned back in her chair, looking grim. "I suppose I must tell Raysa." She brightened. "Do you want to do it?"

"I can, if you think it's a good idea. You're sure she shouldn't hear it from you?"

"She probably should, but I won't be able to bear the look on her face. She'll think I've betrayed her."

Harsh and unpleasant as Ottilya could be, Raysa was her soft spot. It was clear to everyone but her daughter that she loved her very much.

"All right. I'll talk to her."

"Go now. The sooner the better."

"I'm a bit of a mess." Gwynneth was dying for a hot bath and change of clothes.

"Better that you are. She won't be so intimidated."

That was probably true. Gwynneth went straight to Raysa's room. The girl sat in a corner of the room, using the light from the tall window to stitch a magnificent tapestry.

"Princess Gwynneth," she said startled, dropping her needle. "I didn't expect to see you so soon."

Gwynneth crossed the room and sat down next to her. "The crossing was faster now that the weather's better. I also came to a quick agreement with King Lennart."

"So it's done then," Raysa said in a small voice.

"Yes." Gwynneth softened her voice and took one of Raysa's thin hands in hers. "It will be all right. Truly. Lennart is kind and has no wish to make you unhappy."

"I can't get used to the idea," Raysa whispered, tears forming in her dark blue eyes. "Everyone always said such dreadful things about him."

"Well, he used to be the enemy. Now he isn't. I understand it's hard to get used to. It will improve once you become better acquainted. Do you realize I

366

nearly married him, some years ago?"

"You did?" Raysa clearly hadn't heard the gossip.

"I was your age and he was my most distinguished suitor. My parents were wild for the match."

"What about you?"

"I won't lie—I found him intimidating. But he was quite attractive, very well-built and manly, and still is. He looks the perfect king, and you will look perfect next to him." It was true. Unlike both her parents, Raysa had delicate features, was tall and slim, with waves of pale blond hair. Her nose was too short and her chin too prominent for true beauty, but she was still rather striking. Gwynneth knew Lennart would be pleased, and felt a twinge of jealousy.

"I must do my best not to disgrace my family," Raysa said.

"You won't. You've been raised for this, as was I. And Lennart is better than any Briansk prince you might have married, if your mother had had her way."

Raysa shuddered. "It's true that would have been worse. Briansk is not our enemy, but I've heard the men are barbaric."

"You needn't worry about that with Lennart. He can be loud and rough, but he's terribly good-natured. I think you'll come to like him. Perhaps you'll even fall in love."

"That doesn't seem like a good idea. Mother always says it's best not to fall in love with your husband so you can keep the upper hand."

"Oh, that's nonsense. I fell in love with my husband, and there's nothing nicer. And I still like to think I keep the upper hand most of the time."

"When do I go?"

"I'm not sure. The treaty will go back to Estenor and then there'll be preparations for a big state wedding."

"Will it be here?"

"Most likely. And I imagine that's when your mother and King Lennart will formally sign the treaty. Raysa, I know this is hard for you but you must realize you are making something wonderful possible. You are bringing peace to your own country, and that means there might be peace in mine too, before long."

That brought a tiny smile. "I like that perhaps I can help you and your family this way. I feel so useless otherwise."

Gwynneth squeezed her hand again. "You are far from useless and I appreciate what you are doing. I'll go straight to the temple from here and pray to the Mother and to Vica for your happiness."

ANTON

Once they made it over the bridge without the hussars getting them, it was easy to reach King Arryk. He'd chosen a good spot to range his troops, but it seemed he'd be outnumbered unless Emilya Hohenwart reached him soon.

"Kurant isn't coming," King Arryk told the count, his face grim. "He tried to take on that infernal wolf woman and she killed him."

The count swore. "What's happened to his army?"

"Scattered in all directions. I received a message from a Duke Trystan, one of Princess Martinek's sons. Seems he was with Kurant and is trying to gather them up again. I doubt he'll succeed. I've heard he's just eighteen or so. How much can a boy do?"

Anton frowned. He wasn't that far from eighteen himself and reckoned he could round up scared soldiers and make them fight again.

The king and the count put their heads together over a big map and Anton went back to the stable, keeping an eye out for the Duchess Maryna. He found her in Skandar's stall, her brother in tow.

"We heard you'd arrived," she said, feeding Skandar a gnarled carrot. "I hope you don't mind we let ourselves in to say hello."

Anton didn't mind one bit. "I didn't know if you'd be here, since your uncle is getting ready to fight."

Maryna sighed. "There was a big argument between my uncle and my nurse and tutor. My nurse wanted to take the four of us somewhere safer, but Uncle Arryk needs Mama here as soon as she arrives. He's worried if he sends us away, she'll go straight there instead."

"You'll be safe enough," Anton said. "I won't let anything happen to you."

"That's so kind," Maryna said politely. "But I'm afraid you'll be busy with the battle. Devyn and I will have to manage on our own and help the little ones."

"I'm a good sword fighter," Devyn said, a belligerent thrust to his lip.

Anton believed him. Though the duke was small, he seemed very fierce.

"Do you know how to shoot?" Anton turned to Maryna.

She shook her head. "Isn't it terribly frightening?"

"It's not so bad. Loud at first, and the pistol bounces around, but you get used to it. You'd want a small one. I can show you."

"Would you?" Maryna looked excited and Devyn threw himself into the straw with a gleeful squeal.

"If I'm allowed. I even have pistols you could use." He had a small pair in mind, though he'd have to ask the count. He reckoned the count would be happy to help the princess's children. "Be sure you get permission, though. I don't want any of us to get into trouble with the noise we'll make."

The count was astonished when Anton asked if he could borrow his set of small wheel-lock pistols to teach the little duchess and duke how to shoot. "You sly little devil. I've never known anyone so good at making friends. It's a great idea. I don't know why the king brought them along. He should have sent them into Galladium where they'll be safe."

"The king wants the princess to come here as soon as she can," Anton said. "He reckons she might go to her children first if they're not here."

The count smiled. "Well, I want her to come here too, so the king did right. The princess will be pleased when she hears we're looking after her children's safety."

Anton stared at the count. "Are you still in love with that princess? I was sure you'd be over her by now."

"I was sure I would be too." The count looked puzzled. "It's strange. I don't think of her nearly as much, though I still love her, of course. I'd hate for her to come back after all this time and find I've still failed to free Prince Kendryk."

"Maybe you can do that after the battle," Anton suggested.

"Yes, perhaps. We'll head south after, no matter what happens with Mattila. I still have no idea how I'll do it, but it would help to be closer to Atlona. I'm sure I'll come up with something."

"You always do."

"I do, don't I?" The count looked pleased with himself. Knowing the princess might be close had put him in an excellent mood.

King Arryk sent scouts out every day to report on Mattila's movements. He had chosen his position and wanted to draw her close. "She doesn't engage unless she is sure she can win," he told the count.

"Then let her think she will. Line up about half your force in front of that hill and keep the rest hidden in the woods. If she thinks your force is much smaller, she might engage."

"My force is smaller," the king said, looking unhappy.

Anton hoped it wouldn't matter too much. He hated losing.

JANNA

Before attending a temple service, Janna thought she should learn more about what was taught there. The little book intimidated her, with its closely-packed print and thin pages, but the sermons were easier to read. She had to admit, the words of Edric Maximus were compelling. She wished she had heard him speak while he was still in the city.

By the time the doctor came for her in the early afternoon, she had read three short sermons and almost finished a long one. She hoped it was enough to help her understand what the priestess was talking about. Doctor Marsel took care to bundle Janna warmly into his carriage, and told the driver to go slowly over the bumpy cobbles. Birgid had agreed to stay home with Iryna, though Janna suspected she would have liked to go too.

Though the temple was one of the largest in the city, it was at least half full by the time Janna arrived, and when the service began just a little later, people stood in the aisles. While she waited for the service to begin, Janna looked around. The building itself was old and beautiful, stone arches soaring to a ceiling so high, it hurt Janna's neck to look at it long. Sunlight filtered through the tall stained glass windows and cast dancing colors across the congregation, as though a goddess had scattered jewels over them. But for all that, it seemed strangely bare.

Janna turned to Doctor Marsel. "Where are the hangings and icons?"

"Put away," the doctor said. "Edric Maximus says they distract from correct worship. They also offer an excuse for the temple to take from the poor. Such luxury is not needed to honor the gods, and the money saved can help those in need."

That made sense to Janna, though she missed seeing the beautiful works of art. And she found prayer without an icon in front of her strange and uncomfortable.

The service began simply, without music or ceremony of any kind. The priestess spoke from a raised pulpit, so Janna could see her well even though she was far away. Mother Ilsa was surprisingly young, not much older than Janna herself. Her pale face was sharp, her eyes intense and her deep voice echoed around the temple's vast pillars.

She started by reading a passage from the Scrolls. Janna was surprised at how much she understood. She had always thought the Scrolls full of long words that only scholars comprehended. Every now and then Ilsa came across one, and she would pause and explain what it meant before reading on.

The passage Ilsa read explained how the gods wanted to be worshiped. They required no great ceremony or complicated rites. They asked only that each person come to them as a child comes to a parent; to expect love, to ask for comfort, to offer respect. Janna found the words touching and resolved to ask the doctor to show her where to find the passage so she could read it again. Even if it wasn't true, it was comforting to hear.

Ilsa put her little book down; it looked identical to the one the doctor had brought Janna. "I realize this passage may seem an odd choice considering our present circumstances," she said. "But I believe that in these difficult times we must never lose sight of the reasons for our suffering. It's possible the suffering will become far worse, and for some of us, might even end in death.

"My children, you must not fear it. We stand here with our Norovaean allies against the forces of evil and we shall prevail. But we must not falter, not even for a moment. Conditions in our city might get much worse. We may run low on food, plague may come. Our walls may be bombarded and perhaps the enemy will even breach those walls one day."

Noises of dismay swept through the temple and Ilsa paused. She continued, her eyes brighter than before. "There is still nothing to fear. The gods might defend us from the enemy. Their swords might be turned and their muskets falter. But even if that doesn't happen, your death at their hands means your immediate salvation. For it is written that those who perish in defense of righteousness will be the first to enter the halls of paradise and will be raised in the sight of the holy parents.

"We also read of the great battle in which the forces of evil will mass against all of the righteous. We do not know when that battle will be, or where. We only know that it will come soon and that a prince will come from the north to defend us. He is already here. Arryk Roussay stands against the armies of the empress and Imperata and has sent his trusted lieutenant, the Duchess Karsten, to be our protector."

Janna squirmed. She did not care for all of this talk about suffering and death, although the faces around her were rapt. She didn't want the city and the Norovaeans to hold out until there was no one left. She wanted them to make an agreement with the empress so Braeden could enter the city peacefully. But it seemed no one else wanted that.

"So what did you think?" Doctor Marsel asked, as he tucked her back into the carriage after the service.

"It was very interesting." Janna kept her misgivings to herself, since the doctor and everyone else seemed so excited about Mother Ilsa's words. She changed the subject. "The priestess was so young. I was surprised."

"Oh yes. Most of the followers of Edric Maximus are quite young. In Ilsa's case, she served a priest who had been here for many years. A kind enough old fellow, but firmly in the Imperata's pockets."

"What happened to him, and the others who didn't agree with Edric Maximus?"

"Most left the city when the Norovaeans came. A few who didn't go peacefully were locked up in the fortress. I imagine they're still there."

Janna shuddered. Perhaps it was safest to avoid religion altogether.

KENDRYK

Ulla ran into Kendryk's study. "Visitor for you, sir," she said, out of breath.

Kendryk smiled at her. He was a little out of breath himself, since he'd just come inside from sword practice with Karil. He'd be happy to see any visitor who wasn't Teodora.

A short, wide, gray-haired woman with a regal bearing swept into the room. "Your Grace," she curtsied. No one had addressed him that way in a long time. "Charlette Bouley, at your service." She spoke Galladian.

Kendryk grinned some more. "Please Madame, be seated. Ulla, bring refreshments." He settled into a chair and waited for his visitor to do the same. Ulla bustled in a moment later, bearing a tray with tea and some sweets. Bouley looked at them and sighed. "Oh, the pastries in this city will be the death of me. I wasn't expecting to find any up here, I must admit."

Kendryk laughed. "I wasn't either. But Ulla's mother is a baker and keeps us well-supplied."

"How marvelous." Bouley bit into a biscuit and sighed. "But I must speak with you first. I am here on the request of Natalya Maxima and King Gauvain. I wish to know if you are well and if your treatment is acceptable."

"I am well," Kendryk said. "And I have no complaints about my treatment."

"Good, good." Bouley leaned forward. "Are we at liberty to talk here without being overheard. Can you trust the servants?"

"Not really," Kendryk said. He felt bad about that. Ulla and Dolf were friendly and helpful but he constantly reminded himself that they worked for Teodora. "But I know what to do."

He asked Ulla to send for Karil Andarosz. "He's a trustworthy fellow prisoner and will make sure no one approaches that door while we talk."

With Karil stationed outside, the heavy door fell shut.

"There is much news," Bouley said. "We aren't certain, but it looks like your wife is on the verge of success in brokering a peace between Estenor and Sanova."

Kendryk shook his head and grinned. "She's marvelous, isn't she?"

"I agree. No one else has managed it. So it's possible that Estenor will enter the war within the next year. Naturally, Lennart will need time to finalize the peace and gather his troops. He will also make diplomatic overtures into Kronland. Galladium is not directly involved but will not stand in his way and will try to offer as much covert support as possible."

"Tell the king I thank him," Kendryk said. "He doesn't need to do this."

Bouley looked at him long. "He feels he does, but perhaps for reasons that aren't altogether clear to all of us. Natalya sees far, and makes provision for things most of us don't even consider."

"What is your connection to her?" Kendryk was curious.

"I manage her correspondence. I used to be a priestess but found the life was not for me."

"Understandable. What brings you to Atlona? Officially, I mean."

"I'm bearing documents finalizing the marriage agreement between the Archduchess Zofya and King Gauvain."

"How is that going?"

"Well enough. The little archduchess is surprisingly eager. The king has sent her a number of lovely gifts and kind notes. I think she's in love with him already."

Kendryk grinned. "He was always good at that sort of thing. Besides being lovable to begin with."

"Indeed." She glanced at the closed door. "There's more. We must consider your safety, which I fear will be compromised if Lennart invades. You haven't served Teodora as a hostage so far, but she might react strongly in the face of a more formidable opponent. We will try to get you out of here before anything happens."

"It's impossible," Kendryk said, even as he felt a small flicker of hope. "This place is impregnable. There's no way I'll get out if Teodora doesn't let me."

"Nothing is impossible. Just start thinking about it and be ready."

TEODORA

It took almost a month, but finally they were prepared to attack. The weather had turned to unbroken rain which made digging go even more slowly than usual.

Teodora was ready to pick up a shovel herself. "I want to hold a pistol to someone's head." She snuggled into Demario's arms. "That would make them dig faster."

"Everyone is already afraid of you. They couldn't work more quickly if you stood above them with a whip."

"You're just saying that."

He laughed. "You're the only woman I've ever met who would consider that flattery. That's why I love you."

She caught her breath. He had never said those words in quite that order. "That's why no one else does." She tried to say it lightly, though it was too true. Since she had been a little girl, she had always known that no one loved her. Usually, she didn't mind too much, since she didn't love anyone either. But this was different.

"Are you all right?" Demario asked, tapping her chin with his finger after a moment of silence.

"Very much all right." She smiled up at him. "I must find a way to keep you with me always. I would go mad right now if you weren't here. How many of these sieges have you lived through? I couldn't bear it."

"You get used to it. Find other occupations. That's why so many soldiers gamble. Just imagine how bored they are out there."

"Do you suppose we'll take the city tomorrow?" Everyone had agreed upon a plan and the assault would launch the next evening.

"If we're lucky. If not, it will be a good way to test the defenses. Then we can adjust our plans depending on what we find."

Teodora was surprised and annoyed at how stoutly the Norovaeans resisted. Large guns fired from the top of the stockade, but Ensden's barrage took down a part of it and troops streamed through the gap.

Teodora stayed back, since both generals had insisted. "There is nothing for you to do, Your Highness," Ensden had said.

"I can scale the walls."

That brought a wide grin from Demario. "I know you can. But we cannot risk you. Can you imagine what would happen if some Norovaean gets off a lucky shot as you come over the top? It would be a disaster."

"I suppose you're right." Teodora chewed on a nail. "You aren't going, are you?" It was the most she would say in front of everyone else. She couldn't stand the thought of seeing his bloodied, lifeless body.

"Me?" Demario laughed. "I'm much too old for this sort of thing. I'll walk through the gate after my hot-blooded youngsters open it from inside."

She stayed as close as she could, though it became difficult to see through the smoke from the guns. Once the earthworks were breached, Teodora's troops set to scaling the walls. They nearly succeeded, but Norovaeans came out of the sally ports and pulled enough ladders down that it was no longer possible to get enough troops over the wall.

"You can offer Karsten terms," Ensden said afterward.

"How? Now she knows we can't get in, I doubt she'll take them."

"Perhaps not right away. But we took a few prisoners and according to them, conditions inside are deteriorating. They are going through their food quickly. If the weather warms, there will likely be plague as well. If she knows there is an offer on the table, she might take it sooner than you think."

"But if I offer terms, I'll have to let Karsten live."

"True." Ensden looked amused. "It's a rare commander who'll agree to terms that will bring about their own death."

"I cannot allow her to live. It's unacceptable."

"Very well then. We'll wait." Ensden was impossible to disturb. "Just remember we have little food here too."

"So annoying. I came here to fight, not worry about stuffing these lazy oafs."

"People must eat if they are to fight." Ensden's voice remained calm.

"I suppose you're right. Send to Arcius and have Princess Zelenka send, well, you know how much you need." Frankly, Teodora found the amounts of everything needed to feed, clothe and house an army unbelievable and far too expensive. "Tell her she'll be paid from Kersenstadt's plunder. We'll do the same for

Prince Herryk. It's a good chance for these Kronlanders to prove their loyalty to me."

One of Ensden's adjutants was already taking notes which meant messages would soon be on their way.

That done, she asked, "When do we attack again?"

Ensden looked surprised. "We need to regroup. It's best if we wait at least a few weeks. As conditions become more unpleasant inside, there's still a chance of surrender."

But he was wrong. Karsten did not surrender and sent out raiding parties to attack the outer edges of Teodora's camp. Some even stole wagons laden with food and other supplies. Now that it was summer and rather hot, she couldn't imagine that those in the city were happy to stay there. Surely the population would put pressure on Karsten to surrender.

"I know you don't want to, love," Demario said one hot night, as they played cards in Teodora's tent. "But you should make an offer. Make it clear that if the city is taken by storm, every Norovaean will be killed, and likely many civilians."

"I don't want Karsten thinking she can survive this if she surrenders." Teodora looked at her hand and wrinkled her nose in disgust. She really shouldn't play and talk at the same time.

"But it's customary." Demario was insistent, then played the winning hand. Teodora wondered if it was an omen. "She can expect imprisonment and a high ransom offer."

Teodora threw her cards on the table. "You know Arryk will pay any amount to ransom her. I'd rather he never saw her again."

"You can always throw up obstacles to negotiations, and plenty of prisoners die in captivity."

"Not enough of them," Teodora grumbled.

Demario chuckled. "I hope you never come to hate me. I doubt I would survive the week."

JANNA

Janna's baby came on schedule. Doctor Marsel had prepared for complications, but this time there were none. Janna wondered if it was because of the siege and the gods were granting her a little mercy. She still wasn't sure if she believed, but was grateful for an easy delivery and big, healthy baby boy. She named him Braeden, even though she knew his father wanted to name him Vluda, after Prince Novitny. They could always change it later if Braeden still felt the same way when they saw each other again. She had to believe they would.

A week after little Braeden's birth, Janna had fallen into a fitful sleep when an enormous crash awakened her. She jumped out of the bed she shared with Birgid and fumbled for a light. Iryna was screaming.

Birgid was up as well and lit a candle first. "Holy mother, what was that?" she asked, her hands shaking, making the shadows on the wall tremble.

"I don't know," Janna said, scooping Iryna out of her bed and holding her close. They stood quietly, holding their breaths. Another crash. This one seemed farther away. Boots pounded on the stairs as the Norovaean officers came down. Janna stood in the doorway and watched them go. Major Ellert came last. "Are we being attacked?" she asked as he went by. She was still frightened of him after he'd taken her money, though he'd remained as polite as ever.

"Seems so," he said, buckling on his sword belt. "Go down to the cellar and stay there until it's quiet. It's an artillery barrage. The house is sturdy enough, but you could still get hurt from shards of glass or pieces of stone." And then he was gone.

Janna wasted no time slipping on some shoes, wrapping Iryna in a blanket, then stopping in the parlor to get her cloak. Birgid had already snatched up little Braeden and waited for her in the stairwell with the candle. There was another crash as they went downstairs, closer again. Hilda and the maid huddled in the kitchen.

"Into the cellar," Janna said. "We'll wait until it's over."

Hilda brought another lamp with plenty of oil and Janna was grateful that they didn't have to stay in complete darkness for hours. Sitting down here, on sacks of flour, the sound of the guns was muffled.

"Will they break down the walls?" the maid asked, trembling.

"I doubt it," Janna said. "Doctor Marsel told me the duchess had great earthworks built up all around the walls. The guns won't be able to break through. Some might shoot over the walls, but this house is sturdy. Major Ellert said we should stay down here so flying glass and stone wouldn't hurt us."

"What if the house falls down on our heads?" the maid asked.

"It won't." Janna hoped it was true. And even if the house fell, perhaps they could survive down here.

The crashes continued for what seemed like hours, intermittently, sometimes near and sometimes far. Iryna fell asleep against Janna's shoulder and after a time, Janna fell asleep as well. Every now and then she slid back into consciousness and heard Hilda and Birgid softly singing hymns. It helped her drift back to sleep. To her relief, the baby slept peacefully throughout.

When she opened her eyes again, a faint bit of light came through the little window at street level. Janna put Iryna on a sack of flour and went to look out. The cobbles at eye level were damp and a light rain fell. She couldn't see any debris, and there didn't appear to be anyone about. "How long since the last blast?" she asked the others.

"At least an hour or two," Hilda said. She and Birgid had stayed awake the whole time. "I think it's safe to go up. We can stay in the kitchen for awhile and I'll make us all some breakfast. That way we can easily come back here if we need to."

Janna picked up Iryna, who was finally waking, and carried her upstairs. The maid built a fire and Hilda made porridge and tea. Janna wished for a fresh egg, but there had been no eggs for at least a month now. When another hour went by quietly, Janna decided it was safe to go upstairs and get dressed.

It was well after dark when the Norovaeans returned. One was missing and the woman had her arm in a sling. Janna ran to the parlor door and intercepted Major Ellert. "What happened?" she asked.

Ellert's face was blackened with grime, his eyes hollow. "The empress's troops made a run at the wall. They had ladders, but we were able to throw them off. Some of us came at them from the sally ports, but we took heavy losses. Olsen was one of them."

That must have been the one who didn't return. "How terrible. Do you think they'll try again?"

"Probably. They were testing our defenses this time. As far as we could tell, it was all Maladenes and Ensden's mercenaries. No sign of Sanovan cavalry."

Janna breathed a little easier, though now she wondered where Braeden was. Still, this was worrisome. It was one thing to huddle inside the walls, and another to be attacked. A question had been eating away at her for some time now, though she'd been afraid to ask Ellert. But now there was little left to lose. "Major Ellert, would you come in and sit down for a moment? I sent for tea just before you arrived. I must ask you something."

Ellert followed her into the parlor and collapsed into a chair. She had never seen him look so deflated. Janna poured a cup of tea for him and waited until they'd both had a few sips. "I don't wish to trouble you, but don't suppose there's much point in waiting any longer." Janna twisted her hands in her lap. "I've heard stories about sieges and how sometimes those inside will send out the poor, women who can't fight, and children, those they consider useless mouths."

Tired as he was, Ellert didn't miss her meaning. He barked out a short, humorless laugh. "And I suppose you're wondering if you might be turned out? I understand, in your situation it might be helpful. I'm sure you'd quickly find your friends out there." It went unsaid that things went badly for those who knew no one on the other side, which never wanted more mouths to feed either. The unfortunate outcasts were often reduced to eating what weeds they could find outside the walls until they froze or starved to death. Janna was willing to take that risk.

"I'm very sorry," Ellert said. He'd probably spotted the hope in her eyes. "But Duchess Karsten gave specific orders some weeks ago. No one leaves. Teodora will be held responsible for the deaths of all innocents in the eyes of the gods. If she wishes to spare those lives, she will retreat."

"She won't retreat." Janna knew the woman she had met would sooner die than back down. "And all the responsibility in the world won't do the dead innocents any good."

"I know." Ellert put down his empty cup. "I am very sorry, Madame. You have been such a kind hostess and I wish nothing more than to spare you and your children what's coming."

"It will be bad, won't it?" Janna whispered.

"There is still hope. King Arryk has surely been on the move since early spring. I am sure the armies of Brynhild Mattila stand in his way, but as soon as he defeats her he will come here and lift the siege. And once things have settled down, your husband can send you instructions on where you might meet him."

"What makes you think King Arryk can defeat Mattila? I've seen her army. I've seen her. She's even more frightening than the empress, and that's saying something."

"You forget; King Arryk doesn't fight alone. Emilya Hohenwart and Seward Kurant will have joined him, and Ruso Faris will be back in the field. Arian Orland will be with him as well. All of them together will create one of the largest armies ever seen in the empire."

Janna nodded. To get herself and her children out of here alive, Teodora needed to be defeated. But Teodora's defeat would also mean Braeden's. It was hopeless.

TEODORA

The rain ended, but within days the burning sun felt worse. The little grass that had grown soon died and Barela's cavalry had to forage over twenty leagues away. The stench of the camp increased and at least two different types of plague broke out. Rations were short in spite of more supplies coerced from the local nobility. Teodora didn't know how much longer they could hold out.

She sat at a table set up in the shade of a lone tree with her generals and Livilla, who had returned from her visit to Mattila's army. No relief would come from that quarter. Mattila was determined to engage Arryk soon, though she was having trouble pinning him down. Teodora wished for a stronger force, but she didn't want Mattila coming here and taking over. Kersenstadt would fall before that, and Teodora would take the credit.

"We must attack again soon," Teodora said. "As dreadful as things are for us, they must be far worse in the city."

"We can try." Barela shrugged. "We still see many Norovaean soldiers on the walls. Likely they are getting what little food is left and will be able to hold out a bit longer. They are very determined."

"Let's wait a few days," Livilla said. "I'm waiting for someone who can provide more information."

"What do you mean?" Teodora demanded. She had given the order that all sources of information be made known to her.

"I mean there are people loyal to us inside the city."

"Are you sure? How will they reach you?"

"There is a way. Few inside the city know of it and if my source still lives, he will use it. Long ago, we agreed that he would make contact on the first full moon after midsummer night. That will be two nights from now."

Teodora wanted to demand why she hadn't been told. She might have averted a sleepless night or two. But she didn't want to appear petulant in front of everyone. And she was just the slightest bit frightened of Livilla. She had never given her reason, but Teodora had seen what she was capable of and didn't want to test her.

Livilla took a small escort to meet her source. "I will bring him to you," she said. "A large party might draw the attention of the city watch."

She returned an hour later with a bedraggled priest in tow. Teodora wondered if it was possible to swim across the river, though getting to it from the city wall must have been quite a feat."This is Father Galen," Livilla said. "He is one of the original members of the League of Aeternos, sent to recruit in Kersenstadt."

"Did you succeed?" Teodora asked, though the man was still on his knees before her.

"Beyond our wildest hope, Your Highness. At least thirty League members still live inside the city."

"How did you survive?"

Father Galen frowned. "We pretended to embrace the Quadrene heresy, even preached it when necessary."

"You will be absolved, all of you, when this is over," Livilla said.

"Thank you, Maxima. We have continued the proper worship in secret and our resolve remains strong. We are prepared to do whatever is needed to see the true faith prevail. The gods are already punishing the heretics. Some are starving while plague spreads unchecked. Hundreds die every day."

"Good." Things were finally going Teodora's way. "Can you open the gate?"

Father Galen blanched. "Perhaps. Though it will be difficult. The gate remains heavily guarded with the most fanatical of the Norovaeans. There may not be enough of us."

"Find a way. We cannot take the city unless the gate is open. Unless there is another way. Such as the way you came out."

"No, that would be even more difficult. I took a great risk in leaving the way I did and can only hope I will be able to return unnoticed." He looked miserable for a moment, then his eyes cleared. "We will open the gate Your Highness, even if it costs us our lives."

"Good. You will be rewarded richly if you succeed, in this life or the next."

"We will say a thousand prayers for all who are lost, and erect a golden altar to Vica in their honor," Livilla added. That seemed to satisfy the priest.

"How soon can you do this?" There was no point in delay.

"Soon. We should wait for the new moon. We will have a better chance of success under cover of darkness."

"Very well. On the night of the new moon, open the gate right after dark. We will be ready." Teodora stood. "You may return, Father Galen. Oh, and someone get the man something to eat. I want him to make it until the new moon." He rather looked like he might not.

JANNA

Janna tried not to notice the nightmare around her. It was hot, but she kept the house shut up tight, hoping that if the front door never opened, the horror outside might not get in. Of the four Norovaean officers, only Major Ellert remained. A few others had moved in, probably from less comfortable accommodations.

"Likely from plague-ridden houses," Birgid whispered.

Janna pretended not to hear. She refused to think about it. To think about it made it real and it couldn't be real. Not after everything she had been through. She read all the pamphlets Birgid brought her. By now she'd read through the Holy Scrolls twice and was starting on a third time. She prayed five times a day, once to each member of the Holy Family separately, then prayed to all of them together. At first she found it difficult without the icons, but the Scrolls were clear that those weren't needed.

Her doubts weren't gone, but she pushed them into the farthest corners of her mind. They wouldn't serve her here. Doubt was the killer. Now that she had two little ones counting on her she must be strong. She had failed her stepchildren; she would not fail these. If the Faith offered salvation, she would take it, and believe to the best of her ability.

Mother Ilsa had become a frequent visitor since little Braeden's birth. Doctor Marsel had asked her to come bless the baby, and she stayed for hours after, talking to Janna. After that, she came often. Once plague broke out, there were far fewer visitors to the temple, so Ilsa reduced the number of services by half. Instead, she visited her congregation when she could, and passed notes and prayers through windows at those houses she wasn't allowed to enter.

Janna liked to see her. Everyone else, including the Norovaean officers looked haunted and fearful, but Ilsa stood erect and her eyes sparkled with life even as her cheeks had sunken. It was as though she had been born for this type of crisis.

"Ah, seeing these two does my heart good." Ilsa ruffled Iryna's head and took baby Braeden from Janna, kissing him on the cheek. "They seem to be well, thank the Mother for that."

"They are," Janna said. "We finally slaughtered the donkey. The major felt we should do it before he got any skinnier. Be sure to get meat from Hilda before you go." There was still a little food in the cellar and Major Ellert imposed strict rations on everyone so it might last a bit longer.

"Thank you. Fresh meat will be welcome, even if it's from the poor old donkey. Be glad you have no dogs or cats. Those have already reached a fair number of tables."

Janna shuddered. "I don't think I could bear it." She'd always had pet cats as a girl, and kept a mouser in her Kaleva kitchen.

"Oh, that reminds me." Ilsa dug in the pockets of her robes. "I brought a little something for our tea. I officiated at a wedding yesterday, and they served ginger cake. It's not much, but we can stretch it to the four of us." Birgid and Iryna usually joined them for tea. Even after food ran out, it seemed they would have tea. One big bale from the black market warehouse had been tea of various kinds.

"Someone got married? Now?" It seemed ridiculous under the circumstances.

Ilsa shrugged. "It was a Norovaean soldier and the daughter of the house. He reckoned he'd get away with it, but she started to show and her parents kicked up a fuss. Went straight to the duchess and she ordered him to marry the girl."

"Oh dear. Not the happiest situation then."

"Maybe not, but it was a good excuse for a little neighborhood celebration. We drank up the last of the wine and forgot about reality for a few hours."

"I would love to do that."

"Do you have wine?" Ilsa's eyes twinkled.

Janna had to smile. "The Norovaeans drank it all long ago. They finished it off after that second attack. I worry they won't hold out much longer."

"They may not. But the whole city prays they will stay strong until King Arryk arrives."

"I'm not sure I want that." Janna had already explained about Braeden.

"Do not be troubled." Ilsa took Janna's hands in hers. "You've told me your self how your husband has been a soldier for twenty-five years and has never had more than minor wounds. Ercos will keep him this time as well, no matter how fierce the battle."

"I still can't see how this will work out." Janna felt bad that her faith flagged, but it seemed weak even on the best days.

"It's not up to us to know the ways of the gods. They take care of us and make plans we cannot foresee." Mother Ilsa seemed to understand Janna's need for comfort. "Remember that bit of the Scrolls I read to you the other day, about the holy martyrs who died for their faith? The Mother took all fear and pain from them during their darkest hours. They suffered the most dreadful wounds with smiles on their faces, praising the Holy Family all the while. It will be the same for us, should the worst happen."

"How do you suppose it is for small children, those too little to understand about the gods? Surely they wouldn't be allowed to suffer just because they were too young to pray properly?" Janna thought of Anyezka dying in the burning farmhouse.

Ilsa leaned forward, clearly eager to make Janna feel better. "The little ones are free of sin. Any faults they have are because of their parents. The gods will take children to them before they can be harmed."

"I wish that were true." Janna leaned back against the chair's cushions, tears leaking from her eyes. "There isn't much that I'm afraid of anymore, but I'm terrified for Iryna and the baby."

"There's no need. None at all." Ilsa patted Janna's hand. "And if you just believe and pray to each of the Holy Family in turn, as is proper, there's nothing anyone out there can do to hurt you."

The days dragged on, hot and still. There hadn't been an attack on the walls in over a month. Janna hoped they weren't just biding their time. She only heard rumors about the army besieging the city. It was said they suffered nearly as much as those inside since the plague had come to them too. Food was short for them as well, and everyone hoped that if they ran out altogether, they would leave.

In Janna's house, everyone was hungry all the time. All that remained in her cellar were a few sacks of weevily flour and the massive bale of tea. They ate just enough bread to stay alive and Janna sometimes went out with Hilda to look for greens. Hilda knew which herbs were edible, so they would range out into the neighborhood, looking for abandoned gardens and weeds growing in every possible corner.

If a house bore the black mark of the plague on its front door, it was safe to say the garden would be deserted. Even in the unlikely event that anyone lived inside the house, they could not come out for fifty days after the last case died or recovered.

Janna wondered how Doctor Marsel was faring. After little Braeden's birth he had paid a rather formal call, a leave-taking of sorts. "I'm going to minister to those in the plague-houses," he said, his voice calm, his eyes resigned. "I won't be back until it's over, since I can't risk exposing anyone in a safe house."

"But you'll die." Janna was aghast. "You don't need to do this."

"Oh, but I do. That I haven't has long weighed on me. The only thing that's kept me from it is that I promised your husband and Doctor Toure I would see your child born and you safe. I've done that and now I must go to those who need me more. My nurse will look in on you and can handle any emergency."

"I still wish you wouldn't," Janna said. "Surely there are others?"

"There are no others." Doctor Marsel shook his head. "The few doctors who survive cannot help all of the new cases. I spoke with Mother Ilsa and she agreed I will be doing the will of the gods in this work."

There was nothing Janna could say to dissuade him. She hoped he was still alive and that when this was over, she'd see him again.

TEODORA

Teodora could hardly sleep for excitement in the nights leading up to the new moon. The weather continued hot and dry, though she didn't care. It could rain frogs and cattle and she would take the city. In spite of the heat, she had her light armor on by late afternoon.

When Demario saw her he frowned. "You should enter the city of course, but only once it is secure."

"No." Teodora folded her arms. "I want to be first through the gates."

Demario sighed. "Very well. I will stay by your side."

She smiled. "I would like that."

Thanks to Father Galen's plan, she'd had time to call in all the troops from the surrounding area. No doubt their hosts were glad to be rid of them and the soldiers themselves seemed eager for action. Teodora had ordered them brought in under cover of darkness so the defenders wouldn't notice any changes in the camp. Unsure of the number of Norovaeans inside the city, she was leaving nothing to chance.

All of her forces had assembled near her camp. They stayed there until the sun went down, then made their way toward the main gate in silent, dark columns. She sent more troops to take the other, smaller gates which would be opened from the inside by those who got through the main one.

Teodora was very clear. "I want Larisa Karsten taken alive." She saw Demario's satisfied expression and said, "So I can kill her myself, slowly." Demario shook his head, and she smirked. "Give no quarter to any Norovaean of rank."

"No hostages then?" Ensden asked. Ransom of noble hostages was one of the best ways for plundering soldiers to raise cash.

"No Norovaean hostages. If you find rich civilians, help yourselves. I want to see no live Norovaeans by morning, except for Larisa Karsten. Is that clear?"

Teodora crept forward at the head of the first column, a pistol in one hand and a sword in the other. Her heart pounded so loudly under her breastplate she was almost surprised it didn't clank. She hoped Livilla's people could pull this off. Everything depended on them.

Demario held a small timepiece. She didn't know how he could read it in the dark. He turned his back to the city and someone struck a tinder. "Ten o'clock five minutes ago," he whispered.

Why was nothing happening? Teodora stood motionless, willing the gate to open. Suddenly, torchlight flickered from the wall and she heard shouting. Next came gunfire and screaming that went on for an unbearable eternity.

"Come one, come on," Teodora muttered under her breath and slowly moved forward. Her hand gripped the pistol so tightly her muscles cramped. She willed herself to relax. She counted backwards from one hundred and licked her dry lips. It seemed no one around her was breathing either. The shouting and screaming inside didn't let up, but at last the gate swung open.

"Go!" Teodora shouted and ran for it.

By the time she reached the gate, Father Galen and all of his people were dead. Norovaeans came from all directions and several tried swinging the gate shut again. Teodora and Demario fired their pistols at the same time and two soldiers went down. She grinned at him. This was how it was supposed to be. Perhaps from now on she would insist on fighting with him every time.

The Norovaeans had been taken by surprise, so the only opposition at the gate came from those who had been on duty. Others would come soon enough. Meanwhile, imperial troops surged around Teodora and flowed into the side streets. "Find Larisa Karsten," she screamed, hacking at an officer in front of her. He was blond and tall, probably just like Arryk, but she ran him right through the middle and he fell like any other man.

She spotted a flash of golden braid and hoped for a moment it was Karsten, but it turned out to be just another soldier. Teodora hoped Karsten wasn't one of those silly leaders who liked to dress plainer than her officers. It would make her hard to find; all of these foreigners looked so alike.

Even though the Norovaeans were out in force by now, there was no question they were severely outnumbered. Who knew how many had succumbed to plague and starvation?

Teodora cut down everyone in her path. No one could stand against her. Suddenly, she stood in a square far inside the city, and there was no more enemy. She was breathing hard, sweat running down her face and prickling her scalp. She yanked off her helmet, took a deep breath and looked around for Demario.

He was right behind, and took her arm. "You must take cover. They might regroup. And for Vica's sake, put your helmet back on."

She grinned at him. "It's marvelous, isn't it?" She left her helmet off. "We're winning, aren't we?"

"Of course we are. The Norovaeans are in terrible shape. I don't know if you paid attention, but those we faced were nearly skeletons and many looked sick. Pray you don't get the plague."

"I can't. I won't." She felt invincible. She *was* invincible. "I want to kill more people. Where are they?"

"Running away, I'm afraid. It will turn into a sack soon, I'm sure."

"Good. Let this lot see what happens when they defy me."

"We shouldn't let it get out of control. I'm sure you don't want the city too badly damaged."

"Oh, I don't know." There was a commotion coming closer, but they were her troops.

An officer flung a body at her feet. "Larisa Karsten, as requested, Your Highness."

Teodora poked at the body with her foot. "She's not dead, is she?"

"I don't think so. Just knocked about the head a bit."

There was a groan and Karsten staggered to her feet. Teodora had heard the duchess was very beautiful, but she didn't look it now. Her face was a dirty, bruised mess. Blood ran from her lip and nose and her hair stuck out in all directions, like straw. She was only half-dressed. They'd probably caught her getting out of bed.

"On your knees, bitch, and surrender." Teodora snapped. "Now."

Karsten spit a gob of blood onto Teodora's breastplate. "Never. You might as well kill me because I won't surrender to you."

"Oh, I will kill you," Teodora smirked. "But you'll surrender first." She nodded at the officer who'd brought Karsten. "Captain, make her do it."

The officer's metal-clad fist struck Karsten on the left cheek. There was a loud crunch. Her looks wouldn't recover from that one, if they weren't ruined already. Karsten staggered, but didn't fall.

"I doubt King Arryk will want you back after this." Teodora was enjoying herself. "In fact, if you don't surrender right now, I'll let these fine gentlemen have fun with you until morning, or until you die, whatever comes first."

"Your Highness," Demario whispered in her ear. "I'm sure the king will take her back in exchange for concessions."

"I don't want his concessions!" Teodora screamed. "I want him dead, and I want all of his people dead."

She was in such a rage, she didn't notice Karsten coming at her until it was almost too late. The girl had no weapons, but her fingers were strong, and long enough to fit around Teodora's throat. Teodora staggered back, but didn't fall. She still held her sword and it slid into Karsten's body easily enough.

Her fingers loosened and she fell back. Teodora pushed her until she fell onto the cobbles of the square. It was hard to say if she still lived. Blood spread all over the front of her dirty white shirt. Teodora slashed at her throat until it she'd opened it completely, just to be safe.

After the excitement so far, it was oddly unsatisfying.

JANNA

One warm evening, Janna had just put Iryna to bed. Baby Braeden was already asleep. He was not as quiet a baby as Iryna had been, but he balanced active days with long naps. Janna needed the rest. She feared she wasn't eating enough to provide him with milk, but he seemed to be growing and didn't act hungry.

She went back into her parlor and lit the candles on the little altar she had created on a side table. There were no icons, but the candles reminded her of quiet prayers with her sisters in a Kaleva temple. But now she no longer prayed only to Vica. Out of habit and comfortable familiarity she started with Vica, but then she prayed to the other three in turn.

She begged Vica for the wisdom to be resourceful enough to survive whatever lay ahead, and to guide the city's leaders. She asked Ercos for strength and most of all to keep Braeden safe, wherever he might be. She also prayed for strength for the Norovaean defenders. She hoped Ercos understood if she prayed for both sides. She begged the Mother to watch over her children, no matter what happened to her. And she asked the Father to breathe new life into an earth become violent and corrupt.

Janna's prayers finished, she went to bed, though the summer sky was still light. She was awakened much later by shouts in the street and sat up in bed listening, then heard the pop of musket-fire. It sounded far away. Without thinking, she jumped up and snatched the baby.

Birgid grabbed Iryna by the arm and dragged her out of bed. "We must go downstairs right now," Birgid said. Iryna started crying, but followed along, clutching her rag doll. The kitchen was empty, but the other women were already in the cellar.

"Does anyone know what's happened?" Janna asked.

"Some Norovaeans ran by just before we came down, shouting that the city has fallen," Hilda said.

"Oh Holy Mother, what's to become of us?" The young maid burst into tears.

"It's all right, " Janna said. "We'll hide down here. I'll check the doors." She felt cold inside, and shaky, but this was her house and her responsibility. Hopefully she'd have time to double-check the back doors and make sure the bolt on the front door was secure.

Back on the ground floor, the gunfire sounded closer and there were screams and shouts coming from some of the houses around hers. Surely the empress's forces hadn't already come this far? Of course, Janna didn't know how long they'd already been in the city.

She felt the smallest bit of hope under her fear. Perhaps Braeden was already inside the city. Surely he would be near, once he had known she was trapped inside the city. But if she locked up and went into the cellar he wouldn't have a way into the house. She knew he had a key for the front door, but a heavy iron bolt barricaded it from inside.

Janna stood frozen in the corridor, trying to think of what to do when there was a great pounding on the door. She listened for Braeden's voice, but the shouting sounded like Maladene. The door shook, but held. Janna decided it was best to hide in the cellar until they had gone. She came back through the kitchen just as there was a tremendous blast from a pistol very close by. Janna shrieked as the back door burst open. She looked straight into the dark eyes of a grinning musketeer. "Your house?" he asked, in heavily accented Olvisyan.

Janna nodded, though it might have been the wrong response. She couldn't think.

The man shouted at a few others still outside and four Maladene soldiers trooped into her kitchen. Janna shook all over, but she raised her chin and said, "My husband is a personal friend of your general, Demario Barela. Take me to him right now."

TEODORA

"Damn the bitch." Teodora wiped blood from her face. It wasn't hers. "I wanted to take my time, after everything she put us through."

Demario shook his head. She couldn't read his eyes, and it frightened her, though she would never show it.

"Ah well." Teodora sheathed her sword. "Shall we see how the rest are doing?"

"Certainly." Demario's voice was tight. It appeared he wasn't having as much fun as she was.

The city was in chaos. There were no Norovaeans in sight and imperial troops streamed in from all directions. By now, invaders had entered the other gates, eager to get their share of the spoils, and something else. Teodora felt as though her anger had radiated out from her, spreading to all who entered the city. Rage at its citizen's defiance, at being miserable for so many months soon turned into a mass frenzy of retaliation.

"How long should the sack go on?" Demario's voice was in her ear.

"A while, I should think. Why not? They've earned it after the horrid summer they've had."

"Perhaps. But if we let them run wild too long, it will be hard to gain control of them again. Especially if they start drinking."

"What of it? Are you worried about Arryk surprising us?"

"It's unlikely. But in my experience, one should never be caught unprepared, for any reason."

"You are probably right." Teodora sighed. "How about giving them until mid-morning?"

"I must round up troops now so I can enforce it later."

"Do that then." She felt she should do something to make him happy, because he clearly wasn't.

He turned away to shout orders and Teodora felt someone plucking at her elbow. It was the youngest member of her guard. The girl looked terrified, even though they had won. Perhaps she found the sight of so much violence disturbing.

"What?" Teodora snapped.

"There's a priestess here who wants to speak to Your Highness."

"What kind of priestess?" These days, one needed to ask.

"Says she's from the big temple in the east of the city."

"I'll speak to her."

A small, blond young woman stepped forward. "I am Mother Ilsa, head priestess at the East Temple, Your Highness." She curtsied correctly enough.

"Are you a Quadrene heretic?" Teodora doubted any League members had survived.

"I serve the true faith and the Holy Family, Your Highness." The young woman's voice shook, but her pale eyes looked straight into Teodora's. She had a sudden unpleasant recollection of Edric Landrus's piercing gaze and shuddered.

"What do you want, heretic?"

The priestess swallowed. "I would beg Your Highness to stop the violence now. The Norovaean soldiers are dead and now only the innocent are harmed."

"Innocent? How can any person who listened to your heresy and believed it be innocent?"

"Your Highness, your soldiers are raping young girls, they are killing babies still at the breast. Surely those little ones cannot be considered heretics. Please make them stop."

"I think not. These rebels must suffer the consequences of heresy and disobedience."

"Please, Your Highness. The gods will look kindly upon any mercy you show."

"The gods look kindly upon me killing heretics." Teodora's patience was at an end. Her sword whipped back out and the false priestess slumped to the ground, her throat cut. "No more petitioners," she snarled at her guards.

She suddenly felt very tired. Perhaps it was time to find lodging. She didn't care to return to camp right now. She opened her mouth to order a search for a suitable house when there was a thundering crash at a distance. Another followed it seconds later. "What was that?" Teodora looked around. She couldn't see because of the tall houses looming around her. "Someone go see what's happened."

A guard ran off toward the noise. After a time, black smoke filled the sky above the houses, blocking out the gray light of early morning.

The guard returned at last. "Exploding munitions magazines, Your Highness." She gasped, between coughs. The smoke billowed across the rooftops and Teodora could taste it.

"Damn it. I need those magazines. Who set them off?"

"Hard to say. Several houses were on fire nearby and the flames might have spread."

"Who set the fires?" With the Norovaeans so fanatical in their resistance, Teodora wouldn't be surprised if they'd set fire to the city themselves.

"I don't know." The girl coughed some more.

The smoke was becoming thicker, making it difficult to breathe. "We should leave." Teodora had a sudden craving for the fresh air outside the walls.

Demario appeared from somewhere at a run, followed by a large troop of soldiers. "You must leave the city now," he gasped. "As fast as you can." His face was black and streaked with perspiration.

"What? I've just taken it. I'm not going anywhere."

"The city is lost." He shouted an order to his troops and they made for the gate at a run.

"Lost? Whatever are you talking about?"

"Fire. There were at least eight magazines in the city, stuffed with munitions and powder. All of them have exploded. The warehouses by the canal are in flames along with that quarter of the city. Soon the fire will engulf all of it. Please go, Your Highness. The flames are moving faster than you can run."

Now the roaring sounded closer and a strong wind blew thick smoke and heat into her face. Teodora coughed and Demario grabbed her arm, pulling her with him as he made for the gate.

"The troops inside the city?" Teodora choked out through her coughing.

"Perhaps some can get out. Many will not. But we must." He had shed his cuirass and helmet and she pulled hers off as she ran. Behind her the wind shrieked, although it might have been the screams of those left behind. The roaring, now very close, was the worst. A few guards disappeared, lost in the black smoke. Teodora's lungs burned, but she kept running. She hadn't realized how far she had come into the city.

When she thought she could go no further, she saw the open gate ahead. Demario never looked back, but as they neared it, she yanked her arm away and turned around. Guards and a few infantry troops scuttled past her. The flames stood in a wall at the end of the street. Surely they would stop at the gates?

Sweat streamed down Teodora's face and her lungs ached. It became even harder to breathe, as though the flames were pulling away every last bit of air. Teodora gasped and fell to her knees. The gate was so close and yet she couldn't move. Anger surged through her. An empress couldn't die like this. There would be nothing left for a state funeral. With one great effort, Teodora used her last strength to struggle to her feet. The heat scorched her face and burning ash landed on her hair. Still no way to draw breath. She swayed and fell back to the ground.

JANNA

The mention of Barela's name seemed to take the men aback. They stopped in their tracks and huddled in a quick conference. One of them shut the broken door and another helped him slide a dresser in front of it. They didn't act like they wanted to take her to their general.

"Well?' Janna asked, hoping she sounded more confident than she felt. "My husband is expecting me."

After more muttering a man stepped forward. It seemed his Olvisyan was better than the others. He swept off his hat in a bow and said. "We are very sorry Madame, but you will remain our guest until your husband can make the proper payment."

"But he's on your side." Janna didn't understand. There were stories of wealthy people being held for ransom during sackings and she realized these soldiers must consider her wealthy based on the size of the house and its furnishings. "He's a commander in the Sanova Hussars. He won't be pleased if you ask him for money."

"He won't mind too much once he gets his share of the plunder. I'm sure the high officers will get so much he won't miss a few thousand."

"A few thousand?" Janna didn't know where Braeden would get an amount like that since soldiers were likely sacking the factor's house right now.

"It might take him a few days, but he'll manage. They always do. Now, who else is in the house?"

Janna hesitated just long enough to know she wouldn't get away with a lie. "My children and the servants are in the cellar."

The man barked something at the others and four soldiers headed for the cellar door. Janna barely kept her knees from buckling. She reminded herself that she was responsible for the well-being of the others in the house and must stay strong.

She kept her head high and fixed her gaze on the man who had spoken to her. He smiled and shrugged as if to apologize again. She heard the children crying and a moment later Iryna ran to her and a man quickly put a screaming Braeden into her arms. Janna collapsed into a chair, pulling Iryna onto her lap.

The other women were crying. "You must let the servants go," Janna said as firmly as she could manage. "My husband will ransom them too."

"It doesn't work that way," the man said politely. "Money in a few days is nice, but the empress promised us some fun right now after all of these wretched months sitting outside your walls."

The soldiers dragged Hilda, Birgid and the maid down a corridor and a door slammed followed by the most dreadful screaming. Janna tried to cover Iryna's ears with one hand and struggled for composure. For all she knew, she was next. She desperately tried to think of ways to help the servants, but realized it was too late. Now she had to concentrate on saving her children.

"You're in luck," the man went on, showing off a mouthful of brown teeth. "We've found ransoms are paid more willingly when the family is left unharmed. You'll of course tell your husband how well we treated you." He took a step toward Janna so he loomed over her.

"Of course," she said tightly. "What happens next?"

"We'll take your servants along and what things we can carry. The general hasn't been so good at paying in coin, so we have to make do. A few of us will stay here to keep you safe until your husband comes. He can find the house?"

Janna nodded. She shut every other noise out of her head. If she stayed quiet and didn't make a fuss, Braeden would be here soon. Even if the Sanova Hussars hadn't been part of the besieging force, she was sure they would come as soon as they'd heard the city had fallen.

After an eternity, the screaming stopped and Janna saw people going out the front door. She didn't understand why they had to take the women with them, but didn't want to think about it. Through the open kitchen door she saw most of her furniture coming down the stairs and out the front door. Someone had brought a cart and was loading it up. It didn't matter. Braeden would be here before long and take her away from this awful place.

The baby cried and Janna fed him. Iryna cried from hunger too, but there was nothing to eat. "Papa will be here soon," Janna said. It looked like daybreak was near and the streets were noisier than they'd ever been at midday. Soldiers were carrying off everything they could. Janna was glad she didn't know what was happening in the houses around her.

Both children fell asleep and Janna dozed in the chair, still holding them close. She awoke with a jolt. It was light outside and her leg had fallen asleep. She put both sleeping children on a bench and went to the window. Soldiers were running to the east, away from the direction they had come. They abandoned carts and dropped whatever they were carrying.

The rising light was to the west. Janna frowned. It couldn't be the sun. And then she smelled it. Smoke. It seemed some houses had caught fire, unsurprising considering the chaos. Even though the more expensive houses were stone, most in the city were half-timber and thatch.

Janna took a deep breath and walked out into the corridor where two drowsy Maladene soldiers kept watch. "It seems there is a fire." She hoped at least one understood. "Perhaps we should leave. There is a large stone temple to the east ..." She had to get the children to safety.

One of the men understood her well enough. He shook his head. "No. You stay here. This house is safe. Go in the cellar if you are afraid."

"I think I will," Janna murmured, hoping they wouldn't follow her down there. After what they had done to her servants she did not want to spend any more time close to these men. Perhaps the fire would frighten them off.

She awakened Iryna and looked out the window one last time. The orange light filled the sky now, smoke rising in great black billows above it. Janna put her head out the window and jerked it back in when the hot gust of wind hit her face. It was almost unbearable. "Into the cellar," she said to Iryna, giving her a push and picking up the baby, who was screaming again. When she glanced into the corridor the Maladenes were gone. Perhaps they'd run off after all.

She wondered if she had time to get water from the pump in the kitchen and decided against it. The fire looked like it was close now, and moving fast. She hadn't realized there would be so much fuel and hoped her house's stone walls and slate roof could withstand the heat. The cellar was without question the safest place.

She settled herself and the children on the flour sacks once more after she'd made sure the door was securely shut. She wished she could lock it. "Let's say a prayer," she said to Iryna, who was still crying.

She held Iryna's hand and prayed for Braeden's safety and for theirs. "And Holy Mother, keep us safe, and all of the good people in the city. We have followed you faithfully and will serve you to death and beyond. Look down upon us, your children and bless us." The roaring overhead was loud, the air scorching. "Holy Father, keep us safe from the fire and the soldiers." Nothing now but the heat and roar of the flames. It was hard to breathe. "Ercos, give me strength," Janna gasped as the wall of flame passed on the street outside.

ARRYK

Arryk knew the dream was coming, but was unable to stop it. Try as he might to stay awake and conscious, the darkness advanced again, faster and heavier than in the last dream. This time there was no armored woman, but a whole horde of screaming riders, sabers raised and dripping blood.

And then he saw Larisa, like a golden beacon against the dark. Joy flooded him as she came toward him, wearing her battered armor, her wedding wreath on her head.

"Thank the gods," he gasped.

Her eyes turned sad and she stopped before reaching him. "Saying goodbye is hard," she said. "But I must. Know that I regret nothing. Everything happened as the gods ordained it." And then the horde was on her, sucking her into the blackness. The shrieking in his ears was unbearable, but ended suddenly, with a rush of blood across the floor.

It built up into a wave, lapping at the edge of his bed, then running across it. He could not move or escape. But this time, he woke up before the blood reached his mouth. He sprang up, and had his sword in hand before his feet touched the floor.

Arryk slashed at the black, still fading into the wall, waded through blood to reach it. He slipped against the wall and slashed at it until his sword got stuck. He heard voices, and someone picked him up by the arms, someone else grabbed his legs and carried him back to bed.

"The king is ill," a voice said, sounding far away.

"Not ill," Arryk muttered. "Bad dream."

"I'll say," another voice said. "You had a bad dream because of a fever. I'll send for the doctor."

"Don't need the doctor," Arryk said, but no one seemed to pay attention. A moment later the door closed, but now several lamps were burning. Arryk looked down at his feet, expecting to see them covered in blood, but they were bare and dry. He rubbed his eyes and his hand came away wet. At first he thought he'd see blood there, but it was only sweat that dripped from his face. He gritted his teeth and lurched to his feet again, reaching for his clothes.

The door opened again and a doctor entered. "Your Highness, you must go back to bed," he said, looking at Arryk with some alarm. "You have a fever."

"I do not," Arryk said. "Go away, and get Magnus Torsen."

"That's not wise," the doctor began.

"I don't care," Arryk shouted. "I'm ordering you to go away. Now do it."

The doctor opened his mouth, closed it again, and backed out the door. Sometimes it was good to be king. But it wouldn't help if he couldn't get to Larisa. He had to do it now, before it was too late. He was certain the gods were sending him these visions. Why would they do it if they didn't want him to act?

He stumbled into the corridor shouting for Magnus, who arrived a moment later, out of breath and still struggling into his clothes. "They say you're not well, Your Highness," he said.

"I'm fine," Arryk gasped. "But we must go now."

"Go where?" Magnus asked, alarmed.

"Kersenstadt."

"Your Highness, we've already discussed it. We can't go. Mattila will expect us to do exactly that."

"I don't care. We need to go to Kersenstadt first. We can handle Mattila if she comes."

"But you must wait for Hohenwart," Magnus insisted.

"Tell her to meet us at Kersenstadt. I won't tolerate any more delays."

"Your Highness, please." Magnus looked so frantic Arryk would have felt sorry for him if he had been able to overcome his own panic. "You're not well. Let's discuss it in the morning."

"The gods have spoken and we must act now." Arryk pushed a door open and lurched into a room that held a table and a few chairs. He fell into a chair and laid his head on the table.

In the distance, Magnus said, "I believe he's gone mad. I'm sure it's the fever. Would someone find that doctor?"

Arryk shook his head but didn't have the energy to protest. It didn't matter. Fever or not, they had to follow his orders even if they didn't understand. Even if he didn't understand. He wished the gods had chosen someone else.

He thought hard, even though it felt like the hammer of Ercos was pounding inside his head. He did his best to remember the prophecy from the Scrolls, since he was certain the dream had to be related to that. Perhaps the gods were guiding him to his proper role by sending him the dreams.

And if he was the ruler in the prophecy, he would win this battle, wouldn't he? He'd had Maryna read the passages from the Scrolls to him several times, but now he couldn't remember who won the battle at the end. Surely he would? Wasn't that the point? And at his wedding the priest had said Larisa was part of it, so he needed to get her first.

Arryk stumbled back into the corridor and spotted a cluster of officers in the distance. "Give the orders," he shouted, "We move out right now."

"Move out where?" someone asked.

"To Kersenstadt."

"But," someone else said.

"Shut up!" Arryk screamed. "I'm the king and I give the orders and we're going to Kersenstadt. Get my horse ready."

TEODORA

Teodora opened her eyes, then quickly closed them again. The light burned. Everything burned. She swallowed. Her throat was raw and dry so she asked for water, but no sound came out. Even though it hurt to breathe, she did it anyway. That she could breathe at all came as a tremendous relief once she remembered what had happened.

She scrambled to sit up, though she kept her eyes screwed shut. She was alive. Teodora forced herself to recall the wall of flame, the roar of the wind, the billowing black smoke. She'd expected to die, but somehow she hadn't.

She opened her eyes to a squint, and realized it was quite dark; a small lamp burned on a corner table. Slowly, she opened them all the way. She was inside her tent, on top of the covers of her bed, still wearing grimy, sweat-and-smoke-stained clothes. Strange, that no one else was about. She tried shouting again, but little more than a croak came out. She needed water.

Brytta burst into the tent. "Your Highness! You must not stand until we can help you."

Teodora wanted to bark at her that no one could tell her what to do, but again, no sound came out.

Brytta tutted, then poured water into a cup and handed it to Teodora. She drank it quickly and Brytta refilled it.

After she'd emptied the second cup she could speak. "What happened? How did I escape the city?"

"Your guards dragged you to safety after you'd fallen. You gave us a terrible shock, Your Highness. We were certain you were dead for the first few minutes."

Brytta did not look nearly as horrified at the idea as she ought.

Teodora scowled. "What about the city? Is it badly damaged?"

Brytta shifted to her other foot and chewed her lip. "I'm not sure. Shall I fetch General Barela? He will know more."

Teodora nodded, feeling weak with relief. She hadn't dared to think about whether he'd survived. One of the last things she remembered was letting go of his hand, then seeing nothing but fire.

She lowered herself back onto the bed, feeling winded and tired. Demario came quickly. He'd changed into clean clothes, but looked grim and haggard.

He pulled a chair up beside her bed. "Thank the gods you survived. After you let go, I couldn't see you; I'm so glad your guards stayed close."

Teodora wondered if she should be angry with him. It would have been far nicer if he'd been her rescuer. "Hmph," she said, fixing him with a hard stare. "I'm glad they did too."

"I noted their names," Demario said. "Though one of them is still unconscious. It seems she breathed a great deal of that terrible black smoke. I was sure you'd want to reward them."

It hadn't occurred to Teodora, but appearing gracious made a better impression. "Certainly," she said. "I'd like nothing better." She pushed herself into a sitting position. Demario did nothing to help, though it was true he looked half-dead himself. "Now tell me what happened in there."

"We're not sure. No one has been able to re-enter the city in the past few hours. The fire is dying down but it might be days before it cools off enough for us to go inside."

"The whole city burned?" She didn't understand; Kersenstadt was nearly as big as Atlona.

"All of it. It's possible a few areas were spared, but we won't know until we can go look."

"So it's completely destroyed." She let her head fall back against the cushions.

"That's what it looks like."

Teodora licked her dry lips. "What about my army? There must have been thousands inside when the fire started."

"Many did not survive. General Ensden and I are still counting and we're still seeing stragglers trickle in. It seems a number escaped from the other gates and are making their way back to camp. We'll know more by morning."

"Morning? But it was morning when the fires started."

"Yes." His voice was flat and his eyes held none of their usual sparkle. "You've been asleep all day, and night has fallen again."

Teodora's head pounded. "The city is ours then, but it's gone. Is this a victory or a defeat?"

Demario's eyes hardened. "Both, I suppose. Your enemies are dead, but so are many of your own troops. And nothing remains of one of the richest cities in Kronland."

Teodora sat up suddenly. Her head swam and black spots danced in front of her eyes, but she refused to faint. "This is all Mattila's fault," she said. "If she hadn't left the city so poorly fortified, it would never have fallen to Karsten." Then she remembered, and brightened. "At least Karsten is dead. Has anyone let King Arryk know?"

Demario's gaze was unreadable. "We were waiting for you."

"Then let's not waste any time." Teodora wanted to spring to her feet, but restrained herself. "Call Brytta and tell her to bring my writing things. I must send the king a message he'll remember the rest of his life."

BRAEDEN

Mattila had located Arryk Roussay's force and was prepared to engage him as soon as she could pin him down. Even though she had sent a detachment north to block Hohenwart, she still outnumbered Arryk and he had stumbled into a bad position after suddenly changing direction.

Braeden had just sent Trisa to the blacksmith with an armful of swords and knives that needed sharpening when Franca ran up to him. "Sir, there's news from Kersenstadt."

He opened his mouth to ask if it was good, but saw by the look on her face that it wasn't.

"I'm so sorry, sir. You're wanted at Mattila's headquarters, you and the prince. Kersenstadt has fallen to Teodora."

Knowing what Braeden did about sackings, the bile rose in his throat. His ears roared.

"Sir, you'd best sit," Franca said, sounding far away. She grabbed his elbow and guided him to a camp stool. Once she made sure he wasn't about to topple over, she pulled up another stool and sat across from him. "I don't know specifics so you might learn more from Mattila. But it seems the city was heavily damaged when Teodora took it. I didn't want you to hear it from anyone else."

"Thank you." The roaring in Braeden's ears grew louder and he wondered he could speak at all. He was glad he hadn't heard this while conferring with Mattila. He might have attacked the little Archduchess Elektra by way of revenge. He still might. Next, all he could think was that he would kill Teodora somehow.

"We haven't received any official word yet so we don't know details, and of course it's possible General Barela was able to help." Franca still sounded far away.

Braeden attempted to pay attention and respond, but no words came. Finally he managed, "I need to go to Kersenstadt now."

"You can't." Franca put a hand on his shoulder. "I'm sure the prince will let you go after the battle. A day or two won't matter. Maybe we'll get a message from Barela in the meantime. Come now." She stood and pulled him up by the arm. "Maybe General Mattila will have more news." She guided him all the way to the inn that Mattila was using as her headquarters. Braeden stumbled along as in a dream.

Novitny waited for him outside. "It's a bad business," he said. "You'll go as soon as the battle is over, and take as many troopers as you like."

Braeden nodded as Franca gave him a gentle push toward the door of the inn.

The mood inside was a mix of festive and nervous. Everyone was glad that Kersenstadt was back in imperial hands, but everyone also reckoned Mattila would be angry that Teodora had pulled it off. Braeden seated himself and concentrated on taking one breath after another. If the battle went well, he'd be on his way to Kersenstadt soon.

Mattila came in, the Archduchess Elektra right behind her. Braeden eyed the girl. Short and dumpy, she looked too pathetic to kill. Her eyes were red-rimmed. The general had likely been making her pay for her mother's sins. Braeden almost pitied her. He wondered if Teodora cared about her child the way he cared about his. He hoped so.

He stared at Elektra so intently she turned her gaze on him and frowned. He looked away with an effort, hoping he didn't appear too menacing. Since the girl never took a step without at least six imperial guards at her side, getting to her would be tricky. He'd have to work it out later.

Mattila was already talking and he tried to pay attention. She was in a real lather about Teodora but trying not to show it. "The empress has done us a great service." Her lips stretched into an unnatural smile. She almost never smiled, so any expression like one was bound to be false. "Kersenstadt is ours once again. Unfortunately I have no idea how much materiel can be recovered. It seems Quadrene fanatics blew up a few weapons depots, but I'm sure we'll find out more later. I've sent numerous messages to the empress requesting more details."

Braeden desperately tried to recall where the weapons and powder had been housed and couldn't remember any specific locations. As far as he knew, none were all that close to his house. With any luck, Janna and the children had stayed inside and were safe.

"The empress has done us another favor." Mattila went on. "She killed Duchess Karsten and has let King Arryk know. If he cared as much as everyone thought, he might not be feeling quite in fighting condition right now."

There were chuckles around the table. Braeden glared at some who did so and they quieted. He understood exactly how the king felt, being in the path of Teodora's destruction. The woman ruined everything she looked at.

"That's a shame," Prince Novitny said. "Having Duchess Karsten as a hostage might have persuaded the king to return to Norovaea without a fight."

"Yes, I thought of that as well." Mattila's voice was tight. "But we cannot bring the duchess back to life, so we'll take what advantage we can from the situation. I always expected an easy victory but now it should cost us very little."

ANTON

Now that King Arryk had changed his mind and marched on Kersenstadt, bad news followed on bad. First came word that Mattila had sent part of her force after Emilya Hohenwart and defeated her. She'd been caught on the march and annihilated. Scouts reported that Hohenwart had retreated into Floradias, though no one knew where.

Even worse, a messenger arrived with the news that Kersenstadt had fallen.

"How could that happen?" King Arryk had turned pale. "What of the garrison? Did Duchess Karsten send you?"

"No, I'm afraid not. The main gate was opened by treachery and my commanding officer sent me out the east gate before the city was taken. I heard fierce fighting, but there were too many imperial troops. I don't know who fell or who was captured."

King Arryk slumped into a camp chair. "Perhaps the duchess got away. If not, I'm sure Teodora will send a ransom demand soon enough. She must, don't you think, Count Orland?"

"Oh yes, I'm sure she will." The count sounded certain, but Anton knew he didn't know what the empress would do.

Anton was very sorry for the king. There was nothing worse than having someone you loved in danger when you weren't able to do anything about it.

The king got a determined look on his face. "Alert the pickets to allow through any messenger from the imperial armies," he said to one of his adjutants. "I hope someone comes soon," he muttered to himself.

An imperial courier arrived the next day, a white flag waving under the Inferrara standard. She was brought directly to the king. Anton wasn't there, but he heard that the king sent everyone else out. There was a commotion and the courier burst out of the tent with a drawn sword and a bloody lip, shouting,

"Your king is completely mad." Then she ran for her horse and departed the camp in a hurry. No one went after her.

Things became very strange. The king's guards allowed no one in his tent, even though scouts were arriving with news that Mattila was drawing near. Without the king to give orders, no one was in charge, so the count took the scout's dispatches. He stood outside the king's tent for a while, trying to get him to come out, but there was no response and he couldn't make the guards let him in.

"I'm sure he received news that Karsten is dead, or badly wounded." The count shook his head. "He must pull himself together."

Anton wondered how well the count would pull himself together if he'd heard that Princess Gwynneth had been killed. It was true the count was tougher than King Arryk, but he would likely drink himself into a stupor, if the past was anything to go by. Maybe that's what the king was doing right now.

The count went on."Mattila will be upon us by tomorrow noon at the latest and we must move into position. I'll speak with the other officers." He stopped and thought for a moment. "I'll need your help with the Bernotas children. I doubt their uncle is thinking about them and I will not allow them to fall into Mattila's hands. That would be the end of everything. You must arrange guards. Here." He pulled off his glove and removed the signet ring he always wore. "Show this to anyone who gives you trouble. Tell them you're authorized to arrange for the children's safety."

Anton slipped the ring on his thumb, pleased to be given such responsibility. He put on his best coat and most of his armor to appear bigger and more impressive. He had Skandar saddled up with his beautiful trappings. They were very like the ones King Arryk's battle mounts wore, so that might help impress the Norovaeans.

It was a few leagues' ride to the manor house where the children stayed. "Someone take this horse," Anton said, imitating the count's manner as he approached the guards. He jumped from Skandar's back, pulled off a glove and showed the officer in charge the count's signet ring. "Count Orland has sent me to arrange transport for the young duchesses and dukes."

"We haven't received orders from the king," the officer said, trying to look down his nose at Anton. It didn't work, since Anton was just as tall.

"The king is busy and has asked Count Orland to assist in battle preparations." Anton lifted his chin and squeezed the words through his nose, the way the nobles liked to do it. "He wishes to see the children safely out of reach of the enemy army, which draws near." He thought it best to say nothing about the king staying in his tent. That would be bad for morale. He held the ring under the officer's nose and huffed impatiently.

The officer nodded and another guard opened the front door. Anton didn't know what to do next, but walked into the main hall as if he did. "Please announce me to the Duchess Maryna," he said, keeping the tone he'd used outside with a liveried footman who also tried looking down his nose.

"The duchess is at her lessons," the footman said. "She is not to be disturbed."

"Disturb her. I'm here on an urgent mission from the king." Anton let his hand slide to his sword belt. The count always did that when anyone gave him trouble.

"Anton!" Maryna stood above him, looking down from a gallery. "What are you doing here?" She started down the stairs and Anton walked toward her.

The footman tried to intervene, but Maryna said. "It's all right. Master Kronek is a close personal friend of mine."

"No, he's my friend," Devyn shouted, clattering down the stairs behind his sister.

"I'm honored to be considered friend to both of you." Anton kept his formal tone.

Maryna laughed. "Why are you speaking so strangely? You sound very funny."

"I'm here because your uncle sent me," Anton said, remembering to talk like he usually did, now he was among friends. "The enemy is close and he wants all of you away from here as soon as possible."

"But I want to fight." Devyn looked dismayed. He wore a short dagger at his belt, but he was so small it looked like a sword on him.

"You might still have to." Anton kept his face straight. "You might run into the enemy at any time, and your guards overrun."

Maryna's eyes grew wide. "Does Uncle Arryk expect to lose the battle?" She dropped her voice, but her words still echoed through the cavernous hall.

"Not at all." Anton had no idea what her uncle expected, but it didn't do to be anxious. "He expects the battle to be hard-fought. It might range all over the area, so he wants you away from the worst of it. Duke Devyn will of course keep you safe should you run into the enemy."

Devyn nodded, setting his chubby face into a fierce scowl.

"Edric Maximus is here with us. He must come along," Maryna said. "We can't have any harm coming to him either. He's far more important than any of us."

Anton had never known such a serious child. It was as though she already felt responsible for everyone. "Of course he'll come along," Anton said.

After that, things went smoothly. Maryna fired off orders and Anton made sure they were carried out. Once the guards saw how serious both of them were, it didn't seem to matter they were children. Not that Anton was a child anymore, being nearly fourteen and almost as tall as the count. Still, it helped to have a duchess giving orders, even if she was very small.

Edric Maximus was helpful too, making sure all of the adults were packed and ready to go within a few hours. Little Stella's nurse was frightened and crying, but Edric made her sit down and pray with him, and after that she was all right. By late afternoon, the three smaller children were bundled into a carriage. Devyn had first thrown a tantrum because he wanted to ride with the guards, but Anton persuaded him that he and his sword were needed inside the carriage should the guards be overcome.

Maryna had mounted her mare, dressed in boy's clothes, a pair of pistols holstered in her saddle. The count had made her a present of his smallest set after Anton taught her how to shoot and reload. With all that, she still looked so small and girlish Anton wanted to laugh, but her face was so set and sober he didn't dare.

"Will you come with us?" she asked as Anton rode up next to her.

"I must return to the count, but I'll escort you to the main road." Everyone had agreed they should take the road north toward Aquianus. If Mattila's troops were still nearby after the battle they could make for Floradias and the nearest Zeelund garrison. They would be safe there until the king or their mother came to get them.

Maryna frowned. "I would much rather you came. I'm sure my uncle won't mind."

"I can't miss the battle. The count needs me." Anton was torn. He was excited about the coming battle, but worried for the children. Even though they were flanked by over two hundred guards, it wouldn't be enough if they ran into a large detachment of Mattila's troops. That they had Edric Maximus with them made the situation that much more dangerous.

"I suppose you're right." Maryna sighed heavily and gave Anton her hand in its fine leather glove. "I will pray to Ercos for your safety and that you defeat the enemy. I hope we will see each other again soon." She blinked tears out of her eyes.

Anton felt his own lip tremble and squeezed her hand, bowed his head, then rode off without saying another word.

BRAEDEN

"Can't say I've ever seen you look less happy about a battle." Prince Novitny looked concerned.

"I'm not happy. I doubt I'll be much good to you," Braeden said. "You don't suppose I can leave?" He didn't know why he bothered to ask, since he knew what the answer would be.

The prince sighed. "That's the one thing you can't do. I already asked the general and she says you're too valuable to spare on the morrow. Once the battle's won, though, you can go."

"With any luck, it will go quickly."

"It ought to." Novitny clapped him on the shoulder. "Now get a bite to eat and some rest."

There was no point in Braeden telling him that neither one was possible. The thought of food made him sick and the pounding in his chest ensured he wouldn't sleep. He'd never gone into battle in such a state. He almost wished he would die, but couldn't, since he had to find out what happened to Janna and the children.

Braeden didn't want to imagine the worst, and it might be the worst hadn't happened. Surely many people had survived. With any luck, the imperial troops noticed she had money and were keeping her safe until he arrived to pay them off. He didn't care if they asked for everything he had. Plenty of wealthy people were held for ransom after sackings; it was customary. That cheered him a bit, though not enough that he could eat or sleep.

Long after most had gone to sleep, Braeden sat by a fire and kept it burning. After a time, Trisa joined him. She would serve as his page on the morrow and he could tell she was nervous. "It's not your first time fighting," he said. "You know what to do."

Trisa frowned and chewed on the end of her braid while staring into the fire. "It's just different when it's a really big battle. I've never stood against an army of that size before. Or those big guns." She shuddered.

"You needn't worry about the guns. Even if we're in range, we won't be for long. Where we'll be sitting, on the left flank, there won't be any friendly infantry in our way. We can go forward as fast as we like."

"Will we be facing Orland's cuirassiers?"

"Most likely. He's done well with them. It should be a good fight, though they're outnumbered."

"I hope we get him this time." Trisa poked the fire with a stick and sparks shot into the dark sky. "I'm still sorry that I stopped you right before you had him."

"Don't be. Even if I'd gotten him, the bridge would've blown up with me on it. Or I'd have chased him across and been on the wrong side when it went. Either way, I wouldn't be here now." Braeden attempted a grin and almost managed it.

When her eyes drooped, Braeden sent Trisa to the tent. She'd taken over Janna's corner, though she was considerably noisier and messier. Braeden didn't mind. It was better than having no one but Gergo. Once he had the girls again, he'd never make the mistake of leaving them somewhere. The tent might be crowded, but at least they'd be here.

He woke up in front of the cold fire, the sky turning gray as the camp came to life. Franca clanked by, pulling on armor as she went. "The Norovaeans are already in the field, sir, Orland's lot grouping up on their right. Better get to it."

For an instant, the usual excitement before a battle rose inside him, the feeling that anything could happen, the heightening of the senses, knowing there was a chance of never seeing, hearing or smelling all that was familiar again. But as soon as he stood still, as soon as Gergo and Trisa started strapping on his armor and he had a moment to think, it all came back. His limbs were already so heavy he wondered if armor was a good idea.

"Are you all right Sir?" Trisa asked. Her eyes were wide and her face pale.

"I'm fine. You?" He winked at her and she managed a small smile.

"I think I'm scared."

"You should be. It's only natural. You'll be fine once the action gets started." He knew that was always true. At least it always had been true in the past and he hoped it would be today.

By the time they were mounted and reached the field, the sun had risen. Braeden saw Orland's purple banners dead ahead, but there was no sign of the count himself. Braeden left Reno in charge and cantered to the center where Mattila and her staff stood on a small rise overlooking the valley and her front lines.

"Seen Orland?" she asked the moment she spotted Braeden.

"No, though it looks like his force is in place." He nodded at the archduchess, mounted on a stallion that was too big for her, though the bright gold armor suited her well enough. To her credit, Elektra looked nervous, but not frightened. Braeden felt a small pang, realizing she must be about Trisa's age, and decided he'd be no better than Teodora if he harmed a little girl.

"Odd." Mattila frowned. "There's no sign of King Arryk, either. Best we can tell, there's a colonel in charge and he's already mucked things up."

"Oh?" Braeden took the glass Mattila handed him and focused on the center. Several small streams criss-crossed the narrow valley floor and a village stood at the base of a hill. The streams were no obstacle, but the village offered the enemy some cover. Pike bristled between the houses and there were likely muskets at every window.

"See his problem?" Mattila asked.

Braeden chuckled and handed back the glass. "We can't get in there, but he can't get out."

"Exactly. I want you to move on it from the left as soon as you can. If Orland gets around you, let him. He'll run into my reserves and give them something to do. I want you on that side of the village and stop any of Arryk's reserves from getting through. It shouldn't take much."

"I agree. Think they'll fight without the king?"

Mattila shrugged. "Not well. Why would they? It seems Teodora was right for once and she's managed to stop him."

"Poor devil." Braeden was probably more sympathetic than he should have been. "She likely sent him a message telling him how she killed his girl and that knocked the stuffing right out of him." Perhaps everyone would be better off if they called a truce while Braeden and the king drowned their sorrows in a jug of wine.

"Surely that wouldn't keep him from fighting?" Mattila shook her head. "If it were me, I would be eager for revenge. I might not be Teodora, but I'm here." She grinned, an unsettling, wolfish smile ill-suited to her otherwise grim features.

"Might be he's in shock." Or maybe his limbs felt heavy like Braeden's did and putting on armor was too much altogether. He'd heard the king was on the slender side.

"There he is," the archduchess said, as a cheer went up from the Norovaean troops.

"Orland too," said an officer who'd been watching through a glass the whole time. "Though he's continuing on to the right flank."

"Time for me to go then. Best watch yourself, General," Braeden said. "The king might come for you after all."

"Oh, I hope so."

ARRYK

It was dark and quiet inside the tent and Arryk lay on his cot, burrowing into the blankets and staring at the wall. He craved oblivion. From time to time, he heard noises outside his tent, voices raised in anger or fear, but they always went away again. Most sounded familiar, but he couldn't identify them and he didn't care. It was over. There was no point in fighting anymore. He'd done what he came to do, and freed Gwynneth, but he should have gone home right after. Then Larisa would still be alive and none of this would have happened.

He took comfort in knowing that if the coming battle was the last one, it would soon be over. Even if he was the ruler prophesied, he had to do nothing but stay right here for the end to come all the more quickly. He tried mustering up sympathy for the many who would die, but it was better for them this way, even if they didn't realize it yet. The numbness he felt was better than the pain and horror that had nearly overwhelmed him earlier. Still, he reckoned death would be even better.

Suddenly there was shouting outside and then light flooded the tent. It was Count Orland, his page close on his heels.

"Help him with his armor," Orland said to the boy, who started sorting through a pile on the floor.

"I'm not fighting," Arryk said.

"You are." Orland drew his sword.

"You can't threaten me."

"I'm not threatening you. I'm making you do your duty."

"There's no point." Arryk lifted his head. "She's dead. The empress killed her."

"I'm very sorry," Orland said, though he didn't sound sorry. "But do you think she would want you to sit here while your troops fight and die? Do you think it's what she would do if she were in your place?"

That hurt.

Arryk sat up, even though his limbs were so very heavy. "You're right. She would never falter." He pictured Larisa here now, laughing about something as she strapped on her armor. He stood. "But she was always so much stronger than me. I can't do it without her." He sat down again.

Orland hauled him back up by his collar, and Arryk was too tired to protest. "You're stronger than you know. You might not have her, but thousands of men and women out there followed you all this way and they will die if you don't lead them."

Arryk didn't know what to say to that, so he nodded, then let Orland and the boy get his armor on him. His eyes wouldn't focus and he felt listless. Someone brought bread and wine and Orland nearly forced it down his throat. Arryk was sure he'd be sick, but it all stayed down.

The two of them shoved him out of the tent and onto his horse. His vanguard was waiting for him and a cheer went up when he appeared. He lifted his hand and attempted a smile. Maybe Orland was right and he shouldn't let down his brave troops. He saw Larisa's bright eyes regarding him. "Stop being such an idiot," she would have said.

He took a deep breath. He would do this for her. Teodora would love to think she had broken him, but he wouldn't let her.

The sky grew light in the east and there were the first reports of the big guns. The gods were with him and he would find a way to win.

BRAEDEN

He'd given his troops Mattila's instructions and passed the word to Prince Novitny. Now Braeden waited for the battle to start. A puff of smoke appeared in a line from the top of a small hill opposite them and an instant later cannonballs shrieked overhead. Trisa started, but stayed put. It helped that her experienced horse didn't mind the noise.

"They've gone right over our heads, like I said they would." Braeden kept an encouraging tone.

"Who's behind us?"

"Infantry reserve, most like. Poor devils."

"Can they get away?" Trisa looked pale.

"No. They have to stand there until they're called up, or the barrage ends."

"Stand there and die?"

Braeden nodded.

"That's why we're not infantry," Franca said.

"Thank the gods." Trisa shook her head, her color returning.

"Enough chit-chat," Braeden said. "Orland's finally up there. Remember, he's mine."

Mattila's center moved forward and another cheer rose from the Norovaean side. Perhaps King Arryk was making a counter-move. Knowing Mattila, she'd go slow and draw him in, then strike hard.

She outnumbered Arryk in any case. It didn't help he'd jammed up all of his reserves behind the village. It was Braeden's job to make sure they didn't get out.

From what he could tell, Mattila's right flank had already engaged. Smoke drifted over the field as the great guns kept firing at ragged intervals now, but steadier than Braeden would have liked.

Braeden gave the signal and the hussars advanced. Out of the corner of his eye, he saw Trisa keep pace with him. They walked the horses until they got closer to the enemy line. No point in using lances, since the cuirassiers would have none of their own. Their armor would be thick, so it was best to get in close. After spending their pistols, it would be saber and axe. Braeden recognized the thrill of anticipation and worries about his family moved to the back of his mind.

These moments just before engaging were the most tense. Kazmir splashed across a creek, nearly dry from the summer heat, and Braeden spotted Arian Orland ahead, the purple plume waving from his black helmet. He raised his pistol, but knew he was still out of range. It was hard to wait. But even worse to fire too soon and miss, then have your pistols spent while the other fellow still had his.

Braeden pushed his visor down. Orland stared straight at him before clapping his down as well. With such heavy armor, Braeden would have to get very close to deliver a killing shot. He'd get only one chance, and then he'd have to continue on to complete his mission. He urged Kazmir into a canter and hoped Trisa kept pace, since he'd lost his peripheral vision.

Orland had a pistol raised. A page rode at his side, so he was sure to have more loaded. Braeden kept his eye on the count and raised his pistol, aimed. He fired at the purple falcon on the middle of Orland's chest and felt a great blow on his at the same instant, knocking the wind out of him. Braeden doubled over, gasping for air and when he looked up, saw that Orland had halted as well. Braeden wondered if he'd scored his own hit. Orland seemed to recover and lifted another pistol while Braeden fumbled for his. He didn't know what had happened to it.

Kazmir kept up a smooth canter, and a pistol materialized in Braeden's left hand. Trisa was right there. But when Braeden took aim, Orland had disappeared. Cuirassiers thundered past at an angle, engaging Novitny on the far left.

He heard a far-away voice and pushed up his visor. He felt sick and needed to breathe.

"Are you all right, sir?' Trisa shouted in his ear. The gunfire was deafening. "Did he hit you?"

"He did." Braeden looked down and noticed a large dent in the middle of his cuirass. "If he'd been three feet closer I'd be dead."

"So would he," Franca said, coming up on his right. "Looks like they're moving on. Shall we make for the village?"

It was nearly impossible to see since the little valley had filled with smoke. The guns were still blasting, but most likely, Mattila's reserves were now out of range as they took on Orland. The hussars knew to keep an eye on their rear just in case the pike didn't do their jobs.

Braeden had to slow down. The ground was soft and some infantry had already fought here. Braeden wondered how long it had taken him to get here.

Plenty of dead and wounded, horse and human were scattered about, some still dangerous. "Shoot anyone who moves, wounded or not," he told Trisa. They held pistols in both hands now.

Finally, he could see the village's rooftops outlined in the smoke. "Hold up," he said. There was no reason to get within musket shot. They only had to stop the reserves behind from coming forward.

On his right, there was pandemonium. He caught glimpses of Mattila's standards, and none of Arryk's. Had it turned into a rout already? If so, those in the village didn't know. Some tried to break out, but by now the hussars were there in force and it wasn't an even contest.

A rising wind blew the smoke around and from time to time Braeden spotted the pike formations behind the village. Then he looked once again and they were gone. All that remained now were those in the village, and they would run out of shot and powder soon enough at the rate they'd been firing.

Braeden waited for orders to start the cleanup.

GWYNNETH

Gwynneth left Sanova over land, accompanied by a hundred Sanovan guards headed by Count Tarka. "We can't have you captured, now you've gone to all this trouble," Queen Ottilya said. Gwynneth felt as though they had nearly become friends. Ottilya also replenished her supply of coin, depleted after many visits to couturiers and paid out in bribes for her new friends.

Gwynneth regretted no longer being able to travel on the *Rusa* incognito, but she needed to get her children and worried going by ship would take too long. She insisted on traveling on horseback and covering at least thirty leagues a day. The weather was bad, the roads muddy, but they managed it most of the time.

She approached the Terragand border with her heart in her mouth, worried she would see devastation everywhere. To her surprise, things were calm. There'd been fighting in the south, but all was quiet further north. "We'll go to Birkenfels," Gwynneth told Count Tarka. "It's out of our way, but I might find messages from my brother there."

She had hoped Arryk would keep her informed while she traveled, but he'd never been a good correspondent. Besides, it would be nice to see the castle again. Her heart ached when she thought of Birkenhof's blackened ruins, but she understood why Kendryk had done it. She told herself they would rebuild a nicer palace when all of this was over and they were together again. She had to believe they would be or she couldn't go on.

It was a dark, gloomy day when they approached Birkenfels, and the towers didn't emerge from the mist until they reached the ruined village. It had never been rebuilt. Gwynneth hoped its inhabitants had been able to start over in Runewald.

As they neared the drawbridge a small armed party clattered across to approach them. Gwynneth rode ahead and was happy to see Merton's friendly face. He was pleased, and astonished. "Your Grace! Is all well? We had thought you with King Arryk."

"Well enough, considering." She fell in beside him as they crossed the bridge and explained what she'd been doing. "Is Count Faris here?" she asked.

"Just returned a few days ago," Merton said frowning. "I'm afraid there's bad news from your brother."

"Oh gods." Gwynneth felt herself turn pale. "Is he all right? Did Mattila kill him?"

Count Faris hurried to meet her as she entered the courtyard. "It's why I'm here," he said, his face grim. He had aged a great deal since Gwynneth last saw him. His hair and beard were white, he walked with a terrible limp and needed a cane. He was accompanied by Trystan Martinek, a sharp-faced youth with dark red hair falling to his shoulders and unsettling green-gold eyes.

"Tell me," she said, taking a seat across from his desk, the same one Edric had occupied years before. She did her best to ignore Martinek's strange stare.

"I have little information," Faris said. "But I do know Mattila defeated Arryk in battle, although it seems he survived."

"Thank the gods," Gwynneth said, unable to keep her voice from trembling. But she couldn't worry about her brother just now. "I'm afraid to ask. What about my children? Did my brother send them to safety before the battle?"

"I'm not sure." Faris looked sympathetic. "I have no news of them, though I'm sure we would have heard something had Mattila captured them. So as far as we know, they are safe, though I don't know where."

It wasn't the worst news, but it wasn't good. "I have to find them. I must take them to Galladium with me."

"Of course." Faris looked sympathetic. "We will help you in any way we can."

"I'm afraid I don't quite understand why you're here. Didn't Arryk send for you before the battle?"

Faris sighed. "I was in Lantura, trying to get Daciana Tomescu away from Seward Kurant's army. Tomescu's numbers are increased to several thousand irregulars. We're not sure where they came from, but it's said Teodora has been paying unemployed soldiers to join Tomescu's ranks."

"Why not hire them for her own army?"

"Oh, these are the dregs. Mercenaries who can't keep a job because they drink too much, or are too stupid or stubborn to follow orders. They'll work for cheap and are well-suited to Tomescu's methods. They're easy enough to defeat out in the open, but it's hard to get them to fight there. We had some luck when we could take them by surprise, but Tomescu is too smart to let that happen more than a time or two. In any event, she fell upon Kurant before he reached your brother, killed him and scattered his army."

"Oh dear," Gwynneth said, though she didn't give a fig for Kurant. Anxiety for her brother and her children threatened to overwhelm her, and she gripped the arms of her chair until her hands ached. She couldn't fall apart right now, not in front of these two, Kendryk's last remaining allies.

"After that, I prepared to join your brother. Duke Trystan has rounded up the remnants of Kurant's force and plans to regroup from here. But by the time I reached the border with Lantura, I received word that Mattila had engaged your brother and defeated him."

Gwynneth couldn't speak for a moment. "But surely," she said. "Surely Arryk has some troops left. He can regroup."

Faris shook his head. "It was a complete rout, and your brother is making for the Ummarvik ports, hopefully before Mattila catches him and finishes him altogether."

"What about Hohenwart and Orland? Can't they help fend her off?"

"Orland is gone, probably to Tirovor, and Hohenwart was picked off before the big battle and is licking her wounds in Floradias."

Gwynneth silently cursed Orland for the treacherous dog he was, for all the good it did. But she reminded herself that all was not lost and told Faris and Martinek what she had been doing.

Duke Trystan brightened. "That's excellent news," he said. "I have great faith in Lennart Ostberg's capabilities. We must hope he can mobilize before Mattila overruns everything."

"He thought it might take more than a year."

"That might be too late," Faris said grimly. "But in the meantime, let's try to find the children. We can assume they are with your brother, unless you left instructions for him to send them elsewhere."

"I didn't," she said miserably. "Though I should have. I didn't expect to be gone so long. I should have left Maryna in Galladium and sent the little ones after her." In fact, it would have been wiser altogether to have sent them to the safety of Norovaea when the war first started, but Gwynneth had been certain that would look like admitting defeat. And there was no question the children had been helpful in raising the soldiers' morale. She resolved to stop blaming herself until she found out what had happened to them.

"You couldn't have known how it would turn out," Faris said. "Things looked much rosier when you first left."

"Yes, they did. I must go right now if I'm to catch Arryk before he reaches the ports. If he can't find enough ships there Mattila will catch him and that will be the end of it."

"Stay tonight and rest, Your Grace. You can leave at first light. I will send a few scouts out at once to ride ahead and find your brother. In the morning, you can leave."

"I must send my escort back to Sanova." She had promised the queen she would return them as soon as she gained her own troops in Terragand. "Can you spare a few guards? I want to travel fast and light."

"I understand, but the way is dangerous, so I insist you take at least three hundred. I can spare that and more since we had few casualties in the south."

"Thank you." It was lovely to deal with Faris again, so competent and efficient after Arryk's endless dithering. "Might I take Merton along? We've always worked well together."

"Certainly. I'm sure he'll want to."

Gwynneth took a deep breath and told herself all would be well. Just to make sure, she spent the hour before bedtime praying to the Mother to keep her children safe until she could find them.

BRAEDEN

"I can't ask you to come along, any of you." Braeden's throat was still raw from the smoke of the battlefield. "I don't know how long I'll be there or what I might find."

"Novitny said any of us who want can go with you," Reno said. He, Senta and Franca stood with Braeden while servants took down his tent and packed a small bag for him. He would travel light and sleep in the saddle. Trisa was getting Kazmir saddled. "Of course we're coming."

"I'll follow as soon as the wagon is packed," Senta said. "I can be there a few days behind you with your things, so everything is ready when you find them. I'm sure you will need me to help." Senta refused to accept anything except that Janna and the children were fine and waiting for Braeden, though they might be a bit hungry. He loved her for that optimism. It gave him hope.

Novitny had taken most of the hussars to chase Orland south. After engaging the Sanovans, Orland's cavalry tussled briefly with Mattila's infantry, but turned tail and ran as soon as the extent of Arryk's defeat became clear. Braeden didn't blame him. No point in sacrificing his force in a hopeless cause. Mattila had gone after Arryk, who'd taken the remnants of his army north, headed for the Ummarvik sea ports.

But now Braeden couldn't think of anything but Kersenstadt. The small party rode fast and reached the outskirts after nightfall the next evening. It was dark and impossible to see the city. Braeden smelled smoke, but it seemed stale. Perhaps people were conserving fuel and not lighting lamps after dark. Braeden needed to get light and someone to help him find his way, but had no idea where to begin. All he knew was that he would kill Teodora if he ran into her. As it turned out, she had returned to Atlona with Count Ensden, so Reno led them to Demario Barela's encampment instead, asking for the general's headquarters.

The camp was in appalling shape, with drunken soldiers everywhere and no sign of military discipline. The stench was unthinkable. Any troops still sober wandered aimlessly, looking sad or surly. Strange for a victorious army.

They asked an officer on duty to notify Barela and he came out of his tent at once. Braeden was shocked at how much he had changed. His normally merry dark eyes were flat, his face thin and haggard and covered by a scraggly beard.

"Please, come in," he said to Braeden. He snapped his fingers for an adjutant and said, "Take the others to the colonel's tent and get them something to eat and drink." He looked at Reno and the girls. "I don't wish to be rude, but I must speak with Commander Terris alone. You will join us later."

Braeden knew this couldn't be good and laid a hand on Trisa's shoulder when she made a small noise of distress. Reno took her away and then Braeden and the general were alone.

"What happened here? You've taken the city, haven't you?"

Barela shook his head and waved Braeden to a chair, then seated himself. "We did. But someone blew the munitions depots."

"I heard about that."

Barela looked at Braeden, then reached for a bottle of something, poured two glasses and pushed one at Braeden.

"I don't want it." Braeden shoved it away, sloshing golden liquid onto the table.

"You need it." The general knocked back his glass, poured himself another and topped off Braeden's. "Trust me. You need it."

Braeden sighed, then drank it down. He didn't want to argue; he needed to find out what had happened. He expected the drink to burn, but it was deliciously smooth. He'd never tasted anything like it.

A pleasant warmth spread through Braeden's chest, loosening up some of the tightness he'd felt around his heart for the past several days. It became a little easier to breathe.

Barela poured more, and waited for Braeden to drink that too before speaking. "It got worse. The fire spread, or others were set. We still don't know and we never might. The city is destroyed, all of it." Barela clenched his teeth. "There is no building left undamaged and most are destroyed altogether. I am very sorry."

"What happened to all of the people?" Braeden had to keep his teeth from chattering. If he hadn't been sitting, his knees would have buckled.

"Dead." Barela poured himself another drink, and another for Braeden. "Drink. Please. It's the only way I can bring myself to tell you this."

Braeden obeyed. He wondered if the drink was causing the numbness, or something else.

Barela drank again, then took a deep breath. "I sent a party of soldiers to look for your house and secure it, but they never returned. I even went myself once I could get away from Teodora but was driven back by the fire. Afterward, we found a few survivors, but very few. I have interviewed each of them, but haven't found your wife. Those who made it were dragged out by my troops who intended to ransom them. They just happened to escape before the flames spread."

"I'd hoped maybe ..." Braeden's tongue felt too large. "I'd hoped someone would see the size of the house and try to ransom her."

"They might have. But if they did, they did not get out of the city in time."

"Surely there are people alive inside. Have you checked the cellars?" Braeden tried to stand, but failed and had to sit again.

"We've started to. Most didn't make it that far. The various fires created a great storm and the flames moved too fast, creating a great wind. The empress herself narrowly escaped being engulfed and was saved only because one of her guards dragged her to safety."

"Damn," Braeden muttered.

"Yes," Barela said, his tone flat.

Braeden looked up, surprised. "I thought you and she ..."

"Yes, we'd been friendly." Barela's jaw worked. "Let's say I feel less friendly at this point, though she doesn't understand why. But let's not talk about her right now. It will make both of us angrier."

"I'll drink to that." Braeden held out his glass. "I know drinking is a bad idea, and I ought to make a plan instead, but I can't think right now."

Barela poured the last of the drink. "It's understandable. You need to wait until it's light anyway. Just sit right there and I will send for your friends. Together we will come up with something." He stepped outside the tent and spoke to someone, then came back.

They sat silently for a few minutes until Reno, Franca and Trisa filed in. Judging by the looks on their faces, they knew about the city as well. No one spoke, or would look Braeden in the eye. Trisa sniffled quietly, though she tried to hide it.

Finally, Barela cleared his throat and reached for a rolled-up paper at the edge of the table. He unrolled it, setting the empty glasses on the corners. "This is a map of the city," he said. "But before we go any further, know that you are causing yourself unnecessary pain by doing this. I do not advise anyone to go in there and see what's happened unless they're required to."

"I have to," Braeden said. "I have to be sure. And if there's even a small chance, I have to find them before someone else does, or before they starve to death, or ..." He didn't want to consider any other possibilities. These were more than enough.

"I think Trisa shouldn't go," Franca said. In all the years Braeden had known her, he had never heard her voice shake.

Trisa tried to speak, but a sob caught in her throat.

"She'll go." Reno's voice was rough. "If she's old enough to go to war, she's old enough to see this."

Trisa nodded tearfully.

Braeden wasn't going to argue though he didn't want her to come either. He didn't want any of them.

He looked at the map. "I should be able to find the house easily enough without it."

Barela sighed. "You don't understand. There are nothing but ruins and one looks much like the other. Many streets are gone and those that still exist are paths cleared through rubble. You will not recognize the neighborhood. You must show me what it was close to and we can go from there. You will need all of us and I will bring more to help."

"I don't want help."

"Then you will never find them. Please let us do this for you."

Braeden was too tired to fight, so he nodded and tried to concentrate on the map. His head swam from the liquor, or perhaps from fatigue. He hadn't slept in nearly a week. He finally focused on the river. "About five streets in that direction, right behind this square." He pointed at the map.

"Good. We can narrow it down. We might not be able to get to every house since some have collapsed completely.

"It was solid stone. Surely the walls still stand?"

"They might. Not all of the stone fell. We will do our best. Now go to sleep, and we'll start at first light."

GWYNNETH

Gwynneth and her escort headed straight west, through the mountains. Until they reached them, everyone reckoned there was little chance of meeting Mattila accidentally. Still, they remained cautious and sent outriders in all directions before proceeding. Gwynneth felt exhausted from so much travel, but now they were in real danger, her nerves were on edge. She still wondered if she'd made the right decision. With favorable winds, Captain Brun might already have reached Zeelund.

Something occurred to her. "Why wouldn't Arryk go to Zeelund?" she asked Merton.

"They might not let him in."

"Aren't they friendly?"

"Yes, but they're not allies and I doubt they want to tangle with Mattila. Still, it's a possibility. If there's no sign of the king by the time we get halfway across Ummarvik, we can assume he's at least trying Zeelund."

"I hope he does." She preferred her children in Bonnenruck than some fishing village on the Ummarvik coast. She hoped the Zeelund authorities wouldn't allow them to fall into Mattila's hands once they were safe inside its borders.

As they moved west, the weather improved, and a series of sunny autumn days did much to dry the muddy roads. The mountain pass was quiet, though they traversed that only after all scouts returned safely.

"Bandits are everywhere," Merton said. "Even in Terragand, outside the towns no one can travel without a large escort. I do wish you'd taken ship, Your Grace."

"I probably should have, but it's too late for that now."

Now they were beyond Terragand's borders, they had to be especially cautious. They were as likely to meet Mattila as they were Arryk. Once they emerged into the flatter lands of Ummarvik, they looked for signs of a passing army but saw none. "We'll go straight for the Zeelund marches," Gwynneth said. "If the king is going north we'll cross his path sooner or later."

Now they hurried, staying too close behind the scouts. If they happened upon Mattila, they would need luck to avoid her. But then, Gwynneth had almost always been lucky. And if there'd been setbacks, she felt her luck had turned for the better again in the past months, though the same couldn't be said for her brother.

They were nearly on the border with Zeelund when they saw signs of a passing army. Merton questioned a local farmer.

"They was Norovaeans," he said, pausing from digging potatoes. "And in a right state too. Took all the food we'd already harvested, the devils. I couldn't understand much of their chatter, but if they came through here, they're headed for Zeelund, mark my words."

"Thank you," Gwynneth said, giving him a handful of coins. "You and your family should leave here. The army of Brynhild Mattila will be near."

The farmer looked dubious, but took the coin gladly enough. She doubted he would leave in the middle of harvest, though that was hardly her concern. At least she'd warned him.

"Let's hurry," she said to Merton. "If there's trouble at the Zeelund border, maybe I can help."

She had been right to worry. They came upon Arryk and a few thousand troops at a Zeelund border fortress, camped in front, not allowed to pass. Gwynneth found Magnus Torsen trying to set up a perimeter with a few shoddy-looking troops. "Where is the king?" she asked, wondering that he wasn't supervising preparations to dig in. If Mattila came upon them here they would all die. They had to get into Zeelund.

BRAEDEN

They rode all the way to eastern gate hoping to find the shortest route to Braeden's house. Even on the outside, the stone walls of the city were blackened.

"We thought the flames would rush right over the top, cross the ground and consume us all." Barela looked at the remnants of the charred gate. "Fortunately there was no fuel outside. Great chunks of burning wood fell onto the ground but didn't catch." He fell silent as they went inside.

In thirty years of warfare, Braeden had seen nothing like it. So many cities sacked, so many houses destroyed, their inhabitants killed. But none came close to this. While a few buildings still stood, their walls were nothing more than charred stone with the insides gutted, the roofs collapsed. It looked like something out of a nightmare, everything black and dead, and it got worse as they traveled further down the street and saw charred bodies. Kazmir sniffed at one, then stopped and refused to move forward.

Barela dismounted. "We can leave the horses here. They don't like the smell." Several grooms had followed them and they took the reins after everyone else dismounted.

Braeden finally dared to glance at Trisa. "It's all right if you need to be sick," he said. "There's no shame in it." He saw that Franca and Reno weren't feeling their best either, but they'd rather die than show it. Trisa gritted her teeth and shook her head.

Braeden was glad now that Barela had insisted on coming. He kept the party moving so they didn't linger over all of the dead bodies. They worked their way down to the river, clogged with debris and still water, as though it was dead too. Using the map, they looked for Braeden's street. Or a street that seemed like it. With so much rubble it was impossible to tell where houses ended and streets began. They finally found the square Braeden knew and that helped narrow it down. Still, they might have to search dozens of houses. Or rather, piles of rubble.

"This could take weeks," Reno said, looking at all of it.

"Perhaps." Barela shrugged. "Though it doesn't matter since I'm in no hurry to rejoin the empress in Atlona." His tone was bitter.

Braeden clenched his teeth. "I'll do it. I won't ask anyone ..."

"Stop it," Franca said sharply. "We're helping and that's final. You know there's no point in arguing with us."

It was difficult, dirty work. Braeden started with the first likely-looking house, but it wasn't the right one. Though narrow and made of stone, it was so blackened it was impossible to tell what shade the stone had been or any other distinguishing feature. He became certain it was the wrong one when he worked his way far enough in to see there had been some sort of shop on the ground floor. That meant he wasn't even on the right street.

So he wandered over to where Barela was directing a crew of soldiers. The day was warm and most had shed their shirts. Covered in soot from head to toe, they looked like demons.

"They've reached the front room." Barela wiped sweat from his nose, leaving a black streak across his face. Braeden imagined he looked even worse himself, digging in the rubble as he had been. "Do you want to go see?"

Braeden walked through the path they had cleared and stepped between what remained of two walls. He shook his head. "No, the stairs are in the wrong place."

Barela waved everyone over and they took a rest while Braeden figured out where to search next. He checked on Reno and the girls who were working on one of the first houses he'd chosen. "We have to try another street," he said. "This isn't the right one."

Franca looked at him, then back at Reno, who shrugged.

"What?" Braeden asked.

No one seemed to want to speak. Finally Reno said, "We got to the cellar on this one."

Another long silence.

"And?"

"They tried hiding in there," Franca said. "A family of six and two servants. They didn't make it."

"I don't understand. Surely the fire didn't reach the cellar?"

"It didn't need to," Reno said.

"We've seen this before." Barela had come up next to Braeden. "Hundreds so far, untouched by fire but dead all the same. The flames took all the air, and eve ryone suffocated. That's why you needn't do this. Even if they were lucky enough to reach the cellar, there's no chance ..."

It took a few more seconds for the meaning of his words to sink in. Braeden sat down heavily on a large stone fallen from a wall. "So no one in the cellars survived?"

"None that we've found." Barela's tone was sympathetic. "I should have told you last night, but it was bad enough."

"No, you're right. I needed to see this." Braeden thought he understood how it felt, not being able to breathe. He got up and stumbled over to where a heavy wooden cellar door stood open. He looked down. The sun was already high in the sky and he could see in quite well. A whole family lay on the floor, as if asleep.

"They're dead," Trisa said, answering his unspoken question. "They look like they're asleep, but I shouted at them and even went down there. It stayed cool, and it's only been a few days."

In other words, the bodies hadn't started rotting too badly. He backed away, stumbled, and Reno caught his arm, guiding him back to where he could sit. Everyone stood around quietly.

Braeden couldn't think. He wouldn't accept there was no hope at all. And even if there wasn't, he needed to be sure.

"Reno and Trisa already know about this." He was surprised at how rough and strange his own voice sounded. "But Janna had two children before we found her. The little girl died when Daciana Tomescu set their farmhouse on fire. Janna never found her body because the house collapsed. She always worried that maybe the little one survived somehow, but died afterward because Janna didn't find her. I always told her it was ridiculous of course." His voice shook and he stopped. When he continued, he had to pronounce his words deliberately. "So you see why I have to be sure."

"I always knew Tomescu was the devil," Barela muttered, then said more loudly, "Of course we understand. That's why we're here. So we keep looking."

After consulting the map again, Braeden picked another likely house. This time everyone worked on it so they could learn more quickly if it was the right one. It wasn't. Braeden had never realized how similar all of the streets were and how many houses the city had. They worked until it was dark, stopping only to eat a quick bite from the supplies that some other soldiers brought them. Barela had thought of everything.

"We come back in the morning," Barela said as they rode back to camp.

"It might take weeks at this rate," Braeden said.

438

"It doesn't matter. I'm happy to stay here for some time. We keep looking until we find them, or until we've looked in every possible place they might be."

"I appreciate that you're doing this, but I don't understand why. I can't ever repay you for helping me like this."

"You're my friend so naturally I want to help. You'd do the same for me."

"But you'll never be in this position. Now I realize how smart you were to never marry."

"Stop that." Barela's tone was sharp. "As awful as this is, you cannot forget the years of happiness you had."

"I want to forget them now and kill Teodora for this. Most likely I'll die trying."

"I don't blame you." Barela's tone was crisp and businesslike. "But let's find them first. Later we can talk about giving Teodora what she deserves."

ARRYK

"Hello Gwynn," Arryk said. "You're a bit late." He sat on the floor of his tent, since no one had bothered to unpack or set up furniture, waiting for Mattila to come finish him off. He wished she would hurry.

"I know, I'm sorry," Gwynneth said, sinking to the ground in front of him, kneeling and taking his hands in hers. She looked tired, but it was clear she had no idea of what had befallen him. "Count Faris told me about the battle. I doubt I could have helped you there."

"Likely not." It was hard to make himself speak. "It was worse than that. What have you heard about Kersenstadt?"

"A few rumors, dreadful ones."

"It was terrible. Something like thirty thousand dead. At least a fair number of imperial troops perished too. But they got Larisa."

"Oh Arryk. I'm so sorry." Gwynneth pulled him to her.

"The empress killed her personally," he said, resting his head on Gwynneth's shoulder. "Sent me her head." So far, he'd not spoken of this to anyone.

"What? That's monstrous."

"And that wasn't the worst of it. She beat her to a pulp beforehand. If I hadn't memorized every last inch of her face I wouldn't have recognized her."

"Oh gods." Gwynneth kept her arms around him and stroked his hair with one hand. He felt like a child again.

"It was right before the battle," he went on. "I tried to kill the messenger, though she got away. But then I couldn't move."

"You fought, surely?"

"Only because Orland forced me to. Not that it did any good. I don't think it took Mattila more than a few hours to trounce us completely. Orland took off after a short skirmish with the Sanova Hussars, and I don't blame him. I wanted to die out there, along with everyone else, but they wouldn't let me. They dragged me off my horse, threw me in a carriage and joined the retreat. Not that I care one way or another."

Gwynneth took a deep breath. "I'm so glad they did that; I can't bear the thought of losing you. But now you must tell me how the children are."

Arryk looked up at her. Normally, he'd feel guilty that he hadn't thought of the children once since Orland had told him he'd ordered them sent away before the battle. Gwynneth's anxious face should have upset him more, but he was numb. "Count Orland ordered them to head for Floradias before the battle, but I don't know where they are and I have heard nothing."

He had to look away again because the shock and despair in her eyes was too much to bear.

"I'm so sorry, Gwynn," he mumbled, hanging his head.

But she was so much tougher than he was and after a moment's silence she said, "Surely we would have received word if they'd been captured. Mattila wouldn't waste any time taking advantage of the situation. So they must be safe somewhere. I will leave right away to find them. In the meantime, you must get home."

"Can't," he said. "Zeelund won't let us in and we don't have money to buy boats in Ummarvik. We're too weak to take them by force, which is what I'd do if I could."

"What about Prince Ossian? Won't he help?"

Arryk barked a laugh. "He's scared of Mattila now, with his guard dog Hohenwart stuck in Floradias. He won't help."

"Traitor," Gwynneth said under her breath. "You can get money in Zeelund, can't you?"

"Yes. Should be enough to hire ships if not buy them outright. I've sent a message to Arenberg for Classen to send as many as he can, but they'll land in Zeelund, with no way to get word to send them here instead."

"I see," Gwynneth said. "I'll talk to the Zeelunders. If I can broker peace between Sanova and Estenor, I can get them to let you in."

"You did that?" He should have been surprised, but perhaps it was a measure of his trust in Gwynneth's abilities that he wasn't.

Gwynneth nodded. "Lennart is to marry Raysa Sikora shortly. He plans to invade Kronland as soon as possible."

"He's welcome to it." Arryk shook his head. "I wish I'd never come."

"I'm glad you helped me, and I'm sorry it's turned out so badly. I'll try to help however I can."

"You can," Arryk said eagerly. He'd been waiting for this opportunity. "I'll abdicate straight away and you can rule Norovaea."

"I can't." She shook her head. "But Aksel will help. I made him get to work while I was visiting there and according to Classen's letters, he's doing well. You can rely on him."

"Not like you. You were born to it, Gwynn. Please." Returning to Arenberg like this and being expected to rule was beyond imagining right now.

"We'll talk about it more later." She disentangled herself from him. "Now I need to talk to the garrison and persuade them to let you cross the border before Mattila gets here."

BRAEDEN

They looked for two long hot days before Braeden found the right street. They had to dig through the rubble of another row of houses, but he recognized the way it curved. His heart pounded. He knew it was too late, but something inside him remained convinced of the possibility of a miracle. Perhaps it was because Senta had arrived and refused to believe the worst in spite of Reno and Trisa's accounts.

"I have prayed to the Mother," she said, calm as could be. "She always answers my prayers."

Braeden had never believed in any such thing, but now he grasped at every possibility. He even offered up a few prayers himself. Not proper ones, but he reckoned if the gods paid attention as the priests claimed, they'd listen to him as well as anyone in front of an icon.

Recognizing the street seemed like an answer to those prayers. The houses here were better-built than most and many walls still stood. So it took very little time to locate his own. He recognized the front step and what remained of the front window. There'd been a little bench built in, and though it was gone now, he saw where it had been. He'd sat there with Janna in that very spot.

Everyone grew quiet, but set to work. Braeden stayed in front of everyone, helping lift stone and beam as they worked their way through the front of the house. No matter what they found, he needed to be first to see it. All of the interior walls had fallen, so if anyone still lived, they wouldn't have been able to open the cellar door from the inside.

Braeden knew the cellar was large and that he'd left Janna enough money to stock it. He hoped that even after a siege enough food remained to keep a few people alive for a few days. He tried not to think about what they would have done about water.

After a few hours of work, they reached the kitchen. Braeden took a deep breath and worked harder. He'd spotted the blackened ring of the cellar door

443

when Trisa breathlessly scrambled over the rubble to work next to him.

"Don't," he said.

"I found her for you the first time; I should be here now."

Braeden wanted to say Trisa was just a little girl, but since the battle and af-ter what she'd seen here, there was nothing of the child left in her. Braeden looked into her dark eyes, calm and resolute, and realized she had grown up. So he nodded, and they worked together silently until they cleared all of the rubble from the door.

The door opened smoothly. It was just about noon. The sun stood directly overhead and no other light was needed. Everyone stopped working and stood, holding their breath. There was complete silence from below and Braeden re-membered to take a breath before going down the stairs.

It was a relief almost, to see them, and realize they hadn't been hurt. Even though his friends tried to protect him from them, Braeden still overheard the stories of the atrocities committed before the fire swept the city. Women raped dozens of times before being killed and small children thrown from windows, or heads smashed against stone. At least now he knew that hadn't happened to his.

Janna sat propped against a barrel, her head cocked to one side, her eyes wide open. She held a small bundle in one arm, and the other held Iryna against her side. Iryna's eyes were closed, her thumb in her mouth. Braeden sat down on the floor, and pulled the bundle out of Janna's stiff arms. He unwrapped it slowly, and kept unwrapping until he saw it was a boy. Then he wrapped it back up and put it back on Janna's lap.

He heard voices, but they seemed very far away. Someone was crying, but then that went away. It was quiet for a while and the light faded. There were footsteps on the stair behind him and someone took him by each elbow and made him stand.

"It's time to go, sir." Franca's voice was soft in his ear.

"We'll take them outside the city." Barela's voice was in his other ear. "Somewhere nice, and give them a proper burial tomorrow. But you must come now."

Braeden wanted to protest, but his voice refused to come and his limbs didn't move. He let them drag him up the stairs. Someone brought Kazmir and he mounted him without realizing it. Somehow he got back to Barela's tent and someone put him on a cot and tucked him in. He was shivering and sweating. Someone said something about a fever and Braeden tried to tell them he wasn't sick.

He tried to order his thoughts. He had endured worse surely, so long ago when all of his family had been killed. No, his sister had survived, he was certain of that. He remembered seeing her on the boat they'd put them on, huddled in a corner, crying. Braeden had wanted to comfort her but didn't know what to say. That was probably how his friends felt right now.

Surely this wasn't as bad. He'd hardly known Janna five years, Iryna only a few and the little boy not at all. Braeden wondered what Janna had named him.

They mostly left him alone. Someone came to mop his brow with a cool wet cloth and much later, poured something awful-tasting into his mouth. When he finally slept, it was to nightmares of screaming, yellow-haired men with wolf-eyes running at him out of a great wall of fire.

GWYNNETH

Gwynneth was tired and dirty and hardly looked or felt like a princess, but there was no time. She had to get Arryk into Zeelund, or she really would be Queen of Norovaea in short order. She laughed to herself. It was what she'd always wanted. Since she'd been a little girl, she knew she'd be far better at ruling than Arryk, and plenty of others had hinted as much. Even after her marriage to Kendryk, she thought ruling Norovaea and Terragand jointly would be advantageous for both.

But right now, she couldn't do it. If she went to Norovaea, it would need her full attention for years to come. Its finances and military required a great deal of repair while she would have to face the monster she had just created—a peaceful Estenor and Sanova, their attention turned toward their richest neighbor in disarray. Without the distraction of Kronland, Estenor could gobble up Norovaea straight away. She had no choice now but to get Lennart into Kronland and keep him there until Terragand was Kendryk's again.

A strong Terragand would create a counterweight and make it impossible for Lennart to dominate the north. Gwynneth's head ached. One problem just bred another. And now she had Arryk on her hands, a shadow of his former self. She was desperate to get to the children, but needed to see her brother safe first.

She took Merton and a small escort and asked for the garrison commander. A stout, bluff Zeelunder, the captain in charge was surprised to see her. "Where did you come from, Princess? The next lot we're expecting is Mattila's."

"I came from Terragand," Gwynneth said, taking a proffered chair. "My brother needs help."

"I can see that," the captain said, with some sympathy. "But I can't let him in if I don't want Mattila breathing down our necks."

"I understand. But if you don't let him in, there will be bloodshed on your front door."

"I know. But I don't want trouble with the empire, especially when they're doing so well right now."

Gwynneth rolled the dice. "They won't be much longer." She told him of Lennart's plan.

"You don't say?" The captain was suitably impressed. "Though that doesn't do me much good if she's standing in front of me a few days from now."

"Buy her off." Gwynneth pulled out a large purse and threw it onto the table with a clank. "If she's to chase my brother further, she'll need ships and food. Give her this, minus a suitable fee for yourself of course. I'm sure she'll be friendly."

The captain looked at her long. "It's no wonder you persuaded King Lennart. Though I didn't expect you to have money to throw around."

"I have a bit." She had spent little of Queen Ottilya's generous gift and had already asked Merton if he had enough money to get her to Floradias. Once there, she could sell the jewelry she had sewn into the children's clothes. They could live off that for a while.

She hoped this would be enough to put off Mattila, and if it wasn't, she hoped they'd be far enough into Zeelund for it to no longer be her problem.

The captain hesitated. "I should consult with the authorities."

"You are the authorities," she said. "There is no time to delay. Mattila will be here soon. What do you say?"

The captain took a deep breath. "All right," he said. "Get your people together. Welcome to Zeelund."

BRAEDEN

Braeden awoke the next morning with a terrible headache, but got up all the same. The others trod carefully around him, like he was a bad-tempered stallion. But he wasn't bad-tempered. Not at all. Not sad, either. He felt a dull ache in his head and one in his middle. He even ate something put in front of him.

There was a buzz of activity around him and he had an idea it concerned him, but he wasn't sure how. Barela found him, sitting outside his tent.

"Time to go," he said, offering a hand, which Braeden took, and pulled him to his feet.

"Where?"

"There's a nice place further up the river with trees and some grass. Lieutenant Dura knows the words to say if you want it done the Sanovan way."

"Why not?" It made no difference to him. Dead was dead and the words spoken over the bodies wouldn't bring them back.

"Janna was Moraltan, but no one here knows ..." Barela trailed off.

"Oh, I doubt she cared about that. Sanovan is fine."

He got there somehow. A cart had gone ahead and waited for the rest of them. All of this had been arranged without him. A plain wooden box, big enough for the three of them, but not very big all the same, stood on the ground. Braeden had forgotten how small Janna was until he had seen her again in the cellar.

Senta, weeping loudly, was putting flowers on the box. Where she had gotten them, Braeden couldn't imagine. It was surprising enough they'd found a bit of green anywhere near the city. It was nice here. The air was sweet, with no hint of the pestilence and death of the city and surrounding camps. Leaves rustled, birds chirped and the wind blew softly through the grass.

Braeden stood there while words were said in Sanovan, then someone sang a song he'd never heard before and suddenly the box disappeared, replaced by a brown pile of earth with wilted flowers on top. Someone steered him back to his horse. Maybe it was his imagination, but Kazmir moved slowly and sluggishly. Braeden hoped he was all right. He needed him to be strong to carry him far away from here.

As they made their way back to camp, following Senta, still weeping in the cart, Braeden started thinking. The fog was clearing and a sharp pain threatened to overwhelm him, so he made plans to distract himself.

By the time they reached Barela's tent, Braeden had decided. "I can't ever repay you for your kindness," he began and Barela made a dismissive noise. "I will leave now and I don't want to make trouble for any of you. So it's best if I disappear quietly tonight when none of you know anything about it."

"What are you planning?" Barela was surprisingly calm.

"I'm not sure yet. But whatever it is means I can't go back to the hussars, ever."

"I see." There was a long silence and Barela finally said. "If you have a plan that involves our mutual acquaintance, I would like to be involved."

"Are you sure? It's treason. I doubt I'll survive it."

"I don't mind taking the risk either. It's worth it to me. I used to admire her determination and ambition, and I understand that bloodshed is sometimes needed. But she's a monster. Perhaps I'm too angry to be reasonable, but I've had enough." His meaning was clear.

"So if I need help from you, you'll give it?" Braeden asked.

"Gladly. But tell no one else here. We'll say you are taking time off. There's no need to skulk off in the middle of the night. Your comrades can report to Novitny, who I'm sure will understand. They can expect your return when you're ready, or not, as the case may be."

"Yes, better they think I'm coming back," Braeden said. "How can I reach you?"

"I imagine I'll join the empress in Atlona and meet you there. If you need to send any messages out of the ordinary, do it through Brytta Prosnytz. She's friendly."

"Well, I'll be damned."

"It's not what you think. She can be relied upon."

Now he had a plan, it was easier to move. Barela's servants packed his few things and the general gave him a heavy purse. "You helping with this is all the repayment I want," he said.

No one had sent for them, but the other hussars were there when he was ready to go.

"You shouldn't go alone," Franca began.

"No, I should." His voice was rougher than he meant it to be. "Please, I need you to tell the prince I'll be back before long. I'll find you lot wherever you are."

Everyone exchanged glances, but it seemed they knew he wouldn't be swayed. Perhaps this was a mistake. Looking at their faces, Braeden realized they were family too and he was throwing that away as well. He couldn't think about the prince—his oldest friend—at all. It didn't matter, since he didn't see any way he could survive what he planned to do.

ANTON

After the battle, Count Orland made his troops ride hard and fast. They needed to get far from the battlefield as quickly as possible. Anton was glad Skandar was young and in such good condition, because anyone unable to keep up was left behind.

"I wanted to head to Tirovor and get to Galladium from there." The count gathered his officers when they made camp in southern Fromenberg, still on high alert for those who might pursue them. "But I need to do something else first."

"The Sanova Hussars will be hot on our heels, no matter what you do," one officer said.

"I'm sure they're expecting me to go to Tirovor."

"Most likely."

"But I won't do that. I'm going to Olvisya."

"You're changing sides?" another officer piped up.

"No, though that's not a bad idea. There's a duty I've neglected too long and I need to do it before it's too late."

Anton rolled his eyes, knowing that the count was talking about the whole princess thing again. Personally, he thought rescuing Prince Kendryk might be fun, though it seemed crazy too.

"You can't be serious," the first officer said. By now, everyone knew about the count's promise to Princess Gwynneth. Many officers had already placed bets on how long it would take the count to forget about her. "I don't see how you can pull it off."

"I'm sure I can," the count said.

"So what's your plan then?"

"Haven't got one yet." The count shrugged. "But pretending to change sides is a good idea. If the empress thinks I've gone over to her, she'll let me into the city, or even into the fortress where the prince is held. Maybe even more." The count smiled suggestively.

"You'll have to kill the empress," Anton told the count later, when the others had gone.

"Didn't ask you."

Anton ignored this. "Even if you rescue the prince, how will you get yourself and all of your troops out of the city? It doesn't seem like you can, unless you kill the empress and all her guards."

"Hmm, now that you mention it, wouldn't that be something. Perhaps I should try that too."

"If it were that easy, someone would already have done it. You'll need a really good plan."

"Of course I will." The count threw a boot at Anton's head. He ducked and it went over. "I'll come up with something."

Anton was sure they shouldn't just march into Olvisya without a plan and some inside help if they could get it, but he didn't know what else they could do right now. He didn't like the idea of running for Galladium either. He'd have to find a way to help the count. And he had to admit the prospect of getting close to the empress was tempting. She'd probably still see him as just a boy, a page of no consequence, and there was no telling when he might get his chance.

BRAEDEN

Braeden took his time on the road to Atlona. It was crowded with soldiers and refugees and he needed time to put together a plan. Knowing he could count on Barela helped, but it wasn't enough. There was perhaps a tiny hope that Teodora would enlist Braeden as a bodyguard again or request a private meeting as she had a few times in the past, but it was unlikely. Surely she would find it odd if he showed up at her palace alone, offering his services.

Kazmir trudged along the road, his head down. Braeden wondered if he realized what had happened. At the least he sensed Braeden's mood. They'd been together a long time. Neither one of them was paying much attention when Kazmir nearly ran into a wagon in front of them. They stopped. Braeden didn't mind the delay, but after a while, he wondered why they weren't moving again.

The wagon ahead of him belonged to a family. All of their worldly goods were piled into it, a few little girls perched on top of everything while their parents and a boy walked. The boy ran ahead and came back after a time, breathing hard. "Big wagon. Broke down," he said. "They're trying to fix it, but it'll be awhile. It broke down crossways, so the other side is blocked too."

Braeden sighed. Kazmir stamped and snorted. Neither of them liked standing around all that much. And Braeden knew another way. He'd learned a lot of the smaller trails in this area while playing cat and mouse with Orland. It would be easy to detour around the broken-down wagon and get back on the road. He knew it was dangerous off the road, but he wore some of his armor and his weapons were ready. On such a short stretch, no one was likely to bother him when there were far juicier victims nearby.

He pointed Kazmir toward the trees, knowing there was a footpath just on the other side, running next to the fields. It was nice to be off the road, though the farms were a depressing sight; last year's unharvested crops trampled by thousands of military horses that had come this way. In the distance, he saw a burned-out homestead.

When Braeden had passed through these parts for the Landrus trial in Teo-dora's entourage, this had been a rich, welcoming country, with tidy villages and farms dotting the fertile farmland. Now it looked like no one had lived here in a long time. It was hard to say where all the people had gone. Fled, most likely, or dead, if they'd been unfortunate enough to take refuge inside Kersenstadt.

Braeden turned his mind away from that city again. He was learning how he might survive long enough to kill Teodora. He wouldn't die of grief or guilt and they wouldn't drive him mad either, if he could think about other things. And planning how to kill the empress gave him plenty to think about.

Kazmir picked up the pace, since there was no one to block their path. Braeden thought about Atlona and the Palais Arden, trying to recall every detail. He wondered if he should enlist Brytta's help and leave Barela out of it. He was willing to die on this mission, but didn't want harm to come to the general who'd been such a good friend to him. He just wasn't sure he could do it himself.

"Halt!" A voice came from nowhere and Kazmir dutifully came to a stop.

Braeden looked around. Two cavalry troopers emerged from the trees, one of them holding a pistol and the other hurrying to grab Kazmir's reins.

Embarrassment washed over Braeden. He'd stumbled into an ambush like a rank amateur. Even Trisa would have had better sense.

He shook his head, banishing the fog that had settled over his mind and looked the troopers over. Familiar—the black cuirasses and Maladene horses. He chuckled.

"What's so funny?" the one with the pistol asked.

"Orland's Cuirassiers, am I right?"

"We're the ones asking the questions," the one holding Kazmir's reins said.

"Ask away," Braeden said. For some reason, he wasn't the least bit worried. He wondered if Arian Orland would kill him. That would be a good way to go, though it would be annoying to think the empress still lived.

"You ain't one of us," the one holding the pistol said, "and that armor looks Sanovan. You might as well admit you're one of Novitny's hussars."

"I am," Braeden said mildly. "Smart of you to figure it out."

"Where are are the rest of you?"

"I'm alone."

"Liar." The pistol-holder advanced on him. "You're a scout, aren't you?"

"I'm not."

"Then what are you doing out here by yourself?"

"Headed to Atlona on personal business."

"You make no sense. We're taking you to the general."

"Orland?" Braeden asked, enjoying the surprise on the fellow's face. "Sure, I'll come along." He was curious about the man he'd tried and failed to kill twice. As far as Braeden knew, no one else had ever been that lucky.

TEODORA

Teodora's life was perfect. Or nearly so. She had returned to Atlona in triumph, the victor of Kersenstadt. After what had happened there, the mere mention of her name would be enough to terrify anyone into submission. Now all that was left was to mop up what remained of Arryk Roussay's army and put Mattila out to pasture.

Though Mattila sent little correspondence, Elektra was more reliable. It seemed her priestess friend, Mother Luca, had impressed upon her the importance of loyalty to family above all else.

According to Elektra, Mattila had chased Arryk to the Zeelund border, where he'd escaped her clutches. "The Zeelunders handed over a great sum so she would leave them alone," Elektra wrote. "And with that money, General Mattila hired ships in Ummarvik and set sail for Norovaea."

Teodora was displeased at Mattila again for disobeying orders, but it would be a blessing if she finished Arryk once and for all. There was no one to take his place. In theory, Princess Gwynneth would succeed the Norovaean throne, but she had disappeared. Teodora suspected she had died, or perhaps run off with a lover. No one had heard from her in months.

There was a younger brother, but everyone seemed to think he wasn't interested in governing. Perhaps he could be persuaded to become her puppet, or he might retire to the country with a nice income. She wondered if Count Ensden might like being promoted to Prince of Norovaea. He would be a loyal vassal.

She was about to call for Ensden when Brytta announced Livilla Maxima. Teodora hoped it wasn't bad news. Even while things went well, doubt niggled at the back of her mind. Events had a way of turning around quickly.

Livilla entered and sat down right away. "I realize you're busy, but one of my agents just returned from Sanova with worrisome news."

"What has my brother done now?" Teodora frowned. Her spy network in Sanova spent most of its time watching Atinos hatch endless plots to overthrow her. They were never workable, but Teodora worried he might get lucky someday.

"Nothing this time." Livilla looked at the piece of paper she held. "But I have it on good authority that Princess Gwynneth just spent a great deal of time in Novuk, some of it in private with Queen Ottilya."

"So that's where the princess ran off to. Does anyone know what they talked about?"

"No one is certain, but there is a rumor she was trying to broker peace between Sanova and Estenor."

A cold chill ran up Teodora's spine, but she shook her head. "That's ridiculous. There's no one more difficult or stubborn than Ottilya, and King Lennart isn't the sort to compromise. I'm not surprised at the princess trying something, but I can't imagine that she would succeed."

"You're right, it's hard to picture," Livilla said, though her face remained grave. "Still, we must stay vigilant."

"What reason does Lennart have to invade Kronland?" Teodora was sure the King of Estenor harbored no great feelings of friendship toward her, but she didn't see why he should be actively hostile.

"Nothing concrete aside from the usual wish to expand his sphere of influence." Livilla shifted in her chair. "But there's something else that concerns me. I've heard rumors that Lennart has gone over to the Quadrene heresy. He hasn't enforced its practice in Estenor, but that hasn't been necessary. Most temples turned away from the true faith on their own. It's possible he would invade Kronland to protect what heretics remain there."

"That seems rather fanatical, and unlikely." Teodora refused to be upset by the news. "And if he invades, he can't have a large force. Where would he get the money? The biggest annoyance is that I'd need to keep Mattila on longer, though I suppose I can live with that."

Now that her peace was disturbed, even in such a small way, she noticed another fly in her ointment. Demario had just returned from Kersenstadt, and Teodora was certain he was behaving oddly toward her. She couldn't decide exactly what was different, but he was no longer as warm and his formerly ready smiles were scarce.

She sat with him in her private study, playing chess. "I have heard from Queen Beatryz," he said, taking her second knight. Teodora gritted her teeth. "She thinks it unlikely they will extend the Floradias truce. So she might call me back."

Teodora looked up. "She can't. I still need you."

"Not really." He was looking at the board, not at her. "You are in no more danger. In a few months you won't even need Mattila."

"Yes, but ..." Teodora made a move, a bad one. "You know what I mean."

"I do." He still wouldn't meet her eye. "But I can't stay here forever."

"Why not? I have a plan for Count Ensden once Arryk Roussay is deposed. You could take over as my commander-in-chief. Beatryz can't give you anything comparable."

"She says she will make me field marshal."

"Pfft. Not while old Montanez is still around. She's just saying that so you'll come back."

"I have to go back," Demario said. "I still work for her, in the end."

"I will write to her. She really doesn't need you, I'm sure." Fear clawed at her insides. He was right. He worked for Beatryz. What worried her even more was that he didn't seem bothered at the prospect of leaving her so soon. She wondered what was wrong. She peered at him from under her lashes. His eyes remained fixed on the board. Had he tired of her? Was there someone else? Teodora clenched her fists in her lap as he made another move. She wouldn't allow it. He would stay here with her. She would write to her cousin and offer her whatever she wanted so she could keep him here.

GWYNNETH

Gwynneth didn't wait to see Arryk to Bonnenruck where he could get ships after seeing his banker. Even though he didn't seem capable of managing bankers and hiring ships, she had to trust that those around him would help. She was still appalled that no one knew where her children were. No matter what had happened to Larisa and to Arryk's army, these were his nieces and nephews, the heir to Terragand among them.

"Why didn't you send them to Galladium before the battle?" Gwynneth asked Arryk. "Once you realized I wasn't coming, you shouldn't have waited."

He stared at her, hollow-eyed.

"Didn't you get my letters?" she asked impatiently.

"I suppose I did, though I was distracted. I'm sorry Gwynn. I'm sure they're fine. Count Orland arranged for them to travel with a large armed guard."

"Did you send money to pay that guard? Did you give them orders where they were supposed to take them? Or what to do once they got there?"

Arryk looked at her blankly, then hung his head. She stamped her foot and left the room before she shouted at him. She wanted to be angrier with him, but he was in such a pathetic state, she found it difficult to scold him. So she compensated by abandoning him more quickly than was decent.

Since Arryk seemed to think the children had headed for Floradias, she worked her way down the frontier fortresses on the western side. To her dismay, the first several she visited had no idea what she was talking about. On the one hand, she was glad her children were so well-hidden, but on the other, she worried because they seemed to have disappeared altogether.

After nearly two weeks, and visiting six different forts, she finally received a small clue. "Emilya Hohenwart is in Megen," a garrison commander said. "Your children might be with her, or she might have news."

Gwynneth didn't know why she should, but at least it was something. When she reached Megen, there was little sign of a military camp, though the town was

459

fortified. Gwynneth found Hohenwart ensconced in a grubby tavern, recruiting.

"There you are," Hohenwart said, standing up as Gwynneth entered the room. "I was hoping someone would show up. I'm getting ready to move out in a fortnight and couldn't figure out what to do with your children."

"They're here then?" Gwynneth could have hugged her, but Hohenwart looked down her nose at her forbiddingly.

"Been here for some time," she said. "Came flying in from Arcius with Mattila's vanguard on their heels."

"Oh Holy Mother." Gwynneth collapsed into a chair.

"You should have a seat, Your Grace," Hohenwart said, draping her rangy frame across another chair. Her tone wasn't at all the thing. "They're fine now, but they had a good fright."

"So they're well?" Gwynneth found her throat was parched.

"Believe so." Hohenwart shrugged. "They've got that Maximus fellow with them and he's been keeping an eye, thank gods. Never been much good at managing brats myself. Give me an artillery crew any day."

Gwynneth bit her tongue. She'd forgive this woman her rough manners as long as the children were safe. She took a moment to master herself, then said, "Thank you for your trouble. I'll see you're compensated when I come into funds."

Hohenwart waved her away. "Don't bother. I didn't do anything. But I must be on my way soon."

"Are you going back to Kronland?"

Hohenwart barked a laugh. "Not for anything. I'll stay well clear of Brynhild Mattila, thank you very much. But the truce in Zeelund is nearly up and they'll need soldiers again. I plan to have a force ready when that happens."

Gwynneth told her that Lennart was likely to invade.

"He's welcome to it," Hohenwart said. "I'm done with Kronland and northern princes."

"Perhaps he can change your mind." Gwynneth stood. "He could use a general with your experience."

"I doubt it."

"Thank you anyway," Gwynneth said, then hurried to the temple where her children stayed.

Gwynneth approached the little temple and realized she was still terrified. What if the children here weren't hers? Or they were ill, or some other dreadful thing had happened? She would never forgive herself.

The novice on duty took one look at her and broke into a smile. "We're happy you're finally here, Your Grace. Come in and I'll send them to you."

She led Gwynneth into a small room behind the temple proper and sent another novice after the children. Gwynneth let relief wash over her and smiled when she heard Devyn's voice echoing off the stone walls of the corridor long before she saw him.

She stood just as they burst into the room and gathered them into her arms. When she sat down again the three oldest piled onto her lap while little Stella looked at her curiously from the nurse's arms.

"You must tell me all about your journey here," Gwynneth said. "It sounds like you had quite an adventure."

"It was very frightening," Maryna said calmly. "But we made it in the end."

"Those soldiers almost caught us," Devyn said. "But I can fight them."

"I'm sure you can." Gwynneth smiled. "Is Edric Maximus here?" The priest at this temple was an old friend of his.

"I sent him a message when I heard you'd come," Maryna said. "He'll be so pleased to see you." No doubt he was eager to stop playing nursemaid.

Edric entered the room a few minutes later, interrupting Devyn's confused account of their journey here.

Gwynneth stood. "I can't thank you enough." She took Edric's hands in hers, returning his smile. It still seemed odd sometimes that they were friends.

"I was happy to escape too, since I doubt Mattila would have dealt kindly with me," Edric said smiling. "I thank the gods for Arian Orland. At that moment before the battle, your brother had half lost his mind. Orland stepped in and sent his page to arrange the children's escape. If he hadn't, Mattila would have caught us far too easily."

"I can't bear to think about it." Gwynneth shuddered. "I'm so glad they took you in here. I worried because I knew you had little money."

"The gods always provide," Edric said. "And your Maryna is most resourceful. She remembered the names of several distant relatives on the way in whose castles we could stay when we needed to rest."

Maryna beamed and Gwynneth kissed the top of her head.

"What are you planning next?" Edric asked.

"I must go to Galladium immediately. King Lennart has converted to the new faith and wishes to enter the fight, but he needs money. He hopes I can persuade Gauvain to provide it."

Hope sprang into Edric's eyes. "That is excellent news. To be honest Princess, I've been close to despair. I had hoped your brother would be able to help, but it seems he was not the one we hoped for. With him defeated so completely and Kronland nearly overrun, I didn't see how we were to move forward."

"It will take a few months, but Lennart will be a formidable opponent for Teodora. He's the only person right now who is a match for Brynhild Mattila. Will you come to Galladium with us?'

"Let me think on it," Edric said. "I'm anxious to get back to Kronland and continue my work, but I would like to speak with Natalya Maxima further. She has ideas that bear exploring. But I worry about the state of the faith in the areas Mattila has overrun. Livilla has sent many clergy along to bring every temple back in line. I fear that the faith of most is not strong enough to withstand that kind of pressure, especially if it's backed by violence."

"I worry about that too," Gwynneth said. "I wish I had the answer. But know that Lennart will back you completely. Even if some backslide now, you can change that when he comes. You needn't decide right now. It will take me a few days to raise funds so we can travel. I will send most of my guard back to Terragand, so we don't need to house and feed them."

When she arrived at the children's quarters in the temple, she sent the smaller children off with a sweet-looking young novice, asked Maryna to stay with her and shut the door.

"What are you doing with my clothes, Mama? Are we packing already?"

"Look," Gwynneth said, spreading a cloak across the bed. "Do you see the hem?"

"Something is in there." Maryna picked it up. "I thought it seemed heavy to wear."

"My jewelry." Gwynneth smiled. "It's all sewn into your winter clothes. Help me get some of it out."

"What for?"

"I must sell it. We have to travel to Allaux very quickly and we need money for that. We will have to live there for a few months too."

Maryna's face fell. "I hoped we could go home soon."

"We will darling, I promise." Gwynneth pulled her down on the bed next to her as she ripped at the cloak's seams. "We just have to wait a bit longer. Then King Lennart will bring his army and defeat the empress."

"But what about Papa?"

Gwynneth bit her lip. "I don't know. I will talk to Natalya Maxima and find out what she can do. It seems she wasn't able to help him as I had hoped. Still, we must not despair. If King Lennart succeeds, the empress will have to turn your father loose."

"I hope so," Marya said gravely. "Oh Mama, must you sell these? They're so pretty." She picked up a pair of sapphire and diamond earrings.

"Yes, I must." Gwynneth sighed. They'd been a gift from Kendryk at Devyn's birth. "But don't worry. When the war is over, I'll get it all back somehow."

"I hope so." Maryna's voice quivered.

Gwynneth was appalled at how little she got for her jewelry. The Floradian money changers drove a hard bargain. At least she had plenty of it. She just needed to make it last as long as possible and hope she could save at least a few pieces for Maryna and Stella to inherit someday.

Within five days, they were ready to leave for Galladium. Gwynneth sent Merton and the guards back to Terragand and Edric elected to go with them. "I might not be able to do much," he said, "but I'm more useful there than in Galladium. I believe Natalya has things well in hand."

"I hope so," Gwynneth said. "Be careful with him." She smiled at Merton, though she was sorry to see both him and Edric go.

BRAEDEN

Braeden was in luck. The troopers took him straight to Arian Orland in a camp surprisingly well-ordered under the circumstances. In front of a tent, a gangly dark-haired youth sprawled against a pile of blankets, polishing a sword. He jumped to his feet when Braeden appeared.

"You caught a Sanova Hussar!" he said, his voice starting deep, but rising to a shriek. Braeden stifled a chuckle.

"We did," one of the troopers said. "The general will want to see him, I'm sure."

"You got that right," the boy said, disappearing into the tent.

He was back a second later, Orland right behind him. Braeden had never seen him up close without his visor down. He certainly looked the part of the romantic hero, making Braeden wonder if the rumors about Princess Gwynneth were true.

Orland walked up to him. He was almost as tall as Braeden, though not as burly. "I know you," he said without preamble.

"I know you too," Braeden replied.

"You should come in," Orland said, turning back toward the tent. "I have a few questions for you."

"All right," Braeden said. "I've got time."

"Are you a scout?" the boy asked, following Braeden into the tent.

"Shush," Orland said. "Bring us some ale."

The boy pulled a face and left the tent.

Orland rolled his eyes. "It's a difficult age."

"Is he yours?" Braeden asked, sitting on a proffered chair. Aside from the dark hair, he didn't see a resemblance.

"Oh gods, no. At least, I don't think so. He says he's from Moralta, and I wasn't there at the right time to father any children of his age. He's surprisingly belligerent for someone not related to me, though."

464

"Sometimes you get lucky with your pages," Braeden said.

"Where's yours? I recall a fierce little girl at your side the other day."

"She's gone to join Novitny and the others. They're looking for you, though you seem to have taken a different path than expected."

"I'm going to Atlona, or close by."

"Have you lost your mind?"

"Yes." Orland was very serious. "I'm so in love I will do anything she asks, even face Teodora herself."

"Princess Gwynneth?" So the rumors were true.

Orland nodded, his dark eyes nearly liquid. "It's miserable. It's been years now and I can't seem to get over her."

"What does she want you to do in Atlona?" It seemed odd to Braeden that he was asking the questions.

By now, the boy had returned with a jug of ale and pewter mugs. He set them down and filled them to overflowing, mostly because he was too busy staring at Braeden. Braeden winked at him and the boy blushed, stumbling over his too-big feet as he tried to back away.

Orland took a long drink and sighed. "She wants me to rescue her husband of course."

Braeden nearly spit out his ale. "And you'll try it? You really are mad, aren't you?"

Orland shrugged. "I must try, or die in the attempt. But never mind that. What are you doing here? You say Novitny is looking for me?"

"We all reckoned you'd make for Tirovor."

"I suppose that makes sense, if I weren't crazy."

Braeden glimpsed the boy shaking his head and rolling his eyes and hid his own smile.

"People seem to think you're sane," Braeden said. "Should help your cause, I imagine. You've sent the Sanova Hussars on a wild-goose chase."

"Excellent." Orland smirked and held out his mug for more ale. Braeden's was topped off too. "Why aren't you with them?"

Braeden was surprised that Orland believed him so readily, but he believed Orland as well. They had taken each other's measures long ago.

"I'm going to Atlona to kill the empress," Braeden said. There wasn't much point in concealing his mission from Teodora's enemies.

The boy gasped, but Orland looked at Braeden for a while then said, "I'll admit, I wasn't expecting to hear that. Why do you want to kill her?"

"My wife and children died when she sacked Kersenstadt." Braeden said it quickly, then took a drink to cover the sudden rush of emotion.

"Ah," Orland said, taking a drink as well. "You have my condolences, though I'm sure killing the empress would be far more rewarding. How do you plan to do it?"

"Not sure."

Braeden told him what he'd considered so far and hinted he could expect inside help, though he didn't yet want to expose Brytta or Barela.

"It seems we ought to be able to help each other, though I'm not sure how just yet," Orland said after Braeden had finished.

"I was hoping you'd say that." Braeden grinned for the first time in weeks.

After their conference, Braeden followed the page to a small tent erected not far from Orland's. A single guard followed them, and though Braeden was certain he could overcome him, he had no wish to get away just yet.

"I rubbed your horse down," the boy said. "He's magnificent. What's his name?"

"Kazmir."

"I like that. I have my own warhorse too. His name is Skandar. He was a gift from King Arryk."

"Is he a Norovaean? I'd like to take a look at him."

The boy's face lit up. "I'll take you to him later, after I've finished the count's armor."

A few hours later, Count Orland called Braeden to dine with him.

"You're in luck," the count said. "I sent out scouts and your story holds up. I must confess I was suspicious, but there are no enemy troops for leagues around. But I do have to wonder if you work for Teodora directly."

Braeden stared. At first he wasn't sure how to respond. Finally he said, "The only way I would work as her spy would be if she had my family for leverage. And they're dead." Whenever he talked about them, the words caught in his throat. He looked away and swallowed the pain down again. He reckoned if Orland didn't believe him there was nothing he could do about it.

There was a long silence while the page cleared the dishes away, brought brandy and glasses. After pouring some for each of them he disappeared and Orland and Braeden drank. Orland drummed his fingers on the table, then said, "Maybe I shouldn't, but for some reason, I believe you, and I'm usually right about these things." He emptied his glass, poured another round, then said, "Kronek here tells me you want to see his horse."

The name hit Braeden like a jolt. "Who?"

"Kronek, my page. His horse is worth seeing. He's full-grown now, a pure-bred Norovaean ..."

"What did you say your page's name was?" Braeden felt as though his throat might close on him. The shaggy dark hair, the lanky build—he realized he'd seen it before.

"Kronek. Anton Kronek. He's Moraltan. Are you all right, man? You're looking rather green."

"I—" Braeden's voice caught in his throat. It had to be a coincidence. But the name, combined with the looks seemed beyond question.

"Here, have a drink." Orland slid his glass closer.

Braeden shook his head. "Might I speak with him?" he finally managed.

"Certainly." Orland cocked his head. "Why don't you go to your tent and I'll send him there? I assume it's a personal matter."

Braeden stumbled back to his tent. He slumped on the edge of his cot, his head in his hands. If this boy was who he thought, the gods were beyond cruel.

The tent flap rustled as it lifted, and then the boy stood before him.

"Sit," Braeden said, his voice rough.

The boy sat on the floor, crossing his legs and looking up at Braeden wide-eyed. "What is it, sir? Have I done something?"

Braeden shook his head. "Please tell me your name and the names of your parents."

The boy looked surprised. "Why?"

"I'm sure I knew them."

"I'm Anton and my parents were Dimir and Elena Kronek, though my mother died when I was little."

"Did your father remarry?" Braeden's insides tightened up and he had to remind himself to breathe.

Anton nodded. "He married Janna. She felt more like my real mother, though she died in Marjatya. You knew her?"

Braeden swallowed hard. It was some time before he could speak. "I'm very sorry," he said. "It's true, your mother is dead, but she died just a few weeks ago."

"I don't understand," Anton said blankly.

"She survived Marjatya. I found her in the woods."

Anton's hand flew to his mouth. "Was she all right?"

"Frightened and half-starved, but well enough otherwise. The wife of one of my officers took care of her." It was hard to keep talking, but he had to.

"So why did she die now?" Tears rolled down Anton's face and ran into his mouth.

"It's a long story," Braeden said, but then told him all of it. Once he started, it got easier, and he found he liked talking about Janna with someone who'd known her long before he met her.

By the time he'd finished, Anton was sobbing. "I'm sorry." He sniffled. "I'm not sure why I'm crying. I was sad about it years ago, but I hadn't thought about it in a long time."

"It's all right," Braeden said, wishing he could cry too.

Anton wiped his tears with his sleeve, then looked at Braeden. "So she was happy?"

"I think so. At least until I took her to Kersenstadt. She didn't want to go, but I was so worried about her and the baby. It was the worst mistake of my life."

"It seemed like the right thing to do at the time, I'm sure." Anton's voice was oddly calm now that the shock had passed. Janna had often mentioned his composure. "You couldn't have known what would happen there. Oh gods." He stopped suddenly. "I was there too, for a while. I came with Larisa Karsten when she took over, spent several days wandering all over the city and I might have walked right by your house. What if she saw me and didn't recognize me?" He was becoming agitated again.

"No," Braeden said. "She would have known you. She was sure you were alive and always kept an eye out for you. Anytime she saw a boy your age, she looked closely. "

Anton nodded. "I would have noticed her too, I'm sure."

Braeden didn't know what to do next. Naturally, if Anton wanted him to, he would take care of him. But he wasn't at all sure what the boy wanted.

Finally, Anton stood. "Well," he said. "It seems we both have good reason to hurt the empress. I'm glad we can do it together."

ANTON

After his long talk with Braeden, Anton wasn't sure what to make of it all.

When he told the count what had happened, he laughed. "So you have a stepfather, do you?"

Anton had never looked at it that way. He liked the fellow well enough, but sometimes he got a look in his eyes even more frightening than the count at his worst. He wasn't sure he wanted him to be family. And now he remembered his mother again, he was sad more often. He didn't like it.

"Would you believe this fellow if he said he wanted to kill the empress?"

"Yes." Anton didn't need to consider it for more than a second. "My mother hated the empress after she killed my father and sent that awful woman who killed my little sister. She wouldn't have married anyone who'd want to help her."

That settled it then. The count and Braeden put together a plan to kill the empress and rescue the prince in one busy afternoon. To his delight, Anton had an important part to play.

"Is he old enough to help?" Braeden nodded in Anton's direction, and Anton stuck his chin out. Of course he was old enough.

"He is. Saved my life in Zeelund recently. Can think on his feet, and that's what we need," the count said, and Anton felt very proud.

Braeden shrugged and Anton decided not to be too offended. It was nice having someone worry about him a little bit like a parent.

"We might get more help," Braeden said. "General Barela is Teodora's lover, but he wants to get rid of her now too. He hinted we could expect help from one of her ladies-in-waiting as well."

The count was pleased. "That she makes so many enemies is finally coming home to roost. I can't believe her own lover would turn on her this way."

"You would if you saw Kersenstadt. Barela's a tough and experienced soldier, but what happened there was beyond imagining and how the empress reacted

469

made him sick," Braeden said. "Also, he's my friend and helped me find ... my family." He barely got that out, but the count pretended not to notice his discomfort and just continued.

Anton swallowed down the lump in his throat and stared up at the ceiling until he could blink the tears away. He didn't want to imagine his mother dying there, along with the little sister and brother he would never get to know. He was glad he hadn't been the one to find them, though he felt terribly sorry for Braeden. He was a tough fellow, but it was easy to see how sad he was.

While they laid plans they stayed on the move in southern Tirilis so no one could find them. Once they were ready, they'd get into Olvisya quickly and quietly. Braeden would go first.

"I'll go to Atlona. No one will think anything of it," he said one evening. They had to travel during the day, but spent the nights huddling around a brazier in the count's tent, poring over maps.

"You're sure? Even without the hussars?" the count asked.

"Why not? I'm taking a break and Demario Barela is my friend. It's natural I'd spend time with him. Who knows, I might even get a surprise crack at the empress that way."

"That would make things a lot easier. Once she's dead, it'll be easy to spring Kendryk in the confusion."

"My thoughts exactly. But I doubt I'll get close. Or at least, I won't count on it. Now, let's talk about Brytta Prosnytz. I know her best of the empress's ladies-in-waiting. She's her personal secretary and all correspondence goes through her. I imagine she can get me an order to let me into the Arnfels on some pretext."

"Once we rescue Kendryk, what do we do with him?" the count asked. "We can take him overland to Tirovor, but there's a good chance the empress's forces will catch up if they pursue."

"We go by sea. Take him to Galladium. Everyone knows the king there is his good friend. "There's a little port here at Capo." Braeden pointed at a spot on a map while Anton peered over his shoulder. "We'll have a ship ready; something small and fast. If you can afford to hire one, that is."

"I'll plunder more temples around here if I must," the count said. "But I'll have enough money."

TEODORA

"Are the Sanova Hussars in Atlona?" Elyse asked Teodora as they walked the garden paths. It was depressing out here in mid-winter, but Teodora needed to get out of the close, cloying atmosphere of the council chamber.

She paused in front of a frozen fountain. "No. Prince Novitny is still looking for Arian Orland. Though I'm sure he'll turn up here before long. With any luck, he'll kill the count or bring him as a prisoner. Why do you ask?"

"I could have sworn I saw Braeden Terris the other day. He was riding out to the hunt with General Barela."

"Are you sure? I can't imagine why he didn't announce himself. We are old friends after all." That was a stretch, but Teodora was certain she left a lasting impression on the men she met. Once she did, they often had trouble staying away. Terris was likely no different.

She remembered to ask Demario when they met that evening.

"Oh, he's on leave," he said with a shrug.

"You should ask him to dine. Why hasn't he appeared at court?"

"He's in mourning," Demario said, a bit brusquely. "His wife and children were killed recently, and he's taking time off."

Teodora tried to remember who his wife was. She recalled some little mouse of a girl he'd once brought to the palace, but couldn't imagine such a dull creature keeping his interest for long. "I suppose I understand why he doesn't want to socialize. Send him my condolences." She wondered if she ought to include a gift, but that might be in poor taste.

"I'll tell him," Demario said, then changed the subject.

"Your Highness, I feel it is my duty to tell you these things," Elyse said a few days later, clearly nervous. She had dared to interrupt Teodora at her work and was likely prepared to have something thrown at her head.

"Tell me what?" Teodora put her quill down carefully, even as dread rose inside her.

"It might be nothing, but it seemed odd," Elyse said, twisting her hands in front of her.

"Well then, out with it."

"I came upon General Barela and Brytta this morning," Elyse said.

Teodora sat up straighter. "Oh really? Where?"

"They were in the garden." Elyse swallowed. "In that little pavilion by the upper fountain."

"I know it." It had been a favorite meeting place in the early days of their affair, when Teodora was still trying to hide it. "What were they doing?"

"Just talking. I even moved closer so I could watch them. They sat side by side on a bench. Just talking."

"What did they say?" Teodora braced herself for the worst.

"They spoke in very low tones, not quite a whisper, but I wasn't able to get close enough to hear without being found out. It seemed best to come to you."

"You were right," Teodora said. "You can leave the rest to me."

Elyse left in a hurry, and Teodora slumped back in her chair. She might have known. Brytta was so pretty, so sweet. Men loved her, even though Teodora thought she seemed rather stupid and was always in tears about one thing or another. She didn't know what to do, so she called for Livilla.

She needed her seldom these days, but Livilla still came quickly. "Oh dear," she said, as soon as she saw Teodora's face. "Has he ended it?"

"He wouldn't dare," Teodora said. "But it looks like he's taken a mistress. One of my ladies-in-waiting."

"Are you certain?"

"Quite. They were seen together in the upper pavilion."

"Doing what, precisely?"

"Just talking. But what possible innocent reason could they have for whispering together there? Especially when it's so cold outside, there are a hundred more comfortable spots for an innocent conversation."

"I can't think of any reason for either of them to have an innocent conversation with each other. I'm so sorry, my dear."

"I don't know what to do." Falling in love had been a huge mistake. She had always feared something like this and now it had happened. All her triumphs turned to ash. Why hadn't she sent him away before it came to this?

ARRYK

By the time Arryk got into Zeelund, visited his bankers and procured boats, Mattila was close behind. He barely had time to land in Norovaea and shore up the coastal defenses, paltry as they were. One large, somewhat dilapidated fort commanded the southernmost approaches to the capital. Arryk landed all of his boats there and put his troops at the disposal of the garrison. Perhaps they could hold off Mattila here. Perhaps there would be a miracle and she wouldn't come, bearing thousands of troops in dozens of ships.

"Your Highness must go on to Arenberg," the grizzled commander at the fortress said. "If Mattila's force is of any size we won't hold her long here. You must see to the city defenses."

"What defenses?" Arryk asked miserably. Arenberg was a relatively new city and had never had walls. He couldn't believe the first invasion of Norovaea in four hundred years was happening on his watch.

"Whatever you can come up with," the commander said. "Now go on. We'll be all right."

Arryk knew that couldn't possibly be true, but he could hardly tell his own forces to surrender without a fight. He borrowed the commander's horse and hurried on to Arenberg with only a few trusted officers.

Word of Mattila's progress had come ahead of him and the city was in a panic. He found the palace in an uproar while Norvel Classen oversaw an evacuation.

"There's no point in trying to defend this," Classen said. "For one, we don't have the troops, and even if we did, the fortifications won't hold."

Arryk had to agree, just glad that Classen wasn't throwing this in his face. "At least it's winter," he said. "It'll be hard for her to leave the city."

"I doubt she'll leave it before spring. But that gives us time to build up our defenses in the countryside. I believe you should make Vastivik fortress your headquarters."

"Whatever you say," Arryk said, "I'm getting my brother."

He found Aksel at work in his laboratory.

"Come on man, pack up what you can."

"I'm not going." Aksel scribbled in a notebook and wouldn't look up.

"You have to. They'll capture you, and you don't want that."

"I'm sure it won't be that bad." Aksel finally looked at him. "Don't you think it best one family member stay behind to treat with the enemy?"

"Treat with the enemy? What are you on about? We need to drive her back into the sea as soon as we can. There will be no negotiation."

"Don't be ridiculous," Aksel said, putting his quill down. "There must be. You can't fight her and win."

"We'll draw her into the countryside, wear her out. Shouldn't take more than a few months."

"What if she doesn't go into the countryside? She can wait you out right here, until you're starving. Someone needs to talk to her."

"It won't be you. Come on. Pack up your things. That's an order."

"I won't do it." Aksel had never been so stubborn. "You can't make me."

"I can," Arryk said, his patience thin, "and I will. If you aren't ready to go in an hour, I'll send someone to get you. You have to go."

"I'm sorry, but I won't. You'll have to carry me out."

"I will then," Arryk said. "I've already lost nearly everything, I'm not losing you too." He turned on his heel and slammed the door behind him. As soon as he spotted one of the palace guards he said, "See that Prince Aksel is packed and ready to go within the hour. If he resists, carry him out."

He noticed the guard's raised eyebrows as he turned to go. Arryk turned back. "I mean it. Gather up several sturdy fellows and make my brother leave."

TEODORA

"Surely, you can appreciate Mattila's accomplishments," Solteszy began.

"Don't even start with me," Teodora screamed, throwing the letter onto the floor and stomping on it. "I specifically told her not to do that. I don't need her to subdue Norovaea. I need her in Kronland to take Birkenfels, bring Terragand into line and subdue Podoska. And I must be sure that Lennart has no plans to invade."

First came Mattila's message that she was staying in Norovaea until she had completely defeated Arryk. That was followed by the news that Lennart Ostberg had married Raysa Sikora in a magnificent wedding in Novuk. Teodora was floored. Even though she was on bad terms with her brother, Raysa was her niece, and she should have been invited, not informed by a spy after the fact.

"What is Mattila playing at?" she raged. "Does she think to rule Norovaea herself?"

"I doubt it," Solteszy said, staying well out of Teodora's way. "If she occupies even part of Norovaea, you should be able to get very favorable terms from Arryk Roussay."

"I don't need favorable terms from him if he's slunk off back home. I need him to stay there and I need Mattila to mind my borders. If there's peace between Sanova and Estenor I can't imagine what they're up to. What if Sanova makes a play for Terragand? What if Lennart grabs Helvundala?" Teodora clutched at her head, which had been aching for some time now. It seemed she was never to get so much as a moment's respite.

"You're correct that the peace is worrisome, far more than Mattila's actions. It might be wise to deploy Ensden and Barela into Kronland, just to be safe."

"I'll send Ensden, but I want Barela here. I can't risk trouble from another quarter and you know how it likes to pop up."

"Indeed," Solteszy said, though he seemed unbothered. "Though it's possible that Sanova and Estenor are simply exhausted. I wonder why a marriage has

475

happened now. Everyone seemed certain Raysa would marry a prince of Briansk and secure that border."

"It was Princess Gwynneth." Teodora stamped her foot. "I'd heard she was in Novuk and never imagined she'd succeed in this. It makes me wonder what kinds of promises she extracted from Lennart since I'm certain she'll want him to act against me." Teodora wished she could confide in Demario, but it wasn't possible now. She needed a friend. And then she remembered. "Did Daciana get here?"

"Yes, she did. I made her disband her people, though, and come here alone. She has accumulated the most disreputable horde."

"Disreputable, but effective. I think she might be able to neutralize Podoska by herself. At least I won't need Mattila for that. Send her in."

It was good to see Daciana. "How is it you still look like a girl?" Teodora asked, after they'd embraced and settled into chairs with glasses of her best wine.

"I bathe in the blood of virgins." Daciana grinned.

Teodora assumed she was joking, though you could never be sure. "I would do the same, but there aren't any in Atlona. And ruling is giving me gray hair. It's dreadful."

"Yes, fighting is much easier." Daciana refilled her own glass and topped off Teodora's. "Such a viper's nest around here."

"You have no idea." Teodora dropped her voice. "I can't trust anyone."

"Not even your man?" Daciana's tone was derisive.

"Especially not him. He's having an affair with Brytta."

Daciana spit out her wine. "What? He betrays you with one of your own ladies? Shall I kill him for you?"

"No, I haven't decided what to do about him, but I'll do something."

ANTON

"So it's all clear to you?" The count wasn't taking any chances it seemed. He and Anton were both mounted, armed and armored and ready to go their separate ways.

"Yes, we've been over it a thousand times." Anton was impatient to get going. This was a serious mission, with serious consequences if it failed. This time, it wasn't just the count who would be killed if they were caught. It would include Anton himself, Braeden, and many other important people. Anton still wasn't sure what to make of Braeden, but he wanted him to live for his mother's sake. It felt good to help someone who'd loved her very much.

"All right then. I need to go." The count looked grim, which was unusual for him. He'd sent nearly all of his troops into Tirovor. From there they would make their way to Galladium, where with any luck, they would be reunited after the mission. The count was taking only a few hundred of his best fighters into Olvisya.

He paused before turning to the road. "One more thing. Once you have the prince and Commander Terris on board, I want you to go, even if I'm not there yet."

"But—" Anton began.

"No, listen. If all goes well, I'll be right there with them. But I don't want to risk the mission if I'm delayed."

"How will you get away?" Anton shivered. The count was the only family he had. Or at least the only family-type person aside from a surprise stepfather.

"You know me." The count shrugged. "I always get away. I'll have money and will take another ship, or make for Marjatya if that doesn't work out. I'll get to Galladium in any case. You can wait for me there. Or you can go with Commander Terris if you'd rather."

Anton was taken aback. He hadn't so much as considered the possibility. "I'd rather go with you, sir."

The count looked at him long, his eyes unreadable. "I appreciate that. You're a better sort than anyone in my family ever was. But you must take care of yourself first."

"I will." Anton said it so the count would just go already. Anton had his own work to do. He rubbed Cid's nose one last time, then turned Skandar aside to join his own escort of ten troopers.

The count disappeared into the woods. He and his troops would stay in them, off the main roads until they were close to Atlona. Once there, they would wait for Barela's signal. Anton had to move fast if he was going to have everything ready in time.

He headed straight south, for the port of Capo, just a few hours' ride from Atlona. Once they got the prince out of prison, they would bring him there, put him on a ship and sail all the way around Cesiano and Maladena to Galladium. Anton found the thought of a sea voyage exciting, even though they would stay in sight of land most of the time.

At the port, Anton had one of the men find lodgings while he went straight to the docks. Once he showed his coin, it was an easy matter to find ships for hire. He needed a fast one. "Can you be ready to go within the week?" he asked the captain of a likely-looking one.

The fellow was a Maladene, proud and haughty, who tried looking down his nose at Anton. "I'm ready to go now," he said. "You pay extra if you want me to wait."

"I can do that," Anton said, making a point of looking him in the eye. He was glad now he had grown so tall, though he wished the rest of him had caught up and he weren't so skinny. "You must be fast, too." He dropped his voice. "There will be a small chance of pursuit."

The captain looked unimpressed. "This is the fastest ship here. No one will catch her. If there is no wind, my crew can row. They are very good at this."

"All right then," Anton said, laying a heavy purse on the table between them. "You'll get another when we reach Galladium safely."

The captain still affected nonchalance, but was clearly taken aback by the weight of the purse and that it was full of gold. "How is it a youngster like yourself has come into such funds?"

Anton tried to look bored. "That's hardly any of your business." The count had given him enough money to hire two ships, but he hated being questioned because of his youth. After his brief brush with poverty in Zeelund, Anton always had money. Sometimes he got it from the count, and he also got his share whenever they plundered a town or temple. While many fellows grabbed the first things they saw, Anton took his time and waited for gold or jewelry. It took a little patience and willingness to search in places no one might expect.

As a result, Anton could now afford to dress like a young lord, with fine lace at his collar and around his boots. He also had a large hat with an enormous feather and felt he looked quite the dandy. Though hopefully, a tough dandy with a sword, two daggers and a pistol at his belt. He couldn't help but swagger just a little.

KENDRYK

Kendryk was walking in the garden with Karil when he saw a flash of blue cloak and blonde hair. Gwynneth? He came to a sudden halt and Karil ran ahead.

"Someone's come to see you," he said.

No, it wasn't Gwynneth. He was sure, though he hadn't seen his wife in over four years. This woman was shorter, her features not as fine, her expression more timid. Very pretty, all the same. Kendryk smiled widely. "Good afternoon."

"Good afternoon, Your Grace." She curtsied. It had been some time since anyone had addressed him that way. "I'm Baroness Brytta Prosnytz, a friend of a friend."

"Shall we sit?" Though it was cold, Kendryk preferred to talk in the garden with the guards out of earshot. "Karil, can you ask about something to drink for us?"

Brytta sat but said, "I can't stay long. I shouldn't even be here."

"I don't understand. Are you here on behalf of King Gauvain?"

"I am a friend of the king's," she said, looking around nervously. "But I'm not here in an official capacity. I came to warn you." She looked around once again and pulled something from her sleeve. "Take this."

Without thinking, Kendryk grabbed it and wrapped it in a corner of his cloak. "What on earth are you doing? And what are you warning me of?" He worried the guards might see, but Karil had somehow diverted their attention from his intriguing visitor and was keeping them occupied.

"Someone may try to kill you soon," Brytta whispered. "It's also possible someone else will help you escape."

"What? That makes no sense at all."

"Things are coming to a head," Brytta said. "I won't be back, I'm sure of it. But someone else will come and when he does you must do as he says."

"This person won't try to kill me?"

"No. We hope he can come undetected. But if he is found out, it's possible the empress will try to have you killed. So keep that dagger close to you always."

"All right," Kendryk said, finding the story fantastical beyond belief. Then something occurred to him. "Did my wife send this person to help me escape?"

Brytta cocked her head. "I'm not sure exactly who's behind this. I just do as I'm told. I'm worried though, that I'm about to get caught and that's why I'm here. It's not part of the plan, but it will be several weeks before your next scheduled visitor and I can't wait that long. With any luck, you'll be gone by then."

Kendryk wondered if she was mad. Brytta had lovely blue eyes, but they glittered feverishly and she seemed terribly nervous.

"Thank you," he said, unsure of how to respond.

"I must go," she said, standing.

Kendryk rose with her.

She took his hand, the one that wasn't holding the dagger still awkwardly wrapped in his cloak. "Be ready," she said. "And give my love to the king when you see him."

"All right," Kendryk said, still feeling puzzled, and then she was gone.

Karil hurried over while the guards gawked after her. "Who was that?" His eyes were wide. "Was she a princess? She was very beautiful."

"I'm not sure," Kendryk said. "But she gave me this." He showed Karil the hilt of the dagger, taking care to turn his back to the guards. "She says I'm about to be rescued, or assassinated."

"Doesn't she know which?"

"Seems not."

"That's odd."

"Yes. I suppose if I'm not rescued soon, I might be killed. Or perhaps I'll be killed before I can be rescued." It felt to Kendryk like he was talking about someone else.

"That mustn't happen." Karil's expression was grim. "I will watch over you when you sleep, and I'll hold that thing. I know how to use it."

"No," Kendryk said, shaking his head. "It's too risky. Whoever is after me, you should stay out of it. Although ..." He came to a sudden stop. "If someone is going to rescue me, I'll make sure they take you along."

"Oh, please do," Karil said. "I'd do anything to get out of here."

"So would I," Kendryk said, a sudden vision of Gwynneth and the children before him. He hardly dared hope. He couldn't imagine how anyone could pull it off. But he had to pretend it was possible so he'd stay alive long enough for them to get to him.

"Do you know who might come?" Karil asked. They stayed away from the guards and kept their voices low. The guards were still busy talking about Brytta.

"No idea," Kendryk said, "though I suspect they might work for my friend, the king of Galladium."

"It must be good to have a king as a friend," Karil said.

BRAEDEN

Braeden wondered if he was spending too much time in Atlona taverns, though it seemed to be part of Barela's plan to keep him busy. They spent the days hunting in the woods outside the city no matter how terrible the weather, and the evenings drinking and playing cards. It reminded Braeden of his life before Janna, and he wasn't interested in returning to it.

Sometimes Barela was called to the palace, but he joined Braeden as often as he could. One evening, he found Braeden at his card game much later than usual, then walked him back to the rooms he had taken in a nearby inn. "Teodora knows you're in the city," he said, once he made sure no one was around to hear.

"I haven't been trying to hide." Braeden wondered if he should be worried.

"She wanted to invite you to the palace, but I said you were in mourning and weren't going out."

"Why? It might have been the perfect opportunity for me to get close to her."

"No better than the opportunity I get most evenings." Barela paused in the street, looked around to make sure it was still empty, but dropped his voice anyway. "Listen, we've decided we'll do this in a way we might all survive, and rescue Prince Kendryk while we're at it. Slaughtering the empress in her rooms or at dinner won't accomplish that."

"I could do it," Braeden said. "And you can rescue the prince in the confusion afterwards. I don't care if I get away."

"That's what you think right now. But someday, you might be glad to be alive again. And some of us like having you around," Barela said, giving Braeden an affectionate punch in the arm. "Besides, Brytta told me that Livilla has a plan in place should anything happen to Teodora while she's in the city. The moment Livilla hears of her death, she will order the city shut up tight. No one will get out while Livilla assumes the regency on behalf of the Archduchess Elektra. Nothing will change and the prince won't escape. No, the plan you and Arian

483

Orland came up with is much better and will give Brytta a chance to see to her own employer's interests."

"Don't you wonder what those are?" Braeden didn't care what happened once Teodora was dead, but was still amazed at the responsibility Brytta carried.

"I'd rather not know," Barela said as they stopped near Braeden's inn. "I suspect they are not in Maladena's interests and with more information I'll be forced to act. My priority right now is Teodora."

But there was a hitch. "Brytta is gone," Barela said two days later, a mere three before they were to set the plan in motion. He and Braeden were riding in the woods again, followed at some distance by Barela's guards.

"What do you mean, gone?"

"I mean, she's not there. She's usually at Teodora's side, and now she's not. She comes in the mornings when I leave, but today she didn't and she wasn't there last night either."

"Did Teodora say anything?"

"No, though I'm not sure she would."

"Maybe she's sick."

"I doubt it. Not right now. There's too much at stake." Barela pulled his horse to a stop and looked around a bit furtively. "What if Teodora knows?"

"Surely she wouldn't. You weren't followed, were you?"

"I'm sure we weren't, though I don't know how careful Brytta has been."

"Even if she's been careful, there are many ways this can go wrong. Perhaps the two of you were overheard accidentally. Or the two of us."

"Gods, I hope not." Barela's horse started moving through the foggy woods. "Should we call it off until we're sure?"

"We can't. Orland is nearby now and we have no way to warn him." Braeden had wondered if they'd see any sign of Orland in these woods by now, but they were silent except for the occasional dripping of moisture from the trees' bare branches. He sighed. "Perhaps we should put our other plan in motion."

"That's a good idea. We can hope it's a false alarm but it doesn't hurt to be ready. You can use one of my messengers."

Barela reported that Brytta had returned by the next morning. "I asked her what had happened and she said she had taken ill." He frowned. "I'm not convinced. She wasn't herself."

Braeden wasn't about to mistrust the instincts of such a famous soldier. "I'll send the message and hope the boy keeps his wits about him." He was surprised that Orland trusted Anton to such an extent. He seemed bright enough, but he was still so young. And Braeden had to admit, he was worried. This was Janna's son, and he felt a certain responsibility to keep him from harm, even though Anton didn't seem to expect anything from him.

Braeden wrote the message and used the cipher Orland had given him. He hoped no one in Teodora's court knew it. He also hoped the messenger was trustworthy—a Maladene girl attached to Barela's headquarters. There were far too many people involved to make Braeden feel very comfortable. But if Anton followed orders, they'd have a way to escape, no matter what happened.

ANTON

Once Anton hired the ship, there wasn't much to do but wait. Fortunately, the port was an interesting place, swarming with people from all over the world. Anton enjoyed himself in other ways as well. The serving girl at the inn where he stayed always saw that he got the best of everything and even hinted that she'd like to spend time with him in private.

"Don't get a big head, young fellow." One of the other men laughed after she'd brought him an ale he hadn't even asked for. "She can see you've got money and that always brings the girls running."

"I didn't think it was my pretty face." Anton grinned as he downed another ale. He was joking, but privately reckoned he didn't look too bad. He wasn't handsome like the count, but he'd learned it wasn't looks so much as manner that made the girls stare at you.

Anton let his hair grow into his eyes so he could fling it out of the way while fixing his gaze on any pretty woman he chose. He also had a dimple that showed up if he smiled kind of crookedly and he liked to think that smile had become his trademark. He'd practiced it in the mirror when he was alone, and it seemed to work well enough.

Not that he had much experience. To be truthful, he'd never so much as kissed a girl. The one time a tavern wench had landed in his lap, the count made her get back up, which made Anton mad.

"I'm not too young," he insisted.

"You're right," the count said mildly. "But you haven't learned how to handle this sort. A sweet girl who really likes you is one thing. But these girls—" He swatted the lass on her ample bottom and she bustled off, giggling. "They're dangerous if you're inexperienced, which you are."

"Then I should become experienced."

"You will, but there's no hurry. Just remember that girls who work in these places aren't always honest and they'll treat a fellow with money better. It's not because they've suddenly fallen in love with you."

Anton snorted. Of course he didn't believe that. But it was stupid advice coming from the count, since women fell in love with him whether he had money or not.

But now the count wasn't here, and Anton had time. The other fellows talked of visiting a certain place in town, but refused to take Anton along. Anton knew exactly what went on there, and figured he should get that experience sooner or later. But he couldn't even bribe them because the count had warned them not to and they were scared of him. Sometimes the count was worse than a mother.

After they'd gone he sat at the table alone and stared glumly into his mug. He didn't feel like getting drunk, but it seemed he had no choice.

"Why are you so sad?" someone with a Maladene accent asked.

Anton looked up. A young woman slid onto the bench across from him. Messenger, it seemed. The port swarmed with them, bringing news to and from all of the ships.

"I'm not sad," Anton said, finishing his drink. "I was just thinking."

The girl laughed. "Well, you seem sad. But you're lucky; I'm taking pity on you and buying your next drink." She waved at the serving girl, who slouched over, glowering at her. Anton was pleased to be the object of jealousy and offered the messenger his special smile.

"I'm Lora," she said, downing half her large mug in one long gulp. Anton stared, impressed.

"Anton," he said. "Where are you headed?"

"Right here. And it turns out I have a message for you. It's addressed to an Anton Kronek, so I assume that's you."

"A message for me?"

"Don't look so surprised." Lora reached into her bag and Anton took the opportunity to gawk. She was very pretty. Dark-haired, flushed and windblown from the road. He always wondered how girls like her managed out there by themselves. They had to be both fast and smart.

"Where's it from?"

"Atlona." She pulled out a single sheet and passed it to him across the table. "They wouldn't say who it was from except that you would know and you should use the cipher."

So it was about the plan. Anton's hands shook a little. "Who do you work for?" he asked.

"General Barela."

Anton breathed out, relieved. "Do you work for him personally or are you hired on?" He wondered if she knew anything about the plan.

"You ought to read that instead of asking stupid questions. I'm sure it's important since they paid me double to get here fast."

"I will." Anton stood reluctantly. He had to get the cipher from his room to read the note but didn't want to leave her here. Some other fellow would move in quickly.

She waved a hand. "I'll be here when you get back. I'm to wait in case you need to send a message back at some point. They thought you might not need to reply to this one right away."

That didn't sound good. Anton dashed up the stairs to his room and found the cipher. He took only a few minutes to decode the message. His heart fell into his boots. She had been right; he didn't need to send a reply right now, but what he had to do instead was much harder. He came back downstairs more slowly.

"Are you all right?" Lora asked.

"I'm going to need your help," Anton said. "I have to find someone who's good with explosives."

BRAEDEN

Now that Braeden had to worry about what might have happened to Brytta, waiting was even harder. Fortunately, Arian Orland appeared right on schedule, sending the whole city into an uproar. As expected, Teodora mobilized all the forces inside the walls.

But there was a problem. "Teodora insists that you join us," Barela said, strapping on what armor he could manage on his own. Braeden helped him with the rest. They didn't want to risk anyone else hearing them, even a page.

"I can't." Braeden tried to think and not panic. This was different than going into battle and he didn't like the feeling. "The orders that Brytta drew up for the Arnfels are for me alone. Even if she had time to change them, there isn't anyone else who can do it."

"I know. You must play along and then leave as soon as possible."

"I'll go get armored up. Does Orland look plausible out there?"

"Good enough. He's arranged around the hills and hidden in the trees, so it's hard to get his exact numbers. I told Teodora he would have more than five thousand, so she wants to bring everyone, just to be safe."

At least that was going according to plan. "I can get most of the guards at the Arnfels out of there for a little while. I should be able to handle the rest, though I need to make sure they don't kill Kendryk first." Brytta had seemed particularly anxious about that possibility, though she wouldn't say why.

"Yes, that would put a damper on things."

Braeden wore lighter armor than usual and hoped Teodora wouldn't notice. It took a maddeningly long time to gather the troops inside the city. As they formed up to leave on the palace parade ground, he joined Barela at the head of the Maladene force, then nodded at Teodora when she saw him. He stayed in her line of sight as they approached the gates.

Once through, she and her guard pulled ahead and Barela followed. He turned one last time and waved at Braeden. If all went well they would see each other again someday.

Braeden spurred Kazmir toward the Arnfels. It all depended on speed now. Orland wouldn't be able to hold them off for long, so Barela would have to act quickly. But even if one part of the plan failed, the other might succeed.

Brytta waited for him in an alleyway near the base of the hill, the hood of her cloak pulled up even though the day was warm. She had the papers ready, along with a map she had drawn to show Braeden where to find the prince.

Braeden grabbed her hand. "You must come with us," he said. "You can't risk falling into Teodora's hands."

"I trust General Barela will succeed." She smiled weakly. "I must stay. When Teodora dies, I will have to prevent Livilla from grabbing power. My employer requires it."

"I wish you success then, and thanks. You've done a great thing."

"Only if we succeed." She surprised him by leaning forward and kissing his cheek. "Now go. I'll tie your horse up here and he'll be waiting for you with the others."

Braeden looked down the alley and saw a boy bringing two more horses. One for Prince Kendryk and a spare. Kazmir would do well on a long, fast journey, but most horses wouldn't.

He looked up at the bulk of the Arnfels, his mouth suddenly dry. The fortress itself stood on a mountain, with a long staircase somewhere inside it. Braeden would have to climb it before he reached the castle proper. While he'd been a prisoner inside, escape from such a formidable fortress had never occurred to him. He wondered if anyone had ever succeeded as he strode into the first guardhouse at the foot of the mountain, looking confident.

"I have an order from the empress," he said to the startled captain. "The city is under attack."

The captain spluttered.

"It's Arian Orland, the sneaky bastard." Braeden sighed and threw the order onto the desk. "The empress has taken every last guard out of the city with her. She wants you to bring all your extras to the walls to fill in for those who had to go."

The captain looked puzzled. With any luck he wasn't too smart. "This is highly irregular," he finally said.

"I just take orders, same as you." Braeden shrugged. "I doubt you'll need to leave many here."

"No, I shouldn't think so. There's only a few prisoners in the dungeons and then it's just the prince and the boy. They won't need much of a guard to keep them where they belong, though I'm more worried that someone might try to spring him. You reckon that's what Orland's up to?"

"Wouldn't surprise me, though he's going about it all wrong. Still, I doubt anyone will try it in the next few hours. You can always send some guards back if the walls seem secure. I can stay if you like, round out the numbers."

"Would you? I wonder you're not out there with the empress."

"I'd rather be, but she wanted me to take care of this. Guess I don't have to be in every last battle." Braeden offered a half-smile.

"True. Leave some for the rest of us." The captain went to the door and grabbed his hat. "I'll round up everyone at the main gate. You can head upstairs right away. There'll be off-duty guards in the main floor gatehouse. Send down all except for those on prince duty right now."

"All right." Braeden couldn't believe how well this was going. He was prepared to kill the captain if he had to and anyone else who contradicted him, but the paper with the empress's seal on it did its job. He grabbed it off the captain's desk. It wouldn't do to incriminate Brytta, though he suspected it was already too late for that. The poor girl's only hope now was that Teodora died today.

The captain disappeared down a corridor, shouting orders, and Braeden started the long climb. He kept one hand at the long knife on his belt since he didn't truly believe he'd pull this off with no resistance. He needed to be ready.

The climb took forever, but when he reached the fortress, he found eight guards in the gatehouse. He showed them the order and asked, "Who's with the prince right now?"

"Cramer, Schwarzer and Torrins," the officer in charge said as he buckled on a belt of pistols. Everyone seemed excited to get a change from the boredom of guard duty.

"That should be enough. I'll stay till you lot come back."

"Good man," the officer said, then rushed out the door after the others.

Braeden waited until they disappeared, took a deep breath, drew his knife and entered the castle courtyard. Prince Kendryk stood on the opposite end.

KENDRYK

Kendryk stared at the man. He looked rather familiar and very large, though Kendryk couldn't quite place him. So this was who Teodora had sent. Even with his dagger, Kendryk didn't stand a chance. He wondered if the guards would try to protect him, though he doubted they could succeed against such a brute.

Time slowed and his vision turned into a dark tunnel, with only the big blond man at its end. From somewhere far away, Karil made a noise. "Get away from me, Karil," Kendryk said, his voice sounding hollow in his ears.

The man came closer. He was saying something to the guards, and they were looking back and forth between him and Kendryk. They stepped out of the way. So they wouldn't protect him then. Kendryk pulled out the dagger.

One of the guards said, "See here now. What's going on?"

Kendryk shook his head and focused on the big man, who at least had come no closer. But now he spotted the knife, a great curved thing that dwarfed his dagger. Kendryk hoped it was sharp, so it would be quick. Still, he felt obliged to put up what fight he could. He wouldn't have it said he submitted peacefully.

Suddenly, a guard lunged toward him. Kendryk stepped back just quickly enough to stay out of reach. Instinctively, he jumped to the side as the guard circled around him. Out of the corner of his eye, he saw the other two guards fall. Maybe they had tried to protect him after all. Seemed this one didn't want to.

The guard kept coming, sword drawn. Kendryk thought he might be able to slide the dagger in under the man's armor. He was in good practice after all of the play fighting with Karil. He wondered vaguely where Karil was, hoping he stayed out of the way. The guard lunged at him again and Kendryk danced aside.

"By Ercos, that's enough!" he heard, and they both stopped, puzzled. The big blond man covered the ground to the guard in two steps and cut his throat before

Kendryk could make sense of what was happening. He froze, stunned, then recovered enough to brace himself for what was coming.

"You did it!" Karil said, stepping out from behind the big man. That seemed odd.

"You might as well finish me off," Kendryk said, facing him. The man had killed three heavily armed guards in less than a minute. Kendryk was clearly no match for him.

To his surprise, both Karil and the man laughed.

"You'll forgive me if I don't find this funny," he said, offended and more than a little hurt at Karil's gloating.

"You're right, it's not funny." The man wiped blood from his face, the long knife still in his left hand. "We've got to go before someone raises the alarm."

"What?"

"Braeden's here to rescue us," Karil chimed in, looking at the man in rather worshipful fashion.

"Oh," Kendryk said. "I thought you were sent to kill me."

"No, that would be this fellow it seems," the man called Braeden pushed at Kendryk's attacker with his foot. He appeared quite dead. "I'm here to take you away." He bent down and pulled a ring of keys from the guard's belt. "I hope these open the gates."

"Thank the gods." Kendryk kept his dagger out. He still couldn't believe what was happening. "Where are the other rescuers?"

"There's no one else." The man chuckled, though Kendryk didn't see what was so funny. "We've got to go right now. I'll explain it all to you later."

"I'm coming too?" Karil said. Kendryk noticed the question in his voice and the hopeful look in his eyes. It was clear from the man's reaction he hadn't planned on taking Karil along.

"Of course you are," Kendryk said firmly.

"Yes, yes, naturally," the other man said. "Good thing I brought a spare mount. Now away we go." He herded the two of them down the stairs. Kendryk kept his dagger out, worried they might run into someone on the way out, but no one came. Surely this Braeden fellow hadn't killed all of the guards in the castle with only that knife?

They burst out onto the street and horses materialized out of an alleyway. Kendryk swung into the saddle of the first one, surprised at how his muscles screamed. He realized he hadn't been on horseback in over four years.

"The western gate," Braeden said. "Hurry."

Kendryk spurred his horse to a gallop. The hoof-beats on cobblestones sounded loud enough to rouse the whole city, though the streets were strangely empty. He saw the gate ahead and the clattering sound was joined by temple bells.

"Someone has raised the alarm," Braeden said behind him. "We will have to fight the guards at the gate. Pray there aren't too many."

For the first time in years, Kendryk prayed.

TEODORA

"Deploy your troops on the right," Teodora said to Demario once they cleared the city gates, sounding sharper than she intended. "You'll stay with me, I hope?" She softened her tone and smiled at him.

He smiled back. "I'd like nothing better." He stayed back to issue a few orders, then caught up to her. "Even with Orland at full strength, we easily outnumber him. He might have stolen a march on us, but we can't let him take the initiative."

"I agree. Let's move on him at once." Most units weren't yet in place—many were still coming out of the city—but Teodora was eager to get this over with.

"Shall we send Tomescu out first?"

"No, she'll be better used to mop up afterward. Her riders are most tenacious in hunting down survivors." Teodora smiled to herself. Arian Orland was in for a big surprise.

Straight ahead, she spotted his cavalry. The first column emerged from the trees at the foot of a hill and Teodora ordered her own light cavalry to advance. She only had Zastwar mercenaries, but they would create confusion, and that was all she needed right now. The infantry advanced behind them.

She turned to Demario and smiled again. "It's good to be fighting together again, isn't it? The two of us."

"At least we're not fighting each other, like most couples do." His smile, full of warmth and humor, was the one she had fallen in love with so long ago.

She realized suddenly she would never see it again and that almost made her hesitate. But she reminded herself that he'd been lost to her for months now and that smile was nothing but a ghost visiting from the past.

Now troops surrounded them. The cavalry engaged Orland's vanguard, the infantry right behind them. When Demario looked away, Teodora signaled to her guard. They came in closer, cutting off most of the Maladene general staff. In the confusion, it wasn't very noticeable.

Demario turned back to her. "Shall we advance?" he asked. "I can't see anything from here."

"Of course. You first."

"No, you should have the honor. Your troops expect it."

"If you insist." Teodora pulled forward, conscious of her guards right behind her. She wondered if he noticed that.

Suddenly he was beside her again.

She stopped.

"My dear," he said, "I am so very sorry."

His pistol already pointed at her, but Teodora's captain of the guard was faster. She was on him in a flash, knocking the pistol out of his hand as it fired. The bullet hit someone behind Teodora, but she wasn't about to turn around to see who it was.

By now, two of her guard had pulled him from his horse and held him. The rest kept the other Maladene officers at bay.

"No, I'm the one who's sorry," Teodora said, jumping off her horse. "I should have known better than to trust a man. You're a liar like the rest of them."

"I wasn't always." Demario seemed unperturbed in spite of having seconds left to live. "I really did love you. But you turned into the monster everyone says you are and made it impossible to continue."

"You're the one who's made it impossible with your ridiculous, hopeless conspiracy. And yes, I know who else is involved, since your precious Brytta sang like a lark the moment my interrogator put the screws to her. Braeden Terris will die as soon as I find him, while Arian Orland enjoys Daciana's attentions." Teodora drew her dagger. "Take off his cuirass," she said to the guards. She wanted to do this properly.

Teodora walked up to him and looked straight into his dark eyes. She only now realized they'd held no feeling for her for many months. "I still love you, you know," she said, sliding the dagger between his ribs and into his heart. She pulled him away from the guards and held him as he slumped.

Teodora had thought she'd want to kick and stomp on his dead body, but instead, she felt like crying. She lowered it gently to the ground while the battle raged around her. Then she stood up and looked at the Maladene colonel who was nearest, his eyes round with shock. "It turns out your beloved general was a traitor," she said, wiping the dagger with her sash. "Now you work for me. Anyone who protests can have some of this." She pointed the dagger straight at him. For all she knew he was part of the conspiracy as well, but as long as he behaved himself now, she would let him live until after the battle.

He swallowed hard and nodded. "What are your orders, Your Highness?"

"Call for Daciana Tomescu and finish Arian Orland. She can follow him if he tries to retreat."

Before she returned to her horse, she heard a shout. A messenger was shoving his way through the troops ordered all around her. "Your Highness," he yelled over the tops of several heads. "Someone has broken into the Arnfels and slain the guards."

Teodora could think of only one thing. "Prince Kendryk?" she asked. She should have known Brytta was holding something back.

By now, a path had opened for the messenger. He nodded, breathless. "We still don't know how it happened, but the gates of the fortress stand wide open and the prince is gone."

"Seal the city," she said. "Bar the gates and leave them shut until I order otherwise. No one gets out. Oh, and tell the guards at all the gates to shoot Prince Kendryk on sight."

She took one more look at Demario's body, then faced forward. It was the only way to go.

GWYNNETH

Gwynneth was relieved to be in a pleasant place, with nothing to do except think about what to wear for dinner. All the time and money spent on dresses in Sanova now paid off. She was making an impression at the Galladian court, known for its finery. With her elaborate Sanovan wardrobe, Gwynneth struck just the right note of fashion-forward and exotic. It was gratifying when other ladies copied her dresses.

Natalya had arranged for a little townhouse for them to live in and insisted on paying for it. "It's befitting your station to have your own house," she said. "And I know you have little money right now. It's all right." She took Gwynneth's hand when she made a face. "I'm sure all of that will change soon. And I will always owe you help when you need it."

"Whatever do you mean?"

"Your kindness changed my life when we were girls. I would not be here today if it weren't for you."

"I doubt that."

"No, it's true. You gave me confidence and made me feel like I was worth something. Until I came to Arenberg, I believed I wasn't."

The daughter of an important Sanovan nobleman, ten-year-old Natalya had arrived in Arenberg as part of a complicated hostage deal in the treaty ending a series of wars between Norovaea and Sanova.

Gwynneth remembered how shy and frightened she had been, but they became fast friends and were inseparable until Natalya left for Atlona to pursue a religious education. Gwynneth had missed her friend, but was proud of her accomplishments. She understood better than anyone Natalya's need to distinguish herself. In that, they were more alike than sisters.

Gwynneth's house was in the best part of Allaux, just down the street from the Maxima's palace. Gwynneth and Natalya saw each other daily while Maryna and Devyn both received lessons at the main temple. It was an excellent education and similar to what Kendryk had received at the same age. Gwynneth was beginning to wonder if they would spend the next several years in Allaux.

She hardly dared contemplate it, but she was almost certain that Teodora would kill Kendryk when Lennart invaded. At that point, she would no longer care about angering Natalya. Even though Natalya assured Gwynneth she was working on another plan to help Kendryk, Gwynneth exhausted herself with frantic worry. And now she had less to do, it was too easy to envision the most gruesome scenarios. Natalya advised her to pray, so Gwynneth visited the temple morning and night, but even that didn't diminish the knot in the pit of her stomach.

She also decided it was time for Maryna to spend time at court. At nine, she was a little too young—Gwynneth had been eleven when she first joined her parents—but she would take on her responsibilities soon if Teodora killed Kendryk.

"What did you think?" Gwynneth asked Maryna after her first day in attendance on King Gauvain.

"His job seems very difficult," Maryna said.

Gwynneth smiled to herself. She had expected a little girl to notice the beautiful dresses and jewelry and the tiny dogs that many ladies carried with them everywhere. "Yes, it is difficult, I'm sure."

"Is it the same in Terragand?"

"Not quite. Terragand is much smaller, and your father's court much more informal. He received petitioners in his study or went out to the towns. He had no throne room or hundreds of courtiers."

"That's good," Maryna said gravely. "It's much easier to do one's work when there isn't such a fuss."

"Did you like those little dogs? Do you want one?"

Maryna's face brightened. "I do. Though ..." Her face fell again. "Will I have to leave it behind when we go home?"

"Of course not. That's the point of having one that small. You can carry it everywhere."

"I even saw some being carried around in those tiny jeweled bags. That doesn't seem very kind."

"You needn't do that. Do you want a black one, or a white one?"

"I will have to think about it. Perhaps I'll ask Devyn, since I'm sure he'll want to play with it too."

"Devyn can have one of his own, if he wants. Do you want to tell him?" Of all her children, Devyn was the greatest animal lover and had begged for a pet ever since they left his kittens behind at Birkenfels after the siege was lifted. For months after all he talked about was "visiting" his cats again. Gwynneth smiled after Maryna as she ran off to find her brother, then turned to a pile of letters on her desk.

She saw the one on top had come by messenger from Norovaea, so she opened it first, hoping for news of her brothers. Her smile fled when she started reading.

"You must help us Gwynn," Arryk wrote. *"Mattila followed us to Norovaea and has sacked Arenberg. Aksel, Classen and most of the nobility got away, but we left everything else behind. I worry about the people remaining in the city with that monster on the loose. I'm in the fortress at Vastivik and we must hold out or die. Please persuade Natalya to send help."*

Gwynneth threw the letter down. Mattila's persistence surprised her and she also knew Natalya wouldn't oppose her openly right now. She pondered for a long time, then picked up her quill.

"No one can help for several months," she wrote. *"Lennart plans to invade as soon as he can, but it might be too late. You must sue for peace. Teodora doesn't want Norovaea. Give her your pledge that you will stay out of the empire."*

She felt terrible. Her brother had done all of this to save her and now she couldn't help him. She hoped Mattila could be reasoned with. Even if she couldn't, she would surely leave Norovaea once Lennart made his move. Gwynneth prayed he could do it quickly.

ARRYK

More and more, Arryk wished he'd died on the battlefield. It was what he wanted after losing Larisa. Then Gwynneth would have become queen and someone competent would be in charge here now, instead of him. Anyone but him. It seemed impossible to salvage the situation, but he had no choice except to carry on.

To his relief the Norovaean people were far more resolute than the nobility. With Mattila's forces on their soil, they quickly rallied when called upon. Arryk occupied the largest castle at Vastivik and sent Classen and what remained of his officers to occupy the rest. Mattila held the capital, but she wouldn't get anything else.

Still, it was hard to hold her off. She sent sizable forces into the countryside, stealing food and burning villages. Since it remained bitterly cold, those who lost their homes were in grave danger. Arryk tried to find shelter for most of them in the fortresses no matter how crowded.

The sturdy Norovaean peasants made excellent guerrilla troops and he found some satisfaction in leading raids on Mattila's forces camped all around Arenberg. He couldn't defeat her on the field, but might make her life miserable with endless hit and run attacks in a different area every day. But that wasn't enough to make her leave.

Gwynneth's letter reached him when he'd hit a low point. He read it over several times. What she said made sense, but he didn't want to do it. Most of all, he didn't want to deal with Mattila. The thought of a mere noblewoman gloating over a king was unbearable. He didn't want to deal with Teodora either, because he would probably try to kill her, but he didn't see a good solution.

Arryk hardly recognized himself anymore. He lived in the cold, dank castle, dressed in fur and wool like any peasant, rode one of their shaggy ponies and carried one of their long farm blades. He'd cut his hair short and looked like any other young man from the land. Perhaps it would have been better for everyone if he had been born one of them. He reckoned any number of peasants might have done a better job at being king.

He told himself when spring came he would go talk to Mattila, but not before. The thought of surrender was unbearable and he hoped something would turn the tide. Maybe Lennart would intervene and force Mattila to leave. That would be best for everyone.

He sat around a campfire with a few of the peasant troops who now comprised his army. Sturdy and stubborn, similar fellows had made up the bulk of his Kronland army though too few had returned.

"As soon as I find a way to make peace," he said, mostly to himself, "I'll find someone who can do the job better. My sister or brother most like."

"But you can't, Your Highness," a farmer named Swen spoke up. Arryk didn't stand on ceremony when they were all living in huts and eating around the same fire without so much as proper officers.

"Of course I can. I'm the king." Arryk poked a stick into the embers, making them flare up again.

"That's just it. You're the king, put over us by the gods. You're meant to take care of us."

Arryk barked a laugh. "Fine job I've done of that, haven't I?"

Swen shrugged. "You've made a mistake or two. Likely shouldn't have run off to Kronland like you did. But now you know better. Now you know it's our land you must care for."

"I don't think I can."

"Sure you can. All this trouble you've had, it's a sign from the gods that you're meant to stay here."

"I've had just about enough signs from the gods." Arryk scowled, thinking about dreams and prophecies that had led him into disaster, as if his own incompetence wasn't enough.

"This is different."

Arryk wondered why Swen was so confident. "I doubt it."

"You must. It's your duty."

"What do you know about it?" Arryk was getting angry.

Swen was unbothered. "What we've always known. Roussays belong in Norovaea, taking care of Norovaeans. Any other adventures tend not to end well, even all the raiding out west years ago. Oh sure, it was fun, but it wasn't until the kings came home and settled into Arenberg that we became rich and peaceful."

"We're neither right now."

"But that will change if you stay here and do what you're meant to."

"We'll see." Arryk poked at the fire, but for the first time, it seemed to warm him.

KENDRYK

As they neared the gate, Braeden called them to a stop. "Here," he passed Kendryk a belt of pistols, then pulled something long and sharp from his saddle and handed it to him. "This is an estoc; do you know how to use it?"

"Well enough," Kendryk said. He'd never practiced with one, but knew it was a Sanovan version of a long dagger. He would have to poke, not slash.

"I can use a sword," Karil said eagerly.

Braeden raised his eyebrows. "When I last saw this young fellow, he was just a little thing who couldn't have lifted a sword. He's grown a fair amount in the meantime, but when did he learn to use one?"

"We've spent hours practicing up there in the castle." Kendryk wished Karil could prove himself in a less dangerous situation, though it was true the practice had been meant for a moment like this one.

"Good." Braeden pulled out a saber and handed it to Karil. Kendryk found the number of weapons the horse carried amazing. "And now we go. The guards at the gate might expect us, so we must strike fast and overpower them. If we fail, we die. Take down as many as you can, as fast as you can, no hesitation."

Excitement thrilled through Kendryk—he hadn't felt this alive in years. He knew he should be afraid; he didn't want to consider the odds of success. He didn't care. Even if he died now, he would die out in the open, on the streets of a city he thought he'd never see. He glanced up at the cloudy sky and grinned. No matter how bad the weather, it beat being in the confines of that tiny garden.

They thundered up on the gatehouse, Braeden on his enormous charger leading the way. A guard came out and stepped into his path and the horse rode him down, heading straight for the gate, already barred, three more men standing in front of it. One of them held an arquebus, but Kendryk fired first and he went down. Braeden shot another, and the third sprang aside.

Out of the corner of his eye, Kendryk saw Karil slashing at the third man with his saber. Without dismounting, Braeden fumbled with the gate's multiple bars,

504

but opened them soon enough. From behind them came the sounds of more guards filling the street leading to the gate.

"Go, go, go!" Braeden shouted as the gate swung open. Kendryk spurred his horse and they were through. Karil and Braeden were ahead of him, so he slammed the gate shut behind him. The door was heavy and swung slowly, but it would give them a few precious seconds before their pursuers could shoot at them. Kendryk hunched over his horse's neck and spurred him again.

Now they thundered through the empty streets of the western suburbs. Kendryk wondered why no one was out, though he was glad it made their way easier. He heard gunfire behind him, but no shot reached him. He ventured to turn his head and saw his pursuers. There were at least twenty guards, but none on horseback. They all shouted and fired, but faded into the distance as the horses sped from the city. Still, Kendryk knew it wouldn't be long before they'd be pursued on horse.

Kendryk urged the horse on as the cobbled streets turned to dirt. Still no traffic. When he glanced back again, the street was empty. He was sure that wouldn't last, but didn't understand why more weren't pursuing him. They galloped a few more miles, taking the road along the river, and turned south, into a wooded, hilly area.

At some point, Braeden slowed his horse to a trot, then a walk, Kendryk and Karil following suit. When they reached a small crossroads, they came to a stop altogether.

"We wait here," Braeden said, "But not for long."

Kendryk finally noticed the sounds of battle. "Who is fighting?" he asked.

"Arian Orland and Barela," Braeden said. "Though with any luck, the empress is dead and they're both on our side now."

"What?" Kendryk couldn't make sense of what he'd just heard. "How? I don't understand. I thought you worked for the empress, but clearly ..." It was obvious Braeden had rescued him against Teodora's wishes, but he still didn't understand why.

"I used to work for the empress," Braeden said, his face grim.

Kendryk finally remembered where he'd last seen him; as Teodora's bodyguard during Edric's trial. He laughed to himself, then said, "But you don't anymore."

"No." Braeden's voice was curt. "Neither does Barela. Arian Orland is acting as decoy, to lure the empress out of the city with her troops, clearing the way for your escape."

"So that's why no one followed us," Karil said. "They were busy fighting."

"And from the sound of it, they're still fighting," Braeden said. "That's not good. It should be over by now. We need to go and Orland will have to catch up. It's only a matter of time before the empress sends horsemen after us if Barela doesn't kill her first."

"All right then, let's go," Kendryk said, still unable to believe that Arian Orland was out there, risking his neck to help Kendryk escape. It made no sense at all. But that meant ... well, it meant a lot of things. No matter what had happened before, Kendryk felt a warm rush of gratitude overwhelm any lingering resentment and hoped Arian would make it.

BRAEDEN

"We can't keep galloping," Braeden said once they'd put the crossroads and sounds of battle far behind them. "Especially now we don't have a spare. Let's reload the pistols and slow down. The port is a few hours away."

"I'm glad we're going by sea," Kendryk said. "I didn't think my chances of escaping over land were very good." He pulled up next to Karil. "How is it you know Commander Terris?" he asked.

"He took me hostage," Karil said happily. "Though he was very kind. He and a nice lady named Janna took such good care of me. Do you know what's happened to her, Commander Terris?"

"She's dead," Braeden snapped, more angrily than he meant to. He'd forgotten that Karil and Janna had been great friends. Janna had taken him under her wing when Braeden took him hostage as a little boy of eleven. It was right about then that Braeden had started falling in love with her. A vision of Janna and Karil, laughing together as they rode side-by-side on a windblown Marjatyan road, passed his eyes and he blinked it away.

"Oh," Karil said, but caught Braeden's gaze and said no more about it.

Kendryk diplomatically changed the subject. "You must tell me why you've done this and everyone who took part," he said to Braeden. "You will of course be rewarded, provided we succeed," he added wryly.

Braeden hesitated, looked into Kendryk's clear, kind eyes, then told him everything, starting with Kersenstadt. When he looked at Kendryk afterward, his eyes were damp.

"I'm so sorry my good man," he said softly. "I have little ones too, and I can't think what I'd do if anything happened to them."

Braeden remembered that one reason he agreed to rescue Kendryk was so he at least might get a chance to watch his children grow up.

Kendryk looked at him with sympathy. "I realize there's nothing I can do to make you feel better. That won't keep me from doing my best." He smiled at

507

Braeden, who had to admit that the long stay in the Arnfels had done nothing to diminish Kendryk's charm.

As they rode further with no sign of pursuit, Braeden explained the rest of the plan to them. "We'll sail around to Galladium, where your friends are waiting for you."

"Is there any word of my family?"

"I have received none, though I'm sure they're safe." Braeden hesitated, and told him the last news he'd had of Arryk Roussay.

"That's my fault." Kendryk frowned. "He would never have invaded if it hadn't been for me. And now he must surrender or lose his country."

"You can't worry about that right now," Braeden said. "Let's get you back to your family and then you can figure out how to help."

It was a relief to see Anton and Barela's messenger waiting for them at a roadside inn near the port.

"Were you pursued?" Anton asked.

"Not right away, though they can't be far behind." Braeden made the introductions.

"Where's Count Orland?" Anton looked anxious.

"Not sure. He didn't show up at the crossroads and the battle was still going on long after it was supposed to end."

"So Barela failed." Anton turned pale.

"Maybe, but we can't wait. Especially if he's failed, they'll be breathing down our necks before long."

"I won't go without the count," Anton said with a stubborn set to his jaw.

Braeden sighed. "I know how you feel, but we have to. All this will be for nothing if we can't get Prince Kendryk to safety." Until he ran into Arian Orland, he hadn't realized the importance of Kendryk's freedom if Teodora was to be defeated. He didn't want to think of Orland arriving here to find the ship gone, but he was a resourceful fellow and would surely find another way to escape.

"I agree with Master Kronek," Kendryk said. "I won't abandon the count when he's done so much. There must be a way to help him."

Braeden sighed again. He could say no to Anton, but Kendryk gave the orders now. "I don't know. I can go back and look, but I want you lot on that ship and ready to sail with the tide. If I don't come back by then, go without me." He scowled at Kendryk until he nodded in agreement.

Braeden ordered a bite to eat from the inn's kitchen, then prepared to leave. "Get them on the ship as soon as I leave," he said to Anton.

"I'll wait," Anton said. "For you and the count."

"Don't." Braeden shook his head. "Better only a few of us get caught than all of you. The prince especially. He's important."

"I'm waiting," Anton said mulishly. "You can't tell me what to do and Prince Kendryk will agree with me." Karil stood at his elbow, nodding. Braeden wondered how they'd become allies in the past two minutes.

"I'll come help you," Karil said.

Braeden shook his head as he shoved some stale bread into his mouth. "It's too dangerous."

"Just as dangerous for you. I can help you; I can fight."

"Suit yourself," Braeden said, shrugging. There was no time to argue. He sent Kazmir for a rubdown and ordered fresh mounts for himself and Karil. He was pleased to see that Anton had already reloaded his pistols and transferred Kazmir's saddle to the new horse along with all of the weapons hanging on it.

"Just like the old days, eh?" he said as he and Karil sped up the road. He had to admit it was nice to have the company.

They found the trouble before too long. About a league from the port, Arian Orland and the few of his troopers who'd escaped the battle were fighting a losing rearguard action against Daciana Tomescu. By now Braeden was almost certain that Barela had failed, but there was no time to worry about his friend.

Braeden paused at some distance and told Karil to wait. "He's outnumbered and I don't want you tangling with that woman. I'll distract her, and you grab Orland's horse and get him away from there."

Orland still held his saber, but lacked the strength to use it. One side of his face was a bloody ruin and still more blood ran from a wound in his leg. He'd been fighting off Tomescu and three others, but he was finished. Braeden though of a recent hunt with Barela, watching a magnificent stag brought down at last by a pack of hounds.

He grabbed a pistol in each hand, spurred his horse and shouted, "Prince Kendryk!" as he barreled toward Tomescu. He fired the first pistol and hit the man on her right, but his horse was unaccustomed to the sounds of battle and shied as he fired the second one. As far as he could tell, he'd hit no one, but had everyone's attention. He hoped Karil was getting Orland, but couldn't look right now. Braeden pulled his horse back in line and drew his saber before spurring it on.

He kept his eyes trained on Tomescu, watching her face light up with recognition. She brandished her own weapon, a great curved thing already dripping blood, and then she was upon him. Metal shrieked as their blades met and

Braeden's horse reared. He held on by sheer force of will, wishing for Kazmir. When the horse found his feet again, he bolted away from the fight and down the road, following Karil and Orland, slumped bleeding over the neck of his charger.

Braeden let the horse have his head, hoping that Tomescu and her people had no loaded pistols. When he looked back, he saw they were pursuing him, but their ponies were winded after the long ride from Atlona. Braeden's frightened, fresh horse was eager to return to the port and pounded down the road, soon overtaking the other two.

"Get on the ship as soon as you can," he gasped at Karil. "I don't think any of the rest of Orland's people made it."

"Anton told me there's a new plan," Karil said. "He'll show you the way when we get there. Do you want me to shoot at them in the meantime? My pistols are still loaded."

Braeden looked back. Tomescu was still behind them, but not gaining yet. "No," he said. "Save them for when they get closer. And for Ercos' sake, don't fire them around the horses."

ANTON

Anton and Lora led the prince to the ship and showed him to his cabin. The captain had offered up his own when he heard who his distinguished passenger was.

"Thank you so much," Prince Kendryk said. "I'm very grateful."

He smiled at the two of them and Lora blushed. Anton scowled. Kendryk was much too good-looking and a prince to boot. How was a fellow supposed to compete?

"We'll be back soon with the count and the commander, I hope," Anton said. He didn't add that he'd told the captain to sail with the tide, even if Prince Kendryk was the only one on board. He checked on Skandar one last time, down in the hold next to Kazmir. Neither one of them liked it much there, but Anton had sugar cubes for them and they would be safe at least.

He and Lora headed for the road on foot. She had a brace of pistols and a sword and said she knew how to use them. Anton suspected she might be the perfect woman, though he worried she thought of him as a little boy, being nearly nineteen herself. So he made himself stand tall, minded his swagger, and remembered to keep his voice low, so it didn't squeak.

Once they reached the Atlona road, they waited. Anton was nervous because he knew the ship would sail in about an hour. He didn't want to miss it and he didn't want Lora to miss it either. If General Barela had failed, she would need it to take her back home to Maladena.

They didn't have to wait long before Braeden galloped into view, Karil and the count right behind him. The count was more dead than alive, slumped over Cid's neck.

"Tomascu's right behind us," Braeden shouted. "We'll have to hold her off at the ship."

Anton looked at him so he didn't have to look at the count. "Follow Lora. Hurry."

511

Lora ran ahead to the ship. Anton grabbed Cid's reins. "Leave the horses," he said to Braeden. "Except for Cid. I'll take him."

The horsemen were close now and Anton saw her at their head, her awful eyes glowing, her mouth stretched wide in a yell. He froze, recalling the cold ground of the forest and crying in his mother's arms. Then he forced himself to remember he wasn't that person anymore. He was a man now and wouldn't let his friends down.

Braeden pulled the count down from Cid and threw him over his shoulder like a sack of potatoes.

"Follow me," Lora said, running up the ship's gangplank. Karil went after her, followed by Braeden carrying the count.

Anton jumped onto Cid's back, and nearly slid out of the saddle, it was so wet with the count's blood. Tomescu and her band had reached the end of the dock and were galloping onto it. Anton drew a pistol, then made Cid stop, blocking the gangplank.

For the first time, he got a good look at Tomescu. She slowed down as she approached Anton and her yellow eyes narrowed to slits.

"I'm going to kill you," he said, raising his pistol.

"You?" She threw back her head and laughed, so he saw her sharp fangs. "I've always liked killing babies, and I'll enjoy killing you especially, little boy."

Anton clenched his jaw, thinking of Anyezka, the little sister Tomescu had murdered so long ago. He hoped he'd allowed the others enough time, and put the spurs to Cid. He went straight for Tomescu, forcing her away from the ship and cutting her off from the rest of her troops.

"Onto the ship," she shrieked. "Kill them all." And she pulled out a very long, bloody blade. Anton heard horses thundering up the gangplank behind him but kept his eyes on Tomescu and that blade of hers. She spurred her exhausted pony toward Anton while he raised his pistol. Right before he fired, she laughed, and he aimed straight at that horrible mouth.

There was a loud thump on the wood as Tomescu fell onto the dock. Her pony danced away. Anton had hit her, though he wanted to be sure she was dead. He reached for his other pistol when he heard shrieking coming from the little boat pulling away from the ship.

"No, Anton, no!" Lora screamed. "Go, go, hurry!"

Now Anton remembered that he needed to get away from the ship. Cid thundered along the dock, but wasn't quite far enough away when it blew. Lora had lit the fuse exactly when she was supposed to and Anton had lost track of time.

Burning timbers rained down on them and Cid screamed as one landed on his back. Anton leaned back and flipped it off with his hand while holding onto the reins with the other. The whole dock was on fire, including the spot where Tomescu had fallen. He couldn't see a body and hoped she was dead. He knew the stories said she couldn't be killed, but hopefully those were fairy tales meant to frighten her enemies and not really true.

Their ship was out of sight, behind a few larger ones and Anton reached it before the boat did. He led Cid up the gangplank and into the hold, then came back out.

"Why did you do that?" Braeden asked, the last to come over the side of the ship after handing the bloody and unconscious count up first. "How did you do that?"

"Because of your message," Anton said. "You said we might have been betrayed and to expect pursuit. If someone was hot on our tail, I didn't think we could all get on the ship and get away. Best to let them think they got us and kill some of them while we were at it. I found one of Mattila's old engineers drunk in a tavern and he was happy to show me how to rig it in exchange for a few barrels of ale. We had to find an old ship to blow up, so I've spent all of the count's money. I hope you have enough to get us to Galladium."

Braeden shook his head and said nothing, though he looked angry.

"I helped," Lora said. She pulled Anton close and hugged him tight while he blushed. "I thought you weren't going to make it. You were supposed to distract Tomescu, not go head to head with her."

"You're crazy, both of you," Braeden said. "Getting a drunk engineer to help you blow up a ship and taking on Tomescu like that. Completely insane."

"It worked, didn't it?" Anton grinned, partly because Lora still had an arm around him and partly because he could tell Braeden wasn't really angry with him, just trying to hide how worried he'd been.

"Seems so," Braeden said, then looked at Anton a long time while shaking his head some more. "We'd best see how the count is faring."

"Will he live?" Anton asked, looking down at the mess the count left on the deck. The ship's doctor was at work on him, his hands bloody.

"He might." The man looked up. "Took a bullet in the eye, but it glanced off his skull. Could be he got lucky. We won't know until he wakes up. If he wakes up."

TEODORA

Teodora refused to believe that Daciana was gone. She had gotten out of worse scrapes, and Teodora half-believed the rumors that said she couldn't be killed. In one day, she'd lost the two people she cared about most. Demario had been lost to her for months, but seeing him dead made it real. There would be no turning back, no reconciliation.

And now she had to deal with another viper she'd nursed in her bosom. That Brytta Prosnytz had engineered Kendryk's escape made her sick with anger. The first interrogation had only yielded up half the plot. And perhaps that had been the plan all along—keep Teodora distracted with her treacherous lover while others rescued Prince Kendryk.

Brytta was in the Arnfels dungeon, but Teodora wanted to be present at her interrogation. This time they wouldn't have to worry about visible damage, so they would do whatever was necessary to wring the truth from her.

Livilla accompanied her to the Arnfels in her carriage. "I don't see why it was so important to free Kendryk at this point," she said.

"It's important because of Lennart." Teodora sighed. "I might have controlled him by threatening to kill Kendryk if he moved on us. Now that Kendryk is gone and Sanova is neutralized, nothing stands in his way."

"Mattila does, much as you hate to hear it," Livilla said softly, as if she knew how Teodora would react.

"Not well enough. She's terrorizing Norovaea and won't respond to my messages to pull back. What if Lennart invades before she returns?"

"You must make an immediate settlement with Arryk Roussay. Go over her head."

"Should I do it myself?"

"If you like. Or you can send a representative like Solteszy or me. Once we have an agreement with him, her hands are tied. If she doesn't leave Norovaea then, she'll be considered a rebel by everyone. I'm certain she doesn't want to go that far."

"I'm not sure it's safe for me to leave Atlona." The words were out before Teodora could stop herself. When had she become so afraid?

"Then I will go. I'm sure I can come to an agreement with Arryk. I don't see any reason he can't continue to rule in Norovaea as long as he reimburses your expenses and agrees not to return to Kronland. It will help us if he can't help Lennart."

"Very true. And I don't want Mattila getting her hands on even more money."

"I also need to attend to some of the big Kronland temples, but will do that on my way back."

"I'm so grateful for you," Teodora said, a bit worried she might cry. "I feel so alone in the world."

"We are alone, all of us. We are fortunate to find one or two people in our lifetimes who truly care. Only the gods can give true comfort."

That did nothing to help Teodora feel better.

Inside the Arnfels, the captain led them to the dungeon and had them wait in the interrogation chamber while they brought Brytta.

He returned a few minutes later, shamefaced. "I'm afraid there's a problem, Your Highness."

"Surely she hasn't escaped too?" At this point, Teodora was willing to believe anything. In her nightmares, Braeden Terris haunted the Arnfels corridors, bloody knife in hand.

"Not in a manner of speaking. But I'm afraid Baroness Prosnytz is dead."

"Dead? Who killed her?"

"By her own hand."

"How? Wasn't she searched?"

"Of course she was. But it seems she hid a small blade in her hair. It was enough."

Teodora was speechless. Now she would never be certain who had been behind this.

"We can still make a good guess," Livilla said as they walked back out.

"Can we?"

"Consider this: who has been steadfastly lobbying for Kendryk's release? And didn't you find it odd that Natalya gave in so easily when you refused to let him go?"

"I hate the idea, but you might be right." It was unbearable. Not only had Natalya been a friend, Teodora did not want Galladium as an enemy.

"Call off Zofya's engagement." Livilla urged. "It's worse punishment for them than it is for you."

"What about Dallmaring? We've already started the handover."

"Then stop it. Stop all of it and let Natalya know her interference in imperial matters won't be tolerated."

Teodora wrote the letter, trying to keep from sounding too angry. She sent orders to bring Dallmaring back into the imperial fold, by force if necessary, then sent for her daughter.

Judging by the look in Zofya's eyes, she'd already heard the news. "But mother," she said, on the verge of angry tears. "I'm in love with him. He's going to be my husband."

Teodora smiled. She doubted she'd been so naive at that age. "How can you possibly be in love with a man you've never met? And once you've met him, well, he's Gauvain Brevard. It wouldn't last long."

"You don't understand." Zofya stamped her foot and Teodora had to hide her admiration. Tiny, dark-haired, and spirited, Zofya seemed better than Elektra in every way. Perhaps Teodora could find a way to make her the imperial heir instead. But first she had to get her over her tantrum.

"Stop whining. These things happen all the time. It would have been a political marriage in any case."

"But he writes me the loveliest letters, with poetry," Zofya protested. "And we exchanged locks of hair."

Teodora failed to hide a laugh. "What you don't know is that he has a child with Natalya Maxima."

That brought the girl up short. "That's a lie."

"No, my dear. I'm afraid he's the one who's been lying to you."

Zofya burst into tears.

Teodora almost felt bad, but knew it was for the best. This was a good chance to teach her daughter that no matter who she ended up marrying, she must never give her heart to anyone.

KENDRYK

As they neared the Galladian port of Sarcy, Kendryk found he was nervous. He didn't expect his family to be there, though he hoped they would be, since it was only two days' journey from Allaux. A message from Natalya had reached him during a stop in a Maladene port, letting him know they were all safe and staying with her. He felt a bit guilty, looking forward to a happy reunion when Braeden would have none.

It looked like Arian Orland would live and Kendryk was glad. He found it very difficult to harbor anger any longer after the part he'd played in Kendryk's rescue. Nearly all of the troops he'd taken to Atlona were dead or captured and Arian had lost his left eye. Kendryk sensed it was a blow to his vanity, but perhaps it would do him good in the long run.

As they neared Sarcy, Kendryk got ready. He shaved and considered cutting his hair, which had grown rather long, but left it for the time being. It had a few streaks of gray, but shorter hair wouldn't hide those. Karil helped him dress in his best clothes. They'd made a stop in Maladena and had been able to buy a few things.

As they came into dock, there was some fanfare. Quite a large crowd had gathered, but Kendryk couldn't pick out any individuals from the ship. He pushed down his impatience and waited to disembark in some state.

A man came aboard saying he was the king's representative. "I'm afraid his majesty couldn't appear personally, though he'll tell you all about it later. But your family is waiting for you."

Kendryk couldn't keep the joy from showing on his face. He wondered if any of the children would remember him, or if he would recognize them. They would all have to become reacquainted and he thanked the gods for giving him the opportunity to do so.

The others had all disembarked and Kendryk slowly walked down the gangplank. If he limped, it was mostly because he still felt like he was at sea.

He saw Gwynneth first, standing on the dock. The wind blew her golden hair and her cheeks were rosy from the chill. She was smiling. Next to her stood a serious-looking girl of ten or so and a bright-eyed blond boy. Another boy stood next to him and a nurse held a little dark-haired girl. Kendryk stopped before he came closer, just to look at all of them.

"Papa." Suddenly the older girl broke away and ran toward him.

Kendryk folded Maryna into his arms, unable to speak, and then Devyn was clinging to him. When he looked up, Gwynneth stood across from him.

"Oh my darling," she said, looking into his eyes and stroking his hair. "I was afraid I'd never see you again."

"So was I," Kendryk said, pulling her close. "But you did it. Arian told me everything."

"We'll talk about that later," Gwynneth said, pulling back a little. "I'm sure you remember Andres." She pushed a pale little boy in his direction and Kendryk greeted him politely, since it was obvious he didn't remember him. "And this one you don't know at all." The nurse had put the little girl down and Gwynneth pulled her forward. "This is Stella, and she was born nine months after the battle."

"Hello, Stella." Kendryk went down on one knee.

"Hello, Papa," Stella said, placing a chubby hand in his. She didn't seem the least bit shy. "Will you play with me?"

"Oh, yes," Kendryk said. "Very soon."

Then they were bundled into a carriage and taken from the docks. Devyn crawled onto Kendryk's lap while Maryna snuggled against his side and everyone talked at once. The carriage disgorged them at a house in the town, borrowed for the occasion. They would leave for Allaux the next day.

"I'd like to bring the others along," Kendryk said, once they'd settled into the house's comfortable parlor. "At least until we know what's next. Arian will need time to recover in any case."

"Natalya has asked that we, and everyone involved in the rescue, be the king's guests for as long as we need to. Of course Count Orland will receive the best care we can give him," Gwynneth said.

For some reason, talking about Arian with her didn't bother Kendryk at all. He was certain now that she didn't care about him. The way she looked at Kendryk made it clear there was no one else for her. Just like there was no one else for him. Whatever came next, he hoped he had the time to just enjoy her and enjoy their children.

They would have to worry about getting Terragand back, but that could wait for another day. From what Gwynneth had told him, it sounded like Lennart would soon invade. No matter what kind of army Teodora had, it wouldn't be able to stand against him. Kendryk was sure of it. He hoped to meet Lennart soon and make plans. But for now he looked forward to seeing Gauvain again, talking religion with Natalya and playing at war with Devyn and Stella, already fighting with toy swords in the corridor.

ARRYK

In the end, a negotiator came to Arryk, though it wasn't anyone he'd expected. They met at the secluded home of a friendly nobleman, deep in the forest. Arryk still wore the rough wool and fur of the peasants, but he didn't care. Neither it seemed, did his visitor.

"Aren't you a treat for the eye?" An older woman rose as he entered the room.

"If you say so." Arryk grinned, surprised at how easily a flirtatious tone still came to him when he needed it. "And you are?"

"Livilla Maxima."

He'd guessed as much based on the Maxima's robes she wore, but he wanted to be sure. "And the young lady?" He smiled at a nervous, awkward girl of sixteen or so, standing behind Livilla.

"The Archduchess Elektra." Livilla pulled the girl forward, who dropped a quick, clumsy curtsy. "Empress Teodora's eldest daughter."

Arryk gestured toward some chairs, then took a seat. Perhaps his manners had suffered after all. Once they were all seated he asked, "Are you here on behalf of Brynhild Mattila?"

"No, we are not." Livilla shook her head. "I am here to represent the empress and no one else."

"Interesting," Arryk said, though he didn't understand the significance of that.

"Indeed," Livilla said. "It may come as no surprise to you that the empress and General Mattila are not on the friendliest terms."

Arryk almost said he didn't think anyone could be on friendly terms with a monster like the empress. Then he remembered he was speaking to her confidant and her daughter, so he bit his tongue just in time. "Hm," he finally managed.

Livilla went on. "These negotiations are occurring without Mattila's knowledge, although by now I'm sure she has noticed the archduchess's absence from Arenberg."

"Will Mattila abide by any agreement we reach?" That worried Arryk.

"Oh yes," Livilla said. "I know she'd prefer to make her own agreement, but she is the empress's employee and must do as she's told."

Arryk shrugged. That was not his problem. He wondered what Livilla wanted, but didn't want to seem too eager. He hoped it looked like he was content to live the peasant life as long as he needed to.

"So, what do I need to agree to to get your lot to leave my country?" There was no point in putting off the discussion in favor of talking Olvisyan politics.

Livilla looked amused. "Not much, fortunately for you. You will sign an agreement promising to remain neutral in any affairs concerning the empire. That includes intervention in Kronland, or assisting any allies of the rebels."

"I can do that. I have no interest in getting involved there again."

"There's also a financial aspect. The empress requires you reimburse her for expenses incurred due to your invasion. We've decided two hundred thousand Taler will be sufficient."

Arryk laughed heartily. "I can't pay that back in a hundred years."

"I expect not," Livilla said, a glint of amusement in her eye. "You'll sign an agreement to pay it in annual installments. Between you and me, it's understood that some years you won't be able to pay the full amount, if at all."

Arryk stared. "Did you just tell me how to cheat the empress?"

Livilla smiled. "I'm telling you whatever I must to make you sign this agreement. How you adhere to it after doesn't interest me right now."

"If only the empress were as reasonable as you." Arryk decided to get this over with. "If I sign right now, when will Mattila leave?"

"Within a month."

"Not soon enough." For the amount Teodora wanted, Arryk felt he ought to demand faster results.

"I understand, but you must also understand that she has a force of some size scattered all over your country and limited ships to take them back."

"She can use my ships if it will make her leave faster."

"Kind of you to offer, but you shouldn't trust her with them. She's more likely to sell them to Zeelund than return them to you."

"Thanks for the warning. Still, I'd like her to leave as soon as possible."

"So would we all. And she will, though it will take a few weeks to complete the withdrawal."

He could live with that if there was an end in sight. "Where do I sign?"

"Elektra darling, can you hand me that pouch?" Then Livilla turned back to Arryk. "There's one more thing. I must return to Atlona with a hostage. Someone of high rank and close to you."

"No," Arryk said. "Isn't my word good enough?"

"It is to me," Livilla said. "But the empress requires assurances."

"The empress can rot," Arryk said, angry now.

Livilla sighed. "Without a hostage, there can be no treaty. You have my word, and the empress's that they will be treated as befitting their station. After five years' time, if your behavior has been exemplary, the treaty will be revisited and the hostage most likely returned."

"The empress's word is worthless to me," Arryk said, surprised that his voice shook. "I don't wish to insult you Maxima, but it's hard for me to trust anyone associated with her."

"I understand."

"Do you?"

"I know what happened at Kersenstadt and I am sorry," Livilla said. "The empress has a temper and often does things she regrets later. If it would help, I'm sure I can persuade her to offer formal condolences."

"You must be joking. No, it's impossible." Arryk stood up suddenly.

"There is another possibility," Livilla said. Arryk had to admire her calm. But then anyone who dealt with the empress regularly would have to be.

Arryk sat back down. "I'm listening."

"Instead of a hostage, there might be a marriage."

"Whose marriage?" Arryk had a bad feeling about this.

"Yours, of course. To the archduchess."

The girl gasped and Arryk realized she hadn't expected this any more than he had. He almost laughed, wondering who believed he would ever accept Teodora as his mother-in-law, but he didn't want to insult the girl, who looked ready to cry. Arryk was sure he didn't look like anyone a young girl would want to marry with his rough clothing and the shaggy beard he'd let grow all winter. He took a breath, then said, "Impossible."

Livilla raised an eyebrow and said nothing.

Arryk went on. "No offense to you, Archduchess." He paused until he caught the girl's eye and gave her what he hoped was a reassuring nod. "But it's impossible for me to marry, now or ever."

"I see," Livilla said. "I hope you can change your mind one day, for both yours and your country's sake. But I had to ask. It would have been a tidy solution."

Arryk caught Elektra's relieved sigh and winked at her. It was hardly fair for a young girl to be hitched to a wreck like himself. There was no question in his mind it would have ended badly.

"That brings us back to the question of a hostage," Livilla said. "Without one, I'm afraid there can be no deal."

Arryk wondered if he ought to send Norvel Classen, though it seemed rather cruel.

"I'll go," Aksel said, coming into the room behind him.

Arryk turned to him. "Are you mad?"

Aksel shrugged. "Probably. But I don't mind doing it if it helps you out."

Arryk found himself unable to speak while Aksel turned to Livilla and Elektra and introduced himself. He could play the charming prince when he wanted to.

"I can't let you go," Arryk said, thinking he would have no one left in the world if Aksel went.

"Why not? I'm not useful to you here."

"You helped a great deal while I was in Kronland."

"Barely. I can't keep it up." Aksel turned to Livilla. "Maxima, do you suppose I might bring my scientific equipment with me and set up a laboratory in Atlona?"

"I don't see why not," Livilla said.

"You're a scientist?" the archduchess asked. It was the first time she'd spoken and Arryk didn't miss the interest in her eyes.

"An amateur." Aksel flashed her a smile. "But it passes the time well enough."

"I don't want you developing explosives for the empress," Arryk grumbled.

"Don't worry. There are many other things I can work on. I'll send you all my useful results, if I come up with any."

"I don't know," Arryk said again.

"I do," Aksel said. "Please, let me do this. It means we'll get our country back before summer, and I'll have an adventure."

Arryk didn't know what else to do. "All right," he finally said. "Let's sign this treaty."

ANTON

The count was still in bad shape and the long voyage hadn't helped. He would probably live as long as infection didn't set in, but it was hard to say if he would walk again, let alone ride or fight. Most worrisome to Anton was his attitude. He felt very sorry for himself and rather hopeless, not at all like his usual self.

"No woman will ever look at me again," he said glumly, sitting up in bed in his fancy chamber in the Maxima's palace in Allaux. His empty eye socket looked dreadful and an ugly scar ran down his cheek.

"But the patch looks good," Anton said, and it was true. With the patch and the scar, he looked rather dangerous and even more dashing than before. But he needed the posture to match and he was so dejected he couldn't manage it. Even Princess Gwynneth's visit didn't help.

Anton had been sitting outside the count's chamber, cleaning his pistols. It wasn't as though he needed to guard his door, but it was an old habit. Besides, the count didn't want visitors and this way Anton was able to keep them out. He had scrambled to his feet when he saw who it was.

"I need to speak to the count alone," Princess Gwynneth said, her voice soft, but firm. She was very beautiful and Anton remembered to close his mouth and not stare too hard. She seemed used to it, though and gave him a kind smile. "You're Maryna and Devyn's friend, aren't you? They told me how you helped them escape before the battle. And of course you were so brave during Prince Kendryk's rescue. We're very grateful."

Anton nodded, his mouth dry, and let her into the count's chamber. It didn't occur to him to keep her out. He pressed his ear to the door, but the princess spoke so softly he couldn't make out any words and the count said little.

She didn't stay long, and gave Anton another dazzling smile when she left.

Anton poked his head cautiously inside the door. "Are you all right?" he asked.

"No," the count said, slumped back against the pillow. Anton was glad to see he was wearing the patch, though he guessed the princess wouldn't have flinched at the sight of worse. For all her pretty softness, she seemed rather tough.

Anton moved quietly about the room, picking up a few dirty cups and putting them on a tray, since the count now drank more than ever. Sometimes he wanted to talk and sometimes not.

"Well, that's it then," he said after a while. "I did as she asked, even though it took years. But now what? She has her husband back and is happy. Naturally, she's most kind and grateful and so on, but that doesn't do me any good."

"First you need to get better," Anton said. "Get your army back together. Then you can go fight for that king that's coming from Estenor. "

"I don't want to fight," the count said. "For the first time in my life, but there you are."

"You will when you feel better."

It was hard for Anton to believe the count wouldn't want to fight. Still, he understood a little of what the count was going through since he'd just fallen in love for the first time and had already lost the girl.

It had happened quickly once they were on the ship. There was nothing to do on the long voyage around the Cesiano peninsula but sit and talk. So that's what Anton did. He got to know Karil, but he was already friends with the prince and Braeden, so Anton and Lora spent a lot of time alone together. At first, she didn't take him seriously.

"You're so young," she said. "At my age, I need a real man."

"I am a real man," Anton insisted. "I've killed people and been in battle loads of times. I can also hold my liquor better than most fellows."

"I can still drink you under the table."

"I know; that's why I love you." He caught her eye and held it, even though his face turned so hot he thought he might explode.

She narrowed her eyes as if she were challenging him. "Have you even been with a woman?"

He wasn't sure if she was mocking him, but he stared straight back at her. "No I haven't, though girls have liked me."

"What's stopping you then?"

"I'm picky."

Lora laughed. "I'll bet you are. You're an arrogant bastard with your pistols and your lace and that walk of yours. You learned some bad habits from the count and you want to be just like him, don't you?"

"Well, yes, though I'd never be stupid enough to fall in love with a princess who couldn't marry me."

"Ha," Lora said. "That just shows what you know."

"I don't care about princesses anyway. I like real girls who can fight."

"Like me?" She was suddenly very close, and they were alone at the starboard rail, the ropes and sails creaking in the wind.

"Exactly like you." Anton decided to be bold, slipped his hand around her waist and pulled her toward him. She was a little smaller than he was and didn't resist. She even laughed a little before he kissed her. Her lips were chapped and salty from the sea air but Anton reckoned his were no different. He was a little surprised when her tongue pushed into his mouth, but it felt wonderful, so he pushed his back.

After that, they kissed a lot, whenever they had some privacy, which wasn't that often. Anton wanted more, but he was a bit scared too and the stolen moments were perfect. He refused to think about the future because he couldn't picture life once they got off the ship.

It all fell apart when they reached the first big Maladene port.

"I need to go home," she said, the night before they sailed in.

"Why?" Anton asked. "You should come to Galladium with me."

"And do what? You're stuck there until the count gets better. If General Barela is dead, I must get home and find another prospect for myself. My mother's dead, my father can't work, and I have two little brothers. I need to make money to send them."

"I don't want you to go." Anton was determined not to cry, even though he had a terrible pain in his chest.

"I don't want to. But I must. I'm sorry. You can come to Maladena with me." She grinned at him. "Plenty of cavalry officers there need a good page. There'll be war with Zeelund again soon; perhaps even with Galladium."

"I can't leave the count." Anton knew the count would tell him to go to Maladena, but he couldn't leave him alone while things were so bad for him. "I'm sorry too."

Then they kissed a lot more, almost all the way into port, and he was able to hold back the tears when she left.

GWYNNETH

Gwynneth hadn't been so happy since the early days of their marriage. And with Kendryk recovered from his ordeal they needed to go to Zeelund soon to arrange funding for Lennart's invasion.

"It's best if it comes from you," Natalya said. "I'm having enough trouble with Teodora as it is. The last thing I need right now is to look like I'm supporting Lennart in any way."

"I'd like to see Gauvain before I go," Kendryk said. The king was with the army trying to prevent Teodora from taking back the Dallmaring provinces. He had provoked a stalemate until they reached further agreement.

"He wants to see you too," Natalya said. "I received a message this morning that he's on his way back."

Kendryk's face brightened. "We'll go soon after."

Gwynneth looked forward to traveling again now she was going with Kendryk. They would leave the children here so they could travel more quickly. With Arryk besieged by Mattila, they needed Lennart to distract her at the first possible chance. And that would only happen when he received enough money to launch an invasion.

Gwynneth slipped her arm through Kendryk's as they walked back to their house from Natalya's palace. "Can I have you for the next hour?"

"Certainly, though I told the children I'd come get them after their lessons."

That much hadn't changed. Kendryk still spent as much time as he could with the children and she no longer minded. At first she worried they would be strangers to each other, especially after parting under such difficult circumstances.

And when she first saw him coming off the ship, she'd been shocked at how much he'd changed. He no longer looked soft and boyish. The planes of his face had sharpened and his eyes were sadder. His hair was longer than she'd ever seen it with a few streaks of gray. That alone made him seem older than his twenty-five years.

He also moved like someone much older. That was because of the wound that hadn't perfectly healed, although it was a miracle he walked at all. She shuddered when he described the wound to her.

"I was sure you were dead," she confessed.

"I came very close to death and was lucky that Teodora's physician was so committed to keeping me alive. She did far more than she needed to, not just to heal me but give me encouragement. I don't know why she did it."

"Perhaps she was an instrument of the gods, or perhaps she came to love you, just as everyone who knows you does."

"Teodora would disagree," he said, grinning.

"But she's the only one." Even the young Marjatyan boy imprisoned with him seemed to regard him as a father. And Braeden, the big Sanova Hussar who had rescued him, also seemed fond of him. Gwynneth rather envied the bond between those who'd taken part in the escape and then shared the long voyage together.

Now they saw a lot of Arian's page, Anton. Kendryk had insisted that he attend Natalya's school with their own children and Maryna and Devyn never stopped talking about him. Gwynneth worried just a little. Maryna was still so young, but there was no mistaking the adoration in her eyes when she talked about Anton. There was nothing wrong with a girlish crush, but Gwynneth would soon have to tell Maryna that the future Princess of Terragand must make a political marriage. With any luck she'd be like her parents and find a husband she also loved, but he would have to be a prince, or a duke at the least. Falling in love with a commoner of any kind needed to be discouraged, even at her age.

"What are you worrying about now?" Kendryk grinned at her. She must have been frowning to herself.

"The children of course. The situation is still so unstable."

"I'm sure it will come right before Maryna is an adult. I can't thank you enough for everything you've done. Getting Lennart to help was a stroke of genius."

"It was Natalya's idea."

"But you made it happen. You made my escape happen too."

"That was mostly Natalya," Gwynneth said. "I was astonished that she had both the empress's lady-in-waiting and General Barela in her pay. What I wouldn't give for a network like that." She was more than a little envious of the resources Natalya had to spend on spies, though she'd now have to replace those Teodora had killed.

"I disagree." Kendryk slid an arm around her waist. "Nothing happened until you came to Galladium. I can't imagine where I would be without you. And now that you believe in Edric's teachings, you're even more perfect than before."

"Believing in his teachings has shown me how imperfect I am."

"Just right for me, though." Kendryk pulled her in for a kiss.

Gwynneth was glad they still had time before the children appeared. She also decided to wait to tell him she was pregnant since she didn't want him to keep her from traveling with him. She knew it would be all right. Now they were together and believed the same things she was certain the gods would bless all of their actions.

BRAEDEN

"I can't pay you as much as you're accustomed to," Kendryk said. "But I'd be honored if you'd work for me."

Braeden didn't know what to say. He liked Kendryk and who wouldn't want to stand around and stare at Princess Gwynneth all day? But he felt restless, and attending a non-fighting prince would be boring. He'd had enough of body-guarding. Besides, after everything they'd done, Teodora still lived. Braeden couldn't really relax until he'd found a way to kill her. After hearing what she'd done to Barela, he was even more certain he needed to do it.

"I'm the one who's honored," he finally said. "And it would be a pleasure to work for a ruler I admire. But I'm afraid another mission calls me, with your permission of course."

"You don't need my permission." Kendryk laughed.

They were walking in a shady part of the Maxima's garden on a warm summer day. The fragrance of thousands of flowers rose into the air.

Braeden should have enjoyed that, but couldn't enjoy anything anymore. The days were dull, no matter what he did. "I'd like to take Karil Andarosz home," he said.

"What a splendid idea. Though I'd be happy to keep him here too, if he wanted it."

"We've talked it over." Karil was no longer a small, scared child. At sixteen, he was still short, but with a sturdy, powerful build to go along with a stubborn, intelligent character. "He's enjoyed staying with you, but understands you have your hands full with your own children."

"Karil is always welcome in my household," Kendryk said warmly. "He's like a son to me. I don't mind having another child around."

"I think he knows that, but he worries about his own family. Things have been hard in Marjatya and the only way for him to find out if they're all right is to see for himself. "

"I understand that. It's possible his father is no longer alive and he will need to take over the estate. He learned a lot in the Arnfels and I'm confident he'll make an excellent ruler."

"You did well with him," Braeden said, though he was thinking of sword-fighting rather than book learning. Karil could talk theology with the Maxima if he wanted to, though he got tongue-tied around Natalya, who Braeden had to admit was handsome in a way that didn't seem proper for a religious leader.

She wasn't beautiful like Gwynneth, but she exuded a sensuality no man anywhere near her could miss. Braeden reckoned it might be even worse for a sixteen-year-old. He'd thought Karil might have a bit of fun with the pretty Maladene messenger girl on the ship, but Anton had that all sewn up.

Braeden had watched Anton carefully, looking for any signs of Janna. He realized he wasn't hers, although she had raised him. But he didn't notice any similarities. It was as though Anton had an almost opposite personality. He was tough, outgoing and rather arrogant. Braeden had to admit he liked him, but mostly because Anton was good at getting people to like him. He didn't need to be Janna's son for that to happen.

Braeden was relieved. At first he worried he'd form an attachment which he didn't want or need right now. As it was, he could say goodbye to Anton and wish him well without it being too hard. And it was clear enough that Anton considered the count as some sort of father. He had family if he needed it.

Karil seemed sad to leave his friends, but told Braeden he was happy to go on another adventure after years of boredom in the Arnfels. Kronland was peaceful for now, but a lack of fighting didn't make it safe. Braeden sold all of his hussar armor and replaced it with plain but heavy plate. He cut his hair and shaved his beard. He refused to change his name, but no one looking at him would recognize Braeden Terris of the Sanova Hussars.

"You won't go back to the hussars?" Karil asked as they left the walls of Allaux behind them.

"I can't, even if I wanted to." To his surprise, Braeden felt the same dullness around that as he did around everything else. It was better that way. That he'd never see Novitny, Franca and the Torresias again might have been too much to bear.

"What will you do then?"

"First, I'll get you home. Then I'll see. I won't be far from Atlona and Teodora isn't dead yet."

"True," Karil said. "I'll help you kill her if I'm not needed at home."

"I might take you up on that," Braeden said. It gave him something to think about, something to look forward to. He doubted anything would ever give him pleasure again, but sliding a blade into Teodora Inferrara's body just might do it.

EPILOGUE

Elektra hadn't felt so happy in, well, maybe her whole life. It was a relief to be out from under General Mattila's thumb. She'd learned a great deal from her, but in recent months, the general had been so angry with the empress, she liked to take it out on Elektra. When Livilla had come to Arenberg in the dead of night and spirited her off to the Norovaean countryside, Elektra was more than eager to go.

The momentary prospect of marrying King Arryk had filled her with dread, but to her relief, he seemed even less interested than she was.

"That wasn't very gallant of him, was it?" Mother Luca asked, amused.

"I don't mind one bit," Elektra said. "You should have seen him. I would have been terrified to marry him."

"But isn't King Arryk rather handsome?"

"I heard he was, once. But he looked like a wicked barbarian to me and had the most awful, frightening eyes."

"The poor man." Luca sighed. "He suffered a great tragedy. Your mother murdered the woman he loved, didn't she?" Luca was inclined to be sentimental.

"That's what I heard too, which is another good reason not to marry him."

"You're probably right. And Prince Aksel is ever so much nicer, don't you agree?"

"Oh he is." Elektra wouldn't say any more, but her cheeks warmed. Aksel was nice and best of all, he seemed interested in Elektra herself, always asking her questions about all sorts of things. She was glad he was coming back to Atlona with her, even as a kind of prisoner.

They had traveled a long way already and finally reached Arcius. Now they would be in Atlona within days. The convoy came to a halt. "What's happening?" Luca asked, trying to see over the heads in front of her.

Elektra had no idea. Perhaps something blocked the road. Most of the roads throughout Kronland were in terrible repair because of the war. It was getting dark, so she hoped they'd make camp. It was tiring, sitting in the saddle all day, though bouncing in a carriage was no better.

Suddenly there was the crack of gunfire and the guard next to Elektra pitched forward, then fell off her horse. Elektra looked around and watched her other guards peel off toward the noise. She wondered if they were under attack. Kronland ought to be subdued right now except for a few pockets of Terragand, so perhaps bandits were attacking the convoy. She wondered if it was better to get off the road so she urged her horse toward the trees on one side. At least she wouldn't be as clear a target. "Come on, Luca, " she said, trying not to worry. Her guards could handle any threat.

She had just entered the shade of the trees when someone pulled her from the saddle. An enormous hand covered her mouth before she could so much as squeak. She struggled, but it was pointless. Before she realized what was happening, a man threw her on the ground. It was then she noticed another. One of them stuffed a foul-smelling rag into her mouth, while the other bound her wrists and ankles.

She tried to see through her terror, but it was dark in the trees and then something even worse-smelling was pulled over her head, leaving her in darkness. The bigger man threw her over a horse, knocking the wind out of her. She cried and gasped for air, and feared she might suffocate between the rag in her mouth and the sack over her head.

But she didn't suffocate, and after awhile became accustomed to the jolting of the horse. She breathed through her nose and tried to calm herself down and think. Judging by the jarring motion, she was moving at some speed. Surely her guards would find her soon.

Time passed; so much she knew the guards hadn't found her trail right away. They must not know which way she had gone. She tried not to cry, but tears soaked the sack over her head and her whole body ached as the horse trotted for what felt like hours. When they stopped at last and dumped her on the ground, then pulled the sack off, it was well after dark.

Elektra saw a boy her age building a fire. She wanted to ask his name, but the rag was still in her mouth. She started crying again.

"Stop that," a gruff voice said. "Crying won't help." Someone sat on the ground next to her and turned her head by the chin to face him. He looked familiar, but she couldn't place him. He pulled the rag out of her mouth. "No hard feelings, sweetheart," he said.

She looked at him some more and then relief washed over her. She wondered why he'd shaved his beard and where the rest of the hussars were.

"Of course," she said eagerly. "You're one of the Sanova Hussars. Are you taking me to General Mattila?" It would be typical of the general to snatch her away from Livilla like this.

"I'm taking you to your mother, in a manner of speaking," he said.

Elektra tried to catch his eye; he'd always seemed friendly. But now he frightened her. His voice was calm, but his eyes as hollow as a dead man's, worse even than King Arryk's.

"Oh, good," she said uncertainly, though she couldn't work out why he'd take her to Atlona when she was going there anyway.

"This really isn't personal," he said. "But it's time your mother learned what it's like to lose a child. Karil, bring me that sword."

Thank you for reading Valley of the Shadow!

Please don't forget to give this book a quick review on Amazon. Even just a two-word, "Liked it" or even better, "Loved it" review helps so much. Positive or negative, I am grateful for all feedback from my readers.

The story continues in Book Three of The Desolate Empire series:

Hammer of the Gods
COMING SPRING 2016

Sign up to be notified at christinaochs.com

CAST OF CHARACTERS

Kronland

Kendryk II Bernotas, Prince of Terragand
Sibyla, Teodora's personal doctor

Gwynneth Roussay, Princess of Norovaea and Terragand, Kendryk's wife.
Their children: **Maryna, Devyn, Andres, Stella**
Linette, lady-in-waiting to Gwynneth
Edric Maximus, religious leader in Terragand, formerly known as Father
Edric Landrus
Merton, Captain of the guard at Birkenfels
Catrin, Gwynneth's maid

Evard Bernotas, Duke of Terragand-Emberg, Kendryk's uncle
His son, **Balduin,** a prisoner inside Birkenfels

Rheda Bernotas-Falk, Princess of Helvundala, Kendryk's aunt.

Ruso Faris, a general leading the remnants of Kendryk's army.
Aidan Orland, Duke of Kaltental-Terragand
Arian Orland, Count of Hornfels, son of Aidan, mercenary general support-
ing Kendryk and Gwynneth
Ossian Schurtz, mercenary officer in the employ of Arian Orland
Anton Kronek, a horse-boy in Arian Orland's army
Cid, Arian Orland's battle charger
Skandar, Anton's horse

Emilya Hohenwart, mercenary general allied with Arryk
Seward Kurant, a mercenary general allied with Arryk
Trystan Martinek, Duke of Podoska, youngest son of Princess Edyta

Flavia Maxima, religious leader in Isenwald

The Kronland Rulers

Eldrid Benda, Prince of Lantura
Floreta Bensen, Princess of Brandana
Ossian Dahlby, Prince of Ummarvik
Dristan Fabrey, Prince of Aquianus
Bronson Falk, Prince of Helvundala
Viviane Kasbirk, Princess of Isenwald
Keylinda Marthaler, Princess of Fromenberg
Edyta Martinek, Princess of Podoska
Herryk Peloso, Prince of Tirilis
Galena Sebesta, Princess of Oltena and Kendryk's aunt
Alarys Zelenka, Princess of Arcius

Norovaea

Andres V Roussay, King of Norovaea, Gwynneth's father
Arryk Roussay, heir to the throne
Aksel Roussay, Arryk's and Gwynneth's youngest brother
Norvel Classen, chief adviser to King Andres
Larisa Karsten, an army officer and Arryk's mistress
Magnus Torsen, an officer in Arryk's army

Olvisya

Braeden Terris, mercenary commander with the Sanova Hussars
Janna Kronek, a Moraltan refugee
Iryna, Braeden and Janna's daughter
Anyezka Kronek, Janna's step-daughter (deceased)
Prince Novitny, general of the Sanova Hussars
Reno Torresia, a captain in the Sanova Hussars, his wife **Senta** and their
daughters Adela, Cara and **Trisa**
Miro Blavic, a lieutenant of the Sanova Hussars
Franca Dura, a lieutenant of the Sanova Hussars
Gergo, servant to Braeden
Kazmir, Braeden Terris's horse
Zoltan, a retired warhorse, Janna's mount

Nisa Retter, a friend of Janna's, wife to a Sanova Hussar
Ashia Toure, a doctor in the Sanova Hussars

Kersenstadt

Alen Marsel, a doctor
Birgid, a servant
Hilda, a cook
Klaus, a servant
Mother Ilsa, a priestess in a Kersenstadt temple
Holgar Ellert, Norovaean officer

Teodora Inferrara, Empress of Olvisya, Queen of Moralta and Marjatya
Raynard Ahrend, consort to Teodora
Their children: Elektra, Zofya and Rudofo
Mother Luca, Elektra's personal priestess
Livilla Maxima, religious leader in Olvisya
Daciana Tomescu, guerilla commander and friend of Teodora
Ahbert Solteszy, Head of the Imperial Council and Teodora's closest political adviser
Meryl Biaram, an adviser to Teodora
Brytta Prosnytz, secretary and lady in waiting to Teodora
Elyse Rastell, lady-in-waiting to Teodora

Demario Barela, Maladene general working for Teodora
Niklas Ensden, Teodora's primary military commander
Brynhild Mattila, a general working for Teodora
Andor Korma, Marjatyan rebel leader

Beatryz Inferrara, Queen of Maladena, cousin to Teodora, her daughter, the Enfanta Johanna

Karil Andarosz, a Marjatyan hostage
Ulla and Dolf, servants in the Arnfels

Galladium

Gauvain Brevard, King of Galladium and childhood friend of Kendryk
Natalya Maxima, religious leader in Galladium

Zeelund

Vrouw Belsen, a tavern owner
Kamyla Melchor, a wealthy Bonnenruck business owner
Peter and Gretel, two Bonnenruck children

Estenor

Lennart Ostberg, King of Estenor
Ludvik Meldahl, his chief adviser
Kelsi Brun, captain of the *Rusa*

Sanova

Ottilya Sikora, Queen of Sanova, married to Atinos Inferrara, Teodora's brother
Raysa Sikora, her daughter
Bendik Tarka, a royal guard
Zytka Hylek, a courtier

The Faith

Teodora the Holy, ancient founder of The Faith
Quadrenes, followers of the reforms of Edric Maximus
League of Aeternos, a group of clerics specially trained to counter the Quadrenes
Vica, the sister goddess
Ercos, the son god

ABOUT THE AUTHOR

Christina Ochs is the author of historical fantasy novels Rise of the Storm and Valley of the Shadow. Her first series, The Desolate Empire, is based upon the events of the Protestant Reformation and the Thirty Years War (1618-48). Many of her characters are also based on historical figures.

With a bachelor's degree in History and an MBA, Christina uses her writing to indulge her passion for reading and research. Publishing as an indie author provides an outlet for her entrepreneurial side and she is an avid supporter of fellow authors, both independent and traditionally published.

Christina lives in a semi truck full time, traveling the United States with her truck driver husband and two cats, Phoenix and Nashville.

You can learn more about her at her blog: http://christinaochs.com or follow her on twitter @therollinwriter

www.ingramcontent.com/pod-product-compliance
Lightning Source LLC
Chambersburg PA
CBHW051931020726
47501CB00001B/70